Love Like You've Never Been Hurt

Emma and Jack
Summer Lake Book One

By SJ McCoy

A Sweet n Steamy Romance

Published by Xenion, Inc

D0999296

Published by Xenion, Inc.
First Paperback edition 2017
www.sjmccoy.com

This book is a work of fiction. Names, characters, places, and events are figments of the author's imagination, fictitious, or are used fictitiously. Any resemblance to actual events, locales or persons living or dead is coincidental.

Cover Design by Dana Lamothe of Designs by Dana
Editor: Kristi Cramer of Kristi Cramer Books
Proofreader: Aileen Blomberg

ISBN 978-1-946220-07-3

Dedication

For Sam. Sometimes life really is too short. Few xxx

Chapter One

Sitting on the freeway surrounded by thousands of other frustrated drivers, Emma wondered why on Earth she had decided to go to Pete's office instead of just calling him. LA traffic was nothing to mess with and she knew it, but once more she'd succumbed to the need to see a real friend. In what she'd come to think of as the 'fakedom' of this city, she took every chance she could to connect with the few genuine people she knew here.

After taking forty minutes to drive a few miles, she soon forgot her frustration once she pulled into the parking lot of the Phoenix Corporation headquarters. It was a beautiful modern building, all steel and glass. Emma had always loved it; it seemed so fitting to her that Pete had built it. Her childhood friend had always been considered 'most likely to succeed'. The success of the construction empire he had created with his partner had far exceeded any expectations and he continued to go from strength to strength.

Pete's secretary, Judy, beamed as she ushered Emma into his grand office.

"Hey, Mousey," he grinned. "To what do I owe the pleasure of this wonderful surprise?"

"Hey," she said as he wrapped her in a bear hug. "I wanted to make sure that you're okay. That you haven't fallen prey to the evils of the fake city yet." Pete was the last person she could imagine ever losing his sense of self. He was as grounded as a man could be. He'd been that way since they first met when they were eight years old.

"Well, I haven't crumbled in the last ten years. Not much chance of it happening today. So why not tell me what's really up?"

"Nothing up at all, Pete," she reassured him. "You know me, I just wanted to check in with reality. And I needed to let you know that I won't be able to drive up to the lake with you on Friday."

"Aww, Mouse! Why not?"

"Carla's brewing some god-awful meeting and you know how those go. Lord knows what time we'll get done."

"I could wait and we'll leave when you get finished," he suggested.

"Thanks, but I think I'll come up Saturday morning. Get there when the fun starts."

They were both looking forward to the fourteenth birthday party of their godson, Scot, on Saturday. Scot's mom, Missy, was the third member of their 'gruesome foursome', and Ben was number four. Emma smiled, grateful that the four of them were still so close after all these years. They had formed such a bond at the little school in Summer Lake when they were eight. It had stayed strong for twenty-three years and counting.

"I really don't mind," said Pete. "I could get a few more hours in here while I wait."

"Oh, no you don't. I'm not going to be the one to explain to your mom why you got there so late. You know she loves it when you're there the whole weekend. And besides, I'm too scared to roll in late at night now."

Pete raised an eyebrow.

"Gramps might shoot me!" she laughed.

Pete joined her laughter, remembering last summer when Emma's grandfather had become a little too eager to defend his property.

"I guess it probably would be safer to come up Saturday then, but if you do get finished early you could always come over and sleep at the guest house. The key is still in the same place it's always been. You wouldn't disturb anyone out there, or get shot at, and that way we could still all do breakfast on Saturday."

Emma put her hands on her hips.

"Ah, she's considering it," smiled Pete. "I knew the mention of breakfast might swing it."

It was something of a tradition for the four friends that, whenever they were all back at Summer Lake, they made it a point to have breakfast together on the weekends. Ben and Missy still lived by the lake. Ben ran his family business, the resort. Missy raised her son and had always worked whatever jobs she could find. A few years ago she had started her own business, cleaning the second homes and vacation houses around the lake.

Emma was all too aware that she was the one who had been missing from the group more and more over the last year. She didn't like it one bit, but her agent, Carla, had been keeping her nose to the grindstone with one project after another. A few years ago Emma wrote a screenplay adapting a best-selling novel into a major movie. Since then she'd been in high demand for adaptations and rewrites, but hadn't really enjoyed any of it. Her time and energy were engaged to the full, but she wished she could say the same about her creativity or sense of achievement. She frowned; it irked her that yet again she'd be missing out on what she really wanted to do in order to do something she didn't.

"Sorry if I touched a nerve, Em," Pete's voice broke her train of thought.

"Oh, it's okay. You know how to push my buttons. Maybe I'll drive up really early on Saturday and get there in time for breakfast."

"Don't sweat it, just get there when you can. We can do breakfast on Sunday...I was only winding you up. No need to go into Super Mouse mode, flying up the freeway in your mouse-mobile at the crack of dawn, cape blowing in the wind!"

Emma took a step towards him, shaking her finger in the air, about to give him hell for mocking her with his childhood nickname for her. At that moment Pete's intercom buzzed.

"Sorry to interrupt," came Judy's voice, "but I've finally got Mr. Bowers on the line for you."

"Great," said Pete, suddenly all businesslike, "put him through." He smiled up at Emma and whispered, "Saved by the bell!"

Emma did her best to flounce from the room. She often hung out in Pete's adjoining meeting room when important calls interrupted her visits with him. This time, still feigning indignation, she stuck her nose in the air, turned, and flung the double doors dramatically wide open, only to hurtle into someone on the other side. She ran straight into a broad chest, which she noticed smelled wonderful... sandalwood. Unfortunately that was all she had time to notice before she realized that their feet were somehow tangled together and her momentum was carrying her off balance. She felt a strong arm latch around her and pull her close. The next thing she knew she was on the floor, cushioned by that big arm which was attached to the most handsome man she had ever seen. Huge, deep brown eyes were staring down into hers; for a moment they were both lost.

"Are you okay?" he asked.

She nodded, unable to speak, entranced by those eyes still staring into hers. She watched them fill with concern when she didn't respond.

"I...I'm okay," she stammered.

The moment of magic was broken by a snort from Pete's office. He'd seen the whole thing through the open office doors. Hand over the mouthpiece of his phone, his face was red from the effort of trying not to laugh.

"Super Mouse!" he squeaked, before lowering his voice several octaves to continue his conversation.

Emma scrambled to her feet, ready to slam the doors shut. But before she did so, she stuck her tongue out and turned and wiggled her backside at him. No sooner had she slipped back into that moment of shared childishness than she remembered the man on the floor. She felt her cheeks flush as she looked down to where he still sat.

"Oh no, are you okay?" She rushed to help him to his feet, hoping he wasn't hurt.

"I'm stunned."

She frowned, beginning to worry. He laughed, a deep, slow, sexy laugh that made her catch her breath.

"I'm stunned because I've never seen Peter the Great have a door slammed in his face before! I've never seen him lose his cool on the phone and here you are, making him snort and wiggling your tushie at him!"

Emma felt the heat in her cheeks again. In this city she was used to projecting calmness, composure and elegance. Now here she was with this gorgeous man sitting on the floor laughing at her childish behavior. She took a deep breath.

"I'm so sorry. Pete and I have known each other since childhood and we occasionally revert to old ways." She extended her hand, this time all cool composure. "Let me introduce myself in a more traditional manner. I'm Emma Douglas."

"Oh, I know who you are." As he looked into her eyes, she had a crazy urge to open them wide so he could see her soul. She made herself snap to; that was ridiculous!

"I'm afraid I don't know who you are," she replied. There went that smile again, those lips. She couldn't help but wonder what it would be like to kiss them. Oh my goodness, Emma! Stop it!

"Forgive me...Jack Benson," he said as he got to his feet and towered over her. He had to be at least six feet two inches tall, powerfully built, all muscle and controlled energy, short dark hair to go with those smoldering eyes and everything packaged in a crisp white dress shirt and black suit pants.

"So, Mr. Benson. We finally meet," she smiled up at him coolly.

"Wow!" he looked surprised and, could it be, disappointed by her switch to coolness? "You don't seem too thrilled to finally meet me. Does a reputation I don't know about go before me?"

"No, sorry. I'm pulling myself together from the fall."

He reached out and touched her shoulder. "You okay?"

She took a step back as his touch sent an electric current zapping through her whole body.

"I'm fine, thank you." Her voice sounded much stronger than she felt.

"Well, okay then." Jack stepped back himself.

At that moment the door flew open and Pete appeared.

"Are you two all right?" he asked. Obviously believing that they were, and not seeming to notice the tension between them, he went on, "Sorry, Mouse. I should have warned you that Jack was still in here."

"Mouse?" echoed Jack as Emma blushed yet again. She hadn't blushed this much since high school. This time she wasn't sure if it was caused by anger at Pete or embarrassment in front of Jack.

"It's Em's..." Pete began.

Emma cut him off. "It's Pete's attempt to be funny," she said, giving him a stern look, "and it's not working."

Pete smiled, seeming to realize he'd made her uncomfortable. "Sorry Em. I'm still too much of a kid when we get together, I guess. I forget that you're all grown up and dignified these days."

She rolled her eyes at him, unable to stay cross for long.

"Let me make the formal introductions more befitting of the adults we are," he grinned.

"Aww," said Jack, "I liked our first introduction best. Could we try that one again?"

Emma looked at him as he and Pete began to laugh.

"You're as bad as he is," she said, smiling in spite of her embarrassment.

"Oh, no. He's much worse than me," laughed Pete.

Emma shook her head at the pair of them.

"Okay. I am going to take what is left of my dignity and leave now. I'll see you on Saturday, Pete. Nice to meet you, Mr. Benson."

"Oh, Mouse. At least call him Jack!"

"I think after rolling around the office floor together we should probably be on first name terms, don't you?" Those eyes were laughing down at her again.

She shook her head. "Let's try this again. Pete, I will see you on Saturday. Nice to meet you, Jack." With that she turned and left quickly.

As she stood in the elevator, she ran through the events in Pete's office. How on Earth had she managed to knock that man over? He was so big and strong. Oh, Emma, you sound pathetic. She laughed at herself, glad she was alone in the elevator. So big and strong... and so darned sexy, she couldn't help adding.

So, she had finally met the mysterious Jack Benson. He'd been Pete's partner for years. They'd met in college and founded the Phoenix Corporation together not long afterward. Admittedly, he'd mostly worked out of their offices in Texas and on the East Coast, but he must have been in LA for a year now. She'd have to ask Pete why they'd never been introduced before. She felt her whole body tremble as she remembered today's introduction. On the floor. With that big arm around her. Protecting her from harm. She tried to chase those thoughts from her mind. See, she berated herself, this is why you stay away from men. You turn into a pathetic, mushy little romantic whenever there is a good-looking one around. And the good-looking ones are all about the superficial. They're all about themselves and how many women they can get into their beds.

As she thought about it, it dawned on her that perhaps she'd never met Jack before because Pete had engineered it that way. He knew her so well, and was protective like a big brother, even though they were the same age.

Jack is probably the kind of man who could really hurt me if I let him, she thought, and Pete knows that.

By the time she emerged from the elevator she had vowed to herself that she would endeavor to stay out of Jack Benson's way. Leaving the building, she stepped into the bright sunshine and set out to do battle once more with the horrible traffic.

~ ~ ~

Jack smiled to himself as he remembered Emma wiggling her rear end at Pete.

"So, what do you say? Jack?"

He looked up to find Pete staring at him expectantly. "Huh? Sorry?"

Pete burst out laughing.

"You haven't heard a word I've been saying, have you?"

"I errr...." Jack shrugged. He had no idea what to say. How could he tell his partner that all he could think about were dancing green eyes and a scent of summer breeze? He could imagine Pete's face if he spoke those words out loud. But, man! That roll on the floor with Emma had really shaken him up. Pete was still staring at him, curious now.

"Tell me this isn't what I think it is?"

"What do you think it is?" Jack played for time. He and Pete were close, but he knew how protective his friend was towards Emma. He wasn't sure how he would react.

"She's really gotten to you, hasn't she?"

"Well, um...."

"Why did I never think of this before?"

Jack pulled himself together, glad the reaction wasn't what he'd feared.

"What do you mean, 'thought of this before'?"

"You and Em of course. Two of my favorite people who might just hit it off together."

"You probably haven't thought of it because I don't do relationships, remember?"

"Yeah, but only 'cos you attract man-eaters that you wouldn't survive a relationship with. You never get the chance to meet any genuine women and believe me, they don't come more genuine than Em."

"Is that so?"

"Yes it is. You know, in many ways you two have similar stories. You've both worked your butts off to achieve success and neither of you have achieved any of what really matters."

"Hey, is that the pot calling the kettle black?" asked Jack, keen to deflect the focus away from the issue that bothered him the most.

He had worked hard, damned hard, all his life. His father had drunk himself into an early grave and Jack had determined that he would not take after him. He'd worked since he was thirteen, any job he could find. He'd worked his way through college where he'd met Pete. The two of them had founded this company that was now a multi-million dollar enterprise, but somehow it all felt hollow. All he'd ever wanted was to achieve success. By most people's standards he'd done that in a huge way. He loved his mom and brother, and he'd done all of this to support them. But Dan didn't need his support any more, he was doing great himself, and Jack had already set his mom up so she'd never want for anything the rest of her life.

Yet somehow it wasn't enough; there was an emptiness that couldn't be filled by his work, his success or even his family. Of course, there had been women, and plenty of them if he was honest. But they never seemed to add anything to his life. In fact, they ended up detracting from it. Like Pete said, he attracted man-eaters. They wanted to take—his time, his attention, in most cases his money. He realized Pete was watching him.

"Maybe I am the pot and you are the kettle bro," admitted Pete, "but at least I know it. We've done great things since we started this place. To me, for now, it's enough. I know I'll add a special someone into the mix when the time is right, and that won't be for a few years yet. In the meantime, I'm content with my lot, I'm engaged in it, I love every minute. I'm not the one who is burned out and looking for more meaning, am I?"

Jack had to admit, if only to himself since he wouldn't give his friend the satisfaction, that Pete was right. He had worked himself into the ground the last few years. His demons had driven him to the point of exhaustion, mental and physical. He'd been working on projects in Houston, Miami and New York. Pete had probably saved him from a breakdown when he'd insisted Jack come back to LA last year. He gave Pete a rueful grin.

"Okay, Peter the Great. No need to point out, yet again, that you've got it all figured out and I'm just a crazy mixed-up kid."

"Ah, come on. All I'm saying is that if you really want to find some joy in life you might have to lift your nose from the grindstone to see what else is around."

"Okay. Point taken. Now back to business, can we? Before giving me this little life lesson, you were about to run a new project by me, right?"

"I did run it by you," laughed Pete, "but you didn't hear a word 'cos you were too busy reminiscing about rolling on the floor with Em!"

Jack had to laugh. "Okay, so a pretty lady caught my eye. What can I say? But that's the end of it; your friend is very attractive, end of story."

"If you say so, we'll leave it there, for now. Although it may come up again since she'll be at the lake this weekend too."

"The lake?"

"You really weren't listening at all, were you? The new project I was talking about?"

Jack shook his head and grinned sheepishly. "Didn't catch a word."

"I want you to build me a house up there. Since there's nothing new starting here 'til the fall, I thought we could kill two birds with one stone. Get you a summer by the lake to get you back to full strength and, to keep you out of mischief, you can build me a house while you're there."

"Wow, so you're banishing me to the boonies?"

"Yep. Of course, it's all in my best interests really. I get you fully recovered, I get the house I've been after and I get the excuse to spend more time up there myself this summer. I win all 'round."

"I don't know," mused Jack "there are a few things I wanted to do here while we're quieter."

"I know," said Pete quickly "and joking aside, I'm not really steam-rolling you into this. I just thought it might work out. All I'm saying is, come up with me this weekend. There's the party, but there will still be time to look around, see what you think. There's something special about that place, I think it might do you some good."

"Okay, why not? I didn't have any real plans for this weekend anyway. I'm not promising anything though." He hesitated a moment. "And you say Emma will be there?"

"She sure will. So, I take it that seals the deal?"

Jack smiled and nodded.

Chapter Two

Emma answered the door to her apartment and greeted her friend, Holly, with a hug.

"Do I smell cookies baking?" Holly asked, with a look of mock horror.

"You certainly do," beamed Emma. She loved to cook, to bake especially. She always made cookies or muffins or delicious cupcakes for her friends when they came over.

"I've warned you about this," laughed Holly. "You must not make me eat gazillions of calories every time I come over or I will have to stop visiting you."

"Well, we both know that's not true. So, come in," said Emma pulling her friend into the den, "and sit down." She pushed her down on the huge sofa, "And have a cookie!" She thrust a plate into Holly's lap.

"Mmm," Holly munched on her cookie. "So what's new with our movie writer lady? Anything interesting on the horizon?"

"Not much. Carla is gearing up to something, not sure what yet, but she's arranged a meeting with some producer on Friday."

"Ooh, that sounds so cool." Holly was always curious about the movie world and thrilled that her friend was a part of it. More thrilled, it seemed, than Emma herself.

"To be honest, I'm more interested in leaving town early on Friday and heading up to the lake for Scot's birthday."

"Oh, I'd forgotten you're up there this weekend. It's been a while, hasn't it?"

"Too long. And I had to tell Pete that I can't drive up with him after all." Emma smiled as she remembered her visit to Pete's office.

"Now that's the kind of smile I haven't seen on your face in a very long time," said Holly. "Spill the beans!"

Holly knew her too well...there was no point trying to hide anything.

"Well," she began, "I went to see Pete at his office and I guess you could say I bumped into his partner, Jack Benson."

"And?"

Emma told her how she'd knocked the man over and ended up on the floor with him.

"So, is he good-looking?"

"Gorgeous! Tall, dark, bottomless brown eyes, muscular, big strong arms and he smells...." She stopped herself short and looked at Holly. "Remember why I stay away from men? This is exactly why. I go completely gaga over a good-looking one and manage to blind myself to the fact that the personality isn't as appealing as the packaging. I can't be trusted!"

Holly touched her arm.

"It was only once, Em, and it was years ago."

"Yes, and I married him! And I thought that meant we would live happily ever after. Pity he didn't believe in the 'forsaking all others' part."

"Em, you were young. That's the past; you've grown and learned since then. He was a jackass, but some day you're going to have to get past the fear that all men are like Rob."

Holly had helped Emma put herself back together after her short but disastrous marriage to a movie director.

"Oh, I know they're not all like him, only the really good-looking ones. Honestly Holly, yesterday, lying on the floor with that man's arm around me, feeling him so close, I felt like that stupid love-struck girl I was all those years ago. And it frightens the hell out of me! I intend to avoid him at all costs."

"Well, it sounds like that shouldn't be too hard to do. He's been Pete's partner for so long and been here in LA for almost a year already and this is the first time you've ever met him."

"I've been thinking about that too. I think maybe Pete deliberately made sure we didn't meet."

"Why would he do that?" asked Holly, puzzled.

"Because Mr. Benson is no doubt a womanizer. Looking like he does he could have any woman he wants, and as many as he wants. I'll bet Pete is protecting me and keeping his own life simple."

"You really think that?"

"You said yourself, Jack's been in LA for a year already."

"Well, in that case, do you think I'm maybe a gold digger or a wild woman?"

Emma stared at her, confused. "What on Earth are you talking about?"

Holly laughed. "It's just that if I follow your logic that Pete never introduced you to Jack because he's a womanizer and a heart breaker, then perhaps you've never introduced me to Pete because I'm a gold digger or a Jezebel."

"Holly! You know that's not true."

"Yes, I do. I'm simply trying to point out that what you're thinking about this Jack may not be true either."

"Oh, it doesn't matter either way. He's gorgeous. I'm an idiot when it comes to gorgeous men, and I have no intention of letting one destroy me ever again. Therefore I'm going to make sure that I don't bump into him again. What does matter though, is that you have never met Pete. I can't believe that. You two would be perfect for each other."

"Now hold it there. That's not where I was going at all. I was using the example to show you that it's perfectly normal for people from different areas of your life to never meet."

"I know, but you accidentally gave me the wonderful idea of getting you two together."

"Forget about it, Em. I'm too busy with the store to make room for a man right now, and by the sounds of it Pete has a really busy life too. Between his construction empire, spending so much time at the lake with his folks and your little gang of four I'm sure he has no time for a relationship either."

Emma smiled sweetly and nodded her head.

"Just leave it, okay?" said Holly.

"Oh, I'll be good. Anyways, enough man talk. They're more trouble than they're worth. Tell me what's going on at the store."

The two chatted about Holly's fashion boutique for a while, always glad to catch up on each other's lives. All too soon it was time for Holly to leave, promising to be in touch soon.

~ ~ ~

Jack headed to Pete's on Friday afternoon, wondering what he was getting himself into. Did he really want to spend the weekend in a sleepy little town by a lake, going to some teenager's birthday party? Would he even consider spending his summer up there? If not, what was the point in going? Who was he trying to kid? He knew what the point was. Ever since Tuesday he'd kept thinking of Emma. Those eyes filled with concern when she'd thought he might be hurt. Flashing with amusement as she'd slammed the doors on Pete. The way he'd felt her heart beat when he held her as they fell to the floor. The protective surge he'd felt making sure she'd come to no harm. The other surge, the one in his pants, as he'd held her soft body against him. The blush that had spread across her neck and cheeks when he'd talked about rolling around on the floor together. He shook his head, trying to clear the images of her that kept crowding in.

If he was honest with himself, he was going to the lake with Pete because he wanted to see her again, plain and simple. At various moments in the week he'd convinced himself that it was just to prove himself wrong. That he'd see her and there would be nothing there, only an attractive woman. The rest of the time, though, he was hoping, really hoping, that she would make him feel the way she had on the floor of Pete's office: amused, aroused, protective, wanting to know more. He hadn't felt any of those things in a long while, and had never before felt them all at the same time about the same woman.

He pulled into Pete's driveway and grabbed his bag from the back of his SUV. Pete came around the side of the house from the pool.

"Hey, man, you're early. Eager to go?"

Jack wasn't about to admit how eager he was. "Yeah, sorry. You know what the traffic's like. Give yourself extra time and you sail through."

"Not complaining. We can hit the road early, suits me fine."

The two of them loaded their gear into Pete's truck and headed out towards Summer Lake.

Emma was so glad this week was almost over. All she had to do now was get through this meeting with Carla and she'd be free for the weekend. She was really looking forward to Scot's birthday party. She had almost resigned herself to never having children of her own. She couldn't imagine being a single parent, even though Missy managed it so wonderfully. And since she had sworn off men, remaining childless seemed a foregone conclusion. Her godson Scot was as close as she would get, and she loved him dearly.

As she battled with the traffic once more on her way to Carla's oceanfront home, she smiled as she thought of Missy. They'd just finished their senior year of high school when Missy had confided that she was pregnant. At the time it had seemed like the end of the world for her. The father had been a seasonal worker at the lake and had left before Missy even knew she was pregnant. When Emma, Pete and Ben had gone off to college, Missy had stayed behind to raise her son, and she had raised a fine young man. Scot was quiet, a real computer wizard and he loved his mom. Missy had made her three best friends his godparents, further cementing the strong bonds that tied them together. Tomorrow, fourteen years on, they would all be there for his birthday.

She arrived at Carla's palatial home and was surprised to find no other cars on the sweeping driveway. Often, a Friday afternoon meeting at Carla's turned into a Friday evening party with the rich and the beautiful dropping by, along with assorted wannabes and hangers on. As she got out of her car, Carla came down the stairs from the front door to greet her.

"Darling Emma!" she boomed and draped Emma in an elegant embrace. She was a statuesque beauty, standing almost six feet tall, with dark curls falling around her shoulders. Carla Messini was as close as it gets to royalty in Hollywood. She came from a long line of actors and directors that stretched all the way back to the heydays of the studios and to Italy before that.

"There is a change of plan, *bella*. I wanted you to meet Mr. Schumacher, who wants to make an adaptation of Geraldine's Way, but he was called unexpectedly to New York."

"Oh. Okay."

"Darling, do not be disappointed. We have rescheduled already. We shall meet on Tuesday."

"Oh, no. I'm not disappointed, really." Emma wondered if she should tell Carla that she would be less disappointed if the meeting had been canceled altogether. She had read Geraldine's Way when the novel was riding high on the bestseller lists and really hadn't thought it warranted all the hype that surrounded it. She couldn't imagine being the one to write the screenplay for it.

"I am so sorry I didn't call you," said Carla, though she didn't look very sorry at all. In fact, she was beaming. Emma smiled, waiting for the explanation she knew would come.

"I received a call from Leandro. He is wanting to see me—this evening!" Emma smiled even more, she knew what this meant. Leandro Pereira had starred in two of her movies and Carla was absolutely besotted with him. Imposing as she was, Carla had a heart of gold. With her height and booming Italian accent, she was an Amazonian in the jungle of Hollywood, but underneath she had the heart of a true romantic and for months now that heart had been yearning for Leandro.

"Oh, Carla. That's wonderful."

"You are not angry?"

"Not at all. I hope you have a lovely evening!"

"But you should be angry. I bring you here for a meeting, I lose you the meeting. I have no party and I abandon you for a man. I would be angry!"

Emma laughed. "Well, when you put it like that maybe I should be, but I'm not. I'm going to go now so you can get ready for your date, and do you know what? I'm going to start my weekend early. I'm off to the lake, and I think I'll leave tonight instead of waiting till morning. So you see, it's all perfect, no problems, no need for anger."

Carla smiled. "You are too even tempered, darling. But this time it is for my good. So you go, enjoy your lake, and I shall enjoy my Leandro." As Carla air kissed three times around Emma's ears, Emma couldn't help but pity Leandro. She had no doubt Carla would enjoy him. Eat him alive more like.

Driving back to her apartment, she looked around at the other drivers as they crawled along. She made up stories for the people she saw. The stressed looking guy talking on his cell phone in the Audi beside her was making excuses to his wife as to why he wouldn't be home in time for dinner with her parents. Claiming it was work instead of admitting he was on his way to see his mistress. The beautiful young Hispanic woman in the VW behind her was a Colombian heiress who had fled from her father's insistence that she marry the son of a neighboring landowner. She'd met a medical student here in LA and was madly in love with him. She was on her way to meet him, not knowing that the father's mercenaries awaited her, having taken the boyfriend hostage.

Emma had always been curious about what people's stories might be; where they were going, what they were doing. For a moment she wondered where Jack Benson might be on this Friday night, where he was going, what he was doing. Ha, that would be more like *who* he was doing! Forget it, Em. Forget him.

She finally made it back to her apartment and collected her weekend bag, glad it was packed and ready to go. At this rate she wouldn't make it up to the lake until gone midnight, but at least she'd be there for breakfast with the others.

Chapter Three

As she drove the last few miles she was growing tired. Grateful she knew the road so well, she followed the twists and turns on automatic pilot. All her life she'd loved this place. It was the only home she'd ever really known. Her parents had died in a car crash when she was eight years old. Her grandparents had brought her out here and raised her in the small community by the lake. She hadn't really known them before the accident, but with all the love they'd shown her, their patience as she had run and hidden from them over and over again, she'd come to love them dearly. When she'd first arrived, newly orphaned, she had felt so alone and afraid, but this place had soothed her somehow. The lake seemed to sparkle just for her and the mountains huddled around, trying to reassure her, comfort her. The horrors of a new school had been eased when Pete and Missy had stepped in on her second day and stopped some boys from picking on her. Missy had taken her under her wing. Pete and his friend Ben had become her protectors and life had started to become bearable. Gramps and those friendships were still her mainstays and Summer Lake had been the backdrop to all of it. As always, she was so glad to be back.

She rolled the window down to get some fresh air and breathed in the scent of pines and lake, the smell of home, of comfort and of Gramps. Her grandmother had died ten years ago. Had it really been that long? Yes, she'd been in college in Oregon when Grandma fell ill. She'd spent that summer back here, sharing her grandmother's last days and helping Gramps through his first days alone. Her grandparents had been married for forty-five years. Emma had wondered how he would ever carry on without her, but Gramps had soldiered on and these days he was doing well. He spent a lot of time with his old buddy, Joe, and between their fishing and tinkering with cars and trucks in his workshop, he led a full life.

Emma wondered again whether she should go to his house now. No, she smiled, she really didn't want to risk getting shot at. She remembered the night last summer when he had threatened her and Pete with his shotgun before he had realized who they were. She took a right turn and headed along the southern shore, out towards Pete's parents' place. To her left, the lake reflected the stars and the skinny moon. That was one more thing she loved up here; no city lights to dilute the brilliance of the night sky. She turned into the Hemmings' property and took the little driveway that led away from the main house and down to the guest cabin which sat on its own little cove at the water's edge.

She parked behind the cabin and looked up at the star-filled sky. It was so good to be here. She wondered, as she had so many times recently, whether she should come up here for the summer. There was nothing to stop her, especially if she told Carla before she managed to sign her up for some project she wasn't really interested in. Ugh, Geraldine's Way! Emma really couldn't imagine writing the screenplay for that novel.

Hmm, novel? Perhaps that's what she should be doing? Writing her own novel, right here. She smiled to herself in the darkness. That felt like the best idea she'd had in a long time – why not?

"Why the hell not?" she asked out loud. She pulled her bag from the car and climbed onto the porch, where she reached under the cushions of the old swing to find the key that lived there.

"Where are you?" she muttered as she scrabbled with her left hand under the cushions. Having no success she plonked her bag down and lifted the cushions – no key! "Well, that's a first!" Pete had told her the key would be in the usual place and it had been kept there since they were kids. This cabin had seen so many antics thanks to that key. "Where on Earth is it?" she wondered out loud. She really didn't want to have to drive back over to Gramps' at this point. She tried the door, just in case, and to her relief it swung open. She returned to the porch for her bag and went inside, planning to simply fall into bed and get some sleep.

Jack lay in bed watching the stars twinkle through the skylight. He had thoroughly enjoyed his evening with Pete's parents. Anne and Graham were both artists, Jack envied Pete's relationship with them. While Pete had grown up here in this little town with doting, older parents, Jack himself had endured a very different childhood. His own father had been a mean drunk. Jack only remembered the beatings, the ones he'd taken, the ones he'd shielded Dan from and, worst of all, the ones his mom had tried to hide from them, her cheap makeup never quite managing to cover the bruises completely. Jack remembered the beatings but he refused to allow himself to dwell on the pain. He'd yearned for his father's love, had envied friends whose fathers took them fishing or came to watch their games. He'd loved his dad so much, but he was a realist and had learned the hard way that love and trust weren't always returned. He'd carried that lesson with him and gave his all to protect and provide for the people who earned his affection, wasting little time on those who didn't.

His father drank himself into an early grave by the time Jack was seventeen. He'd already been working after school for four years by then, and from that day on he'd worked every job he could find to support his mom and Dan. He'd stayed in Austin for college instead of heading to California as he'd hoped. He'd brought the family closer to the city so he could live at home and worked at a gas station, as a day laborer and truck driver to keep his family going. He'd met Pete while they were both at UT; they had become firm friends and later business partners.

As he lay looking up at the stars, he wondered again if this place might be what he needed for the summer. He'd been touched by the beauty of the sunset over the water as they'd eaten out on the deck. As he'd watched the golden light bathing the rolling hills and sparkling on the lake he'd felt a sense of peace creep over him. A feeling he'd never felt before, but one he was pretty sure he could get used to. When Pete's parents had told him about the skylight over the bed in the guest cabin, he'd asked if he could sleep down here.

Pete said this place had some kind of magic. He wondered if it was part of what gave Pete his own unique character. Jack had never known anyone so at peace with himself, so confident yet unassuming. He smiled—Peter the Great. And his parents had that same air about them. Perhaps this place instilled something special in the people that lived here. If he stuck around perhaps he might pick up some of it.

And of course there was Emma; she definitely had something special. He'd managed to avoid peppering Pete with questions about her. He knew she'd grown up here. Most importantly he knew she'd be here tomorrow. Perhaps she'd be here for breakfast with Pete's other friends—he hoped so—but definitely she'd be at the party. He was surprised at himself how often she invaded his thoughts, but he smiled and thought, Why the hell not?

The hairs on the back of his neck stood on end as he heard her voice echo the question. "Why the hell not?" Damn, that sounded real, his imagination was getting carried away.

He decided it was time to get some sleep and give his tired brain a rest. Hearing her voice like that was a little too freaky. He turned on his side and pulled the covers up over his shoulder. As he closed his eyes he heard her again. "Where the hell are you?"

He sat bolt upright in bed, wondering if he was going nuts. He heard a bang on the porch outside and her voice came again, sounding a little frustrated this time. "Well, that's a first!" A wry grin spread across his face. He had no idea why, but Emma really was outside, muttering to herself. Perhaps this place really was magical after all. It'd brought her out here to him in the middle of the night. Then it dawned on him that she no doubt wouldn't be as pleased to see him as he was to see her. What to do? He heard her again. "Where on Earth is it?" What was she looking for? Then he heard the front door swing open and she entered, plopping her bag down.

Oh, shit! thought Jack. What do I do?

He was half amused and half concerned. He was thrilled that she was here, but he really didn't want to frighten the life out of her, or worse, scare her away by announcing his presence. As her footsteps approached the bedroom door he quickly decided on the path of least resistance. He lay back down, pulled the covers up over himself and pretended to be asleep.

Emma had a terrible habit of drinking iced coffee on the drive up here. The first unfortunate side effect being that the bathroom was always the first place she saw at the lake. The second, she realized as she emerged, was that although she was exhausted, her mind was skittery and the sleepiness that had plagued her the last few miles wouldn't translate into real sleep for a while yet. Oh well, at least here in the cabin there was the wonderful skylight above the bed. She could watch the stars until sleep claimed her.

She loved this cabin. As kids, and later as young adults, their gruesome foursome had spent many good times here. She believed Pete's parents, whom she adored, had probably built the place with that in mind. A place for their son and his friends to hang out, have some fun away from adult interference yet still be right there, safe on their own property. She would swear this cabin had a presence of its own; it held happiness and fond memories, it was almost like one of the gang. Tonight its presence felt almost tangible, as if she were sharing space with another living being, as if she weren't really alone. She chuckled to herself as she began to undress. She stepped out of her clothes and folded them neatly, placing them on the chair by the window. Pausing as she walked toward the bed, she looked up through the skylight at the stars. She sighed a happy sigh, it was so good to be here.

~ ~ ~

Jack was trying his hardest not to even breathe. Two seconds after she emerged from the bathroom he realized that pretending to be asleep was probably the dumbest thing he could have done. He should have spoken up when she came in. Damn! Then she started to undress and he had no choice. This was going to be awkward. But, man, part of him couldn't peel his eyes away from her. One part of him was wide awake and standing to attention. Why hadn't she turned the light on? He could have woken, or pretended to, and she would have seen him. Perhaps they could have laughed together about the mix up. But now...now he was watching her undress and there was nothing he could do that wouldn't make this worse. Nothing, that is, except stick with his idiotic plan of pretending to be asleep.

He stayed as still as he possibly could, watching her bare shoulders, the curve of her neck as she stepped out of her jeans. She was so beautiful. Full breasts overflowed from a smooth silky bra. Her waist was narrow above curvy hips and, oh my God, a silky thong. His breath caught in his chest as she bent to remove the thong, showing off that perfectly rounded ass he'd so enjoyed watching her wiggle. His erection strained inside his boxers. Man, she was perfect. He watched, transfixed as she unfastened her bra, freeing those luscious breasts. Jack squeezed his eyes closed. This was pure torture and it was so, so wrong—was he now some kind of creepy voyeur?

He couldn't help it though. He opened his eyes again only to find her standing before him, completely naked, face upturned to the stars above, every perfect inch of her calling out to him as she gave a contented little sigh. That image burned itself into his brain and he knew he would never, ever shake its memory. It filled him with so many emotions. Lust of course; she was incredible. He wanted to smell her, taste her, feel her, take her. But more than that, she looked so vulnerable somehow that he wanted to protect her, and yet so strong he wanted to challenge her. What the hell was wrong with him? She'd never speak to him again if she knew he'd watched her. All the same, he couldn't wait for the moment this very beautiful, very naked woman would slide into bed next to him.

And she did.

Emma climbed into bed and wriggled over to center herself under the skylight. Just as she reached the middle she realized the other side of the bed was warm. There was someone already there! For a second she lay stunned, holding her breath and hoping not to wake whoever was there. Her mind racing, she thought she could probably slide back out without making too much noise or movement. At that moment the body on the other side of the bed rolled over to face her and stretched an arm over her.

Jack Benson! Oh, my goodness! Emma froze. She had to admit she'd entertained a few thoughts about being in bed with this gorgeous man, but this hadn't quite been the scenario she'd had in mind. Could she get out without waking him? She started to edge away from him, but damn if that arm didn't tighten around her and draw her towards him. All of a sudden she was pressed up against his hard naked chest, enveloped in the scent of him, with that muscular arm holding her close. For a moment she breathed him in, imagining what it would be like to be held by this man for real. She felt her nipples go taut and a tingling warmth between her legs. Oh my!

As if the change in her had startled him, Jack opened his eyes, looking dazed and half asleep.

"Emma?" he murmured. "You're a good dream." He smiled down at her with those eyes she wanted to swim in, for a moment she stared back. Then she came to her senses and pulled back.

"This isn't a dream, Jack. I'm so sorry. I didn't know you were here." She scurried to the other side of the bed, covering herself with sheet as she went.

Jack sat up, looking startled. "What the...?" he asked, leaping out of bed and standing to face her.

Emma couldn't help but notice his bulging shorts; that was quite a bulge! Oh, how could she be thinking that right now? She should be mortified that she had crawled naked into bed with him, not admiring the size of his manhood!

"I'm sorry," she stammered. "I didn't know you were here."

"You already said that."

"Pete told me I could stay here if I came in late...I sometimes do."

Jack seemed to be gathering his wits.

"Hey, it's okay," he smiled. "No harm, no foul. It's me that's out of the ordinary. They told me about the skylight and I asked if I could sleep down here. I've always loved watching the stars, ever since I was a little kid. Pete must've assumed you weren't coming as it was after midnight when we turned in."

Emma just nodded at him. Now that the shock had passed she was filled with acute embarrassment. She should have leaped out of bed screaming the moment she realized someone was there. Instead she'd lain still, let him hold her, pull her against him. And the worst thing was that she'd loved every second of it.

"Are you okay?"

"Yes, I'm fine! I should go," she snapped, her embarrassment coming across as anger.

"Whoa," Jack held up a hand. "Calm down and slow down. Where are you going to go?"

"Anywhere." Tears filled her eyes, she felt so stupid. He came around the bed towards her.

"Hey. It's okay." He was standing in front of her. "It's okay, you're tired and you had a shock." He perched on the edge of the bed and put an arm around her. Emma couldn't help it; she relaxed into him and rested her head against his shoulder.

"There, see? Relax," he murmured. "It's okay. You don't need to go anywhere. You can just lay down there and go to sleep. In the morning we'll laugh about this, you'll see."

She turned to look up at him. "If I sleep here, what will you do?"

"I'll sleep right out there on the sofa," he pointed, "unless you have a problem with that?"

"No, no problem," she replied in a small voice. She felt so foolish. Why, oh why hadn't she jumped out of bed? And why on Earth had she lain still as he held her? To her chagrin she felt her nipples harden at the thought of it. She clutched the sheet tighter around them, finding it hard to believe that she was sitting here naked with his arm around her.

"Okay," he said as he stood.

"Okay," she repeated, looking up at him. She couldn't help but notice the dusting of dark hair above perfect washboard abs. Oh, he could be so dangerous. Summoning her practical side to save her from lust and confusion, she said, "They keep extra blankets and pillows in the closet."

"Thanks." Running his fingers through his hair, he disappeared into the closet and emerged to make himself a bed on the sofa. She sat with the sheet clutched to her chest, watching him, admiring the muscles that rippled on his broad back as he spread out sheets and blankets. Once his new bed was made he turned and stepped toward her again. Instinctively, she pulled the sheet higher. He stopped dead in his tracks.

"Don't be afraid of me, Emma. You don't ever have to be afraid of me," he said in a low voice.

She met his eyes and gave a small smile. "Not afraid."

He took another step toward her and leaned down, placing his hands on either side of her hips. She breathed in the scent of him, the scent of man and sandalwood. Being this close, she again felt her body respond, the heat tingling between her legs. She buzzed with anticipation, wondering what he was about to do, knowing that whatever it was, she wanted it. He lowered his head; she could feel his breath warm on her skin, her heart thundering. He placed a light kiss on her forehead.

"Get some sleep, Miss Douglas," he breathed. Then he was gone, arranging his long body on the short sofa.

Snuggling down into the covers, Emma couldn't believe she was so disappointed. Disappointed that the kiss had only landed on her forehead. So much for avoiding the man! Here she was spending the night with him in the same cabin and wishing he was in the same bed. "Get some sleep, Miss Douglas," she repeated to herself. Though she already knew sleep would be a long time coming and not because of the caffeine in her system.

~ ~ ~

Jack lay on the sofa feeling terrible. What kind of jackass was he? He'd lain there and watched her undress when he should have told her he was there. When she'd slid across to the middle of the bed he hadn't been able to resist turning toward her, throwing an arm across her, all the while pretending to be asleep. It wasn't by choice, but by overwhelming desire for her that he'd drawn her to him. Feeling her softness in his arms had almost driven him crazy, feeling the warmth of her against him, breathing her in. And she'd felt it too, he knew it. The second he'd felt her nipples pebble against his chest he'd had to break the spell. He'd wanted to take her that second. And she'd apologized to him! He'd let *her* feel bad. What was wrong with him? But what else could he do at that point? Man, he felt bad. Lying there, with her only feet away from him, he determined that he would make it up to her. Even though she'd never know. He also determined that before too long he would hold her naked in bed again, and this time not only would she know he was there, she would come to him willingly and she'd ask him to make love to her. The bulge in his boxers grew larger at the thought, and he too knew that sleep would be a long time coming.

Chapter Four

Emma opened her eyes as she heard a soft tapping on the door. It took her a moment to remember where she was. Jack's voice brought it all back.

"You awake in there?"

She sat up in bed, noticing a cup of coffee steaming on the nightstand.

"Morning," she called back, "thanks for the coffee."

"I didn't know how you take it, so there's cream and sugar too."

Emma smiled. How thoughtful. "Thank you."

"Your bag is in there too, I thought you'd need it. Pete will be down in half an hour to pick me up."

Emma started. That should prove interesting. What would Pete have to say about them both spending the night out here? Hang on, it was his fault. He'd told her she could stay here and he hadn't told her he was bringing Jack. Still, she didn't doubt he'd have something to say, especially when Jack told him what had happened.

"I'll jump in the shower and be right out."

She was surprised that he had thought to make her coffee and leave her bag ready for her. Was he kind and thoughtful, or trying to avoid her as long as possible? She showered quickly and dressed in cutoff jeans and her favorite pink T-shirt.

Oh well, she thought, here goes nothing. She opened the door to join him outside on the porch.

He looked up from his seat on the swing and smiled. The way his eyes crinkled at the corners set the butterflies swirling in her stomach.

"Good morning, beautiful." She looked at him, surprised. "I'm sorry, but you are." He patted the swing beside him. "Join me?"

"Just let me refill my coffee. Want some fresh?"

"Yes, please." He handed her his mug. "Black, no sugar."

She returned with their coffees and sat down beside him.

"It's so beautiful out here. Especially in the early morning like this."

"It is. You should see it from Gramps' house. We get to watch the sunrise over the lake from that side."

"I'd like that," he smiled. "Last night we watched it set over the water. It's so neat that you get to do both here."

"Listen. I want to apologize for last night."

"Shh. Please, can we just forget it? You apologized last night, I apologized last night, but it was only a mix up. Shall we let it go at that?"

She smiled up at him. "I'll drink to that." She held out her mug in a toast. He chinked his against it.

"Cheers! Although if you want to sneak into my bed again tonight I won't say no."

Emma almost choked on her coffee. She looked up to find him grinning cheekily at her. She punched him on the arm and laughed.

"You are terrible, you know that, right?"

He looked at her with big sad eyes in a hurt puppy dog look that melted her heart, even though he was only playing.

"You're a hard woman, Emma Douglas."

"And you really are terrible" she laughed.

"No, I'm not terrible at all, in fact I'm pretty damn good, and if you sneak into my bed again tonight I'll prove to you how good I am!"

Emma couldn't believe her ears. She looked at him closely and found those eyes twinkling with mischief.

"Did you really say that?"

"Yes, Ma'am."

She laughed and pushed at him again. "Well, I'll have to take your word for that. I'm sure there are lots of lovely ladies who will vouch for your prowess, but I have no intention of becoming a notch on your bedpost!" Though her words were accompanied by laughter, she was deadly serious. Attractive as she found this man, and much as she would like to find out just how 'good' he was, she didn't do meaningless sex and couldn't risk a relationship, not that a man like him was looking for one.

~ ~ ~

Jack was surprised by that comment, but tried to keep it light. "Hey, now that's not fair. You've accused me of being terrible and of being a collector of bedpost notches and you don't even know me. I demand you take it back."

He loved the way her eyes danced when she laughed. "I will not take it back." She raised her chin in defiance. He wanted to take her face in his hands and kiss that defiance away.

"So," he raised an eyebrow, "you are judgmental, jump to conclusions and won't listen to evidence that contradicts you? Is that what you're saying?"

"No, I'm saying I know your sort."

"Same thing. And I demand a fair trial."

"A fair trial?"

"Yes, I submit that I be allowed to take you to dinner next week, to prove to you that I am a decent, upstanding human being and not the kind of guy you have prejudged me to be."

He clenched his jaw while she looked at him, hoping she'd be carried along enough to say yes. She hesitated, then....

"Well, I consider myself to be a fair person, so I suppose I should hear all of the evidence before reaching my final conclusion. When and where might this dinner take place?"

Jack allowed himself to breathe again. "Thursday, eight o'clock, Mario's."

"Okay," she replied slowly, "Thursday it is."

She got up and took the coffee mugs inside. Jack sat grinning to himself on the swing. He was taking her to dinner; she'd said yes! He heard Pete's car approaching. Hmm, let's see how this goes. Maybe he'd wait to mention the dinner date until he saw Pete's reaction to finding out the two of them had spent the night out here.

Pete jumped down from his truck and climbed the porch steps as Emma emerged through the front door. He stopped and did a double take.

"Where did you come from?" he asked, looking first at her then over at Jack, who was still smiling on the swing. Emma decided she'd rather go on the offensive than the defensive.

"I came from LA, where, last time I saw you, you said I could stay at the guest house if I arrived Friday night, remember?"

"Oops! Sorry, but I didn't think you'd arrive after midnight. So...you two both spent the night out here?"

Emma noticed the gleeful glint in his eyes and really didn't want to explain the details of what had happened. Jack spoke up.

"Yes, we did." He threw her a smile and she prepared herself to be teased about crawling naked into Jack's bed. "Luckily, I was still watching the stars when Emma rolled in, so, being the gentleman I am, I took the sofa." He stood up and rubbed his back. Looking at Pete he said, "You owe me one, bro. I ache all over."

Emma was so grateful to him and shot him a smile behind Pete's back.

How about that? she thought. He really is considerate.

She had fully expected to have to face the two of them ribbing her this morning. Instead, Pete was apologizing and Jack really was turning out to be a much more decent human being than she'd given him credit for.

"I'm sorry guys, I messed up," admitted Pete. He looked put out so Emma, who knew he wasn't used to messing up at anything, went and gave him a hug.

"No biggie," she smiled, "but it will be a biggie if we're late for breakfast. My car is round the back, I'll see you there."

Pete grinned. "Okay, Mouse, we'll follow you over."

Emma followed the lakeside road that led into the resort that Ben's family had owned for generations. The sun sparkled on the water and the breeze blew her hair through the open car windows. Spring was giving way to summer, and it was going to be a warm day. She was pleased that there had been no awkwardness or teasing from Pete. Her heart beat a little faster as she thought about how Jack had stepped in to save her any embarrassment. She thought about Thursday and the dinner she'd agreed to. So much for avoiding him, huh? Oh well. She could have dinner with him. It wouldn't be a problem because she was becoming more certain with every minute she was here that she should come and spend the summer by the lake. She had no intention of working on Geraldine's Way, and a few months up here would be exactly what she needed.

She slowed the car as she turned into the square at the center of the resort. The restaurant stood at the lake's edge with a two-story deck over the water. She could see Missy and Ben already seated at their usual table outside. As she got out of the car, Pete pulled up alongside and the three of them went to join Ben and Missy, who stood to greet them with hugs. A waitress brought menus and coffee. Emma sat next to Missy and gave her old friend another hug.

"It's been too long, Em."

"I know. I'm sorry, but I'm here now. There's no way I'd miss Scot's party. How's he doing?"

"Still fast asleep. I think he is naturally a nocturnal creature, you know? Left to his own devices, he'd stay up all night writing computer programs and then sleep all day."

"He sounds like my brother," said Jack.

"Please tell me your brother made it through high school?" laughed Missy. "Sometimes I think I'm fighting a losing battle to get Scot out of bed and off to school every day."

"It was the same with Dan, but don't worry, he made it through high school. He only took afternoon and evening classes in college and now he runs his own software development company in Silicon Valley."

"Hey", said Pete, "we should get the two of them together. It would be great if Dan could mentor him." He looked at Missy who smiled and nodded. Looking toward Jack she said, "If Dan would have any interest I'd be really grateful. It would be great for him to meet someone who understands what he's talking about!"

"I think Dan would enjoy that. I'll call him later. He's never outgrown the nocturnal habit, so eight o'clock on a Saturday isn't the best time to get hold of him."

The waitress returned to take their orders.

"So," asked Ben when she'd left, "how long has it been since we did this?"

"I don't even want to count," said Emma, "especially since it's usually me that's missing."

"Ah, Em, I didn't mean that. I'm just really happy that we're all here."

Emma loved Ben. He was the quietest of their little group. Some folks thought he was a little standoffish, but that was only because they didn't know him well enough. He was great fun to be around and she'd missed him. His grandfather, Joe, was Gramps' best friend. After college, when Emma and Pete had headed off to LA, Ben had returned to run the family resort. His parents had never really loved the place as his grandparents had; they spent most of their time traveling in a ridiculously large RV that Ben hated. All he had ever wanted was to run the resort and restore it to its former glory. He'd done that and more since graduating college. The lodge was now pretty much fully booked all year round instead of summer only. He'd added more cabins, a thriving marina, and a horseback riding operation. When he'd had the double deck built on the Boathouse Restaurant, the resort became the place to eat on the lake. Emma was proud of all he'd achieved here, and perhaps a little envious that he was so settled. He had only ever wanted to be here and he loved what he did. She loved to write, but felt she hadn't yet found her proper path.

Jack watched Emma as she chatted happily with Ben and Missy, catching up on each other's news and making plans for the rest of the weekend. He loved the way she waved her fork around as she recounted a story of a snooty concierge in an LA hotel. He chuckled at her description of some actresses who'd been involved in her last screenplay; he knew the exact type she was talking about. He'd dated quite a few of them. Her assessment of them and what she referred to as the "fakedom" of Hollywood warmed his heart. Having endured nearly a year in LA, he could relate to her frustrations with the place only too well. Perhaps he should seriously consider spending his summer up here. He envied the easy friendships and beautifully serene setting Pete had here. Maybe his friend was right and this would be just what he needed.

He looked up to find Pete studying him closely, realizing he'd been watching Emma the whole time. Pete raised an eyebrow and Jack returned the questioning look as if he didn't understand. The knowing look Pete gave him in response told him he wasn't fooled one bit.

~ ~ ~

"Well," said Pete, a long while after their table had been cleared, "I hate to be the one to break it up, but I've got a lot to do before tonight."

"Me too," said Missy. "I need to get back before Scot wakes up. I want to have a fun day with him and then get set up over here for this evening."

"I've got to go and see Gramps," said Emma, "then I'll be over to see you later, Miss. I want to give Scot his gift this afternoon, if that's OK with you. Then I can help you set the room up for tonight."

"Great, come on over whenever you're ready."

"Mind if I hitch a ride out with you, Em?" asked Ben. "Joe took my truck out to your Gramps' place and I need it."

"Of course. What have those two been up to now?"

"Don't even ask!"

They all headed to the parking lot, where there were more hugs. Emma let go of Missy, promising to see her in a little while and then reached up to hug...Jack!

He wrapped her in those arms and held her close for a second. With his mouth next to her ear, sending shivers down her neck, he whispered, "Sorry, but with free hugs all around, I couldn't resist getting mine." With an innocent smile he stood back and held her at arms' length.

Looking up at him, she had to laugh; he was irresistible. "I'll see you later, Mr. Benson." She got into her car, where Ben was waiting.

As they drove out to the western shore, Ben updated Emma on the antics of their respective grandfathers. From what he told her, they were having a fine old time, fishing, tinkering with cars and drinking whiskey, mostly.

"At times," said Ben, "I think they're more like teenagers than old guys. It's so weird that now I'm the responsible one while Joe is out running round and getting into scrapes with his buddy. It doesn't seem so long ago that it was us giving them gray hair." He ran his hand through his shoulder-length blond hair that did indeed have some gray in it these days.

"Well, they've reached their second childhood by the sounds of it."

"I know." Ben turned to her now, more serious. "Thinking about how the years have passed, how much the roles have changed, it makes me realize that Joe's not going to be here forever. Your Gramps either, you know?"

Emma heaved a big sigh. "That's been weighing on me too, Ben. At least you're here, you're with Joe every day. You're making the most of the time you have with him. Me, I'm down there in the fake city, not getting out here nearly enough, and I don't even know why anymore."

"Come home then. Easy!"

"I've been thinking of doing just that."

"Really?" Ben looked surprised. "Gramps would love it if you did. So would I. I never really thought you would though."

"I never thought I would either, Ben. But I'm so sick of city life and I'm not doing anything I really value work-wise. So, I've been toying with the idea of spending the summer up here at least."

"Could you do it, work-wise I mean?"

"Yes, I've got nothing big going on at the moment and I'd kind of like to take the time up here to write a novel."

"That would be awesome! Say you will, Em. Stick around for the summer, hang with Missy and me. I bet we could even get Pete up here most weekends, he's still rumbling about building a house and coming up more."

"I'm seriously considering it." She turned into the driveway of the house where she'd grown up and her heart filled up when she saw her grandfather sitting on the front porch. She turned to Ben, "Don't say anything yet. I'd hate to disappoint him if I can't pull it off."

"Of course not."

Emma jumped from the car and ran into Gramps' arms, as she always had. He spun her around 'til she was dizzy.

"Here's my Mouse," he beamed.

"I missed you, Gramps."

"I missed you too, Sunshine, but you're home now. Tell me all about the wicked city."

She laughed. "The wicked city is still wicked and it's driving me crazy!"

"Well, why don't you come on home to your Grampy then?"

Her eyes filled with tears, which took her by surprise. Talking to Ben about how long she'd still have Gramps had really hit home. She knew her decision was made. "You know Gramps," she beamed, "I'm going to do that. For the summer at least."

This time it was Gramps' eyes that filled with tears. "You mean it, Mousey?" his voice was hoarse as he asked the question. She wrapped her arms around him and squeezed him tight, surprised by the raw emotion on his face.

"I mean it Gramps." As she held him she felt him tremble. She'd had no idea it would mean this much to him.

"Oh, Em. Oh, my little Em!"

"Toughen up, old fella!" Joe's voice boomed from inside the house.

Gramps straightened up and dabbed at his damp eyes. "Quit yer hollerin' and come out and see my girl!" he yelled back.

Joe appeared at the front door and gave Emma a big hug.

"Good to see yer, young un. Do yer good to stick around a while, I'm thinking. Getting too skinny down in that city. Besides, yer Grandaddy here needs someone to be lookin' after him now he's knockin' on. Yer can cook for him, make him cocoa and the likes."

Emma and Ben both laughed as Gramps sputtered.

"I'm not an old codger yet, Joe Bishop! I don't need nurse-maiding. Anyways, you're older than me!"

"By three whole days," laughed Joe.

"And besides, Emma's got her own place, she'll be staying there."

Emma turned to look at him; she hadn't even thought about that. Gramps stared her down.

"You weren't planning on moving in here and cramping my style were you, Mouse?"

"Well, I...."

"Aunt Martha left you that house 'cos she thought you'd live in it someday. May as well give it a test run for the summer if you're really sticking around."

Wow. This was all taking shape by itself. The big old house her great aunt had left her had been used as a vacation rental for years now, part of a program the resort ran.

"I can switch out any bookings to our other properties, if you want to do that," offered Ben.

The house did rent well, but wasn't one of the most popular, since although it sat in a wonderful location, right by the water's edge with gorgeous views, it really needed renovating and updating.

"Well, I guess if Gramps doesn't want me under his feet here," she knew well enough to play along with his bluster, "then I'd better go take a look at the old place."

"I'll drive," said Gramps.

"I need to get back to the resort," announced Ben, giving his grandfather a meaningful look, "and I need my truck. Are you coming?"

"All right, all right," grumbled Joe.

~ ~ ~

Pete hadn't said much since they'd left the Boathouse, and Jack was starting to feel a little uncomfortable.

"You okay over there?"

"Sorry. Yeah, I'm fine. I was thinking about Scot."

Jack immediately felt bad for assuming that Pete was thinking about him and Emma.

"What's the story with him?"

"He's a good kid. Missy has done a great job of raising him by herself. I just wish he had a father figure around. I mean, Missy's family is great with him. He has her dad and brother and uncles, but, well—and this is going to sound awful— they're locals."

Jack looked at him.

"Summer Lake is a small town. Most people who are born and raised here have a small town mentality. Now, I'm not saying there's anything wrong with that, nothing wrong with it at all. It's just that it doesn't help Scot. It's not what he needs. He's smart and he has so much potential. The kind of potential that's never going to develop into anything in a small town like this."

"People come from worse situations and make good. Look at Dan."

"Exactly. I was thinking of Dan. Dan had you. You may be small town, but no one could ever accuse you of small town thinking. You supported him, encouraged him. Can you honestly say he'd be where he is now if it weren't for you?"

Jack shrugged. He liked to think that Dan had made it on his own.

"There's no one here that can help Scot like that. No one really even understands him, what he's talking about when it comes to computers, like Missy said. I wish I could do something for him."

"Believe me, I get it," said Jack. "I think Dan would love to help Scot out. In fact, I think they would be good for each other. If I stay up here and build you this house, Dan could come visit and hang out with the kid. What do you think?"

"If you do build me a house, what do you think of this as the site?"

They got out of the truck and stood looking at the lake and the rolling hills leading away into the distance. The lot was on a headland and sloped all the way down to the water's edge on a wide cove. Only one house was visible at the other end of the beach.

"Man, it's beautiful."

"Isn't it? Are you serious about staying up here and doing this? You don't have to decide right now, you know."

"I know, but you're right, this place does have a magic about it. I feel at home already."

Pete turned to him, looking him straight in the eye. "And what about Emma?"

"What about her?"

"She doesn't get up here too much you know."

"I know, and if I'm honest, she's the only reason I'm still thinking about staying in the city. I may as well come clean, I've asked her to come to dinner with me on Thursday and she said yes."

"Wow! I wondered how much you'd tell me. The way you were watching her at breakfast kind of gave you away."

"I've got it bad," Jack admitted with a grin. "But she's made it clear she's not interested and, to be honest, I didn't know what you would think. So maybe coming up here out of the way is best all round. And anyway, she does come up here some weekends, right?"

Pete smiled. "Yeah, she does, but be warned, I'm usually with her."

"Hey, I never thought, you don't...you haven't...you're not?" He didn't know how to put it. "I mean I know you guys are all close, and I'd know if you were actually seeing her, but...."

"Me and Em? No, not like that, no worries there, bro. You wouldn't be stealing my girl...it'd be more like you were dating my little sister."

"Whoa. I imagine you would be one hell of a protective big brother!" Jack was only half joking.

"You can bet your ass on that." Pete smiled, but it didn't quite reach his eyes. "Though you know, she doesn't really date much so it's probably not an issue anyway, especially if she's said she's not interested."

"What have you often described as my best quality?"

"Uh-oh, you're going to subject her to the Benson persistence, are you?"

Jack grinned. "So where does that leave us?"

"It leaves you deciding if you want to spend the summer up here. It leaves you deciding if your intentions towards my 'little sister' are honorable. And it leaves me hoping that your answers are yes and yes. In which case you can call your brother and introduce him to my godson!"

"Okay, then. Yes, I'll build your house. Yes my intentions are honorable, and to prove as much I'll stay up here out of the way and give her time to get to know me, instead of chasing her all over LA. Therefore I will call Dan this afternoon and talk to him about Scot."

"All sounds good to me. Now tell me what you think of this lot. I've got three more to show you before we decide, but I really like this one."

Chapter Five

Emma let herself into Missy's house and found Scot on the sofa playing a video game.

"Happy Birthday, bud! Let me know when you can pause so I can give you your pressie." Scot smiled and continued zapping bad guys. Emma wandered into the kitchen to find Missy surrounded by cupcakes, balloons and all kinds of party supplies.

"What can I do?"

"Hi honey. I think I've got it covered for now. Have you seen Scotty?"

"I didn't want to disturb him. I told him to find me when he can pause the game."

Missy smiled. "That's why you're his favorite, you know. The rest of us just talk at him, mistakenly believing that he's here with us. You're the only one that understands that you have to leave a voice mail for him to call you back when he rejoins planet Earth."

Emma grinned, thrilled to think that she was his favorite. "He's such a good kid, Miss. He's a credit to you."

"Aw, thanks, Em. He is a sweetheart. I hope he has a good time tonight. You know he's not exactly sociable normally, but he wanted this party. His whole class is coming and I've done it all the way he wanted – pizza and cupcakes and gallons of Mountain Dew."

"I'm sure he'll have a great time. He really doesn't mind us oldies being around though?"

"It's funny. He said he couldn't imagine a party without you guys. Anyway, you know what it's like up here, the generations all party together. Always have, no doubt always will."

Scot stuck his head around the kitchen door. "Hey, Auntie Em!"

"Hey! Am I allowed a birthday hug?" She didn't want to embarrass him, but needn't have worried.

"'Course you are!" He bounded over to her. He was a wispy kid, with his mom's dark hair and eyes.

"You want to guess what your birthday pressie is?"

"I'd rather just have it."

"Scot!" Missy gave him a scowl.

"Hey," said Emma, winking at Scot, "haven't you always taught him to tell the truth? And now you're going to tell him off for doing just that? Shame on you!"

"Yeah, shame on you, Mom!" laughed Scot.

Missy shook her head at them.

"Here you go." Emma handed him a plain white envelope.

"Thanks!" He took it from her and tore it open. "Oh, wow! Thanks so much Auntie Em! This is great!" He gave another big hug. "Awesome!"

Missy looked at Emma. "New Egg?"

Emma nodded, confirming that it was a gift certificate for the online computer parts retailer.

"So, how much did you get?" asked Missy.

Scot looked at Emma, who in turn looked at Missy, folded her arms and said, "Private! That's need to know information and you don't need to know!"

"You're the best, Auntie Em! Mom, can I get online and start shopping? Please, please, please?"

"Go on then," she laughed. Scot scampered off to his computer.

"You really don't mind?" Emma had made light of it, but she still felt a little uncomfortable about the uneasy arrangement she had with Missy. She didn't want to spoil Scot, but she knew that computer parts were expensive. There were so many things Scot needed to build his systems and really challenge himself, and she knew that often things were quite tight for Missy.

"Honey, you won that argument years ago, remember? And you were right. All I'm going say is thank you, just thank you."

"The pleasure really is all mine and you know that. I wish I could do more practical stuff with him, but he's so much smarter than me. I have nothing to offer him there, but I can finance whatever he wants to build. It would be great if Jack's brother does get in touch with him, don't you think?"

"Yes, I do. That was so kind of him to offer. I hope something comes of it." She took a sly look at Emma. "So, what's the story there?"

"Well, as you know, he's Pete's partner, he's been in LA for a while...."

"Cut the BS," laughed Missy. "I am your oldest friend and you show up here with a gorgeous man drooling all over you, looking like he's going to scoop you up and carry you away at any moment, so don't play Miss Innocent with me!"

Emma blushed.

"Wow! Pink cheeks!" Missy grinned. "This should be juicy."

"There's really nothing to tell."

"Not yet maybe, but there is something and it's enough to make you blush, so tell."

Emma told her about their first meeting at Pete's office. "But you know what I'm like. He's so darned sexy and I reverted to mushy little romantic mode. I can't do that, Miss, it only ends badly for me."

"Oh, come on, Em," Missy echoed Holly's words. "That was once and it was a long time ago."

"I know, I know. But I promised myself I would stay out of Mr. Benson's way."

Missy raised an eyebrow, "And how's that working for you?"

"Okay," Emma smiled, "you win." She told her friend all about the night in the cabin.

"Only you," giggled Missy, "could promise you're going to stay away from a man and then within a week end up naked in his bed without him even knowing you're there! I'm sorry, hon, but between the way he was looking at you this morning and your success rate so far at staying out of his way, I'd say that this is going to get very interesting, very soon."

"Well, you're wrong. Though I am having dinner with him on Thursday...."

"See, I knew it!"

"No, no, no! Let me finish. I'm having dinner with him Thursday, but after that I won't be in the same city as him for anything to happen."

"Oh," Missy's face fell. "Where's he going?"

"Don't be sad. You're going to love this."

"What?"

"He's not going anywhere. I'm coming up here, for the whole summer!"

"Oh, Em. That's wonderful, we'll have so much fun!" The two of them were jumping up and down like little kids. "Will you stay with Gramps?"

"No, he wants me around, but not under his feet. We just went to look at Aunt Martha's house. I think it'll work out great. I'd forgotten how much I love that old place."

"Do the guys know?"

"Ben does. I only decided for certain when we got to Gramps' this morning. I haven't seen Pete yet to tell him, but I'll probably see more of him here than I do in LA anyway."

"This going to be a great summer. Come on, help me get all this over to the Boathouse for tonight. Now we've got an added reason to celebrate."

~ ~ ~

Missy stood leaning on the rail of the Boathouse's upper deck. Inside, Scot's party was going wonderfully. She was so pleased to see him laughing and even dancing with his friends.

"Mind if I join you?" Jack Benson appeared at her shoulder.

"Sure." She smiled. He seemed like a genuinely good guy, and definitely easy on the eye.

"I talked to Dan earlier and he said he'd love to meet Scot. He sounded excited about it, too," he grinned. "If you imagine Scot in another fourteen years, you'll get the idea of who Dan is. I think the two of them could be really good for each other."

"Oh, thank you so much. You are a sweetheart! I love that boy with all my heart, but there is so much I can't share with him. I'm not smart enough, you know?"

Jack nodded. "I do know. I've always felt that way with Dan. He's not much younger than me, but with no father around, I always felt responsible for him and I just couldn't help with the computer stuff. It hasn't been easy for him, but he's managed to do really well for himself. When I told him about Scot he loved the idea of helping him along. He asked if Scot wanted to come down to Silicon Valley." Missy tensed on hearing that. Jack smiled. "Don't worry. I told him it would be better for him to come up here first, let you meet him, let Scot get to know him."

Missy smiled gratefully. "That would be easier. It's not that I'm not grateful and everything...."

"No need to explain, I get it." Jack's face broke into a huge grin. "Anyway, there will be loads of times that Dan can come up and hang out here over the summer."

"Why's that?"

"Because I've agreed to build Pete's house, so I'm going to be staying up here for a while!" He seemed thrilled.

Missy had to bite her lip to stop herself from laughing out loud.

"Is that so?"

Jack nodded happily, looking very pleased with himself.

"And how long has this been the plan?"

"Only since this afternoon. Pete had asked, but I didn't think I was going to do it. Now that I'm here though, I think it's going to work out great."

Missy smiled back at him. This was definitely going to be an interesting summer. "Oh, I think you might thoroughly enjoy yourself."

Pete and Ben emerged into the cool night air and came to join them.

"More beer?" asked Ben. Missy and Jack both nodded and he went back inside only to return moments later with four cold bottles. They sat at one of the picnic benches.

"Scot seems to be really enjoying himself," said Pete.

"He is," said Missy, "it's so good to see him having fun with other kids."

"Yeah." Ben pointed his bottle at the dance floor. "The biggest kid of all is right in the middle of it too." They all looked in through the open doors to see Emma dancing with Scot and his friends. Scot was sticking close by her side and bristling every time one of his friends danced too close.

Missy laughed, "He loves his Auntie Em so much."

Ben grinned at her. "We all do, and like me, he's going to be a very happy boy that...." Missy kicked him under the bench. He got the message. As Pete and Jack looked at him he mumbled, "He's going to be a very happy boy that she's here for his birthday. I just need to check on things downstairs. Miss, will you give me a hand?" The two of them disappeared inside.

"What was that all about?" he asked as soon as they were out of earshot.

"Sorry," Missy laughed, "but it's just too funny. We know that Em's staying up here for the summer, but Pete and Jack don't."

"Oh," Ben looked confused, "and?"

"Jack is staying for the summer too!"

"Oh, wow! Are they...?"

"Not yet, but have you seen him looking at her?"

"Hard to miss, huh? He seems like a good guy. He's certainly got a thing for her."

"In a big way! The funniest part is that she's got it just as bad. But you know what she's like, she's too scared to do anything about it. Says it can't go anywhere and she thinks coming up here will help her stay out of his way."

Ben laughed. "This should be fun to watch. And Pete doesn't know Em's staying?"

"She hasn't seen him since she decided."

"You think we should tell him?"

"Tell me what?" asked Pete as he appeared behind them. "I thought you two were up to something."

"How much do you like your friend Jack?" asked Missy, her eyes gleaming.

"I'd trust him with my life." Pete looked back to where Jack still sat sipping his beer.

"With your life, maybe, but would you trust him with our Mouse?" Ben's tone was laughing, but his eyes were serious.

"You noticed, then?" Pete grinned. "It's okay though, you know what Em's like. She still swears she's staying single. Anyway, Jack is going to be spending the summer up here and she'll be down in LA where he can't get his hands on her."

Missy laughed. "Well, the best laid plans of our Mouse seem to be going awry because she decided today that she is staying up here for the summer!"

"Uh-oh!" Pete frowned, then smiled again. "Maybe I need to be around too."

"Yay!" cried Missy, "we're putting the band back together!" The guys laughed at her excitement.

"I can't stay the whole summer, but I sure can get up here a lot." He looked back at Jack, who was smiling as he watched Emma with the kids.

"Guys, please can I be the one to drop the bombshell on those two?"

"Only if we can watch!"

Emma came back from the bar with two beers for Gramps and Joe. She put them down on the table and smiled. "I'm going outside to catch up with the gang." She'd loved dancing with Scot and his friends and talking with Gramps and Joe, but now she was ready to spend some time with her friends.

She plonked herself down at the picnic table where Ben was making them all laugh with a story about a rich divorcée who had been wooing him all through the off-season. She looked up at the night sky and smiled; she felt happier than she had in a long time. This would be a good summer, and hopefully she'd be able to figure out where her life went from here. She looked over at Jack, who was laughing, head thrown back. Too bad she'd be moving away from him, but she knew it was for the best. She would never risk her heart again, and she knew that Jack, with his deep sexy laugh and gorgeous smile, could shatter her heart completely if she gave him a chance. No, one dinner with him on Thursday and then next weekend she would come up here and begin her summer. Here she had her friends and her Gramps, the beautiful lake and the fresh air. She had Aunt Martha's house to work on and a novel to write. She didn't need a man, no matter how attractive, to get in the way of that. He was part of the LA life, and she was leaving all that behind.

"So," Pete turned towards her, "Ben tells me you were out at Martha's old place today?"

Emma realized she hadn't told him her plans yet. "We were. I'd forgotten how much I love that house."

"It is a beauty, and the best spot there is on the lake. What made you go out there?"

"Well, I've got something to tell you. I think you're going to like this." Pete shot Jack a look she couldn't fathom, and Missy and Ben looked like they were about to laugh. "Have you told him?" she asked them.

"Told me what?" asked Pete. "That you might need some help fixing the place up? Because if that's the case, I might know the very man." She saw him look at Jack again.

"Okay, so I didn't tell you first!" she laughed.

"Tell him what?" Jack looked thoroughly confused by the whole exchange. She looked at him, sad that she'd be leaving him behind.

"That I'm staying up here for the summer." Missy and Ben both burst out laughing at the stunned look on Jack's face.

"And as I was saying," said Pete with a smile, "she may need some help with renovations," he looked at Jack, "if you have time."

Now it was Emma's turn to look confused as understanding spread across Jack's face.

"If you have time?" she echoed. Jack had already recovered and was grinning from ear to ear.

"Since I'm going to be up for the summer, too, building Pete's house!"

Emma had no words. She looked from Jack to Pete and back again, then at Missy and Ben who were still laughing. "Oh!" was all she could manage.

Pete laughed. "I'm so glad you've decided to take some time up here, Em. You need it." She stared at him. "But you didn't tell me," he added.

She gave him a grudging smile. "I didn't know myself until Ben and I saw Gramps this morning." She looked at Jack. "So, you're going to build him a house? Where?"

"Oh, you have to see it. It's a gorgeous parcel on the north shore. It's on a headland with only one other house up there...."

Ben and Missy both collapsed laughing. "Aunt Martha's!" they chorused.

Pete grabbed her hand. "Dance with me, Em." He dragged her inside where the music had slowed and couples young and old swayed together.

She looked up at him. "What the heck have you done?"

"Mouse, I'm sorry. What can I say? My best friend and partner is absolutely crazy about you, and I happen to think he would be wonderful for you. Even so, knowing your weird hang-ups about men and relationships, I did not meddle...."

"Did not meddle?" she interrupted, "You just...."

He buttoned her lips together between his finger and thumb.

"Let me finish?" he laughed as her eyes bulged furiously at him. "Can I let go?" She nodded. "I did not meddle. In fact this afternoon I thought I was sending him away from you. That he'd be up here and not, in his own words, chasing you all over LA."

"He said that?"

"I told you, he's crazy about you. So you see, this really is not my fault and I can't stand for my Mouse to be mad at me. Sometimes fate intervenes you know, Em. Even when we think we know better."

Emma stared up at him. She couldn't stay cross with him for long, and had never been able to.

"Still friends?" he asked.

"Always, idiot," she replied in a ritual they'd shared for over twenty years.

"Good," he breathed a sigh of relief. "I'm sorry I had to drop it on you like that, but you have to admit it was too good not to."

She slapped his arm and smiled. "I have to admit I'd have done the same to you given the chance, and I hope you realize I shall get you back whenever I can. So you're really going to build on my headland?"

"Hell, yeah! We're going to be neighbors, kiddo!"

"So, that man is going to be out there all summer?"

"That man is a very good man and you might want to give him a chance."

For a moment she felt as afraid as she had all those years ago when their friendship first began. New kid in class, newly orphaned, hurting, alone and trusting no one. Pete held her a little closer.

"It's okay, Em. You know I've always got your back. Not all men are like the asshole you married. You're not going to go through that again."

"But, Pete, that's the point! I married an asshole and I thought he was wonderful. I adored him and he broke my heart. I am a terrible judge of character and I can't be trusted. And no, I won't go through that again, ever!"

He tipped her chin and tried to make her smile by whirling her around the dance floor. She managed a weak smile.

"Mouse, you may be a terrible judge of character, but I'm not. I told you Rob was an asshole and I'm telling you Jack is one of the nicest guys you'll ever meet. But that's all; I'm not telling you what to do with it. What matters most is that you enjoy your time up here. Rest, relax, get your sparkle back, okay? And if it's really going to bother you, I'll forget the house, not send him up here."

"Oh, no, Pete. I can stay out of his way. I want you to have your house, to spend more time here yourself. I'm sorry. I'm being silly."

"It's not silly, Em. I understand, just trust me, okay?"

~ ~ ~

Jack and Ben watched Pete dance with Emma. Missy had gone to check on Scot.

"Welcome to Summer Lake, then." Ben slapped him on the back and smiled.

"Thanks. I'm not sure what to make of this, though."

"I'm not surprised. Pete just landed one on both of you!"

"Well, I can't say it was an unpleasant surprise for me, but I'm not sure what Emma made of it." The hurt and confusion in her eyes had touched him. "What's the deal with her being so anti-men?"

Ben looked at him. "She's not so much anti-men, as anti-relationships. She's been hurt."

"No shit?"

"Listen, you seem like a straight up guy to me. I'll be happy to help out and hang out when you come up here. Hell, it'll be good to have a new buddy around. But when it comes to Emma, I think she should be the one to talk to you about it, not me."

"Fair enough," said Jack, liking Ben even more.

"I will say though, that if you can make our Mouse happy, you'll make me and Pete and a whole bunch of other people around here happy too."

Jack smiled. "I'm going to try my damnedest to do that." Standing up, he shook Ben's hand. "Wish me luck!"

He tapped Pete on the shoulder. "May I cut in?" He raised an eyebrow, hoping that neither of them would refuse. Pete looked at Emma, who gave a small nod. Pete stepped away. Jack placed a hand on the small of her back and offered her his other. She smiled as he led her around the floor.

"Ballroom?" she asked. "You do surprise me."

"As I told you already, Miss Douglas, I am not the man you prejudged me to be. I am full of surprises. Good ones," he added hastily. "Let's just say I had to learn ballroom many years ago in order to help someone I care about very much."

"A girlfriend?"

"My little brother, actually, but that's a story for another day."

The music changed to a slow ballad and he dropped his hands to her waist, drawing her closer. He felt his heartbeat quicken as she placed a hand against his chest and looped the other up around his neck. He shifted a little, hoping she couldn't feel how much she aroused him. Man, what was she doing to him? Whenever he'd danced with a woman like this before, the whole point had been to let her know how much she aroused him and move quickly on to what came next. Now here he was, slow dancing in a room full of teenagers and grandparents, hoping not to scare away this beautiful little Mouse.

"I didn't know, you know," he murmured next to her ear.

She raised her eyes to meet his. "I could tell. You looked as shocked as I felt."

"Yeah, but for me it was a good shock."

After a few moments silence he heard her say, "It was a good shock for me too."

He held her a little closer. "Really?"

"Really."

Wow, she'd surprised him again. But he still had to say what he'd come to say. "You know, if you don't want me around I won't come up here."

She jerked her head back and looked up at him, her green eyes dark and unreadable.

"You'd do that?"

"I will do that if it's what you want."

"You'd let Pete down?"

"Pete would understand. He'd do anything for you."

"He would."

"So would I."

Her eyes darkened even more. What was that about?

"You would?"

"Yes."

"I don't want you to stay away."

His heart beat a little faster, wondering what would come next.

"No?"

"No."

"What do you want, Emma?"

"I want you to be my friend. Then we don't have to worry about any of that other stuff."

"Your friend?"

"Yes, like Pete and Ben. Please be my friend, Jack. I'd like that."

The song ended and she stepped back from him. "So, what do you say, buddy?" she flashed him a smile.

"Okay then, friend." They walked back to the others. How had that happened? He didn't want to be her friend. Well he did, but only as part of a much, much bigger package! He wanted to kiss her, to hold her, to make her moan his name, to wake up next to her. All those things that lovers do and friends can't. Damn! What the hell had just happened?

~ ~ ~

Pete was puzzled as he watched them approach the table. Emma was smiling, cute as a button, looking thoroughly pleased with herself. Jack, on the other hand, looked miserable. This, he decided, was a good time to bring a close to this eventful evening.

"Guys, I need to get going." He was surprised how eagerly Jack jumped up to join him. They said their goodbyes to the others, found Scot to wish him one last happy birthday and headed down to the resort's main square. The taxi company that operated from there was on alert to a party night and they took the first of a long line of cabs that stood ready. After Pete gave the driver his parents' address, he turned to Jack.

"So, what happened?"

"She asked me to be her friend, like you and Ben, so we don't have to worry about all the other 'stuff'!"

"Oh, man!"

"What do I do?"

"Not a lot you can do, old man. Be her friend."

"I've been relegated to the friend zone before we even started!"

"Give her time, she's scared."

"Scared of what? What the hell is her problem?"

"She was married," said Pete, deciding Jack deserved to know at least the basic story. "She fell head over heels in love with a guy in the early years in LA. He swept her off her feet and she bought into all the romance and flowers shit. Trouble was, after they got married the guy kept the romance and flowers going with a couple of actresses and a couple of models too. He married Em and kept sleeping with the rest of them anyway. You probably know him. He's a director, Rob Rivera."

"Shit! I do know him, by reputation at least. The guy's well known for it."

"Yeah, he's an asshole of the first order. Em was young and naïve, she wanted her own fairytale. Now though, she doesn't believe in fairytales anymore and she doesn't trust her own judgment. She thinks if she likes a guy then he'll turn out to be another jackass and break her heart, so it's simply easier for her not to go there."

"Oh, man."

"The only positive I can offer is that if she's scared you'll hurt her it can only be because she likes you, a lot."

"Well that's great, but how do I show her I won't hurt her if she will only be my friend?"

"Give her time. Be a real friend and maybe she'll come around."

"Looks like the only option I have."

Chapter Six

On Wednesday evening Emma was baking again as she waited for Holly to arrive. They'd only caught up last week, but since she was leaving for Summer Lake on Friday she didn't know when they'd get the chance again, though she did plan to get Holly up there soon. She hadn't forgotten her plan to get her together with Pete...that would be lovely. Holly was happy and healthy and, unlike herself, free from emotional damage. Emma was sure that the two of them would get along well, perhaps much more than that. She smiled; they would make a lovely couple. Hmm, a lovely couple. Oh, well. That was for other people, not for her. She thought of Jack, as she had so often this week.

What would it be like to make a lovely couple with him?

"Oh, stop it, Em," she chided herself. He was gorgeous, a successful, self-made man who was funny and smart. He traveled all over the country designing beautiful, beautiful buildings – yes she'd checked out his work online and loved what he did. Even the Phoenix Headquarters, Pete's building as she'd always thought of it, was actually Jack's building; he was the architect. But really, a man like that could have any woman he wanted, and as many as he wanted! She wasn't stupid; he might want her right now, but for how long? If she were fool enough to start anything with him she'd be falling for him and dreaming about happily-ever-afters right around the time he was moving on to an actress in LA or a model in New York. No, it was much more sensible to stay friends with a man like that. They could hang out and have fun, and he really was fun to be with. He'd be one of the gang at the lake and there'd be none of the pain or heartbreak. It was a much better idea. So why didn't it feel like it?

The doorbell chimed and she went to let Holly in.

"Oh, no. I smell goodies. I've warned you about this." Holly took off her jacket and came through to the kitchen, "Uh-oh." She was now serious. "What's wrong, Em?"

"What do you mean?"

"Well, I smell chocolate cake, which you usually make to go with bad news and sad times. And you look like you lost a dollar and found a penny."

"Humph! How do you know me better than I know myself?"

"Because, my dear, I am able to observe from the outside while you are so caught up in the inner turmoil you can't see beyond it. So spit it out, who peed on your parade? I thought you'd be full of beans and eager to get up to your lake. Was Carla mean to you?"

"No, Carla was surprisingly understanding." She'd called her agent first thing on Monday morning to cancel the Geraldine's Way meeting and to tell her she'd decided to take the summer off. She smiled, "I don't think she'd let Leandro escape from her bed since I saw her on Friday. She's too loved up to be cross with me at the moment."

"Well, good for her, but what about you? Have you seen any more of the delicious Mr. Benson? I'm guessing not, judging by the chocolate cake."

Emma hadn't yet filled her in on the developments of the weekend.

"The delicious Mr. Benson is now officially my friend. We are having dinner together, as friends, tomorrow evening."

Holly furrowed her brow, "What's this 'friends' thing about? I'm not sure I like this."

"It's the sensible option, given the circumstances," said Emma in a mock pompous tone with her nose in the air. She went on to fill Holly in about the weekend and how she had reached the conclusion that friendship with Jack was the sensible solution.

"Screw sensible! Sounds like the guy is crazy about you."

"He acts like it too," Emma smiled, remembering his hug and his breath on her cheek, "But, as you know, I can't be trusted."

"Em, you've so got to get past this, sweetie. Date the guy! See where it goes. Have some fun—and some hot sex! If it lasts, it lasts. If it doesn't, too bad. It's better to have loved and lost and all that."

"But for me it's not better, don't you see? For me it's better to just not go there. Now move over while I get that cake out of the oven. And why can't you be happy for me that I have a nice new friend? Pete and Ben are two of the most important people in my life, along with you and Missy of course, so how can it be bad to add Jack into that?"

Holly shook her head. "You're crazy. If I met a guy I liked as much as you seem to like this Jack, I would throw caution to the wind and dive right in."

"But Holly, you don't know what it's like to lose the people you love most in the world. The ones you think will always be there for you." Her eyes filled. "When Mom and Dad were killed, I told myself I would never love anyone else in my life, so I wouldn't ever have to feel that pain again. I know that was silly kids' stuff, but obviously it's stayed with me on some level. Then I let myself love Rob and we know how that turned out. So, yeah, maybe I am crazy, but I cope in the ways I can." With that she banged the chocolate cake onto the counter top. Then, ashamed of her outburst, she turned to Holly and rolled her eyes. "Yep, you're right, definitely crazy! Sorry about that."

"No, I'm sorry." Holly touched her arm. "I shouldn't have kept hounding you. It's just that I sense a chance for happiness for you. I so want you to have that because you deserve it more than anyone I know, and because you're my friend and I love you."

"I know you do, and I love you too." Emma bit back a smile as an idea occurred to her. "You know, if you really want to see me happy there is something you could do for me."

"Do I spy a set-up coming on? What do you want me to do?"

"Come visit me at the lake. In a couple of weeks we're having a big party for Gramps and Joe. They both turn seventy-five the same week, so Ben and I are arranging a big cookout for everyone. It'll be so much fun. Since my life is going to be up there for a while, I want you to be a part of it. Say you will?"

"I'd love to. It'll do me good to escape the city for a weekend."

"Excellent! Come on then, time to eat cake."

Chapter Seven

Jack sat at Mario's waiting for Emma to arrive. Goddammit, he was nervous! Didn't that just beat it all? He was waiting for a woman who had openly stated that she didn't want to get involved with him, who had been perfectly clear that they were meeting as friends, yet he was more nervous than he'd been on his first date as a kid. He was freshly showered and shaved with a little extra of his favorite sandalwood cologne. He wore dark jeans and a black short-sleeved shirt that showed off his muscular arms. A party of women at a nearby table kept looking over at him, whispering and giggling. A leggy brunette rose from her table in the corner and sauntered towards him.

"It would be a shame for us both to dine alone," she purred, "why don't you join me?"

"Actually," he gave her a gracious smile, "I'm waiting for my girlfriend."

She put a hand on his shoulder, and smiled. "Your loss."

Jack was used to this; it seemed that women who knew what they wanted often wanted him.

Of course, Emma chose that moment to appear. As the brunette walked away, Jack stood to greet Emma and pulled out her chair.

"Hi."

"Hello, Mouse." She looked at him. "Well, hey, I figure it's what all your real friends call you, right?"

"Yes, it is. Is that a friend of yours?" she asked, looking towards the brunette who was now watching them from her table.

"No."

"Oh?" She obviously wasn't going to let it go at that. Jack had already decided, given what Pete had told him, that honesty in everything was the only way to go if he ever wanted to be anything more than her friend. He sighed; this wasn't the start he'd hoped for.

"She thought I was eating alone and asked me to join her."

"Do you want to join her? I could leave."

"Of course not!" He was horrified. "I want to have dinner with you!"

"Just checking. I didn't want to cramp your style."

Oh, she was infuriating. He'd love to tell her that the only thing cramping his style was her insistence that she wanted nothing more than friendship from him. Okay, calm down. That wouldn't help his cause. The waiter came with menus and returned with the wine Jack ordered. Once he'd nodded his approval he reached across the table to take her hand.

"Let's forget that and start again, shall we?"

"Okay." She smiled as she removed her hand from his and picked up the menu.

"So, how are your plans going for getting out of Dodge?" asked Jack once they had ordered.

"Much better than I expected. I wiggled out of the one looming commitment I had without my agent giving me the hard time I thought she would."

"Well done. How did you manage that?"

She giggled. How could a giggle be so sexy? She went on to tell him all about Carla and the crush she'd had on Leandro for months.

"I think she still had him tied to her bed when she took my call!"

Jack laughed, wishing Emma would tie him to her bed. "That sounds like one scary lady."

"Oh, she is. She's amazing. Most people in the business are totally intimidated by her."

"But not our Mouse," he said gently.

"I'm sorry?"

"I'm picturing all the hotshots and ball busters wilting in the face of the mighty Carla, but the one they call Mouse, she stands her ground and gets her way."

Emma smiled. "That's where Super-Mouse comes in."

Jack smiled, thinking of Pete calling her that in his office. "That, and knocking over men twice your size."

"Yeah, sorry about that."

"Please don't be! I thoroughly enjoyed our first meeting. And our second."

Her eyes flew up to meet his and her cheeks colored, as they did so often.

"I'm sorry about that too. I've been meaning to thank you for not telling Pete what really happened. So, thank you."

"Hey," he did his best shoulder-shaking swagger, "I was protecting the little lady's honor. I told you I was a gentleman, despite what you may believe. In fact, as I recall, wasn't this dinner about giving me the chance to prove that to you?"

"Yes," she smiled, "it was."

The waiter returned with their food.

Once he left Jack said, "So, go ahead, ask me anything. You can interrogate me to find out what kind of human being I really am, how about that?" If she wanted him as a friend then she really should get to know him, and of course he was still hoping she would decide she wanted more and surely this couldn't hurt that. She was adorable as she sat there looking at him, wondering what to ask. Her cream silk crossover top and black pants told him she'd given some thought to what to wear too. Light make-up and small diamond studs in her ears completed her outfit. She looked stunning, but then he'd never seen her look anything else.

"Okay, first tell me about your brother."

He was puzzled by that. "You get to ask anything you want about me and you ask about Dan instead?"

"It's not as weird as you think. It's actually quite a clever ploy on my part."

"And how's that?" He was glad she was playing along.

"First, people reveal their true selves when they talk about their family. They can't help but give away their views and values. Second, normally when you ask someone about their siblings they tell you about their childhood, which gives you a lot of insight. And third, but by no means least, your brother is going to be hanging out with my beloved godson, so I want to know more about him."

"I like the way you think. Well, Dan is three years younger than me and he is definitely the smart one. You have a head start because you know Scot. Scot is just like Dan, and I'm actually excited for the two of them to meet. Over the weekend, I saw Scot struggle in many of the same ways Dan did when he was a kid; how to respond to people, how to make a point so that he would be understood, and how to get the hell out when he'd had enough people time and needed to get back to his machines, which are much easier for him to relate to."

She smiled at his insight and he continued.

"Dan went through all of that as a kid, and over the years he's found ways to cope and to enjoy life more. I'm hoping that in sharing that with Scot he can shorten the kid's years of struggle and, at the same time, get to feel good about himself by connecting with someone he genuinely understands and can help. As for the childhood part, well, we had it tough. I'll leave it at that for now. Let's just say our Dad wasn't the greatest. He died when Dan was fourteen. I already felt more like Dan's dad than his brother and that instinct kicked in even stronger at that point. I'd always felt the need to protect him, then there came the need to provide for him, and Mom too." He paused; he didn't normally talk about his childhood at all. This was strange, but it didn't feel bad. He shrugged and gave her a smile. "How am I doing so far?"

He was rewarded with an admiring look on her face. "Well, I have to admit you are dispelling a few of my judgments."

"Excellent. So what else do you want to know?"

"Why architecture?"

"Because you get to create something from nothing. You start with nothing but an image of what you want in your mind. Then you discover all the reasons why it can't happen and you have to figure out ways to make it happen anyway. There are rules and laws which are unquestionable, but you get to work with them to create something beautiful and functional. You can add to the quality of people's lives without them even knowing it. Whether it's by adding to the skyline of their city or creating the space in which they spend many hours of their time, you touch people's lives with what you build. It's something permanent, too. It will outlast you, and depending on the building, you are contributing beauty, safety, protection, shelter to the lives of thousands of people. That's a good feeling." He stopped again, surprised at how much of himself he was revealing. He was relieved to once again find her smiling admiringly at him.

"You really love it, don't you?"

"Yes, I do, but I wish I could use it for something more meaningful. I know I've found my path, I just haven't found the right way to walk it yet. If I'm honest I've been enjoying the construction side of it more, lately. The design side is great, but to me it's not complete without the actual physical involvement. I worked construction as a kid, day laboring wherever I could, so for me it's like going back to my roots."

"And what about Pete's house? Will you design that or will he?"

"That will be a joint effort. Pete's brilliance is on the business side of things. He has some ideas and he wants me to develop them, but of course it will be his living space, so he'll guide how he wants it. We're both excited to do the work too. I mean, we'll have a crew of course, but we're both keen to do some real work. Pete likes the idea of building his house with his own two hands, and I get that."

"I can't imagine Pete having his own house up there. That place is our childhood and this, well, it's like bringing it into the now. I like it."

"Aren't you doing the same thing? With your Aunt's house...your house?"

"I suppose so. I don't think I've wrapped my head around it yet. It wasn't even really a plan, it suddenly all came together last weekend. I'd been thinking about it, but that was as far as it went."

"What made you decide to do it?" He was intrigued.

She told him about her conversation with Ben on the way to Gramps' house. He was surprised to see her eyes fill with tears and he took her hand again. This time she didn't pull away.

"I can't imagine losing him. He's all I've got. I know he's not going to be around forever and he's had a good run and all that, but still, he's my only family. Talking to Ben really brought it home. All I'm doing in LA these days is bitching about the place, and it became so patently obvious. I don't need to be here, and I do need to be up there. Why would I waste a summer here when I can spend it there with the people who mean the most to me? I can spend precious time with Gramps while I've still got him, and have some fun with my dearest friends."

Jack held onto her hand and looked into her eyes. "And do you want to count me as one of those friends?"

She didn't look away from the intensity of his gaze. "I would like you to be my friend, if you want to?"

Jack swallowed hard and decided to risk it. "Emma," he continued, looking deep into her eyes, "you know I want to be more than your friend." He held on as she tried to pull her hand back. "Will you give me a chance? Find out what we could be together?" He left the question hanging, his heart hammering in his chest.

"I can't do that. I'm sorry Jack, but it's not going to happen."

Disappointed, he let her pull her hand away. She was watching him, waiting to see his reaction.

He shrugged his shoulders. "You can't blame a guy for trying now, can you?" She shook her head. "Good, because if you're not going to blame me for it, I'm going to keep trying." He flashed her his 'sexy grin' and under the table he rubbed his foot against hers. He loved the way she blushed so much. It made him think of how she would look in bed, flushed with passion. It also gave him hope that he was having some effect on her, despite her denial.

Emma stared across the table at him, not knowing what to do with this man. If she was honest, she'd like nothing more than to join in with his flirting, see where this went. She wanted to feel his arms around her again, be close to him and feel safe and protected as she had on the floor of Pete's office – but that was the point, wasn't it? If she did get involved with him she wouldn't be safe or protected, she would be exposed to all the pain a man like him could inflict on her tender heart. Still, she was flattered that he was interested in her. Perhaps she should enjoy the banter until his infatuation passed and he moved on to pursuing some beauty like the brunette in the corner who, Emma noticed, was still eyeing him.

She completely surprised him when instead of rebuffing him, she hooked her own foot around his calf and slowly rubbed up and down.

"You can keep trying Mr. Benson," she laughed, "but it won't get you anything, other than a laugh with your friend."

"That sounds like a challenge to me, and I accept it." Seeing the determination in his eyes, Emma felt a mixture of trepidation and excitement. She already knew he was a man used to meeting challenges head on and coming out with what he wanted.

"It's more a statement of fact, dear friend," she smiled. "And on that note, I think I should be heading home."

Jack called for the check. "May I walk you to your car?"

"You could, but I walked here. I only live around the corner."

"Walk you home then?" He raised his eyebrows suggestively, making her laugh. As she hesitated, he asked, "Would there be any question that Pete or Ben would walk you home?"

"No."

"Well, you're the one that insists I'm to be like them, so there's our answer."

As they walked, Emma caught glimpses of their reflection in store windows. He was so handsome. And she had to admit that they did make a lovely couple, him tall and dark, making her look tiny and blonde at his side. They walked down by the waterfront. It was a beautiful evening and the moon shone on the water. Jack grabbed her by the hand and pulled her across the street.

"Come see the ocean."

They stood leaning on the rail, looking out at the surf.

"I love living by the water."

She smiled. "Well, you'll be living by some different water this summer."

"As will you."

They stood in silence looking out. Jack inched closer to her, and she laughed and edged away. He slid closer again and this time she stood her ground and hip checked him. Undeterred, he edged closer still until their sides were touching. Her heart beat fast as she waited to see what he had in mind. She stayed still, staring out at the ocean as he moved behind her and placed his hands either side of hers, looking out over her shoulder. Her whole body trembled at the nearness of him. Oh my. Sensible was such a silly word! His mouth came close to her ear.

"Turn around, Emma."

She stayed frozen to the railing. With one hand he swept the hair away from the nape of her neck and brushed his lips against the smooth skin there. She felt her knees go weak, grateful the railing was there to support her. His mouth was by her ear again, his warm breath sending goose bumps racing down her neck and arms.

"Turn around, Emma," he said again, this time a little more insistent.

Slowly she turned to face him. He held onto the railing on either side of her and leaned his weight against her. She was amazed by the tenderness in the brown eyes looking down at her. He lowered his lips towards hers, holding her eyes the whole way. She stared back at him, unable to believe this was happening. He paused with his mouth an inch from hers.

"Stop me now if you want to," he murmured.

With a will of their own, her hands reached up and buried themselves in his hair; it felt as soft and silky as she had imagined. She saw the smile spread across his face in the moment before his lips met hers. Slowly he ran his tongue across her bottom lip, waiting for her to respond. She parted her lips and kissed him back, darting her tongue inside his mouth which seemed to ignite him. He let go of the rail, holding her close with one hand at the small of her back and the other cupping the nape of her neck, holding her in place to receive the passionate kiss with which he was announcing his intentions. Slowly he raised his head and framed her face between his big hands. She stared up at him, her heart beating wildly and her mind spinning. A single kiss had never had this effect on her before.

"You didn't stop me, Em."

She shook her head, unable to speak. He kissed her lips again and she let him, surrendering to him, allowing him to explore her mouth with his tongue, meeting him with her own. He lifted his head again and smiled at her.

"See, that wasn't so hard, was it?"

She shook her head dumbly. She was suddenly aware that her hands were still caressing his hair. She quickly brought them down and they landed on his chest where she felt his heart thundering through his shirt. She pushed with both hands against him, but he just held her closer to him.

"Don't push me away, Emma, please?" She looked up, surprised by his tone. He was staring at her with longing in his eyes.

"I'm sorry. I know I shouldn't have kissed you, but I couldn't resist you." She stared at him. "Please say something?"

"I didn't stop you," she stammered.

"See!" he smiled, his confidence returning. "You didn't stop me because you wanted to kiss me too, and don't say you didn't enjoy it."

Emma was quickly regaining her senses. She shook her head. "But we're just friends," she insisted.

Jack's hands fell to his sides. "You kiss me like that and then say we're only going to be friends?" His victorious smile was fading fast.

"Jack, I already told you, you can keep trying all you like, but... we're just friends."

"Okay, how about friends with kisses?" He was trying to make her laugh again. Despite herself, she had to smile at him. She began walking again to her apartment, which wasn't far now. He walked backwards in front of her.

"Friends who kiss sometimes?" he held his hands out hopefully. She couldn't help but laugh.

"Friends who kissed once."

"And who enjoyed it?" he raised his eyebrows.

She shook her head, amused by his playful determination.

"Is that a shake of the head for no?" he asked, stopping dead in front of her so that she walked right into him. His arms closed around her once more. She stepped back, not daring to stay that close to him.

"I was shaking my head at you, not in disagreement with you." She kept on walking.

"Okay, then," he smiled. "Friends who kissed once and enjoyed it. Do I have it right now?"

She gave a small nod, grateful that they were almost to her building. She needed to escape from him now, because she badly wanted to kiss him again and that wasn't how this was supposed to be working.

"How about friends who kissed once and enjoyed it so much they will kiss each other again, deeply and often?"

She couldn't help but laugh. He was nothing if not persistent, and he certainly knew how to make her laugh. She stopped abruptly in front of her building and looked up at him.

"Friends who must say goodnight now and who will see each other with their other friends out at the lake," she said with a smile.

"Friends who are going to have coffee before they say good night?" he asked.

She shook her head. "I'll see you at Pete's this weekend."

He gave her a rueful smile. "Thanks for tonight, Emma. This was good."

"It was good. I enjoyed it so much, Jack. But, it really is best for us to just be friends."

He nodded and gave her a hug. Then he tipped her chin with his thumb and, holding her eyes with his, he slowly placed a chaste kiss on her lips. He stepped back and smiled.

"Friends who kiss goodnight." With that he turned and was gone.

Emma let herself into her apartment and leaned back against the door. She looked down at her shaking hands. "Oh my goodness!" She was more attracted to Jack Benson than she had been to any man her whole life—including the one she had married. The way he kissed her. The tenderness in his eyes when he looked at her. It would be sooo easy to do what Holly said and throw caution to the wind. But, she couldn't do it. She couldn't set herself up for that kind of hurt. It was no good letting herself pretend that she'd be happy with a fling. She was an all or nothing girl when it came to her heart, and Jack struck her as the kind of man to have a girl in every port. She didn't want to be one of the crowd. She couldn't, wouldn't do it. She'd have to find a way to deal with him over the summer. She enjoyed flirting and teasing with him, but she couldn't afford to lose her heart to a man who would only shatter it into a million pieces.

Jack walked back to his own apartment, which was only a few more blocks. He hadn't realized she lived right there. He smiled as he thought of her fingers running through his hair. The way she'd kissed him back; she could say what she liked about wanting nothing more than friendship from him, but the way she'd responded to his kiss told him she wanted a whole lot more than that, even if she wasn't ready to admit it to herself yet. That was okay, he was a patient man. Tonight she'd told him, with her kiss if not in words, everything he had hoped to hear.

He let himself in and took a cold beer from the fridge. Walking through the apartment he looked around. It was all understated elegance; the big leather couches, the modern artwork, everything spoke of a successful man, so why did it leave him feeling so empty? He'd worked so hard, come so far from the kid from the poor neighborhood. The kid that had worked construction to support his family. Was Pete right about him? Had he really achieved so much success without achieving anything that mattered? He led a good life, and he was certainly financially successful. He loved his work, kind of. He just wished it meant more. He got to travel a lot, both for work and for fun. He had no shortage of offers of female company. He thought of the women he usually dated. Like the brunette at Mario's they tended to be beautiful, self-assured and knew what they wanted. He smiled: none of them could hold a candle to his Emma.

He took his beer out to the balcony and looked out at the city lights and the ocean. His Emma? If only. She was so different from his usual type. While they were tall, dark and svelte, she was smaller, maybe five feet six? She was so beautiful, in such a different way. Hers was a natural beauty. She was a breath of fresh air with her wavy blonde hair and dancing green eyes and her curves that drove him crazy. He laughed to think that the types he normally went for were plucked and groomed, manufactured images of beauty, plastic in more ways than one, while Emma was the real thing.

Pete was right, he didn't do relationships, at least not in the usual sense. He was more used to, well, what? Convenient arrangements? Was that it? He guessed it was. The women liked his money and his name, especially in Houston and New York. In Miami and definitely here in LA, where everything was about the beautiful people, he acknowledged that he was as much a trophy date as any woman ever was. These women wanted to show off a handsome boyfriend; most hoped to make him a handsome husband. And what did he get out of it? Well, of course there was sex. He took another sip of beer and shrugged. Hey, he was a red-blooded male after all. But, was that really it? Was he really what Emma thought him to be? A guy who wanted nothing more from women than sex, who moved on when their demands for more than that became too much? No, he shook his head. It was just that he'd never met a woman who had made him want to stick around for more. Until now. Until Emma. She'd touched his heart, as well as his libido. So what did he want from her? Sex, yes. But so much more than that. He wanted to make her smile and laugh, make her eyes sparkle just for him, as they had tonight. He wanted to wake up with her in the morning, watch her sleeping and make her coffee, like he'd done at Pete's cabin. He remembered how her eyes filled with tears as she spoke of her grandfather. He wanted to be there for her when the old guy did pass on, to let her know that she did have someone left in the world. Someone who would love her and protect her. He wanted to show her that it was okay to give her heart, because he would cherish it and never hurt her or let her down.

Damn! He finished his beer and put the bottle down. He really had it bad! And of course it was all for a woman who was too scared to love him back. He shook his head. Love? "Yeah, buddy!" he muttered to himself. "That's what this is starting to sound like." Trust him to fall for the one woman who wouldn't willingly drag him down the aisle at the first chance she got. A woman who insisted she would never be more than his friend. He went back inside and got ready for bed. As he switched off the light he said, "We could have it all, Emma. I'm going to prove it to you."

Chapter Eight

Emma sat on the front deck of Aunt Martha's house watching the early morning sun sparkle on the water. Aunt Martha's house? She smiled: my house. Thanks, Aunt Martha. She'd inherited the house as a teenager when her great aunt had died. It had provided her with some rental income over the years, but other than that she'd never really given it much thought. She'd spent many happy times here as a child. The old lady, Grandma's eldest sister, was the one who'd instilled in her the love of cooking and especially baking.

She remembered Aunt Martha stirring a huge bowl of cake mix and waving her wooden spoon at her saying, "Don't you go getting into those diets and picky eating habits like your friends, young lady. Cakes and cookies are some of life's goodies and you need to enjoy them. Eat what you like, just make sure you always work hard to burn it off. Do the same with life. Dieting is like saying you're going to abstain from the good stuff because you don't want to do the work to pay for it."

It was a philosophy that had sat well with Emma and she still lived by it. She ate well and she worked out every day. More than that, though, she applied it to the rest of her life.

When she'd first bought her apartment she'd looked at others that were smaller, further from the beach and much less expensive. But the one she now owned was what she'd really wanted. She could see the ocean, it had a huge kitchen that she loved and it was full of natural light. She'd gone for what she wanted and then worked her tail off to make sure she could afford it. She felt like it was an upward spiral; she was sure she had been more successful in her writing career than she would have if she'd held back and bought a lesser home.

She looked up as she heard a car approaching. Pete's truck pulled up and he bounded up the stairs to greet her.

"How's it going, Mouse? You all settled in?"

"Not that quickly, no," she laughed. "I only arrived last night. I had dinner with Gramps and Joe out at his place so all I've done here so far is sleep and make coffee. You want some?"

"I'd love a cup." He settled his big frame into one of the chairs. Emma returned with his coffee and a plate of fresh muffins.

"Wonderful," he said, taking a bite. "You know, you could always open a bakery here if you're done with the writing."

She laughed. "No, thank you. I bake for myself and my friends, that's it. And besides, I'm not done with writing, only with that fake city for a while. That novel idea I was telling you about is brewing nicely in my mind and is about to start spilling out through a keyboard any day now."

"Is that so?"

"Yes, sir. It seems this summer is working out perfectly. I can write, spend time with Gramps and see more of Missy and Ben."

"And me!"

"I know. I told Missy I'll probably see more of you here than I do in LA. That place makes everything so difficult."

"Well, I've decided I am going to be up here a lot more, too. We don't have much going on 'til the fall and I want to have the house built by then, so I'm thinking of doing three or four day weekends up here, what do you think?"

"Oh, Pete! That will be wonderful." She was delighted. "It'll be like old times, the four of us hanging out on the weekends."

Pete gave her a sideways look. "Yeah, but there will be five of us, not four, remember? You've not forgotten that Jack will be here too? You know I'm not going to leave my partner out."

Emma did her best to appear casual. "Of course I hadn't forgotten. He's my friend too now. We had dinner the other night, as friends do."

Pete laughed. "So, you're sticking to that road, are you?"

She nodded her head vigorously. "Just friends."

"You are a crazy little lady, you know that? The guy is perfect for you, why won't you give him a chance?"

She looked at him seriously now. "Pete, you know why. I'm not going to lie to you, you know me too well. I find him incredibly attractive...."

"I knew it!"

"But that's the point!" she said, frustrated. "It seems I have some strange malfunction that means I am only attracted to incredibly good-looking cheats and charmers!"

"Oh, Em," Pete sighed, "Jack is neither a cheat nor a charmer."

She laughed, "Oh, he is definitely a charmer."

"Look, Em, if you don't want to go there that's your choice. I think you could be missing out on something special, but that's for you to decide, not me. All I really wanted to do is make sure I've not messed up by having him out here. I don't want you to be uncomfortable having him around."

"It's fine, honestly. He is a really nice guy, he fits in with everyone. It's no big deal, right?"

"And you don't mind having him at the other end of your beach? I'll be a lot happier knowing there's someone out here should you need them. It's a bit isolated up here, you know?"

"What do you mean, at the other end of the beach? He'll be staying at the resort, won't he? Since you don't actually have a house here yet."

"Mmm," Pete started to look a little uncomfortable. "Whenever he's building he likes to stay on site. You know he's bringing his brother up to meet Scot? Well, Dan has an RV so they're driving that up here for Jack to stay in while he works."

"Oh."

"Problem, Mouse?"

Oh my. She certainly hadn't been expecting to have Jack staying out here.

"No, no problem. I just didn't realize."

"It'll be fine. Like you said, he's your friend too now, and I really do like the idea of you having someone else up here if you need them."

"Okay." Emma didn't want to think about it at the moment. "Anyway, what are your plans for today?" she asked, eager to change the subject.

"That's what I came to ask you. Jack and Dan should be rolling in at about three o'clock, so I'm free 'til then. I wondered if you wanted to come walk the lot with me, knock around some ideas for the house and make sure your new neighbor isn't going to spoil your views or anything."

"Oh, that'll be fun. We can walk along the beach from here. Let's go."

Aunt Martha's house stood at one edge of a large cove. Pete's lot occupied the other half of the headland that the cove bit into.

"Isn't it cool that you're going to be my neighbor up here?" she asked as they walked along the beach.

"I'm so glad you think so. When I decided on this lot I wasn't even thinking that you owned Martha's old place, let alone that you'd be living up here so soon."

"I think it's wonderful! I wish your house was already done and you were staying the whole summer too. Imagine how much fun we'd have."

Pete smiled at her enthusiasm. "Don't worry, Em. We'll have fun, I'll be around quite a bit. And once the house is built it will always be here. This place will always be home. When we're old and gray we'll be the batty old neighbors up on North Cove."

"We can have cookouts on the beach!"

Pete laughed, enjoying seeing her happy again. "Yes, we can, Em. I said you should stay up here and get your sparkle back, and you're already sparkling. The last few times I've seen you in the city you've looked down."

"All I needed was to get back here, I just didn't realize it."

"What will you do in the fall? Do you think you'll stay on?"

"I really don't know yet. I'm trying not to think that far ahead. I want to see how it goes for a while before I decide what's next."

"I can see that. Live the moment and enjoy it for what it is."

"Oh, I like that."

"Perhaps you should try it with Jack then."

"Oh, you!" She punched his arm. She really wished that she dared do exactly that, but she'd been through too much pain already. She couldn't willingly set herself up for a whole bunch more.

"Sorry, I couldn't resist. I mean, it is a little hypocritical of you isn't it? That's the one thing you won't even try."

"Give it up, Pete." She didn't want to keep going over all this.

"Okay. Come on then. Help me walk this land and figure out where I can get the best views without becoming an eyesore for you."

~ ~ ~

Jack was enjoying driving the RV. It amused him greatly that his little brother owned this huge vehicle. It was more like a rock star coach than the simple motor home he'd been expecting. He'd packed enough to last him a couple of weeks and hopped a flight to San Jose where Dan had picked him up last night. He was so proud of how Dan was doing these days. His software company was thriving and he really seemed to have a handle on life. Jack smirked to himself, well, other than the questionable decision to buy this RV!

"Tell me again what possessed you to buy such a monster?"

Dan laughed from his spot on the armchair-like passenger seat.

"Don't mock it, big brother. You'll be very grateful for its creature comforts if you're going to be spending a few months out in the boonies. I bought it because me and the guys like to go up to Yosemite when we can. It was getting to be a pain packing ourselves and our gear into someone's SUV then staying in cabins or rental houses. Now we can all pile in here, drive up in comfort and have everything we need to stay connected. We have satellite internet with speeds you won't find in a vacation home, plus we've got servers loaded back there and a wall full of monitors."

Jack laughed. "Every geek's dream."

"You got it."

"So you really don't mind being without it for the summer?"

"We geeks do one-up-manship like no one else. Steven's bought one that's even bigger and has more and better everything than this one. So this would no doubt have spent the summer in storage anyway. Besides," he looked over at Jack, "it's kinda cool for me to able to do something for you for a change."

Jack smiled. He knew that as well as being Dan's protector, he'd also been his hero since they were small. He knew it was good for Dan to be able to make some gesture in return and could see how pleased he was. "I appreciate it, bro. More than you can imagine."

Jack couldn't believe his luck when he'd called Dan about going up to the lake this weekend. He'd thought that they would meet up there. He'd also thought he'd be renting one of the resort cabins from Ben for the summer. In the course of telling Dan his plans, his little brother had offered the RV and now, he grinned to himself, he would get to stay on site, which he liked to do. Even better though, he'd be right next door to Emma, which he liked even more.

"So," said Dan, "tell me more about the kid. Is he cool with me coming up to meet him? I'm not sure I'd have been down with it at his age."

"I think so. I didn't get to talk to him much, just watched him, and he reminds me of you so much. I really think you'll enjoy him. His mom, Missy, is so excited about this. I think you'll like her too."

"She's not one of those pushy moms is she?" Dan looked wary.

"No way. She's really down to earth and she adores the kid. She's had it tough, I think. Had him when she was seventeen, raised him by herself. They're close."

"We'll see. I hope this is going to work out like you think and not leave him feeling like his mom's brought someone in to interfere."

"Don't sweat it, Dan. It's all going to work out great. In fact, when he sees this rig with all your servers and monitors, I bet it'll be hero worship at first sight."

Dan smiled. "If he's as smart as he sounds maybe I'll pull some of the kit out of here and let him work on it. It's not like you'd be using it."

"I sure won't. Listen, we should be there in an hour. Want to stop for some lunch and prolong our little road trip?" Much as he wanted to get to the lake, he was enjoying being with Dan again. They rarely got together these days and he promised himself that would change.

"That'd be great. I'm starving and they're not expecting us 'til later are they?"

"I said not before three, so even if we stop for an hour we'll still be early."

They pulled off into the next little town where Jack maneuvered the huge vehicle around the tiny streets until they found a burger joint with a parking lot big enough.

"My treat" called Dan as they climbed down. Jack smiled to himself. He was so proud of his little brother and loved the way he was trying to prove he could stand on his own two feet now.

A few hours later Jack pulled the RV into the town square at Summer Lake Resort. Dan waved as they passed Pete walking with Emma.

"Damn, she's hot! Is that Pete's new girlfriend?"

Jack grimaced at the thought. "No, she is not," he said, a little too adamantly. "She's one of his oldest friends."

Dan smirked, "So, big brother's got the hots for Pete's oldest friend, huh?"

Jack sighed; it wasn't as if he was going to be able to hide it. He turned off the ignition and turned to Dan. "You're going to enjoy this," he smiled ruefully. "Big brother has got so much more than the hots for that woman and she doesn't want to know."

"But man, they all fall at your feet with their legs wide open!"

"Don't be crude!"

"Well, they do. What woman has ever said no to you?"

"That one. Repeatedly."

"Ho hum, there's plenty more fish in the sea, as they say. Especially for a big cat like you."

"I don't want fish," growled Jack. "I want that Mouse right there." He jerked his head to where she was climbing the steps to the deck over the lake.

"Really?" Dan was surprised. "That much more than the hots, huh?"

"'Fraid so. You stick around here much this summer and I think you'll get to see your big brother make a fool of himself."

"This should be good. I hope this Scot kid wants me around because this I have to see."

Pete appeared at the door and shook Dan's hand as he hit the ground.

"Good to see you, Dan."

"And you. It's been too long."

"It has. I really appreciate you coming to see Scot."

"No problem, man. I'm looking forward to it. He's your godson, right?"

"Yeah, his mom is one of my oldest friends.

Dan looked confused. "Was that her you were with just now?"

"No, that was Emma, another of my oldest friends. She's Scot's godmother. His mom is Missy, and she's going to meet us at the Boathouse. And then there's Ben." He waved as Ben approached from the lodge. "He's the other one of my oldest friends. He completes our little gang of four, and is Scot's final godparent."

Ben came over and shook Dan's hand.

With the introductions complete, Pete asked, "I thought you were bringing an RV, not a mobile palace?"

Jack laughed. "So did I. Blame the boy genius here."

"Hey, quit bitching about it. You've got everything you need in there."

"Everything I need and a whole lot more. Seriously, it's going to be great, thank you."

Ben looked at the RV. "It's like the one my folks travel in, and much as it's not to my taste, I think it's better equipped than my apartment."

"See?" Dan looked at Jack. "You don't have to like it, just make the most of it. Anyway, shall we go and see Scot? Figure out how this is going to work?"

"Yeah, come on," said Ben, "I can only stop a while, I've got to get back to work. The girls are out on the deck already."

They joined Missy, Scot and Emma at a big table around the back. Emma was surprised how similar the Benson brothers were. Dan was a little shorter and had a little lighter build than Jack, but otherwise he was like a carbon copy. She shook hands with him and liked him immediately when he met her eyes directly with a shy smile. She watched as he greeted Missy and Scot. Scot looked a little uncomfortable and she realized this was probably quite an ordeal for him. Missy was talking to Dan, thanking him for coming, so Emma went and sat with Scot, who had already moved to a smaller table by himself.

"You managed to work your way through that gift card yet?"

"Not yet, Auntie Em, but I'm working on it. The external hard drive I wanted was out of stock though so I've got to wait two weeks, which is a bummer."

"Where have you ordered it from?" asked Dan as he sat down next to Emma.

"New Egg."

"Good, that's where I was going to recommend. Most people still don't know about them."

"Auntie Em keeps me in gift cards with them." Scot smiled at her.

Dan laughed, "That's the kind of godmother I need. How many gigs is the one you ordered?"

"It's a terabyte," said Scot, his eyes big, looking thoroughly impressed with himself.

"Wow, that's cool! You've definitely got yourself a good godmother there. Wanna come see if there's something we can fix you up with while you wait? I've got some supplies in the van." He stood and pointed to the RV. Scot looked at Missy, who nodded and smiled. With that the two of them headed off.

"I think they're going to hit it off just great," smiled Emma.

"I hope so," said Missy and Jack in unison.

"I've got to get back to work," said Ben. "What's everyone doing later?"

"I'm waiting to see how those two get on," said Missy.

"Well, that's all he came for," said Jack. "So I think they may be a while, but then with all the gear he's got in there, I think we could roll them anywhere and they wouldn't even notice."

"How about," said Pete, looking at Emma, "we all roll out to your place tonight. My truck is still there and we've got to get the coach up that way anyway. We can leave those two doing their thing in the back."

"That's a great idea," said Emma. "I said I wanted to cook out there for everyone. Steaks on the grill?"

"Mouse steaks?" asked Ben. "Hell yeah, I'm down!"

"And me," said Pete. "I don't remember the last time you cooked for us all."

Missy looked at Jack. "She is the best cook you will ever meet," she explained. "If Emma offers to cook, anything, ever, you say yes."

"In that case, yes."

"And since Mouse does the food, I'll do the beverages," added Missy. "Is Scot okay to stay with you and Dan while I run to the store? I need to pick up a few things and I'm guessing beer, red wine and Mountain Dew will do?"

Jack laughed. "Mountain Dew and tech guys, what is it about that?"

"Easy," said Missy, "it's loaded with caffeine to help them stay awake all night tapping at keyboards."

"Finally, I get it."

"I'll come out after work," said Ben, "I've got to go."

"How about we hang down here and wait," said Pete. "We can all ride over in the coach when you're done and that way there are fewer cars to drive back tonight."

"You know, you can all stay out there if you like," said Emma. "I've got five bedrooms and there's that thing as well," she nodded towards the RV.

"Why not?" said Pete. "That way we can all have a beer."

"Sounds great," nodded Ben. "I'll catch you guys back here when I'm done."

Missy and Emma walked back to her car to head to the grocery store.

"I think Scot is going to do okay with Dan, don't you?" asked Missy.

"I really do. I like Dan already."

"So do I." Missy's smile lit up her face.

"Oh. Now, why didn't I think of that?"

"Beats me," laughed Missy, "I mean, he's like your Jack, only sexier in a quieter sort of way."

"He is not my Jack!"

"Then you're a fool," Missy laughed.

"Oh, I do not need to hear this again," sighed Emma as they arrived at the store. "You, Madam, go and get our booze supplies while I go and get the food. Come find me when you're done. We'll need a lot with all those hungry men to feed."

Chapter Nine

Emma smiled as she bustled around her kitchen. She was at her happiest when was she was cooking and it was so much nicer to have her friends to cook for. Missy sat at the counter with a glass of wine, watching her work.

"Okay," said Missy, "two huge pies in the oven, steaks marinating, potatoes baking on the grill, veggies doing their thing and smelling wonderful already. You are a culinary demon!"

"Don't forget Scot's pizza."

"How could I forget? I feel so bad that you're making all this wonderful food and my kid is the only boy on the planet who doesn't eat steak, or even anything vaguely nutritious, just pizza."

"Oh, come on, Miss. He eats it, but he doesn't enjoy it, and since tonight is about everyone enjoying themselves, then why not?"

"So why not store bought pizza? You have to go and make that great big thing from scratch and make me feel even more inadequate."

"Because," laughed Emma, "as you well know, I blend all the veggies into the sauce so that he still gets all the nutrition you are so concerned about since you are such a wonderful mother. And let's just say that it's such a great big thing because I have a hunch, and leave it at that for now."

"Is there anything at all I can do to help or does Miss Super Mouse have it all covered?"

"You've set up the table beautifully. You've managed to light all the Tiki torches around the deck, which I would never have thought of, and you have a wonderful fire pit set up on the beach for later, so don't make out you've done nothing at all."

"Since you put it like that I can sit back and enjoy my wine then. I hope we'll have a lot of nights like this this summer, Em. It's so good to have you back here."

"It's so good to be here. It feels right. And did Pete tell you he's going to do long weekends while he builds the house?"

"He did. I'm hoping it'll be like old times, the four of us together again."

"Well, here they come," said Emma as the motor coach turned into her driveway. The guys all piled out. Scot came to Missy and hugged her.

"You doing okay, son?"

"Awesome! Dan has a set-up in there that's got more power than I've ever seen and he's letting me have an external hard drive to use 'til mine comes and the server rack has...."

"Whoa, slow down, buddy," Missy interrupted. "Rewind to 'Hello' and explain this to me in words of one syllable or less, please?"

He grinned at her, "It's okay, Mom. All you need to know is that Dan is the most awesome dude I have ever met!" He gave her a big hug. Missy looked over his shoulder at Dan, who had arrived in time to hear the last part. He gave Missy a bashful shrug as she mouthed, 'Thank you'.

Emma was asking everyone's preferences on steaks and came to Scot. "Now then, you'll want yours medium rare, right?"

Scot looked horrified. "I, err...." he looked nervously at Missy.

"Don't panic, buddy," Emma said with a laugh. "I'm only teasing. How does pepperoni, sausage and extra cheese sound? Auntie Em special."

"Phew." Scot swiped at his brow with his sleeve. "Yes, purleez, Auntie Em, you make the best pizza ever."

"Coming up, young man." She turned to Dan. "And how about you? Steak? How do you like it?"

Dan shifted from one foot to the other and looked to Jack, much as Scot had just looked at Missy. He opened his mouth, but no words came out.

Emma smiled at him, "May I take a guess at pepperoni, sausage and extra cheese for you too?"

He looked at the floor, then met her eye with that shy smile. "Would that be okay?"

"More than okay. I made two huge pizzas," she looked back at Missy, "on a hunch. It should even be enough to get you both through the night and breakfast too."

She caught Jack's eye as he watched her put his brother at ease. The gratitude in the look he sent her warmed her heart.

"Anything I can do to help?" he asked, as he followed her into the kitchen.

"You can open another bottle of red, if you would, and take a couple of Mountain Dews out for Scot and Dan."

"How did you know he'd rather have pizza?" asked Jack, eyeing the two huge pies she'd prepared.

"Easy." She smiled. "You told me the other night that I had a head start since he was just like Scot. When I met him this afternoon I understood how similar they are. Anyway, I didn't really know, I covered my options. If he'd wanted steak I would have had a humongous pizza in the freezer for another day."

"Thanks, Emma."

"What for?"

"For having us both here, for all of this," he waved his arm around the kitchen.

"Like I've said before, you're my friend. I think Dan will become my friend too."

"Okay, friend," he smiled, passing her the wine he'd uncorked. "I'll get the Mountain Dew to the tech guys."

Emma timed everything perfectly and, with Pete's help, had it all to the table at the same time. They all laughed as Dan and Scot tucked into their pizza and both said, "Awesome!"

Ben groaned as he bit into his steak. "Oh, man! Mouse steak, it's died-and-gone-to-heaven food." The rest of them nodded their agreement.

"You know, Mouse," said Ben, "I may have to hold you hostage and keep you here when the summer ends."

"I'll help," chimed in Missy.

"And me," added Scot through a mouthful of pizza.

Pete exchanged a glance with Jack. "Maybe some of us want her back in the city."

"Maybe some of you should move up here too. Then we can all eat Mouse food all the time."

Emma laughed, thrilled that they were all enjoying the food.

"Well," said Pete, "none of us can say what will happen when the summer ends, but for now we still have the summer ahead, so I propose a toast." He raised his glass. "To living the moment and enjoying it for what it is."

"I'll drink to that," said Ben.

The others all chinked their glasses and murmured their agreement. Jack's glass was the last to meet Emma's. He raised his eyebrows and held her gaze as he brought it back to his lips.

Emma stood, flustered. "I need to check on the pies," she said and returned to the kitchen.

Was that what she should be doing? Living the moment with Jack? Enjoying it for what it was, as each of her friends had now told her to do? But, what exactly was it? It was a very attractive man who made it plain he wanted her. Did it have to be any more than that? Oh, who knew? Not her, that much was for sure. She pulled the apple pie from the oven, then the cherry pie that Pete loved so much.

She returned to the deck. "Okay, who's for pie?"

Everyone started clearing their own plates and bringing dishes inside until she shooed them all back to the table.

"Go, go, go!" she laughed. "I enjoy doing this part as much as you all enjoy eating it, so please sit and let me play!"

Once they were all served, the table was silent as they ate. Emma beamed. "Now that is the highest compliment I can have. If my pie managed to shut all of you up, then I know it's good."

"This is the best pie I've ever tasted," said Dan, his tone almost reverent.

"Oh no," said Jack, "I know that voice, but I've only ever heard it used when it comes to computer programs that he then obsesses about for months. I have no idea what this will mean when it comes to pie though." He looked at Emma. "Be warned, this could go anywhere."

"Nowhere bad, I promise," said Dan. He smiled at Scot and then whispered to him. Scot nodded his head as a big grin spread across his face.

"Hell yeah!" said Scot.

Missy shot him a look, "Was that 'heck', young man?" Scot smiled and looked back at Dan, nodding encouragingly.

"Let me add my name to the growing list of folk who are going to be spending a lot of time here in the next few months," said Dan.

"Hell yeah!" exclaimed Jack. "Really, little bro?"

"Really." Dan grinned. "I just met one of the smartest guys I've ever known and we have a few projects we need to work on." He looked down at Scot, who seemed to grow two feet taller at the compliment. "I get to hang out with my big brother and get to know a bunch of great new friends." He smiled around the table, holding Missy's eyes a moment longer than the others, "And, I've been fed the best pizza and apple pie I've ever tasted!"

They all laughed as he finished what, for him, was a long speech by rubbing his tummy to accentuate the point.

"Well," said Emma, "if you are going to be hanging out with my godson and using your combined genius to better the world, the least I can do is supply pizza and pies."

"Then we have a deal." Dan dusted his hands together with a 'that's that!' finality. "Now, would it be okay with everyone if we get back to work?"

"Not so fast," said Emma, "I need you to follow me first." She led him and Scot to the kitchen, where she gave them the second pizza and the remaining apple pie. "That should see you through to morning."

The rest of them made their way down to the beach, where Missy had set out chairs around a fire pit.

"Looks like those two have clicked," observed Pete.

"Yeah," said Jack, "I kind of knew that would work out."

"Looks like this whole thing is lining up to work out nicely," added Ben.

"How do you mean?" asked Missy.

"Well, we've got Emma back. We're going to have Pete around more than we have for years. Scot has a guy in his life who can help him in a way none of us ever could. And Jack," he paused, "Jack gets to kick back and hang with us for a few months too. I think we'll all look back on this as a summer to remember."

They all raised their glasses to that.

Emma leaned back in her chair, content to listen to the others talk. It was a beautiful, cool, clear evening, the fire cast a circle of heat and bathed them all in flickering light. She watched Pete entertain them all with a story about his parents and some gallery in Denver. He was a natural leader. He'd always protected the rest of their little group. She was intrigued by his friendship with Jack. She watched the two of them banter back and forth, obviously equals. She'd only ever known Pete in the lead role, so it was interesting to see how easily he shared it with his partner. It was obvious they made a great team.

Pete's words echoed through her mind; "I'm a good judge of character...." and "I think you could be missing out on something special...."

Was that what she was doing? Missing out on something special because she was too afraid to risk the hurt? Watching Jack throw his head back and laugh at what Ben had said, she remembered the way he'd kissed her. Now that had been something special! She couldn't deny that, and she did know she would like more of it.

Missy stood up, bringing Emma back to the moment.

"I'm going to check on those two and then I think I'm going to go to bed, I'm exhausted."

"Want me to show you your room?"

"No thanks, hon. You showed us all before. Bedrooms, bathrooms," she laughed, "I know there's a lot of them, but I'm good. You stay here, I'll see you in the morning."

"I think it's time for me to turn in, too," said Ben. "Some of us around here still have to work for a living."

~ ~ ~

When they'd gone, the three of them sat in comfortable silence looking into the flames.

After a while Pete said, "I think I'm going to like being your neighbor out here, Mouse."

"I already like it, Pete, and as you said, it'll be like this 'til we're old and gray."

Jack was surprised to find himself feeling left out. They had a lifetime of shared history and a lifetime ahead of them. He was only a summer visitor, unless he could convince her to let him be more than that. He wanted to be so much more than that; he wanted to be a part of this place, a part of her life.

"Can I ask something that's been puzzling me?"

"Fire away," said Emma.

"Why 'Mouse'? Where does the name come from?"

She and Pete exchanged a look he couldn't decipher.

"I'll let Pete tell you, it's his name after all," she smiled, but he noticed that it didn't reach her eyes.

"I don't know," shrugged Pete. "It's a childhood thing I guess."

Jack was surprised by the evasive answer but thought it best not to push it.

All of a sudden Pete stood. "I think it's time for me to turn in, too. I've got to be back out to my folks early in the morning." He was gone before they even had chance to say goodnight.

"So," said Jack, "then there were two. Are you going to cry off on me as well?"

"I am not," she surprised him. "This is my first proper night in my new home. I want to make the most of it."

He noticed her shiver as she reached down to put some more wood on the fire. He took off his sweater and offered it to her.

"Here, it looks like you need this more than I do." She only hesitated for a moment before she took it from him and pulled it over her head. She was adorable, swamped by the sweater that was way too big for her. She smiled at him.

"Thank you. This is great. So, how do you like it here so far?"

"I love it. Pete told me there was something special about this place and he was right. And now I'll get to see more of Dan out here too, so it's going to be great."

"Are you going to drive that big thing around everywhere you go?"

"No," he laughed at her mention of the RV. They had towed Dan's Jeep up so that he'd be able to drive back. Jack, however, was going to need to find some other means of getting around. "I talked to Ben earlier and he said there's a dealership about fifteen miles down Route Twenty. I figure I'll head out there on Monday after everyone's left and buy myself a pickup to run around in."

"I'll take you, if you like?"

Wow, this was progress. "Thanks, I'd love that."

"That's what friends are for," she smiled.

There she went again. She sat there looking so damned cute, out here under the stars, firelight dancing over her, snuggled inside his sweater—a sweater he knew he'd never be able to wear again without picturing this moment—and she was still insisting on friendship only. He honestly believed that if he kissed her again now, as he so badly wanted to, he could make her admit that she wanted more too. The way she'd responded to his kiss made that obvious. But he also knew that, if this was going to go anywhere, she would have to decide that for herself.

"Thanks friend," he smiled and shrugged his resignation. He decided it was probably best not to sit out here alone with her for too long. What he couldn't have was driving him crazy. "I think I'm going to turn in too. It was a long drive up here and I'm beat."

"Oh." There went that little word again. Was that really disappointment in her eyes?

"Hey, I'll stay a while if you like." So much for his resolve!

"That's okay," she said, standing and kicking sand into the fire. "It is late, I should go too."

Once the fire was out it was quite dark on the beach. He was surprised to feel her slip her hand inside his and start to lead him up the path to the house.

"I'll show you the way."

His heart was beating faster as he followed her, her small hand holding his tightly, and pulling him on. She stopped before they reached the front deck, at the edge of the shadows. She turned slowly to face him and smiled up at him. She stepped towards him and circled her arms up around his neck. He closed his arms around her and drew her against him, breathing her in. Her lips came up to meet his, tentative at first, but soon they were lost in a passionate kiss, tongues dueling. He held her tight to him, forgetting caution and pushing his arousal against her. He went wild, devouring her with his mouth. She responded, molding herself against him.

Eventually, they came up for air. He looked down at her, trying to figure out what had brought this on, not that he was complaining. She smiled back at him, her cheeks flushed, her breath coming quickly. She ran her hand down his cheek then pressed a finger to his lips.

"Friends who kiss goodnight, Jack." With that she walked up onto the deck and into the light.

Damn!

He followed and caught up to her in the hallway. He caught her by the shoulder and turned her to face him. She smiled again.

"Goodnight, Jack. I'll see you in the morning."

He shook his head and let himself back outside. He'd rather sleep in the coach with Dan and Scot working around him than spend the night under the same roof as Emma and not be able to do anything about it. Where in the hell had that kiss come from? He had no idea. He only knew he wanted more, so much more.

~ ~ ~

Emma lay in bed, wide awake. What had she done? She smiled. Exactly what she wanted to! And she'd enjoyed every moment of it. She'd sat there in his sweater, enveloped in the smell and the feel of him. He'd looked so handsome with the firelight on his face. Out here he looked even more sexy, if that were possible, kind of rugged and like he belonged here. Well, she'd certainly lived that moment. Remembering the feel of his hardness pushing against her, she couldn't deny that his desire for her was very real. Now all she had to do was decide if she was brave enough to live it for what it was, and throw caution to the wind. She wanted to, but was it really worth the risk?

Chapter Ten

Jack walked into the kitchen to find Pete, Ben and Missy sitting at the big table drinking coffee and eating delicious smelling muffins. Emma was busy again. He couldn't help but admire her long legs and rounded backside as she bent to put some bowls in the dishwasher. He caught Pete watching him and lifted a shoulder.

"Pull up a seat," said his partner.

Emma turned and greeted him with a hesitant smile. Oh no. She was backing off again.

"Coffee?"

"Love some, please."

She placed a mug of black coffee in front of him. "Help yourself," she pointed to the muffins.

"Thanks." He bit into one and moaned, "Oh, my God, this is amazing. Is there anything you don't cook?"

"Doughnuts!" chorused the others.

"You don't like doughnuts?"

"I love doughnuts, but I hate having a house that reeks of the oil you need to fry them in. Anyway," she put a hand on Ben's shoulder as she came to join them at the table, "Ben here has me covered since they make wonderful doughnuts at the resort."

"That's right" said Ben, "fresh at five every morning."

Jack felt his throat tighten. That was crazy; how could he hate the idea of Ben having her covered for anything? He was her friend, and they were talking about doughnuts, for God's sake! Nevertheless, he felt an undeniable twinge of jealousy as he watched Ben touch her hand and smile up at her.

"Speaking of the resort," Ben continued, "I need to get down there, we've got a big changeover this morning. Who wants to give me a ride?"

"I can," said Pete, "I promised my folks I'd get down there early. How about you, Miss?"

At that moment Scot came barreling through the door. "Wow, awake before eight on the weekend? What's up, hon?"

"I need to show Dan some of the programs I'm writing. He doesn't believe I've taught myself PHP."

Dan appeared behind him. "Morning."

Emma handed him a glass of orange juice and gave one to Scot.

"Thanks," murmured Dan and downed it in one gulp. Jack watched Emma refill his glass, amused and grateful at how well she read his little brother.

"So, can we, Mom?" asked Scot.

"Can we what?" asked Missy.

"Take Dan home now. He has to leave this afternoon and I need to show him."

"Well, if it's okay with Dan?" Missy looked at him.

"Sure. I can drive us down there, I've got the Jeep."

"Well, okay then, let's go."

Pete looked at Emma. "Could you do me a favor, Mouse? Would you mind showing Jack the site we picked out yesterday? I'll be back in a couple of hours." Emma nodded. Pete smiled at Jack. "That work for you?"

"Sounds great," said Jack, curious whether Pete was engineering him some alone time with Emma or simply being practical. Either way it suited him fine.

When the others had left, Emma poured him a fresh coffee.

"Want to sit out front with these?" she asked.

He brought his coffee and came to sit on the deck next to her. She looked out at the water and he stole a sideways look at her. Her hair seemed even wavier out here, and it fell around her shoulders, wild and untamed. She wore a white tank top and faded, cut-off jeans. His heart ached, she was so beautiful. The throb in his pants ached too, she was so desirable.

"About last night," she said.

He waited, not knowing what to expect.

"I'm sorry."

"Oh, Emma, don't apologize, please."

"Let me finish?" she asked.

He nodded and bit his lip to keep his big mouth shut.

"I want to say, I'm sorry I'm acting so weird. I'm not playing games, I promise you. I don't do that."

He shook his head. She certainly wasn't the game playing sort, he already knew that much.

"I'm just, well, I'm scared," she admitted.

"What are you scared of, Emma?" he asked, relieved that she was prepared to be honest with him.

"I'm scared of you." Her voice was so small, it put a dagger through his heart. He knew only too well what it felt like to be scared of a man.

"Em, please don't be scared of me. You must know I'd never hurt you." He turned to her and took both her hands in his. He looked into her eyes, wanting to reassure her that not only would he never hurt her, but given the chance, he wanted to protect her from any and all harm for the rest of her life. He figured telling her that at this point may scare her even more though. She looked back at him.

"By now, I don't think you would hurt me on purpose. But look at you, you're rich, you're successful, you're..." she paused and smiled, then continued, "the sexiest man I have ever met."

He had to smile at that, thrilled that she felt that way and that she would say it out loud.

"But...."

"Why does there have to be a 'but', Em?" he asked gently.

"Because I'm no good at this," she shook her head.

He lifted a hand to her cheek. "What's the worst that could happen, baby?" She looked so small somehow, so vulnerable.

"I like you too much. It would be too easy for me to fall in...even more in like with you, and then have my heart broken when you go back to your life and your girlfriends."

"My girlfriends? I don't have a girlfriend, Em, let alone multiples. Whatever makes you think that?"

"I'm sure I'm not the only woman who thinks you're the sexiest man she's ever met. A man like you always has beautiful women around, waiting their turn. Like the one at Mario's the other night."

It took him a moment to even remember the brunette. "Emma that's crazy. I admit, women do seem to find me attractive," he shrugged, "but I don't really notice them. You say I'll go back to my life and my girlfriends. What if I were to tell you that since I met you and came up here, the only thing I can think about is wanting to make a life here, a life with you in it? That I'm already falling...." He too hesitated on that one and decided to go with, "more than in like with you. What would you say to that? All I'm asking is that you give me a chance, let me prove to you that we could have something good together, something special."

She looked at him and he saw the surprise and longing on her face, but then it was gone. Those green eyes shuttered over again. Damn. He'd thought he was getting through.

"Men like you say things like that to get what they want, until they want something else."

Oh, she was infuriating. Careful not to show his frustration, he spoke slowly. "That's not fair, Emma. I know the guy you married let you down and hurt you badly, but I'm not him. And you're not giving us a chance when you judge me to be the same as him." He waited, but she didn't respond.

"So, what are you telling me?" he asked when he was convinced she really wasn't going to say anything.

"I don't know. All I wanted to do was tell you that I'm not playing games. Last night I kissed you because I wanted to."

She looked so small and sad. He framed her face between his hands. "I want to kiss you now," he breathed. She lifted her lips to meet his. He wrapped her in his arms and gently explored her mouth with his tongue. Her arms came up around him and she molded herself to him, responding to him in a way that belied everything she'd said. Eventually he lifted his head and looked down at her.

"So where do we go from here, Em? What can I do to convince you?"

"I've been thinking about Pete's toast yesterday."

"How did it go again?"

"About living the moment and enjoying it for what it is."

"I knew I liked that guy. Do you think you can do that, Emma? Enjoy this, live it for what it is?"

She nodded slowly. "But...."

Another 'but'; she wasn't going to make this easy. "But what, baby?"

"But nothing. You're right. We can have some fun for the summer and enjoy it for what it is."

He frowned. "The summer?"

"Is that too long?"

Oh, she was unbelievable. "Too long?" he asked incredulously. "Did you hear what I said? Give me the chance to convince you I'm for real. I don't want just the summer, Em, I want the lifetime."

Her eyes were sad. "I don't believe in the lifetime, Jack. Not anymore. Not with a man like you, especially."

How could she be so stubborn in her mistrust? He closed his eyes and sighed. He knew why. Because anyone she'd loved and trusted had caused her terrible pain. She'd lost her parents when she was a little kid, and when she dared to love a man and trust him, she'd given him her heart completely, and he'd shattered it. He would gladly help her put it back together again. He only hoped it wasn't shattered beyond repair, that one day she'd be able to love him back.

He put a finger to her lips. "How about I work with what you're giving me. You want to have fun with me this summer?" She nodded and he smiled with relief; this was a start at least. "Then let's have some fun but—and now I have a 'but'—I need you to understand that I am going to do everything in my power to make it last much longer than the summer. I will prove to you that you can trust me, that I won't hurt you...I want to make you believe in forever again."

Her eyes filled with tears. "Jack." He loved the way she spoke his name.

"Yes, baby?"

"I'd like to believe you, but I'm not sure I ever will."

"How about we leave it at that for now then? You've been honest with me and I appreciate that, I understand where you're coming from and I'm saying I'd like to prove you wrong. You don't believe me now, but I think I can make you." He gave her his best smile and drew her closer to him, "But it will be by having some of that fun we were talking about, not by talking it to death."

With that he found her lips with his own and kissed her with even more hunger than he'd allowed himself to show before. She opened up and willingly let him in, kissing him back, quivering under his touch as he ran a hand down her back. Hell yeah, this would be a good summer. When they resurfaced, Emma seemed to have recovered somewhat.

"We'd better start the fun by getting over to Pete's lot and showing you around. We don't want him to come back and find us still sitting here. You've got work to do, Mr. Benson." She took their mugs inside and closed up the house. "Do you want to drive that thing around there?"

"Let's walk over first, then I can get a feel for the land before I put that monster in a ditch or something."

"Good thinking. Come on down to the beach then, that's the best way to go."

She ran ahead of him and waited at the fire pit. She looked happy again now, eyes sparkling. Seeing her standing there, his heart clenched in his chest. This was a start; he hoped he really could do enough to convince her to trust again. He knew enough to understand that as well as trusting him, she needed to learn to trust herself. He joined her on the beach and they set out to Pete's side of the cove. As they walked he slung an arm around her shoulders and was delighted when she reached up and laced her fingers through his.

By noon they were back at her house. Jack was sitting on the deck making notes and sketches after seeing where he would build Pete's house. Emma was feeling a little lighter. She really hadn't wanted him to think she was the kind of woman who would play mind games, saying just friends one minute then kissing him the next. Her heart did a happy little skitter as she looked at him sitting out there, absorbed in his work. He wore cargo shorts and a T-shirt with no sleeves that showed off his muscular frame. She watched his biceps bulge as he reached up to run his fingers through his hair, staring out at the lake a moment and then returning to the huge pad he'd fetched from the RV.

She still wasn't sure that this was a good idea. She was afraid she was already falling for him, but she couldn't be the scared little mouse that hid away from life. She'd conquered it in every other area of her life. She wasn't afraid to stand her ground or speak her mind with the powerful men and women in Hollywood, so why was she so cowardly when it came to her heart? She knew the answer only too well; she didn't think she could live through the pain of loss again.

When her parents had been killed, she'd wanted to die too. She'd believed that was the only way to make the pain stop. With time, and all the love and patience her grandparents had surrounded her with, and the friendship of her three pals, she'd learned not to be so afraid. She'd struck out in life, gone off to college and then earned her way in Hollywood and become a respected screenwriter very quickly.

Then she'd met Rob. He too was a very good-looking man and he had romanced her. She'd believed that all the pain and sadness were now behind her, that she'd earned the right to have her own fairytale, to meet 'the one' and live happily ever after. She'd thought herself so lucky that he wanted her and not the beautiful actresses and models that were such a part of their world. She'd been so happy when he'd proposed. She'd always dreamed of a big wedding at Gramps' house by the lake, but he'd surprised her with a quick afternoon ceremony and glitzy reception in the city, filled with people she barely knew, but that the media loved.

She'd believed at first that this really was the fairytale she'd wanted. She'd ignored the little things—the missed dinners when she'd sat alone in restaurants waiting for him to show. The weekends he could never come to the lake with her. The disaster of the one time he did. She'd tried to convince herself that Gramps hated him because he was a city-boy. She'd thought that her three friends were cool towards him because he was intruding on their little group. She remembered Pete trying his best to open her eyes to what Rob was really like. Ha! She'd reassured Pete that he didn't know him well enough. It turned out Pete saw right through him, while she herself had been blind.

It had only taken six months to all fall apart. She'd found him in their bed with an actress when she'd come back early from the lake one weekend. Instead of apologizing or trying to explain, he'd told her to grow up. Told her she was pathetic and she needed to get real. This was how life was and she should get used to it. Oh, what a fool she'd been. She wondered now if she'd ever really been in love with him or had she been in love with the whole idea of living happily ever after with a wonderful man?

She looked out at Jack again; he certainly didn't treat her like Rob had. Even in the beginning, if she was honest, Rob had never been as caring or considerate as Jack. But, where would this go? She poured two glasses of the lemonade she'd been making. Like the man said, talking, or thinking, it to death wouldn't get her anywhere. She needed to stick with Pete's toast, have some fun, enjoy it for what it was and not worry too much about what that might be.

She placed the lemonade on the table and Jack looked up. "Thanks. Sorry, I just need to get this down, I won't be long."

"Take your time. I've got plenty to do." She went back into the kitchen and started unloading the dishwasher. She wondered whether she should invite him for dinner this evening. She took a deep breath, imagining where that might lead. Was she ready to have him out here with all the others gone? The phone rang, startling her. She didn't even have a land line in LA. Who might know the number for this place?

"Hello?"

"It's me," said Missy, "how's it going?"

"Great, what's up?"

"Would you mind very much if we all invaded you again later? Scot and Dan are totally involved in writing some program, so much so that Dan's decided to stay 'til tomorrow. They want to work on the equipment in the RV again later."

"I don't mind at all, that'll be great. I'll do dinner for everyone."

"Thanks, Em, we'll see you later then."

Emma smiled to herself. It looked like she wouldn't get to find out where dinner alone with Jack might lead, at least not tonight. She went outside to tell him that Dan was staying another night. He was gone from the deck and she saw him on the driveway, talking to Pete who had just arrived. They made a handsome pair, equal in height, Jack so dark and Pete much fairer, but no less attractive, although in a different way. She imagined the two of them caused quite a stir with the ladies. She had to stop that. Thinking of Jack being pursued by other women was not going to help her resolve to be brave and try to trust. However, thinking of Pete and the ladies reminded her of her plan. He'd been pushing her and Jack together, so the least she could do was return the favor. She must call Holly soon to make sure she was still coming up for Gramps' birthday.

She smiled as they walked towards the house. Pete grinned. "How do you feel about feeding your old buddy again tonight?"

Jack pulled a face at her behind Pete's back. It seemed that he'd thought about dinner alone too. It would keep, though, they had the whole summer ahead.

"The more the merrier. Miss just called and Dan's staying another night so they're all coming up, too."

"Is that so?" Jack looked pleased.

"They'll be over later. Apparently they still have more work to do in that thing." She nodded her head at the huge RV.

Jack laughed. "You really don't like it, do you?"

"It's not that so much as I don't know what to make of it, it's such a big, a big...thing."

The guys both laughed at her. "I'll try to make sure we put it somewhere it won't disturb you then," said Pete.

"How come you're staying over anyway? I thought you were going back to work tomorrow."

"I just want to. I think I'm getting the Summer Lake bug. The city loses its appeal when all my favorite people are up here. Besides, I spent more time with Mom and Dad this morning than I thought I would and Jack and I have still got a lot to figure out before we can get anything started." He looked at Jack, "I guess we'd better walk over there, leave 'that thing' here for Scot and Dan to do whatever it is they do."

"Sure thing."

"You want to walk over with us, Mouse?"

"No thanks, I think I know every inch of that place by now. Anyway, I need to get to the store if I'm feeding the five thousand again."

"Want me to buy?"

"I'm fine, but you know what, you can do the booze run later. I don't know how Miss is fixed at the moment and she spent a lot yesterday."

"Tell you what," said Pete, "we'll run down and do that first so she can't argue later. Any special requests?"

"The usual. I'll get stocked up when I get the chance to settle in properly."

"We'll catch you back here later on, then." Pete climbed back into his truck and Jack took the passenger seat. He gave her a small wave and a big wink as they drove away.

Chapter Eleven

After dinner they all sat out on the deck. Scot and Dan were back in the RV.

"It's a shame Ben was too busy at the resort to come out tonight," sighed Missy. "Did he tell you guys about that developer who's been sniffing around Joe?"

Emma watched both Jack and Pete prick their ears up at the word 'developer'.

"No," Pete shook his head. "He said this morning there was something he wanted to talk to me about, but his phone kept ringing all the way into town so we didn't get to it. Do you have any idea who it is, Miss?"

"He did say a name, Armstrong, I think it was."

Jack and Pete exchanged a look.

"By your faces I'd say he's not one of your favorite people?" guessed Emma.

"He's a bastard!" said Pete, and Jack nodded.

"He must be." Emma was surprised to hear Pete use that word.

"Tell me Ben's not thinking of doing business with him," said Jack.

"From what he said, Ben doesn't like him much either, but Joe's apparently got it into his head to sell off a big chunk of his land at Four Mile Creek. Says he wants to leave Ben all the money and none of the hassle."

"He'd be setting him up for a whole lot of hassle if he has Armstrong developing out there," said Pete.

"He'd ruin the place," agreed Jack.

The two of them looked horrified. "What do you think, bro?" asked Pete. "We go see Ben first thing in the morning?"

"I was about to suggest it."

Missy nudged Emma. "Looks like our two superheroes are about to save the day," she laughed.

Emma nodded. If they were going to see Ben in the morning she wouldn't be able to take Jack car shopping. She'd been looking forward to that. Oh well. It was starting to seem that since she'd decided to have some fun with him, everything was conspiring to make sure she didn't.

Everyone except Emma was headed back to town. Dan was taking Missy and Scot home, doing something or other with a bunch of equipment he'd pulled from the RV, and then he'd be going home. Jack and Pete were off to find Ben. Emma had some cleaning up to do and then she really wanted to get to work. The characters for her novel were now stomping around in her mind, eager to have their story told. She planned to sit out and write, since car shopping was off the agenda. She hugged Dan before he got into his Jeep.

"It's been so nice to meet you."

"You too, Emma. Thanks for everything. I'll be back up next weekend."

Next came Pete. "I won't see you before I leave, so give me a hug, Mouse. You be good now and I'll see you on Wednesday right?"

"Yes, I'll be down to switch cars, only for the day though."

Jack looked at them. "Switch cars?"

"That old thing," Pete pointed to the station wagon Emma drove, "is not our Mouse's usual transport. She borrowed it to bring her things up here."

"Yes," Emma said, smiling. "And now I want my baby back."

Jack raised an eyebrow. "Your baby?"

"I think you should wait and see," laughed Pete. "I think you'll like the Mouse-mobile. You didn't have her down as a station wagon kind of girl, did you? You're in for a surprise if you did." He went to get in his truck.

Jack leaned in to hug her. She rested her cheek against his chest for a moment and he planted a kiss on top of her head. "See you later, Mouse."

"Later," she smiled.

~ ~ ~

"That looked a bit more hopeful," said Pete as they drove away.

"Hopeful, yeah, but this is going to be a long haul."

"You up for that?"

"More than I've ever been up for anything in my life."

Pete smiled. "So, my hometown is working its magic on you then?"

"It's looking that way, old friend. I'll tell you something though, I hate the idea of Darren Armstrong building one of his sleaze holes up here."

Pete rubbed his chin. "You thinking what I'm thinking?"

Jack grinned, his eyes crinkling at the corners in the way that made Emma's heart skip. "I believe I am, partner. If Ben's old man really wants to sell the land and if new development is really needed up here, then I can't think of anyone better than us to do the job. Do you think it would help the place? I kind of like it the way it is; I'd hate to see it become commercialized and crowded."

"It's something I've toyed with over the years. On the one hand, I'd hate to see it change at all, I want to keep the sleepy little town where I grew up. On the other hand, given that change is coming to the whole area, you know it's going to happen. And given the choice between having Armstrong build an eyesore that will draw the cheap crowds up here or stepping in ourselves to develop something more in keeping with the nature of the place, I know which one I choose."

"It'd be a great project." Jack's mind was already crowding with ideas. A Mediterranean style village with a square down on the lake, red tile roofs dotting the hillsides. "If we took on something like that we'd both need to spend a lot more time up here."

"And I don't think either of us would have a problem with that, would we?"

"No, sir."

"Let's see what Ben has to say, shall we? He might hate the whole idea. After all, whatever we did would kind of be competition for the resort."

"Not if we work it right."

"Uh-oh, I sense the illustrious Mr. Benson is having one of his brilliant ideas."

"Maybe, but only if we want to take on a third partner."

"Go in with Ben, you mean? Not just buy the land from him?"

"What do you think? If we bought the land and built it out, then we'd only sell it on and, you're right, create competition for Ben. I'm thinking we could work out a deal where we retain a stake and he manages the final development as an extension of what he's already got going on here."

"I like it. Sounds like you really want to be a part of this place."

Jack nodded, "I really do. Seriously, if I get my way Summer Lake is going to be central to the rest of my life, so why not invest in it?"

"Okay, then." They had arrived at the resort. "Let's go find Ben and see what we can work out."

Jack was riding in Ben's truck with him on the way to Gramps' house. Ben was thrilled at the idea of going in with Jack and Pete and wanted to talk to Joe straight away. He said they'd find him up at his friend's house. Pete had reluctantly left for the city for a meeting he couldn't miss.

"I really need to get myself a car," said Jack, sad he'd had to postpone car shopping with Emma. He wasn't used to being chauffeured around.

"Well, you know Joe will want to talk to me alone about this, so that will give you something to talk to Gramps about. He's always tinkering with cars out there, and if you ask his advice he'll talk all day."

"What's he like?"

"Oh, he's great, a bit gruff, but like I say, ask his advice and he'll warm to you."

They drove on in silence. After a while Ben said, "I think you and Emma would be great together."

Jack smiled. "I hope so."

"Well, getting on the right side of Gramps will earn you some big brownie points, so let's go get 'em."

They found the two old men in Gramps' kitchen drinking coffee.

"What do yer want?" asked Joe, looking suspicious.

Ben turned to Jack. "Wasn't I just telling you what a sweet-natured old guy he is?"

"Bullshit!" Joe gave Jack a quick grin, then turned back to Ben. "Yer out here on a Monday morning when yer should have plenty to be keepin' yer busy. So I reckons yer up to somethin', so what do yer want?"

"Nothing gets by you, does it, Sparky?" laughed Ben. "What I want is to talk to you about this Armstrong guy."

"Shifty little weasel," said Joe, "but he's offering good money."

"Yeah, Armstrong's a shifty little weasel all right."

Joe looked at Jack. "He a friend of yours?"

"No friend of mine. He's a competitor."

"So, you out here to compete with him then?"

"Yes, sir." He looked at Ben. "Do you want to lay it out for him?"

"Yup." Ben poured himself some coffee and handed a cup to Jack.

"Thanks, I'll take mine outside." He went out to the front porch and Gramps followed him.

"I'd sooner come with you than listen to those two squabble," Gramps said.

He set out towards a little dock on the front of his property and sat on a picnic bench by the water. "Take a load off," he said. Jack sat down beside him.

"So, you're Pete's rich-kid, city-boyfriend, aren't you?"

Jack had to laugh. "Well, I'm Pete's friend, but I'm no city-boy, and I suppose some folks might call me rich now, but I was never a rich kid"

"Where you from then? What's your story?"

"I grew up in Texas Hill Country, that's where I'm from. And my story? Well, I guess I'm the kid from the wrong side of the tracks who had a family to support, so I worked my ass off to make sure I could. Got together with Pete, started a company and we got so busy working it that when we turned around, the 'rich' thing just seemed to have crept up on us."

Gramps smiled. "So why did a kid have a family to support? Where was your Daddy?"

Jack wasn't used to such direct questioning, but he wasn't about to shy away from it. "He died when I was seventeen."

Gramps raised an eyebrow. "You were pretty much a man by then. Why did you work as a kid?"

Gramps was sharp, he wasn't going let him gloss over it. "I started working when I was thirteen. Trying to bring in enough to keep us fed, since anything he ever earned went to straight to the bar."

"Sorry son, don't you mind me, I'm a nosey old man."

"No problem, sir. I don't like the city-boy rich-kids any more than you do. I'm glad to be up here and away from all that for a while."

Gramps nodded and they sat in companionable silence until Jack remembered what Ben had told him.

"I hear you're the man to ask for some advice about a car?"

"Well, that'd depend on what you want to know."

"The best place around here to buy a pickup, and any thoughts you have on what I should get. I'm going to be here for a while, building Pete's house. I don't need anything fancy, just a work horse, something reliable that'll get me around and haul the smaller stuff."

Gramps stood. "Come with me." He led Jack around the side of the house to a huge workshop at the back. Jack was impressed. There was a pit and hydraulic lifts, and all sorts of equipment, neatly kept and well organized.

"Wow! You sure know your stuff, what a great set-up."

"It keeps me out of mischief," smiled Gramps. He led Jack out through a back door to where several vehicles stood. He walked over to a Toyota pickup and leaned against it. It was old, but it gleamed in perfect condition. It was a real beauty.

"See, if you want to," said Gramps, "I'll take you down to my buddy's dealership and we can get you a good deal on one of those shiny new models, if that's your thing. Or there's this one."

"This is beautiful," said Jack, "and perfect for me. How much do you want for it?"

"Oh, she's not for sale. But if you're the man I think you are, then I'll trust you to take care of my little lady for a while, see how things work out." Jack looked up sharply and the old man met his gaze with a set of green eyes that were so familiar. "See, you wouldn't know it to look at her," he continued, "but she got real banged up a few years back. Took us a long time to put her back together." He smiled to himself. "She has her quirks, can be a bit temperamental if you don't handle her right, but I'm thinking you might be up to the job."

Jack looked him straight in the eye, certain now that they weren't simply talking about the truck. "I have no interest in the shiny new ones. I'm honored that you would trust me with her and I give you my word, I'll do everything in my power to take real good care of her."

"Don't let me down, son."

"I won't, sir. One thing though? Would you mind if I come to you for advice when I'm not handling her right?"

As Gramps chuckled, his eyes danced, just like Emma's. "It's a wise man who knows when to ask for help. You come to me, son. Between us I think we should be able to troubleshoot her." He offered Jack his hand and slapped him on the back. "Now, let's go find you the keys and see if those two haven't figured it out yet."

Jack felt happier and more alive than he had in long while as he drove the truck out towards Emma's. In a long while? When had he ever felt this happy and alive? He was thrilled to have Gramps' blessing. He genuinely liked the old guy and intended to make damned sure he didn't let him down. He'd take good care of Emma, and this truck. It also looked like he and Pete would be getting more involved out here than he'd thought. Joe had been eager to set up some kind of deal, especially when he realized that they wanted to go into partnership with Ben, not simply buy the land. There were lots of details to work out, but they'd agreed to all get together with Pete when he returned on Friday.

He arrived back at Emma's, and his heart raced when he saw her sitting on the deck. He shook his head as the blood flow stirred in his pants, as it did every time he saw her.

"Down boy," he muttered as he sat a moment longer, admiring the curve of her neck. Her hair was piled on top of her head in a ponytail. She wore a halter-top the same bright green color as her eyes, the V-neck showing enough of her cleavage to make him shift in his seat as the throb in his shorts intensified. She looked up and waved as he got out, looking a little puzzled to see him in Gramps' old truck.

"How did that happen?" she asked, as he climbed the stairs to join her.

"I met your Gramps."

"So I gather."

"And he's letting me borrow his truck while I'm here."

"Really! Well that's good, he must have taken to you."

Jack smiled, "You could say we reached an understanding."

"I'm so glad. He can be a bit gruff when he doesn't know you. And how did it go with Ben?"

He told her about the meeting and Ben talking to Joe. "We're going to thrash out the details later with Pete, but it looks like it's a go. So, my little Mouse, you'd better get used to having me around."

"I am getting used to it." She smiled shyly.

"And you like?"

"I like."

"Then kiss me." She stepped into his outstretched arms and stood on tiptoe to place a small peck on his cheek. "You can do better than that." She put her hands on his shoulders and pecked his lips. "Better than that," he breathed as he closed his arms around her, drawing her against him. He brought his mouth close to hers and watched her plump pink lips part, as her arms came up around his neck and she kissed him deeply.

"That's more like it," he said, when he finally lifted his head.

"Glad you approve."

"Oh, I approve."

"Well don't get too comfortable, because I have to go to town in a little while and this afternoon I have work to do."

"I have work to do too. I just wanted to say hi. Do you mind if I leave 'that thing', as you call it, over here until tonight? I've got some running around to do."

"Of course, it can stay here as long as you need."

"I was wondering if I could make you dinner this evening, since you've cooked for the masses all weekend." He could see that took her by surprise.

"Oh, no. I really don't mind, it's what I do."

"No problem. Another day." He was determined not to push her any faster than she wanted to take this. She surprised him by placing a hand on his arm, smiling.

"I didn't mean no, I meant I don't mind cooking and since I have a wonderful kitchen and you are living in 'that thing', I thought perhaps I could cook for you."

"How could I say no? Though can I at least do the booze run?"

She laughed, "You're already getting the hang of how things work around here. See you around seven?"

"You got it, baby,"

Chapter Twelve

Emma looked at her reflection and held her hair up, then let it fall around her shoulders. "Up or down?" she asked the mirror. This was ridiculous. She'd tried on five different outfits before finally settling on a white skirt and lilac colored baby-doll top. Everything for dinner was ready to go. Salad and pasta, bread ready to warm in the oven. She'd made a key-lime pie for dessert too. She knew Jack had arrived back at the RV a little while ago. Soon he'd be over here and the fun would really begin. She decided to go half and half and fastened her hair loosely at the nape of her neck.

Had she ever been this nervous about a date before? She thought about the early days with Rob, then decided that was not a comparison she wanted to make. In the last few years she'd dated a little, only safe men though, ones she wasn't really interested in. She'd had a few enjoyable evenings, but a lot more boring ones. More often than not recently she'd ended up pressing Pete into service when she'd needed to take a date along anywhere. It had been a great way to catch up with him and he'd saved her from the dating hell of the beautiful, but superficial, Hollywood crowd.

She rubbed some of her favorite lotion into her bare shoulders, fastened some gold hoops to her ears and stood before the mirror. "Not too shabby," she smiled and headed back downstairs. She wished she could shake the nerves. He'd been here for dinner the last two evenings, it wasn't like this was a first. Oh, who was she trying to kid? Over the weekend he'd been one of the gang, and this was the first time they would be alone together. Goose bumps ran down her arms and she shivered at the thought of being alone with Jack Benson. Where would it lead? His desire for her was obvious, she'd felt it pressed against her when they'd kissed. She thought of the night at Pete's cabin, laying naked in bed with him as he'd pulled her closer. Was she ready for that? She wanted him too, she couldn't deny it, but was she really ready for that? She hadn't slept with a man since Rob. Part of her wanted to throw caution to the wind, but the other part was still afraid. Perhaps it would be better to take this slowly.

"Knock, knock!" Jack shouted from the open doorway.

"Come on in."

As he walked in carrying a huge paper bag, she inhaled sharply: caution might soon be blowing in the wind. He was gorgeous! His muscular legs were encased in faded blue jeans, with leather flip flops on his feet and he wore a white short-sleeved shirt, untucked and open at the collar. Delicious. He plonked the bag down on the island and treated her to that smile that made her knees weak.

"Something smells good."

"Pasta, I hope you'll like it."

He stepped towards her, buried his face in her neck and breathed in. "You, I think," he murmured against her skin, sending shock waves rippling all over her, "and I do like."

Flustered, she stepped back, overwhelmed by the desire that swept through her. If he carried on like that they'd never even make it to the salad. "Just let me turn this down." She ran to the oven.

Jack went back to the bag, making light of the moment, and he pulled out two bottles of wine. "I didn't know which way to go, so I went Sauvignon, one Cabernet, one Blanc.

Emma turned back to him, having regained her composure. "I think the Cab."

He uncorked the bottle and poured two glasses. Handing one to her, he returned to the bag and pulled out a six pack of light beer. "I like to cover my options, so these were for just in case." She smiled; he was irresistible. "You're beautiful, Emma." This time he simply raised his glass to her.

She raised hers back. "You're not too shabby yourself." She reached up and planted a peck on his cheek, hoping he might draw her to him again.

However, he returned a chaste kiss on her own cheek. "Why, thank you purdy lady." He turned back to the bag once more, this time pulling out a beautiful little vase filled with freesia and pink roses.

She clasped her hands together. "Oh, Jack, thank you! They're beautiful, how did you know?"

"Know what?" he arched his brows, trying to look surprised, the humor playing on his lips giving him away.

"That they're my favorites," she laughed.

"Would you believe me if I said it was a lucky guess?"

"Probably not."

"Okay, then I won't say that. How about insider information?"

"Pete?" That surprised her.

"Well, I had to talk to him this afternoon."

"And he knew my favorite flowers?"

"Of course not, he's a guy! But he knows your best friend, Missy."

"I'll have to watch myself if the two of you are going to gang together on me."

"We are a force to be reckoned with," he smiled.

She looked at the pretty little flowers. "Thank you, Jack. That was very thoughtful of you."

"Hey, I thought they'd make you smile, and I like to see you smile. Pete actually came back to me with roses, freesias or daisies, but the daisies at the florist were those huge big ones and they didn't go with the others, sorry."

She laughed as he held his hands out wide to describe giant daisies. "These are perfect, Jack, thank you, and you're right, daisies wouldn't go. I do love daisies, but the regular ones, seeing them growing wild."

"All wildflowers or just daisies?" he seemed to be genuinely interested.

"All of them, but especially daisies. They make me happy. They always look like they're smiling and nodding. Sounds goofy I know, but you have to take your happiness where you can find it."

"I'll drink to that," said Jack and raised his glass to hers.

They decided to eat outside again since it was such a beautiful evening. Jack lit the Tiki torches while she brought the food. He'd wanted to help again, but she'd convinced him that it was part of her fun to cook and serve.

"This is amazing," he said, as he tasted the pasta. "You really are a great cook."

"Thank you, I'm glad you like it. Cooking is one of my very favorite things to do and it all started right here in this house."

"It did?"

She told him about Aunt Martha and learning to cook with her, all the good times she'd had here as a child, learning the old lady's recipes, for food and for life. "Baking is the best though," she said, "and tonight we have Aunt Martha's very own key-lime pie." She went into the kitchen and returned with the pie and two dishes. "Now you mustn't tell Pete you got key-lime without him, he adores this."

"I can see why. Best key-lime pie I've ever tasted and I've had it all over Florida, even down in the Keys when I was in Miami. I take it you like it too?" He watched her lick her fork as she finished her own slice. She saw a little pulse appear in his jaw. Oh my, stop licking the fork, Em!

"How do you manage to stay so," he let his eyes wander down to her chest and then travel slowly over her body before coming back to her face, "so shapely, when you make such great food all the time?"

Emma tried to calm the butterflies which had started to flutter under the heat of that look. Forget the pie, he looked like he wanted to eat her alive right then and there. "I have Aunt Martha to thank for that too. She taught me that in cooking, and in life, we shouldn't hold back. We should indulge fully, allow ourselves to have what we want, and work hard to pay for it."

"I like the sounds of that." The hunger in his eyes made it very clear that it wasn't more pie he wanted to indulge in.

Emma swallowed, hard, trying to stay on neutral ground. "I eat pretty much what I like and I work out every day too, like she taught me."

"She sounds like a wonderful lady and it sure does look good on you."

"Well, I'm glad you think so, because I'm going to have another small piece. Want some?"

"Yes, please, and I don't mind if mine isn't too small."

~ ~ ~

After they'd cleared dinner away they took the wine and went to sit down on the beach.

"This place is good for me," said Jack looking out across the lake. "I can feel the stress evaporating with every day I spend here."

"You do look more relaxed out here. Did you grow up in the city? Is small town life new to you?" she asked.

He realized how little she really did know about him. "Oh no. I'm a small town kid myself." He thought of the rundown little house where he'd spent his childhood. Always anxious not to spark any anger from his father, always looking out for his mom and Dan. "My childhood wasn't exactly as idyllic as this though." He stopped and looked at her; losing her folks wasn't exactly idyllic either. "Sorry, I didn't mean that yours was."

She shrugged. "I had Gramps and Grandma. I lost my parents when I was eight, but I had people who loved me and took care of me."

"Your Gramps is a great guy." He was still thrilled that Gramps seemed to approve of him and of his relationship with Emma, or at least what he hoped would become a relationship. She seemed more relaxed tonight, willing to see where this went.

"He's wonderful, the best man I could have had around after my Dad was gone. You weren't close to your Dad?"

Jack did his best not to show the thoughts that ran through his mind at that question, but must have failed.

"Sorry," she said.

"No problem, want to walk a little?" He didn't want to dwell on that subject.

He took her hand as they walked along the water's edge. "Thanks for a wonderful dinner, Em. I really would like to return the favor though and cook for you soon."

She smiled. "How about you come over and use my kitchen to do it?"

He laughed. "What are you worried about? Have you seen the kitchen in 'that thing' parked in your yard? It's better than most apartment kitchens, you know."

"Really?" She looked surprised.

"You haven't even seen inside yet, have you? Yet there you go, prejudging again." He laughed.

"Hmm, guilty as charged I suppose, but it still can't be as good as my kitchen. So how about tomorrow you can make me dinner in mine?"

"Tomorrow it is then," he said quickly, more interested in locking her in for dinner again tomorrow than where he might cook it. "Come on though, want to take a look inside so you won't need to worry about me 'camping out' in there?"

"Why not?"

They walked back up to the driveway, where Jack opened the coach door for her. "After you," he said and climbed the steps behind her. The intention had been gentlemanly, but the view of her backside made him feel anything but gentlemanly. She stopped dead and turned to face him; the stunned look on her face made him laugh, she was so adorable. He couldn't help it, her eyes were wide, her lips parted. He had to kiss her. When he was finished she looked even more stunned.

"Go on in. Look around." If she kept kissing him back like that, he'd soon forget all about showing her the kitchen.

They walked through the lounge area, past huge leather couches and two enormous flat screen TVs embedded in the walls. The kitchen was fitted with stainless steel appliances and cherry cabinets with granite counter tops.

"That's a full size fridge," said Emma, "and freezer. And a double oven!"

"And it's probably never been used for anything but heating pizza," laughed Jack. "This is Dan's remember, but you can see it's perfectly adequate for making dinner?"

"It is. I don't know what I was expecting, but it wasn't this."

"Let me show you the rest." He went through the kitchen and slid a door open to reveal a bathroom, all done out in marble. Behind the next door was a beautiful bedroom, then another. At the end of a short corridor they came to the master bedroom. "Take a peek."

She went inside and was amazed at the California king size bed facing a wall entirely covered by a huge screen. She peeked around a door to find an en suite bathroom. She imagined Jack showering in here earlier. She could still smell the wonderful sandalwood cologne he was wearing now. She turned to find him standing in the doorway, arms above his head holding the frame.

"So now you know I'm not slumming it in here."

She slipped past him, back into the bedroom. There was a huge desk built under the window. "And you can work in here too?"

"Yeah, in fact, do you want to see the preliminary workups for Pete's house? I did them this afternoon and I know he's going to run everything by you."

"Yes, please. I'm curious to see what kind of house you two are thinking of."

"Take a seat a minute."

Emma sat on the edge of the huge bed while Jack fired up the computer to print off the plans of how he envisioned Pete's new home. As he tapped at the keyboard, she looked around the room. That screen was enormous. She could imagine him, lying on the bed watching a movie... oh, who was she kidding? She could imagine lying on this bed with him! She looked up as he sat down beside her. He looked down at her, eyes full of humor.

"Want to see my etchings?"

She had to laugh. "I thought you would come up with a better line than that!"

His eyes were serious now. "Do I really need a line?"

"No, you don't." His arm came around her, drawing her closer. She reached up and touched his face, looking into eyes filled with desire. His mouth came down on hers and she surrendered to his kiss, feeling her nipples tighten as his tongue explored her mouth. She returned each stroke, feeling a sense of power as he trembled under her hands. Without leaving her lips he groaned and lay back, taking her with him. He drew her closer until she lay pressed to him, his arousal pushing against her. Feeling emboldened she rubbed her hips against him.

"Emma!" His hands tangled in her hair. She slipped her hands under his shirt and trembled herself as she touched rock hard abs. He rolled onto his back, still kissing her, as he pulled her on top of him. In a moment his hands were on the back of her legs, stroking upwards until they cupped around her backside and he pulled her down onto the hardness that was now straining to escape from his jeans. She felt the heat from him spread all through her body and moved rhythmically against him as his hands caressed her. She sat back a little, her skirt riding up around her hips as she unbuttoned his shirt then ran her hands over his chest. She smiled and gently squeezed his nipples, then cried out as he surged upwards in response.

He smiled and held onto her hips as he flipped them so he was on top of her. "Two can play that game," he said, as he slipped his hands inside her top. He bent his head to kiss her once more as his hands worked their way up, over her stomach, then stroking her ribs. She moaned as he cupped her breasts through her bra. He rolled to the side, bringing her to face him and trailed his tongue from her ear down to her collarbone, his hands still teasing her silk-covered nipples. Emma was overwhelmed by the sensations rolling through her, consumed with desire for him. As she pushed at his shirt, he pulled back long enough to remove it, then carried on kissing her as he pulled her own top up. She felt him get rid of it and felt the heat mount between her legs at the feel of his hard naked chest against her.

"Let's lose this." He reached one hand around her back and expertly flipped the clasp of her bra, unfastening it in one deft movement.

Emma felt a little chill run through the heat of her desire. Expertly? How many women had he practiced on to be able to pull that little move off so neatly? Oh, Em, stop it, she thought. She tried to respond to his kiss, but couldn't recall the same excitement as her mind raced. She moved her hands across his chest, but even to her the movements felt mechanical. Did she really want to be doing this with a man who had so many other women wanting, willing and waiting to give him the same thing? Jack had obviously sensed the change in her. His hands stilled and he was no longer kissing her.

"Baby, what's wrong?" his voice with husky with desire. "What happened?"

She couldn't bring herself to say anything, she felt too stupid.

"Emma, sweetheart, what happened?"

She felt her eyes fill with big, stupid, tears. She couldn't exactly tell him, could she?

His big arms closed around her, holding her close, lust now replaced by tenderness. He gently stroked her hair and turned his body to stop the last evidence of lust from throbbing against her.

"Too soon?" he asked gently.

She buried her head in his chest, and nodded.

"I'm so sorry, baby. I should have known, should have waited. I just.... You're so beautiful, so desirable, I want you so much."

She kept her face pressed into his chest, breathing in the reassuring scent of him, listening to his heartbeat slow back down to normal. She still didn't trust herself to say anything. How could he be so sweet, so gentle, when he must be frustrated as hell? She bit her lip as he reached around and fastened her bra. He held her close for a long time, stroking her hair, murmuring how sorry he was, asking for her forgiveness.

Eventually she looked up to meet his eyes.

"Please don't be sorry, Jack. You didn't do anything wrong," The tender look on his face almost made her cry again. "I'm the one that's sorry, I guess I wasn't as ready as I thought."

"I should have known," he began, "Should have...."

She pinched his lips between her finger and thumb to quiet him. "How could you have, when I didn't know myself?"

He could only shake his head as she still held his lips closed.

"Will you forgive me?" she asked.

He tried to talk again, but she buttoned his lips tight until he gave in and nodded his head.

"And," she took a deep breath, "have I frightened you off by being such a prick tease?"

His eyes widened at the term, but he shook his head vigorously.

"Please will you still make me dinner tomorrow?"

Again he nodded.

"I'm so sorry, Jack. Please don't give up on me." She let go of his lips and looked at him, not sure what to expect.

"Never," was the only word he spoke before his lips found hers in a slow, deep, kiss.

They stood on her front porch. She put her arms around his waist and leaned her head against him. "Thank you for understanding."

"I'm sorry, Em."

"Please don't make me button your lip again." She gave him a weak smile.

"All right then. Are you going to be okay?"

"I'm fine. Will you stop by for coffee in the morning?"

"You got it, baby."

"Okay then."

"Okay then."

"And you'll still make me dinner tomorrow?"

"Try stopping me, you offered me your kitchen, remember?" he smiled. "Em, don't worry about tonight, it's not a problem, we went there too soon. It doesn't change anything for me, just that I know to go slower, and I'm sorry."

"Thanks, Jack. So I'll still see you in the morning?"

"Bright and early." He tilted her chin up to him and kissed her long and slow. "Goodnight, baby."

He waited while she let herself inside and he saw the lights go on upstairs. He shook his head; he'd almost blown it. He needed to dial it back and let her make all the moves from now on. He looked down at the moonlit water of the lake. Time for a walk on the beach to clear his head? No, what he really needed was a cold shower.

Chapter Thirteen

Emma busied herself, grinding coffee, squeezing oranges. She'd hardly slept at all. Why, oh why had she been so silly? Of course he knew how to unfasten a bra. What man didn't? The fact that he did it so expertly was just how he was. He did everything with confidence, seemed to be an expert at everything he touched. That was part of what she found so attractive about him. She liked the feeling of having a big capable man around. He gave the impression that he could handle anything with ease.

She checked on the muffins in the oven. Another few minutes and she would pull them out.

By the time the sky had lightened she'd given up on sleep and taken a shower, and looking at her naked reflection when she stepped out, she had reached a decision. Tonight she was going to make it up to him. She was going to finish what they'd started and she wouldn't let any old hurts or silly fears interfere with that.

Now, as she waited for Jack to come by for coffee, she hoped that she hadn't spoiled things, that she would still get the opportunity to show him that she really did want him. He'd been so sweet and gentle, hadn't shown any of the frustration he must have felt, but still, she hoped there would be no awkwardness between them.

~ ~ ~

"Good Morning, Mouse," Jack called from the deck.

"Let yourself in, it's open."

He strode into the kitchen and straight to Emma. He put his arms around her waist and lifted her, twirling her around the kitchen, as she giggled and wrapped her arms around his neck. When he finally loosened his grip and let her slide back down to the floor, she kept her arms around his neck and kissed him.

"How's my Mouse today?" he asked with a smile. He was determined this morning should be light and fun. He didn't want last night's events to cast a shadow over things.

"All the better for seeing you," she said with a smile.

Wow, this was good. She wasn't hanging on to her embarrassment. He reached into his jeans pocket and pulled something out. "I come bearing gifts."

"Oooh, gifts for me?"

"Of course. Now close your eyes and hold your hand out."

Smiling, she did as she was told. He dropped a pebble into her outstretched hand. "You can open them now."

She looked down at the pebble and a huge smile spread across her face. "How beautiful!" It was a piece of flat, smooth rose quartz that sparkled, shot through with pink lines. She looked up at him, "More insider information, I take it?"

He was surprised by that. "No, just one of my little quirks. Ever since I was a little kid I've appreciated natural beauty in all its forms. I may still be a big kid in that respect, but I love pretty pebbles. Walking the beach this morning, I spotted this one and thought you would like it." He was touched by the expression on her face, she looked so happy.

"Come see." She took him by the hand and led him to the living room. On a high, small window sill sat a collection of stones, large and small, some very similar to the one he'd given her. "Aunt Martha and I used to spend hours pebble hunting on that beach. These are the best of our collection. I was surprised to see that they're still set out here." She moved the stones around to give his pebble pride of place in the center. "Thank you, Jack."

"My pleasure," he replied, and it really was. It was such a small thing, but it filled him with hope and happiness that she had placed his gift among her childhood treasures.

Back in the kitchen he sat at the counter, drinking coffee and eating the delicious muffins. "So what does your day hold?" he asked.

"Writing for me. I have to pop over to Gramps' for a while, but other than that I want to get as much writing time as I can in, especially since tomorrow I won't be able to."

He raised an eyebrow.

"I'm back to the city to get my car, remember?"

He did remember. Pete had refused to enlighten him about her so-called 'Mouse-mobile', insisting he would have to be patient.

"So, what do you drive?" he asked, his curiosity piqued.

She smiled. "You'll have to wait and see."

"What's the mystery?"

"No mystery, it's just that they all tease me about my love for my baby car." She paused, "And you probably will too."

He couldn't imagine what kind of car would have the others teasing her, but he could wait until tomorrow to find out.

"Do you have a busy day?" she asked.

"Yeah, I have a lot of running around to do. Arranging permits, talking to suppliers and contractors. Pete wants to hurry things up now, so I'll be greasing the wheels to get all the groundwork done as fast as possible." He looked at his watch. "In fact, I should probably get going soon," he said reluctantly.

"What time are you thinking for dinner?"

He was pleased that she seemed keen to pin him down. He'd feared he may have frightened her off, but it seemed she was doing her best to show him he hadn't.

"I was thinking I could be over here by six. Then you can keep me company while I make you dinner. It won't compare with your cooking, but I think you'll enjoy it."

"I'm sure I will. Do you want me to get anything in?"

"No, thanks. I've got it covered. And no need for a booze run, since I brought double yesterday."

"Okay, then. I shall leave myself in your capable hands."

He waggled his eyebrows suggestively and said, "I'll look forward to that," then immediately wished he hadn't. He looked at her, but she was laughing. Okay, maybe he didn't need to be too cautious. He got down from his stool and kissed her softly. "You have yourself a good day, little Mouse."

"You too." She smiled. "And, Jack, thank you. Thank you for the pebble and for being so...you know, for making this not...." She trailed off.

He planted a kiss on the top of her head. "No idea what you mean," he said with a smile, "but I'm sure glad you liked the pebble. Thanks again for breakfast. I'll see you tonight."

"Later," she said, and her smile warmed his heart.

Emma spent the morning outlining her novel. She knew many writers who simply went with the flow, started to write and went where the story took them. That wasn't her style, though. She preferred to lay out a framework, to plot out the beginning, middle and end. She couldn't begin to write chapter one until she knew how everything would pan out and where all her characters would end up by the last page.

She chewed her pen and stared out at the water. Perhaps that was her problem. In life you couldn't neatly arrange the plot lines to your liking, couldn't always know how things would turn out. You had to let the story unfold and go where it led. She thought about Jack. She couldn't know how it would go, and she shouldn't try to figure it out; life didn't come with guarantees. She'd have to go with Aunt Martha's philosophy, and indulge in what she wanted. She shivered in anticipation. And, she would just have to be prepared to pay for it. If it ended badly, she'd survive. But at least she was going in with her eyes open.

At noon she took a break and called Holly.

"Hey Em. You still coming tomorrow?"

"Yes, I am. Can you manage lunch?"

"I've kept midday clear especially."

"Excellent. And have you kept next weekend clear too?"

"I have. It'll be fun to see your Gramps again."

"He's really hoping you can make it." Holly and Gramps had met on a couple of his infrequent visits to the city and he had taken a real shine to her.

"I'm bringing him some of that whiskey."

"Oh, he'll love you even more!"

"So, how are you settling in up there?"

"So far so good."

"And Mr. Benson? Anything happening there?"

"I'll tell you tomorrow."

"Ooh, so something is happening?"

Emma laughed, "I think tomorrow I will have something to tell you."

"Oh my goodness! Well then, I hope you have a wonderful evening. Get here as soon as you can, but drive safe, okay? Pick me up at the store."

"Will do, I'll see you then."

After lunch she headed over to Gramps' house, eager to tell him that Holly really was coming to his birthday.

"She's a good girl, that one," he said as they sat on the little dock in front of his house. "Been a good friend to you."

"Yes, she has. And can you believe in all the years I've known her, she's never met Pete?"

"Is that so?"

"Yes. Even that time she came up with me, she met Missy and Ben, but Pete was away somewhere. Houston, I think." She realized as she said it that he must have been with Jack. It was strange to think that their lives had overlapped so much already without them ever knowing.

"So, you're going to make sure they meet this time, are you?"

"What do you think?"

"I think you might be on to something, Sunshine. But don't push it. Just put 'em together and see what happens, eh? If there's going to be magic, they have to find it for themselves."

"I know. You're right. As always."

"Any chance you might start believing in magic again?" He gave her a knowing look.

She smiled. "A wise man told me not so very long ago, 'Don't push it. Just put 'em together and see what happens.'"

"That so, huh?"

"Yes, Gramps. That's so."

"Okay then, Mouse. You know I won't push you."

"Thanks Gramps."

They sat a while longer, chatting about events in town and about the party. Emma told him about her novel.

"I'm glad you're wanting to write again."

"Me too, and I really should get back to it."

"Yeah, off you go. Now that you're up here, we can do this anytime. It's not like I have to wait weeks anymore 'til I can see you again. So you get back to your words, and I'll get back to my fishing pole." He walked her back to the station wagon. "Bet you'll be glad to get your own wheels back tomorrow, been a while now."

"I can't wait. It was good of Holly to let me use this old thing for so long, but I want my baby back. Oh, and it was good of you to let Jack use your old truck. It's not like you with someone you don't know, though."

"Oh, I've got his number, Sunshine. I'm just doing my bit. He's a good 'un. I say give him a chance, you might find your magic right there."

Emma stared at him. Gramps had never spoken so openly about something like that. She was surprised.

He ignored her shock and carried on as if he'd mentioned nothing more than the weather. "Now git! You've got work to do and I've got fishies waiting on me." He ambled back to the house, leaving her staring after him.

Chapter Fourteen

Jack stood at Emma's sink peeling sweet potatoes. He ran the garbage disposal until it made a horrible grinding sound and stopped.

"That doesn't sound too healthy."

"Yeah," Emma was sitting at the counter sipping a light beer. "I need to call someone to get it replaced. There are lots of things breaking down in this place."

He looked at her, wondering whether to go there, deciding he would. "Do you want me to pick one up and do it for you? It's an easy job."

"I don't know. I'm kind of thinking about updating the whole kitchen." She looked around. "The whole house really. It hasn't been touched for years."

He decided to risk it. "Pete wasn't kidding, you know. I could do all the work for you." He hoped she would at least think about it. He liked the idea of being the one to help her reshape her home.

"I don't know," she smiled. "I have to figure out what I want to do first."

"Of course." Ah well, he'd keep trying. At least he'd planted the seed. He knew this was going to take a while and, like he'd told Pete, he was in it for the long haul. He was a patient man, and it was rare that he didn't get what he set his mind to. He wasn't so sure that he really could win Emma over, past all her pain and mistrust, but he knew he was going to give it everything he had.

He finished slicing the sweet potatoes and mixed a little pot of kosher salt, paprika and cinnamon with a few other sprinkles of spice. Emma came to stand behind him and leaned against his back. She reached around and ran her hands across his stomach, then up over his chest. As she ran them back down again she slipped a finger inside the top of his jeans and his cock sprang to life hopefully. Whoa! Where had that come from?

After last night he'd decided that any physical intimacy could wait. Wait until she felt more sure of him. The rest of her fingers joined the first and brushed against the tip of him, sending a wave of desire coursing through him. He quickly turned around to face her. She leaned against him, pressing him back against the sink as she looped her hands around the back of his neck and pulled his head down, kissing him hungrily. He returned the kiss eagerly, then her hand was there again, stroking his erection through his jeans. Man, that felt good. Reluctantly he covered her hand with his own and brought it up to his chest. Undeterred, she rubbed her hips up against him, her heat more enticing even than the stroke of her hand had been. Patience. Control. He needed them both as he lifted his head from that kiss and held her at arm's length.

"Wow!" He met green eyes gazing up at him.

"You don't like?" she asked.

"Oh my God, Em. I more than like," he smiled. "I think you felt just how much I like."

She returned the smile and started to reach back to the front of his pants. He caught her hand in his and brought it to his lips. Kissing her wrist he asked, "It's, well, I thought we were going to take this more slowly. Wait until you're sure?"

"I am sure."

"But, last night...."

"Last night I was stupid. I was still a little bit scared, but I'm not now. I'm over it and I want, I want...I want you!" she finished. The desire in her eyes confirmed the truth of her words.

"You know I want you too, Em," he said quietly. He sure didn't want to rebuff her advances, but he didn't want to go faster than she was ready to. When he finally made love to her, he wanted her to be absolutely certain that it was right for her and he intended to make damn sure she would never forget it. "I want you so much." He closed his arms around her, pulling her against him so his bulging pants could prove his point. "But there's no rush, baby, whenever you're ready."

"Jack, I am ready. I want you to make love to me."

Damn! How he'd hoped to hear those words and now here she was saying them and he was the one holding back. Resisting the very real temptation to give her what she said she wanted right there in the kitchen, he lowered his head and kissed her, a demanding kiss that could leave her in no doubt. A kiss that left her clinging to him.

When he raised his head, he smiled and asked, "Will that do as a down payment while we at least have dinner? I told you I would cook for you and I am a man of my word."

She was still breathing a little fast from the passion of that kiss. "I suppose I can wait, but that down payment will be accumulating interest until you satisfy me."

Jack was a little surprised and a lot turned on by this new seductive side she was displaying, but he wanted to be sure, wanted her to be sure, that it wasn't just bravado in an attempt to please him. "Oh, don't worry. I'm more than prepared to pay in full. And you will be satisfied." He kissed her again, lightly this time. "Now, are you going to let me make this dinner?"

She laughed. "Yes, is there anything I can do to speed things along?"

He shook his head in amusement. "Patience, Miss Douglas. The best things in life are worth waiting for."

"Yes, but not for too long, Mr. Benson!"

They sat out front again to eat. "This is wonderful, Jack," said Emma as she bit into the burger he'd made for her. "You may well give me a run for best chef around here. And these sweet potato fries are incredible. You have to tell me the combination of spices you used. I know there was some salt and cinnamon, but what else?"

"You really think I'm going to tell you my secret?" he laughed. "I shall never tell and that way you'll have to come to me whenever you want them."

She laughed herself, liking the sound of that. "And this burger," she took another bite, "I think it may be the best I've ever had!"

"I aim to please. That one's easy though, it's really only about making sure you buy fresh Angus and having them grind it when you buy."

She narrowed her eyes at him. "I saw you shaking some secret ingredient in there too, mister!"

He grinned. "Don't know what you mean!"

Emma was glad now that he'd insisted they eat instead of moving straight to dessert as she had planned. She was determined that tonight was the night. She was going to sleep with him, no more running scared...but this was good. They had laughed and teased while he cooked and the food really was wonderful.

"You look gorgeous in that dress, the green matches your eyes."

She smiled, pleased by the compliment. She wasn't about to tell him why she'd chosen the cream-colored halter neck dress with the little green swirls. The back was open and the top tied around her neck—no bra! She wasn't going to repeat last night's mistake and freak herself out over something so silly as a bra strap. By wearing this dress she'd sidestepped that issue completely. The full skirt flowed as she moved and felt very feminine, so much so that when she'd put it on earlier she'd felt emboldened and removed her panties too. No bra, no panties; she'd never done that before. She'd been acutely aware of it all evening, the fabric against her bare skin, the fresh air between her legs. The sensations were adding to her arousal and to her determination that this evening would end with Jack in her bed.

No rush though, like he'd said. She'd enjoyed every moment of his company. She was surprised by how powerful she felt, knowing how much he wanted her, and she loved that he was restraining himself, making sure it was right for her, that she really was ready. That in itself told her how very wrong she'd been in her first impression of him.

"How about dessert?"

She looked at him with a coy smile. "Are you ready for me then?" She felt the tingling heat spread through her at the hungry look that crossed his face.

"I was thinking of the food variety...for now."

"Okay then, spoilsport. What are we having?"

"Well, I don't bake, but I do have something I think you'll like. He returned a few minutes later with two large dishes. Sliced bananas and dainty little scoops of vanilla ice cream were drizzled over with warm caramel sauce.

"Oh my. You can cook again."

"I am truly honored."

"You have no idea," she laughed.

After dinner they walked along the beach, searching for pretty pebbles, showing each other their finds. Jack looked so relaxed and at ease, she reached up and kissed him. "Thank you for making me dinner."

"Thank you for letting me," he smiled. He ran his fingers across her bare back, making her shiver. "Are you cold?"

It was heat not cold that ran through her. She really didn't want to wait any longer so she nodded and took him by the hand, leading him back up the path to the house. Instead of heading back to the kitchen, she held his hand tightly and led him straight up the stairs. At the top he stopped her, so she held him close and kissed him.

"No more excuses, Mr. Benson." She put her arms around him and slipped her hands in his back pockets to pull him against her. He took out his keys and cell phone, placing them on the little table that stood on the landing. "That's better," she returned her hands, stroking his butt.

He returned the favor, cupping her cheeks in his hands, pulling her close as she rubbed up against him. He claimed her mouth with his in one of those deep kisses that left her senseless. When she came up for air she started leading him into her bedroom.

Jack stopped. Part of him still didn't want to rush this, although that part was losing fast. "We can wait, Em," he said, the pounding of his heart and the straining in his jeans rebelling against his words. That part of him sure didn't want to wait.

"Jack, I've waited long enough. I want you. Now."

The way she emphasized that last word melted any hesitation he had left, until he remembered. Dammit! "I want you too, Em, but we can't."

She looked at him, ready to do some more convincing.

"I don't have any protection."

She looked confused for a moment, then realization dawned on her face. "You mean condoms?"

"I mean condoms," he repeated. How could it be such a turn on to hear that word on her lips?

She met his eyes. "I'm on the pill."

That surprised him. It must have shown because she explained, "I had bad periods as a teenager and I've been on it ever since to help with that."

That made sense.

She hesitated, then added, "I was checked for nasty diseases after Rob and there's no way I've acquired any since then."

Jack's mind raced. Was she really saying that she hadn't slept with a man since her marriage ended? And that they

didn't need protection? In all his life he'd never had sex
without a condom. He preferred to control his own destiny.
He'd never wanted to risk having a woman come to him and
tell him she was pregnant with his child. He didn't fear that
with Emma.

"Well," he said slowly, "I just had my annual physical and
I'm all clear, so...."

"So that settles it then!" She pulled him into the bedroom
and pushed him back against the door. Good God. She was
driving him crazy. She pressed the full length of her soft sweet
body up against him. Sandwiched between her and the door he
swept her hair away from her neck and placed slow open-
mouthed kisses on her collarbone. He was rewarded as a
tremor rippled through her. Encouraged, he laid a trail of hot
kisses up her neck to her ear.

"Easy, tiger," he murmured as her fingers tugged at his
shirt. She unbuttoned it and flicked his nipple with her tongue.
He ran his hands down her back and cupped her rounded ass,
pulling her against him, kneading her cheeks. Reluctantly he let
go to help her get rid of his shirt, which she was trying to push
off his shoulders. Once the shirt was on the floor he brought
both arms back around her and held her close to his bare
chest.

"Are you sure, Emma?" he murmured, hating himself for
asking, but having to anyway.

The desire in her eyes gave him all the answer he needed.
In case it hadn't, her hands were now working on his belt
buckle and freeing him from his jeans. In a moment he stood
before her in just his boxers, and he took great pleasure in the
way her eyes widened at the size of his desire. He held her
close against him, running his tongue along her bottom lip

then thrusting inside her mouth, exploring as she surrendered to him. As he kissed her, he circled her nipples with his thumbs, her little moans reassuring him that she was still with him, that this wasn't what had frightened her last night.

He couldn't resist any longer and, aware that something about this had shut her down before, he said, "One of us is wearing way too many clothes."

She giggled. "Well, perhaps you'd better get rid of them then."

Avoiding her top to start with, he reached down and stroked up her legs, loving the feel of her breasts pushing up against him, her whole body trembling under his touch. He brought his hands up the outsides of her thighs to her hips— no panties. Oh man. He stroked his hand across her stomach then let his fingers slowly walk down into the damp curls that covered her. She bit into his shoulder and let out a low moan as he stroked her.

"Please, Jack," she whispered.

He took the hem of her skirt and lifted the whole dress up and over her head. She seemed to flinch for a moment, but then stood still, beautifully naked before him. He recalled the night she'd stood like this in the cabin, only then she hadn't known he was there. Now, not only did she know, but she was begging him to make love to her. He lowered his head and took her nipple in his mouth, circling it with his tongue. That brought her hands into his hair and she cradled his head, as if to make sure he wouldn't stop. He did stop, but only long enough to transfer his attention to her other breast. His hand returned to her inner thigh, working its way up in soft strokes until again he found her heat. She was so wet for him.

"Please, Jack," she murmured again.

At that he hooked his arm behind her knees and lifted her. She wrapped her arms around his neck as he carried her to the bed. He gently laid her down and moved out of reach as she touched the front of his boxers.

"Patience," he murmured. Taking each of her hands in his, he raised them up above her head and held them there. "Trust me?" he asked.

She nodded as he kissed her neck and returned to her breasts. He let go of her hands and she left them on the pillow above her head as he kissed his way down to her navel. She gave a little yelp as his tongue explored there. He reached up and placed her hands back over her head before continuing on his southward journey. He held her hips as he trailed his tongue down over her stomach. She tensed and her hands came down again as he kissed her inner thigh.

"Relax, baby," he soothed, but feeling her tension mount, he came back up to kiss her lips. As he felt her surrender to the kiss and relax he asked, "Is this okay?"

She nodded, "You don't have to do that though, if you don't want to."

"You don't like it?"

Her cheeks flushed. "I don't know…I don't know what to do."

He couldn't believe it. "You mean, you've never…?"

She shook her head, looking a little ashamed.

"What, baby?"

With great effort, she said, "Rob didn't like it."

The selfish bastard! thought Jack. He'd never hated someone he'd never met before, but he was starting to hate this Rob character. Man, if he ever met him. He calmed himself; time to think of that later. For now he had much more important business to attend to. He kissed her again until she was panting and writhing beneath him.

"Baby, will you relax and trust me? I do like this," he gave her that hungry look, "more than like this, but more importantly, I think you're going to like this. I want tonight to be all about you, making sure you enjoy it, okay?"

She nodded up at him and he felt his heart clench as for the first time he saw trust as well as desire in her eyes. She raised her arms above her own head this time and closed her eyes, offering herself up to him. With his hands and tongue he worked hard to deserve that trust as he made his way back down her body. She was trembling all over as he used his broad shoulders to spread her legs wider.

"You okay?"

"Mm, wonderful," she sighed, then gave a little yelp as he stroked her bud with his tongue. He breathed in deeply; the musky scent of her was driving him crazy, but this was all about her. His own lust could wait, much as his aching cock disagreed with him. He stroked the inside of her thighs then used both hands to hold her open. She moaned and writhed as he blew into her heat then stroked her with his tongue. Her hips left the bed and rose to meet him and he buried his face in her, working magic with his tongue and lips. When he lifted his head her hips fell back down to the bed.

"You like?"

"Oh, my goodness, Jack. I more than like."

He lowered his head again and this time as he did, he reached up and caressed her nipple, gently circling and squeezing. Her hips raised back up to him as he sucked and teased her bud. As she began to move her hips in time with the strokes of his tongue, he rested two fingers at her entrance.

He felt her tense in anticipation. She matched his rhythm and as he felt her getting closer he slipped his fingers deep inside. She was so wet and tight. At the second stroke of his fingers he felt her velvety wetness close around them and she moaned as her orgasm took her. He worked her with his tongue and fingers as she came for him, carrying her through wave after wave.

When she eventually lay still, he came back up to lay beside her, tracing little circles over her chest and stomach. She opened her eyes and he smiled down at her. The sexy, satisfied smile on her face made his heart and his cock throb.

"I more than like." She pulled him down for another lingering kiss and then pushed him on his back. "Now who's wearing too many clothes?" She slipped her hand inside his boxers and as she closed her fingers around him Jack felt himself grow harder still, though he'd thought that was impossible. She pushed his shorts down and he kicked them off. Still holding him in her hand, she peppered his chest with little kisses and started to work her way down his abs. "Your turn."

For a moment he gave in to the pent up desire of the last few weeks. Her mouth burned a trail down his body as she stroked him with both hands. Before he realized she was there, she ran her tongue over the tip of him. No, no, no! He couldn't go there. Not yet, he wouldn't last a minute. He drew her back up to kiss his lips and turned her so she was on her back once more, looking up at him as he held his weight above her.

"You don't like?"

"I'm afraid I might like a little too much."

A troubled look crossed her face. "I do know how to do that."

Jack gritted his teeth as hatred for Rob bubbled up once more. She didn't know how to let a man go down on her, but she knew how to return the favor? What kind of asshole was this guy she'd been married to? He kept his voice steady as he said, "I'm sure you do and there will be plenty of time for that, but tonight isn't about taking turns."

"No?"

"No," he smiled again now. "If you remember, I told you that if I got you into bed, I would prove to you that I am not terrible."

She returned his smile. "So you did."

"And how am I doing so far?"

"Oh, not terrible. Not terrible at all."

"Well, if that's the best you can say, I still have much work left to do here." He caressed her nipple with his thumb and loved the dazed look that came over her face as her breath quickened and her eyes darkened. He buried his face in her neck, then nibbled her ear, the whole time teasing her nipple. She writhed underneath him, torturing his erection as it throbbed to be inside her.

"Jack?"

"Yes, baby?"

"Make love to me, Jack." He held his breath as she spread her legs wider. "Please, make love to me." Still he hesitated. She opened her eyes and looked deep into his. "I'll beg if you want me to. Please?"

Damn!

She pulled his head down to her and he leaned in for another kiss, but instead she brought her lips close to his ear and whispered—two little words that sent him over the edge: "Fuck me." He hadn't expected to hear that dirty word from her sweet lips, but it had the effect she'd hoped for.

Despite the heat coursing through his veins, he steadied himself. He wanted this to be slow and gentle, to make sure she would never forget and always want more—of him. He positioned himself between her legs, which were spread wide, waiting to receive him. He couldn't believe he was about to be inside her with nothing between them, no rubber to mute the sensations.

This time, she questioned him, "Are you okay?"

"Oh yeah, baby."

"What is it?"

"It's nothing, just realizing we're going to do this with no condom."

"Is that unusual?"

"You're my first."

The look on her face told him how much that pleased her. As he looked down at her beautiful face, eyes shining, the flush spread across her cheeks and chest. He had never wanted a woman as badly as he wanted her. He had to make this special for her. His little head was impatient, aching to be allowed to penetrate her wetness after weeks of waiting. He was wary though; she hadn't done this for years and he knew he was a lot to take in. If he was honest, he was hesitant because he was shocked how special this felt to him too, and it was more than going without a condom for the first time.

Using every ounce of willpower he possessed he nudged gently at her entrance, watching her face closely. To his surprise she thrust her hips up to him and he entered her. He clenched his jaw and sweat rolled down his back. The feel of her, the raw sensations as he pulsated just inside her threatened to take him over the edge with the need to thrust deep and hard, but he held out.

"You okay?"

She nodded rapidly and her hands came up around his ass, urging him in. He slid a few inches deeper and watched her face flush. She wrapped her legs around his, resting her feet on his calves, opening herself wider to him. He thrust a little deeper and she moaned.

"All of you, Jack. I want all of you."

He was throbbing inside her, tormented by the self-imposed restraint. Her eyes flew open as he slid a little deeper still.

"Almost there, baby."

She nodded and lifted her hips to receive him. Unable to resist a moment longer he drove all the way home, and man, it felt like coming home. The sensation of her hot wetness, gripping him tight even as she yielded to him. He was determined to set up a slow, gentle rhythm, but she bucked underneath him and within moments he felt the waves of another orgasm take her. He bit his lip as she tightened around him, pulsing over and over.

Eventually she lay still and opened her eyes. "Oh my, Jack!"

Sex looked so good on her.

Then her eyes clouded. "I didn't wait for you. I couldn't. I'm so sorry."

He silenced her with a kiss. "We're not done here yet, Miss Douglas." Holding her gaze he thrust his whole length inside her, drawing a wide-eyed gasp. This time he set up a deep, slow thrusting rhythm. Her arms came up around his back, almost making him lose his steely control. He heard her breathing change and, knowing she was getting close, he stepped up his rhythm, claiming her as his own with every thrust. Just when he knew he must explode at any moment, she drew her legs up high and wrapped them around his back. With a low keening moan another orgasm took her, and this time he let himself go, coming harder than he ever had, a whole body sensation from his scalp to his toes as he pushed deep into her very core.

For a long time he lay, breathing hard on top of her, unable to move, even if she didn't have her arms and legs still clasped tightly around him. She mewled as an aftershock rippled through them both. He buried his face in her hair. "Oh, Emma."

Eventually he rolled to his side and drew her into his arms.

She smiled, a very sexy, very satisfied smile. "What have you done to me, Mr. Benson? I had no idea it was supposed to be like that!" Her wide eyes gave away the fact that she wasn't really joking.

"For once, I don't know what to say, Miss Douglas. You see, I had no idea that it was supposed to be like that either!" He grinned. "But now that I do know this is how it's supposed to be, I think we should keep doing it."

"Oh, most definitely. All the time, whenever we can!"

His heart leaped. "Really?"

"Yes, really. I think I could get addicted to this."

She snuggled closer to him and he held her tight. If he'd thought he was doomed before, he knew now that he'd lost all hope. He'd never known sex this good. She was unbelievable. So innocent and yet insatiable. He realized she was drifting off to sleep and placed a kiss on her lips.

She smiled at him through sleepy eyes. "Stay with me tonight?"

"Try stopping me."

"I have to leave at eight."

"I know."

"But, maybe, before I go, we could...." She trailed her hand down his abs. "I'll make you a proper breakfast, not just muffins."

He laughed. "You'll have to keep my strength up if you intend to keep doing this to me."

"Oh, I will and I do." She turned over and pressed her bottom against him. "Goodnight, Jack."

"Goodnight, baby." As he spooned her he held her close, happier than he'd ever been as he held everything he wanted right there in his arms.

Chapter Fifteen

Emma came to slowly. A smile touched her lips as she remembered the night before. As she moved she realized she might be sore in some interesting places today, but oh, had it been worth it! She tingled all over as she remembered the feel of his hands, and his mouth, caressing her, touching her in ways she'd never known. She reached out, hoping to start this day with some more of him, of the way he made her feel. Her hand touched cold sheets. She opened her eyes and stared at the empty pillow beside her. Feeling disappointed, she got up. She visited the bathroom and brushed her teeth. Looking in the mirror she noticed a little patch of razor burn on her chest. She touched it gently, loving the thought that he had marked her as his own. She put on her robe.

Now, don't get carried away. It's that kind of thinking that gets you in trouble. You are not his own and he is not yours. He is just an incredibly sexy man, who you spent a wonderful night with, and hopefully will spend many more with this summer. She smiled again at the sweet memories of the night.

She went downstairs and was disappointed not to smell coffee brewing. She'd thought he must be doing the same as he had in the cabin, but he wasn't in the kitchen at all. She peeked outside, thinking he may be on the deck. No, no sign of him there. She went out and looked down the beach; perhaps he was walking down there. She didn't see him. Looking up the driveway she noticed that Gramps' truck was gone. Well! She went back inside, her heart racing. He hadn't stuck around for the morning after even when he was practically living on her driveway?! She took a deep breath. Calm down, there will be a perfectly reasonable explanation.

She busied herself making coffee, though her hands trembled as she did. It was only six thirty, there was plenty of time before she had to leave. She would shower and get ready, and by the time she'd made breakfast he'd back from wherever he'd gone. It would be fine. She strained to listen for the truck as she showered and dressed. She checked herself in the mirror, satisfied with the blouse and pencil skirt that were more suitable for her city lunch than the cutoff jeans she preferred to wear up here. She wondered if her appearance gave away the fact that she'd spent the night making passionate love to a gorgeous man. Her eyes shone, maybe her complexion glowed a little, but she wasn't wearing a sign that said 'Screwed Last Night' - or 'Dumped This Morning'.

"Make breakfast," she said out loud. "Act like everything is okay and it will be okay."

She scrambled eggs, fried bacon and sausage, even popped some biscuits in the oven that she had in the freezer from the weekend. When everything was ready she served up two plates and covered them over. Where was he? No note. No call. She checked her cell again, made sure the volume was on and that she had a full signal. Nope, no call. Oh, Jack. Please don't do this to me. She took her coffee and sat outside.

Quarter till eight. She'd have to leave soon. She wondered whether to call him. No, if he didn't want to stick around for the morning after, he wouldn't want her hounding him, and if it were anything else he would call her, wouldn't he? She got the message. At five till eight she emptied both breakfast plates into the garbage. There was no way she could have eaten hers. She gathered up her purse and closed the house.

"Oh well. You were an idiot once more, Emma Douglas."

She got into the station wagon and started it up. She didn't want to believe that this was how it was. After last night, after everything he'd said, was it really only a one night stand to him? Suddenly convinced that she was simply getting carried away by her fears again, she fished her cell phone from her purse and dialed his number. Her heart beat fast as she hoped against hope that she would hear his deep laugh and some logical explanation. It rang and rang then, "You've reached Jack Benson...." She hung up. "So that's how it is then, Jack?" She put the station wagon in gear and headed out for the city.

Inside the house, on the little table at the top of the stairs, Jack's cell phone flashed, 'Missed Call'.

Emma turned the station wagon onto the unpaved county road and headed up to Route 20. At least living up here on the North end of the lake she could use this shortcut and be on the freeway fifteen minutes sooner than if she had to go down through town. Though she would never go this way in her own car. She'd been so excited for Jack to see her car. Now she didn't know if she was more hurt or angry. She'd been such a fool, falling for all his sweet talk, believing that, perhaps, he really might care about her. Giving herself to him so willingly once he'd talked his way past her reservations.

"Damn you, Jack! And you can forget the friendship," she fumed to herself as she sped towards LA.

She'd been on the road for almost an hour, alternating between anger at herself and anger at Jack when her phone rang and her heart leaped. She didn't normally touch a phone when she was driving, her own car had a hands free system, but Holly's old station wagon didn't. She picked it up, hoping it would be him, but instead she saw Pete's name on the display. She dropped it back on the seat.

"Not talking to you," she said. "You vouched for him."

~ ~ ~

Jack cursed as he ran. "Dammit!" he shouted as yet another stone caught in his flip-flop. He stopped, hopping around in the middle of the road holding his foot. Please, God! Would someone drive by and give him a ride? It was seven thirty already! This had seemed like such a neat idea this morning. How had it gotten so badly screwed up? He'd woken early and lain watching Emma sleep, her hair spread over the pillow around her. So beautiful. She'd surprised him last night with her passion, her lack of inhibition once she'd surrendered to him. He'd lain there beside her as the dawn broke, daring to believe that she might come to love him. He already knew he loved her. The trust he'd seen in her eyes had told him he was on the way to convincing her that he was for real. That he wasn't like that...that.... He clenched his fists and started jogging again. He'd used up his whole repertoire of expletives thinking about the man she'd been married to, the man who had broken her heart. Watching her in the gray light of the predawn, he couldn't understand how any man could ever hurt her, let alone treat her like that idiot had. He truly hoped for both their sakes that his path never crossed with Rob's.

He'd wanted so badly to hold her as she slept. She brought out all his protective instincts. He'd wanted to take her in his arms and never let her go. Of course he'd wanted to make love to her again too, but he knew she had a long day ahead. LA and back would be at least eight hours on the road. He'd been surprised, but pleased, that she wasn't staying the night there. Instead, he'd gotten up, gone and sat on the deck as the sky lightened into a new day. Then he'd had what at the time seemed like a great idea and yet now seemed like the dumbest move he had ever made.

He'd decided to take the truck down to the resort to buy her doughnuts. He could be back and have her coffee made before she awoke – or so he'd thought. He hadn't added the truck key to his key ring with the others yet. It was right there in his hip pocket, so he'd jumped straight in the truck, hoping not to disturb her by going back indoors, and headed off to buy doughnuts. She'd said she'd make him breakfast, but he wanted to give her a nice surprise and maybe a snack for her drive. He wanted her to know that he paid attention to what she liked and would go out of his way to get it for her. Ben had said they made doughnuts fresh at five every morning, it seemed perfect.

He'd made it into the resort and bought them no problem. It was on the way back, on the road up the western shore, that a deer had run out in front of him. He'd swerved to avoid it and succeeded but, in doing so, his front tire had gone off the pavement, hit a rock, and blown out. He hadn't even been too worried about that. He'd checked the truck over the first night Gramps gave it to him. There was a decent spare and a jack, he could have it changed in no time and be back, hopefully still before she awoke, but at least with plenty of time before she had to leave.

He'd hauled the spare out and jacked up the truck. The lug nuts were tight but he'd got them off no problem, all six of them. It was when he'd gone to mount the spare that he'd known he was really in trouble, it had eight holes, not six! It was probably for one of the big old Fords behind Gramps' workshop, but it certainly wasn't going to fit on this truck. Great! He'd reached into his back pocket for his phone to call Emma and ask her to come rescue him—not the early morning surprise he'd hoped to give her. But, of course, his phone wasn't in his pocket. He remembered removing it to give her better access to his butt last night. It was still sitting on the little table on the landing along with the rest of his keys.

"Son of a…." He'd thrown the spare back in the truck and locked it up. He reckoned he was still about eight miles from the house. Checking his watch he realized that even at the height of his running days, he wouldn't have made it before eight, especially in flip-flops. He'd set out anyway, hoping that maybe he'd get lucky and someone would happen along and give him a ride. Of course, that hadn't happened and now here he was, jogging along an empty road with a bruised foot while Emma would be speeding off to LA, no doubt believing that he was all she'd feared him to be. That he'd had his wicked way with her and then slunk off into the night.

He jogged on, despite the pain in his foot. He actually believed it was the least he deserved for being such an idiot. Sweaty, his head banging and his heart sinking, he came in sight of the house. For the last mile or so he'd allowed himself to hope that just maybe she would still be there, that she'd decided to wait for his return. After all, wouldn't she have passed him if she'd left? As he came down the driveway, though, the worst of his fears were confirmed. The station wagon was gone, damn. At least he'd left the RV unlocked. He thought of his keys, sitting with his phone on that little table. Maybe she'd left them out for him. He checked on the deck. Nothing. He tried the front door. Locked.

He returned to the RV. He couldn't call her, since the only place he had her number was in his phone. All he could do was call Pete and ask for it. He really did not want to explain why he needed it. He ran his fingers through his hair in agitation as he fired up his computer and waited for it to boot.

"Come on, come on." Thank God he had an internet phone account. He clicked on Pete's cell number and drummed his fingers impatiently as it dialed and then rang.

I need to get her number. I don't need to explain anything at all, he thought.

Pete's voice mail clicked in.

"You've reached Pete Hemming...." Jack clicked the End Call icon, he didn't want to leave a message! Damn you, Pete. Pick up! He clicked on Pete's office phone.

"Good Morning, Mr. Hemming's office, this is Judy sp...."

Jack didn't wait for her to finish, "Judy, is he there?"

"Oh. Good morning, Jack. Yes, but I'm afraid he's in with Mr. Bowers."

"Damn!"

"Is everything all right, Jack?" Judy sounded shocked; he obviously wasn't controlling his frustration too well. "He said no calls, but do you want me to buzz you through?"

He sighed. "Sorry, Judy. No, don't interrupt him, it's okay. What time are you expecting him finished?"

"He said to bring coffee in at ten."

"Great." Jack groaned. Emma would be halfway to LA by then, all the while thinking he'd run out on her. Still, he couldn't go interrupting Pete with Bowers; he'd been working on that deal for months.

"Jack, can I do anything to help?" He was obviously blowing his reputation of being unflappable here.

He hesitated for a moment. Would Judy have the number? Probably not, and he was in no mood to explain himself. He sighed again, regaining his composure.

"Sorry Judy, it's fine, thank you though. Nothing I can't handle." How he hoped that would prove to be true. "Is everything okay there?" He tried to sound more normal.

"Everything's fine."

"Good, well, thanks then, bye." He hung up a little too quickly as it dawned on him that he could look up Missy's cleaning business and call her instead. If he had to explain to anyone about why he needed Emma's number, he figured Missy would be the lesser of all evils.

Back in LA, Judy sat staring at her phone, hoping Jack was really all right. That had been so out of character for him that she had to wonder what was wrong. In all the years she'd worked at Phoenix she'd never known him to get ruffled. He handled everything in a cool, calm, confident manner that she admired greatly, and that she knew caused many hearts to flutter around the building. He hadn't even asked for Pete to call him back. Maybe she'd give Pete a note when she took in the coffee.

~ ~ ~

Jack searched online and found the listing for Missy's cleaning company. He typed the number in and waited, hoping this wasn't a mistake. Emma was no doubt already thinking the worst of him; he didn't want her thinking that he was going around telling people her business too.

"Welcome to Sunshine Cleaning Service," Missy's voice rang out, "Sorry we can't take your call right now…"

Jack clicked to disconnect and sat down heavily. Another answering machine that he didn't want to talk to. Could this day get any worse? As if to answer that question he heard a car approaching and looked out to see Gramps' old Ford pulling in. Oh man. If there was anyone he didn't want to explain the situation to, it was Gramps! How to explain why he needed Emma's number? And oh, by the way, if he could just collect his keys and phone from outside her bedroom door, that would be great too! He shook his head and headed out to meet the old man. He had no idea how to handle this one, but he was going to meet it head on. He was used to dealing with anything and everything that life and business threw at him. He prided himself on stepping in and making things look easy, however, when it came to Emma, he felt he kept messing everything up, bumbling around like a love-struck kid.

"How's it going, son?" Gramps greeted him with a friendly smile.

Jack grimaced. "Let's just say today isn't off to the best start."

"I reckoned as much. And I'm thinking that might be my fault. I went down for doughnuts this morning," he gave Jack a long, measuring look. Jack simply nodded. "They said they'd seen you bright and early. Then I saw the truck out on the West Shore. I stopped for a look and saw that spare. I'm sorry, I must've mixed up my spares when I checked 'em all over."

"That's all right. I should have spotted it myself."

"And she was gone before you could get back?" Gramps jerked his head up at the house.

Jack nodded miserably. "And I didn't have my phone, so I couldn't call her."

"Well call her now, son. I'll get out your hair." He turned to go.

"I still don't have my phone, sir. Could you give me her number?"

Gramps gave him another long look that he couldn't decipher. He met the old man's eyes without flinching, even though he felt like a kid about to be reprimanded.

"Tell you what," said Gramps, "how about, I give you the number, then I'll go up to the house and fix us some coffee while you make your call?" He took a pen and paper from his truck and wrote down Emma's number. "Good luck, son." His eyes twinkled as he handed Jack the paper. "Come on up when you're done."

Jack dashed back in to his computer and tapped in her number, memorizing it as he did. Never again would he be unable to call her.

"Please pick up, please pick up," he murmured as it started to ring.

"This is Emma Douglas. Leave me a message."

Damn! "Emma, it's Jack. Please call me back. I can explain. It's not what you think. I'm so sorry, baby. Please call me back at this number."

He disconnected. What were the chances she would call? Slim to none, he thought ruefully. He'd let her down. He'd wait until Gramps had gone and then try again. He grabbed his tablet and logged into his phone on there so if, by some miracle, she did call back, at least he wouldn't miss it. Tablet tucked under his arm he headed up to the house.

Gramps had two mugs ready when he came in.

"No joy?"

Jack shook his head grimly. "I messed up, Gramps," he admitted.

The old man patted his shoulder. "She'll come around, son. You'll see. You'll need patience though, and you'll need to understand why we call her Mouse."

Jack looked at him questioningly.

"You think of a little Mouse. It comes out of his hole and takes a look around, checks if it's safe to come out. Well, that's her. She'll come out a little way, get some confidence and you see the real Em, then she'll run back in at the first thing that spooks her. It was your friend Pete that came up with it when she first came here, when they were little kids. She was scared of everything and everyone, but he figured her out, always was a good boy that one. Between him and the other two, they got her through that time and pretty much everything since. So you see, when she spooks, she runs off or shuts down. May take a while before she comes back out of her mouse hole, but when she does, it's worth the wait and the frustration. She's so damn cute, just like when she first came to us, tiny little thing with blond curls and big scared eyes. Always wary though, even now, even when she's relaxed or being the city-girl writer. She'll run for cover in a heartbeat, as I think you're finding out."

Jack smiled, understanding only too well. That was exactly how she'd been with him. Coming out of her hole a little way, skittering away from him, then slowly getting bolder and coming closer. Until now. Until she'd woken up alone this morning—not that he would say that to Gramps.

"So what do I do?"

"You wait, son. You let her know you're still out there and that you are there for her, but only if that's what you want. It'll be a long road, make no mistake, so you should quit now if you haven't got the heart or the patience for it. I'd understand that."

"I'm a patient man, Gramps. My heart is in this for keeps. I'll wait as long as it takes, do whatever it takes." His voice was strong with conviction.

Gramps smiled. "I kind of figured as much, just wanted to hear it from you. Now let's go sort out that spare, shall we?"

When they got to the truck, Gramps got inside and took some papers from the glove box. "Might be needing these," he said, as he climbed down. Jack changed the tire with no problems. As he finished up Gramps apologized again for having left the wrong spare.

Jack felt bad. "Honestly, sir. It's no problem. I'd messed up anyway. The tire was the least of it."

"Don't worry, son. It'll work out. Now I'm going to get along, but you give me a shout whenever you need me. I might understand better than you think."

"Thanks. I really appreciate that."

He watched Gramps drive away, deciding he'd drive back to the house before he tried Emma again. He got back in the truck and started it up. On the passenger seat sat the doughnuts that had led to all this. And next to them, he couldn't believe his eyes! Next to the doughnuts sat his keys and his cell phone. Apparently Gramps did understand better than he'd thought. He smiled to himself, thrilled to have such a wonderful ally, then his face fell again as he remembered how much he was going to need one.

Chapter Sixteen

Emma pulled in at a drive through for coffee. She fished out her phone and ignored all the missed calls and messages, just wanting to call Holly.

"Hi, sweetie. What time will you be here?"

"Look out for me at twelve fifteen or so. I'll pick you up at the store."

"Em. What's wrong? You sound terrible!"

"Thanks," said Emma glumly. "I'm fine."

"You don't sound it. Did last night not go well?"

Emma stifled a sob. "I don't want to talk about it."

"Oh, sweetie. Get here as quick as you can, okay?"

"Okay." Emma hung up and looked at the phone. All the voice mails and missed calls were from Jack and Pete. How could he have told Pete? She had decided on the road that the best way to deal with it was not to deal with it at all. She wasn't going to listen to their messages. She was just going to go and have lunch with Holly.

She double parked outside Holly's boutique at twelve twenty and honked the horn. Her friend came running out, straight to the driver's door.

"Scoot over, you sounded like a wreck!"

Emma slid over to the passenger seat, grateful not to have to face the downtown traffic.

"Want to come home with me for lunch?" asked Holly.

She nodded, she wasn't in the mood for any of their usual places. They drove in silence for a while.

"Want to tell me about it?" asked Holly eventually.

"Not really." She knew Holly wouldn't push her, she also knew that she needed to talk about it, despite the desire to push it all away. She could feel the tears building. "I had actually started to trust him!" she blurted out, swiping at a tear that rolled down her cheek.

"Want to start from the beginning?"

She nodded and started to tell Holly everything that had happened with Jack over the last few days. They arrived at Holly's townhouse and went inside. Once they were settled she continued. "Last night, he was so unbelievable. He made it all about me. He made me feel so special. He kept reassuring me, making sure it was good for me," she paused and smiled. "Holly, he made it so good for me, I had no idea it could be like that. I know I'm not exactly an expert at this...."

Holly smiled. "Understatement of the year," she teased.

Emma nodded, "I know. But even I know that he must have had massive willpower to do everything he did for me and not make any of it about, well...." She didn't know how to put it. "You know, about satisfying himself."

Holly sat staring at her. "Help me out here, sweetie? I think I'm missing something. From what you've said, he is a very good-looking, charming, funny man, who has pursued you relentlessly since he met you. He has asked, no begged, you to give him the chance to prove that he's for real. He was gentle and understanding when you led him on and then stopped him in the height of passion and then last night he made sweet love to you for hours and dedicated himself to your pleasure. So, I have two questions."

Emma nodded.

"First, what the hell happened between last night and this morning to turn you into a miserable wreck, when you should be the happiest woman on Earth? And second...." She smiled. "If you really don't want him, please can I have him? I didn't think men like that existed outside the movies!"

Emma managed a laugh at that. "Oh, Holly. Maybe he was too good to be true. When I went to sleep last night with his arms around me I thought I was the happiest woman on Earth. But then I woke up this morning and he was gone!"

Holly frowned, "Gone?"

"Gone. Disappeared. No note. No call. No nothing! I tried really hard to think that he would be back. He knew I had to leave at eight. He didn't show."

"And you didn't call him?"

"I did! Just before I left the house. I thought maybe I was doing what you all tell me I do, getting carried away with my fears, not giving him a chance. Holly, I so wanted him to be for real, so I called him. But he just let it go to voice mail. Didn't even pick up."

"Oh," Holly looked perplexed. "And you haven't heard from him?"

Emma hung her head.

"Well?"

"He left me a message, but not until I was halfway here and Pete left me a message first, so I bet he's told him and that's just too awful."

"Well what did they say?" asked Holly, exasperated.

"I don't know."

"You haven't listened to them?"

"It's too much, Holly. I can't deal with it!"

"Oh, sweetie. You don't know what you're dealing with until you find out what he has to say. You at least owe him that. C'mon, why would he have called you at all if he's the monster you think he is?"

"I don't know, maybe Pete made him."

Holly shook her head, "Em, do you realize how childish you sound? I think it's time for some tough love, sweetie."

"What do you mean?"

"I mean I need to tell it to you like it is and hope you love me enough to know I'm saying this for your own good. I've felt I should do this for a long time, but I've always been afraid to hurt you, maybe hurt our friendship, but you're too important to me. I can't watch you do this again."

"Do what?"

"Be so childish, Em. I'm sorry, honey, but you need to grow up."

Emma looked at her with tears in her eyes, but Holly pressed on.

"I know you've got it together in the rest of your life. You're strong, smart, independent, but when it comes to men, you act like you're still a little girl. You pretend you don't know what you want, but deep down I think you do. You want what most women do. You want a man who will love you, honor you and protect you. Those words are in the vows for a reason, you know. You want to give yourself and your big, big heart to a man who really will forsake all others to spend the rest of his life with you, and only you. But you're too scared to even try it. I know why. It's because you, more than most, already know the pain of losing love. You found out way too young. When you lost your parents you experienced the pain of loss that most of us don't have to go through until we're much better equipped to deal with it. That set you back, but you're strong, and you were prepared to try it again because you believed in love. Rob shattered that belief. He made you think that the kind of love you want doesn't really exist. That it's just a little fantasy of yours, but it's not, Em. It's what most of us search for and a few lucky ones get to have. You bought his lies. You blame yourself, but you were young and he was a master manipulator. He used your fears against you so that you would blame yourself and not him.

But honey, if you stay the way you are, you're letting Rob steal from you. You're letting him steal one of life's greatest gifts, the gift of love. It's yours for the taking, maybe with Jack, maybe with someone else down the line. But finding love involves risk and if you're too scared to take the risks, you'll never find the reward. You have so much love to give and share. I have a good feeling about this Jack. I think he may have a whole lot of love to give you. But it's down to you. It would take courage to risk the hurt—and I know you were being brave to get as far as you did with him. But if you run scared now, if you blame him and decide he's just like Rob without ever giving him chance, then all you're doing is taking the easy way out, the coward's way out. I believe you're stronger than that, but you'll have to grow up, and fast."

Emma stared at her for a long time, tears rolling down her face, but she said nothing.

"You want to chew on that while I fix us some lunch?"

Emma nodded.

Chapter Seventeen

Jack arrived at the supplier's yard. He'd left Emma three messages; he wasn't going to leave any more. He'd ignored Pete's call earlier, not wanting to get into explaining anything. He sighed. He had to get on with his day and this meeting. He sat in the truck a moment, trying to put things back in perspective. He might have acted a little crazy this morning, but he had to get a grip. He was dating a woman—yes, he was dating her, he was not going to let this mess things up—a woman who had some baggage to deal with and who was afraid of getting hurt. He remembered Gramps' description of her as a mouse. She'd run back in to the safety of her mouse hole. He figured he'd have to get used to this. She'd come back out and he'd be there, waiting to move forward. He smiled to himself. He really was patient and he'd never failed at anything he'd set his mind to. Now he'd set his mind—and his heart—on winning Emma for his own. The stakes were higher than any he'd ever known; the rest of his life was on the line and he didn't intend to fail.

With that thought he gathered his usual confidence and headed in to the office to meet with Bill Meyers, the supplier he knew was keen to offer him a good deal. Word had gotten out that the Phoenix Corporation might be starting a new development out at Four Mile Creek. Meyers wanted in on that and was ready to cut Jack a great deal on whatever he needed for the construction of Pete's house.

After a productive afternoon, Jack drove back out to Emma's place. He'd decided that he would move the RV over to Pete's lot. If she wanted to stay mad at him, it would be easier for them both if he weren't living on her driveway. His own preference would have been to stay put, to make her face him. He was pretty certain he could persuade her, he smiled as he thought of ways he could do just that. But he didn't want to crowd her either. She might take longer to come back out of the mouse hole if he was sitting right outside. He also hoped that she might come to him, of her own accord—perhaps that was a little too optimistic, but a guy could hope.

After he moved the RV he walked back along the beach to Emma's to collect the truck. He'd written her a note and he taped it inside the screen door, making sure it wasn't going to blow away or fall. With that done he went down to town for groceries and a six-pack, since he might be spending his evenings sitting alone in the RV. On his way out of the store he bumped into Missy.

"Hey, Jack! How's it going?"

He smiled, "Oh, it's going, Missy. How about you?"

"Only going, huh?"

He gave her a shrug and smiled, not wanting to elaborate. "I'll get there."

She nodded, "I hope so. Please know I'm in your corner—and Ben too, if ever we can help at all."

"Thanks, Missy. That's good to know."

"We can see what you're about. We love our Mouse and we can see that you would be good for her." She laughed. "Even if she can't yet." She looked up to watch a beautiful blue convertible streak down the road. Jack followed her gaze; he was a sucker for a nice car and that one was a beauty.

Missy looked at him. "You might want to work on that dopey, love-struck look you've got going on, though!"

"Sorry, Lexus SC430, nice vehicle."

Missy slapped his arm with a grin. "That's what you may call it."

"It is, I know, I almost bought one when I moved to LA. Not sure I'd want one out on these roads though." His eyes returned to the car as it disappeared around the corner onto West Shore Road.

"Well, around here we call it the Mouse-mobile."

"That was Emma? She's back already? And that's her car?"

"Yes, yes and yes," laughed Missy. "So I imagine you'll be hitting the road up there too."

Jack hesitated. He wanted nothing more than to chase her back up to the North Shore, but he didn't want to pressure her. He'd left the note.

Missy was watching him closely and raised an eyebrow.

"Man, I'll bet Scot dreads that look," he laughed.

"Only when he's messed up. Want to tell me about it?"

"I'm trying to give her some space, that's all."

"Okay, well you can come and hang with me and Scot for a while if you want to?"

Jack looked at her. That would be a really good idea if he could bring himself to do it.

"Oh, you poor soul, you don't know what to do for the best, do you?'

He shook his head miserably.

"As her friend, I say that if you really want to give her some space, come and hang with me and Scot, or go and have a beer with Ben. But," she wrinkled her nose at him, "if there is even the tiniest chance that she might be mad at you for anything, anything at all, then get back up there. Don't go near her, mind. Just let her see where you are so she won't go thinking you've disappeared on her."

Jack was relieved to have it spelled out for him. "Thanks, Missy. In that case, I'll get back up there."

Laughing now, Missy reached up and gave him a hug. "Go on then, and good luck."

~ ~ ~

When Emma arrived home her heart fell as she saw the empty driveway. She'd had a lot of time to think on the drive back from LA. Her lunch with Holly had made her step back and take a look at herself. She had thought she was being brave with Jack, but after talking to her friend she had to admit that she was only pretending to be. She was still looking for any excuse to run and hide, to say that it wouldn't work and yes, to blame him. She'd listened to his messages. The first two had sounded so desperate. The last one, he had sounded resigned. He wouldn't keep pestering her. He'd like the chance to explain. Hopefully he'd see her tonight. She'd listened to Pete's messages too. He had sounded increasingly concerned. The first call this morning, he had just hoped to see her today. Then he hadn't been able to get hold of Jack, wondered if she knew where he was. Then another, he was pissed and now a bit worried as nobody would answer him, so please call him back! She'd smiled at that. Peter the Great, as Jack liked to call him, wasn't used to people not returning his calls. So she'd called him, told him that she and Jack had had a little misunderstanding, that she was fine and neither of them wanted to involve him in it. He'd been appeased by that. She really didn't want to cause any friction between the two of them, or to put Pete in a difficult position. Jack was his partner, and his best friend, but at the same time she knew he was still overly protective towards her. He'd assumed responsibility as her protector in grade school and had never relinquished the role.

She'd decided not to call Jack. He'd said he hoped to see her this evening and she'd rather talk to him in person than on the phone. Only now it was this evening and the RV was gone. Well, she wasn't going to get over dramatic about it. She'd wait and see what happened. Grow up a bit, like Holly said, and wait for the facts instead of imagining the worst. As she opened the screen door she saw his note. She let herself inside and sat at the counter to read it.

Dearest Emma,

I am so sorry about this morning. I can imagine what you're thinking, but it's not true. I've moved the RV to give you some space. You can avoid me if you want to. I hope you don't. I'd like the chance to explain. I'll be on the beach at eight o'clock. I hope you'll join me.

Love

Jack

She put the note down. 'Okay, Mr. Benson,' she whispered, 'I'll see you at eight'. She looked at her watch. There was time to eat something then take a shower. It had been a long, stressful day.

At quarter till eight Jack turned to see Emma emerge from the house and start out on the path down to him. He'd been out here twenty minutes already. He hadn't been able to stand the waiting. He'd lit the fire in the pit and had a cooler with beers and a few other goodies. He took a long swig of his beer as he watched her approach. She was so pretty. Hair tied up in a ponytail, she wore jeans and sneakers and a fleecy pink sweater. She didn't meet his eye as she walked down, but still, she was coming, and early too. Hopefully that was a good thing?

He stood up, "Hey, baby."

She finally met his eyes, "Hi Jack." She didn't come to him, instead she took a seat.

"Want a beer?"

"Yes, please."

He popped the top off a bottle and handed it to her. As she took a sip from the long neck he remembered what she'd tried to do to him last night. Man, this was no time to be thinking of that!

"Emma, baby, I'm sorry. I was trying to do something nice for you and I screwed up."

She looked at him and those big eyes, where last night he had seen such trust, were now shuttered again. One step forward, three steps back!

"Em, I lay there this morning, watching you sleep and I wanted to do something to make you smile. So I went to the resort to get you doughnuts."

She raised her eyebrows. He explained about the doughnuts and the spare and the disaster of his good intentions gone awry.

"But I called you before I left. You didn't even answer."

"Did you not hear it ring?"

She looked confused.

"Remember what we did with my phone last night?"

She nodded slowly.

"When I did finally get back here, you were gone. I couldn't call you because I only had your number in my phone. I tried Pete. I even tried Missy."

Her eyes widened.

"Yeah, that's what I thought, but I was desperate. I was only going to ask for your number though, not explain why I needed it."

"But you have your phone. You called me from it. Not the first time, but the other times."

This was the part he wasn't looking forward to, not sure what she would make of Gramps' involvement. "Gramps rescued me." He explained about Gramps coming to the house and, having decided to stick with complete honesty no matter what, he told her everything, right down to finding his keys and cell phone in the truck after Gramps left him. When he finished he looked at her, expecting the worst for having let the old guy know that they'd spent the night together. Instead of anger though, he was relieved to see a little smile playing on her lips.

"I'm glad you're finding this funny," he said, trying not to smile back. "I've had a pretty stressful day."

"I'm just smiling at Gramps doing that. I'd have been less surprised if he'd run you out of town with his shotgun when he found your things upstairs."

"The same thought had crossed my mind!"

"He must like you and he must trust you, that's all I can make of it."

"That makes me happy, but it would make me a whole lot happier if you liked me and trusted me."

"I do like you Jack, you must know that much...." She hesitated.

"But you don't trust me," he finished for her.

She met his eyes. "I would like to trust you Jack, but it's hard for me."

"I know, baby, I know. Can you at least forgive me for this morning?"

When she nodded, he released the tension he hadn't realized he'd been holding. This was quicker than he'd hoped. He came to sit in front of her and took her face between his hands. He planted a quick kiss on her lips and she smiled back at him.

"I'll do everything I can to earn your trust, Em."

She shook her head, looking sad now.

His heart stopped. "What do you mean, no?"

"It's not you, Jack. It's me."

Oh, no. Not that old line. He really didn't want to hear the 'you're a nice guy, but I don't think I can do this' speech. It was the one he was used to delivering as a gentle let down. He didn't want to be on the receiving end of it. Not from Emma.

"Em, please give me a chance."

"I am, if you'll listen."

"Oh, sorry." He felt a little foolish as she continued.

"What I'm saying is that it's not really you I don't trust. You have done nothing to make me think you are anything other than a decent, honest," and here she smiled, "very sexy, man. I'm having trouble trusting because of my own past, not because of anything you have done."

He was surprised at her insight; it was what he thought, but he hadn't been about to say it so bluntly.

She went on, "I had lunch with my friend Holly today and she very kindly told me I was being an idiot and that I needed to grow up!"

Jack silently thanked the unknown Holly, but said nothing.

"She helped me put myself back together after Rob. She knows me too well. I'll admit. I was a little freaked out by this morning and she talked me down, showed me I was overreacting and that perhaps I needed to listen to what you had to say, instead of listening to all the stuff going round in my head. So, Jack, I want to apologize to you, too."

"Emma, you don't need to."

"Yes, I do. Because I'm taking all my stuff out on you and you didn't cause any of it."

"Hey, baby. Look how big these shoulders are." He mimicked a body builder, trying to make her laugh. "I can take it."

He won a small smile before she continued. "But Jack, you might want to dump me...."

"Emma!" he tried to interrupt, but she put a finger to his lips.

"Maybe I'm starting to understand why I freak out at things and struggle to trust, but it doesn't mean that I'll be able to stop doing it just like that." She snapped her fingers. "You could go and be with any beautiful, uncomplicated woman you want. Why would you stick around to deal with my crap when neither of us knows how long it will take or even if I will ever get past this? Perhaps you should think about that?"

"Don't you think I already have thought about that, Em? As you keep reminding me, I could have any woman I want. I don't know how this sounds, but don't you think I know that? The only woman I want is sitting right in front of me. I already know she's afraid of getting hurt, that she'd rather hide her heart away than risk having it broken, but that doesn't change the fact that she is the only woman I want. It's for me to decide what I want, and I want you. I am prepared to take the risk that you may never want me back in the same way. I know I'd rather be taking the risk to win you than going for a sure thing with anyone else. I know you can't change it all overnight. All I'm asking is that you let me stick around, for all the time it takes. We can change it together, build new memories."

She looked up at him, tears welling in her eyes. He folded her into his arms and felt the wetness on his chest. Her arms came up around him and she clung to him. He nuzzled his head down by her ear. "So, what do you say?"

"I say yes, if you'll have me."

"Oh, I'll have you!" he grinned.

"I'd definitely like *that*."

"I think maybe we should have some S'mores first, don't you?" He opened the cooler to reveal his supplies of chocolate and marshmallows.

"Oh, I love S'mores!"

"Then you shall have them," he said, relieved to lighten the mood.

~ ~ ~

Emma watched Jack as he reached into the cooler to pass her another beer. He was so handsome. Holly had been right; he was like the romantic hero from a movie. She'd be insane to push him away. Even after the craziness of today, here he was toasting S'mores for her, sitting on the beach, telling funny stories to make her laugh. He really was a good man, and she determined to do her best not to mess this up.

Once he'd popped the top on his own beer, she raised her bottle to his. "Here's to S'mores."

"I'll drink to that."

She leaned in and kissed him, running her tongue along his bottom lip. "I'd like s'more of what we had last night, too." She loved the way he looked at her, eyes filled with lust at her words.

"That could be arranged."

She stood up and pulled him to his feet.

"You mean right now?"

"I mean right now." She laughed as he tipped his freshly opened beer and poured it away into the sand. "What my lady wants, she gets," he smiled.

She reached up to kiss him and molded herself against him as he pressed into her, loving the feel of his hard desire.

He broke away. "Let's gather this up and head inside, shall we? Your place or mine?"

"Oh, mine, I think. It's closer."

He laughed at that. While he packed up the cooler and fastened it shut, she kicked out the fire. In the darkness he kissed her deeply. She ran her fingers through his hair, completely aroused, wanting more of him. He hooked his arm behind her knees and lifting her off the ground, carried her up the path to the house. Surprised, she wrapped her arms around his neck and held on tight. At the front door she squirmed to get down, but he held her tighter.

"I've got it."

"What about the cooler?"

"Critters can't get in, it's fastened." He managed to open the door and close it with his heel, then, holding her close to his chest, bounded up the stairs and kicked open the bedroom door.

"So masterful," she giggled, both amused and very much aroused by his caveman act.

He smiled down at her. "Seemed like the quickest way to get here." He lowered her onto the bed and lay beside her. She pressed her lips to his neck and trailed her tongue up behind his ear, loving the sigh it drew from him. Still kissing his neck, she tugged his shirt up and over his head. He pulled her own sweater up and off, then freed her breasts from her bra. He seemed to hesitate before he took it off her, but she was determined she wouldn't spoil this moment, so she pulled his head down to her nipple which was hard and taut, longing for his touch. As he circled it with his tongue she felt the heat pool between her legs. She tugged at his jeans and soon two pairs of denims lay on the floor.

He kissed her hungrily, his tongue exploring her mouth as his hands explored her body. She gave herself up to him, losing all sense of everything except his mouth on hers and the way her whole body ached with desire for him. She tried to turn him on his back, but he gently overpowered her. Pinned to the bed with her arms above her head, she met a hungry look. He held her arms in place and let his eyes wander down over her. She was amazed how her body responded to just a look. She could feel the heat and the wetness between her legs. Her nipples strained for the feel of his hands or his mouth around them.

"Jack," she breathed, "please?"

"I'm hungry," he murmured, his eyes leaving no doubt what he wanted.

A tremor ran through her whole body as she remembered the feel of his mouth on her.

"Jack, please. Take me now, I want to feel you inside me." The look of pure lust told her all she wanted to know. "You make this all about my pleasure. What would please me most is to satisfy you." He hesitated. She knew what he wanted to do for her, but she wanted him to indulge himself, take her without restraint. Keeping her arms above her head, she held on to his hands and began to move beneath him, spreading her legs wide so the part of him that wouldn't argue with her was nudging at her wetness. She moaned; he felt so good. She felt his whole body tense as she let go of his hands and ran her hands down his back. Knowing how hard he was struggling to resist, she looked him in the eye. "Do I need to say those two words out loud again?"

He shook his head and she could see the pulse in his jaw. She loved his gentleness, his restraint, but she knew what he really wanted. She wanted it too and was turned on by the fact that she could give it to him.

"Are you sure? I don't want to be selfish."

"I'm sure." She lifted her hips to him and then tensed as he slid inside her. She breathed hard, feeling the size of him throbbing inside her, the raw sensations radiating out from their connection. Her eyes flew open and she moaned as he pushed deeper still. He was so big. As he touched a place deep inside, she felt herself tighten around him as an orgasm took her fast and hard, leaving her panting. Oh my goodness! He'd hardly even moved. She looked up to find amusement mixed with hard lust in his eyes.

"You like?"

"Oh, I like. Now where were we?"

"I believe you were insisting that I take my pleasure." With a smile he thrust his hips again. She cupped his ass and urged him on. At that he plunged deep and she arched up underneath him, stretching around his throbbing movements. Carried along with his desire she brought her legs up around his back and that seemed to send him over the edge. He nibbled the sensitive skin of her neck, sending currents of electricity zinging through her. He kept up an insistent rhythm and reached underneath her to hold her cheeks in both hands, steadying her as he rode deep and hard. She felt the heat mounting with each determined thrust, amazed as he grew even bigger and harder as he got closer. She moaned as the heat ignited and at the first wave of her orgasm she felt him explode inside her, wave after wave of pleasure carrying them both along as one. She was lost, riding the crest of his orgasm, flying high on sensations she'd never known. Eventually she came back to earth. His head was on her shoulder, breathing hard. She shivered with an aftershock as he still throbbed inside her. They lay joined that way for a long time.

"My Emma," he whispered.

Her arms came up around him at that. How she would love to be 'his' Emma! She certainly felt like it after what they had just shared.

"That was amazing, you were amazing, baby."

"If you still think that was you being selfish, then I hope that you will be very selfish, very often in the future."

He chuckled, "I don't know about being selfish, but more of this can definitely be arranged."

She snuggled close to him, liking the idea of more of this. Lots more.

"You've worn me out." She felt his chest rumble under her hand as he chuckled again.

"I've worn you out? I thought it was the other way around, my little minx."

"Either way, I'm exhausted." she yawned.

"Well, get some sleep, baby."

She tensed as she remembered the night before.

"It's okay, I'm not going anywhere. I'm going to hold you all night long and when you open your eyes I'll be the first thing you see."

She relaxed a little, hoping it was true. "Goodnight, Jack."

"Goodnight, Em."

Chapter Eighteen

Jack awoke as the dawn was breaking. Emma slept with her back pressed against him. His arm was still slung protectively over her. He smiled; even in his sleep he'd kept his word and held her all night. She stirred and he grew hard, his cock nestled against her backside. Since trying not to wake her had gone so horribly wrong yesterday, he decided he wouldn't worry about that. He stroked her hair away and kissed the back of her neck, pulling her closer to him. She quivered as he trailed his fingers down her arm.

"Mm, that feels good," she mumbled.

He turned her to face him, loving the feel of her, soft and warm, in his arms, her full breasts pressing against his bare chest. Slowly she opened her eyes and he smiled.

"Good morning, Beautiful. Told you this ugly mug would be the first thing you'd see today."

"That's no ugly mug." She returned the smile. "I think I must still be asleep and dreaming I've got a fantasy man in my bed."

He chuckled. "Well then, you lay back and enjoy the fantasy." To his surprise she turned over and presented her back to him. Did she really want more sleep? She answered that by wiggling her ass against him, making his cock stand to attention, wide awake and ready for action. He drew her close and pushed against her as he kissed her neck again. She turned her head to kiss him as his hand worked its way down, circling ever lower until his fingers found her opening. She was awake all right, hot and wet and ready for him. She may be running scared from emotional connection, but he loved the way her body responded to him, so willing for the physical connection. He drew her leg back over his hip, opening her up as he continued to stroke, teasing her with his fingers until she gasped with pleasure. Knowing she was close, he slid two fingers inside and felt her surge in response, her body pressed back against him as she came. Seeing the way her hand grasped the pillow in front of her turned him on so much. The moment she lay still, he turned her face down and knelt between her legs. Lifting her hips so that she was kneeling before him, he placed her hands on the top of the headboard.

"Trust me, baby?"

She nodded, still breathing hard. Positioning himself behind her, he held her hips and slowly, gently penetrated her wetness. She moaned and he saw her grip on the headboard tighten.

"You okay?"

She responded by moaning again, pushing herself back against him, taking him deeper. He couldn't help but plunge into the velvety wetness he craved. He filled his hands with her plump breasts as he thrust over and over into her heat. Knowing that he wouldn't last long he reached down and stroked her where they joined, coaxing the bundle of nerves between her legs. He saw stars as he found his release. She cried his name as he took her with him, trembling beneath him as every nerve in his body soared. Finally she let go of the headboard and slumped down on the bed, smiling up at him.

"That was the best morning fantasy I've ever had!"

He grinned, "You can have it every morning if you'd like."

"Well...." she pretended to think about it, then gave him a mischievous little smile, "it certainly beats doughnuts!"

He laughed, pleased she was able to joke about that already. "I'll make you a solemn vow right now, okay?"

"What's that?"

"I shall never again go buy you doughnuts for breakfast—unless you come with me."

She smiled. "That sounds good to me."

~ ~ ~

At nine o'clock, Emma settled out on the front deck, ready to put in a morning's writing. She felt relaxed, relieved to be past yesterday's stress. She'd enjoyed every moment of last night, and this morning. She flushed now, remembering how he'd felt, taking her from behind as she'd clung to the headboard; she'd never known anything like that. Then he'd joined her in the shower, soaping every inch of her body before he took her again, hard and fast against the wall, hot water running over them as they'd both cried out at the moment of climax. He made her feel so sexy and somehow powerful, while at the same time cherished and protected. After their passion he'd held her and kissed her so tenderly, then washed her hair. He was so big and powerfully built, she shivered at the memory of his big body glistening in the shower. Yet he was so gentle, he made her feel so safe. Now that was quite a realization. She'd never truly felt safe in her

whole life, not since her parents had died, leaving her alone
and afraid.

Her phone interrupted her reverie. It was Pete. "Hey,
Mouse! How's it going?"

"I'm good thanks, how about you?"

"You doing better today, then?"

She smiled. He was still concerned about yesterday. "Much
better, thanks. When are you coming back up here?"

"That's good to hear," he sounded relieved. "That's what I
was calling you about. Jack and I have that meeting at two
thirty tomorrow to start working out the Four Mile Creek deal,
but I'm thinking I can be up there by noon. I was wondering if
you had time for lunch with an old friend?"

"I've always got time for lunch with you, Pete. You know
that. Want to meet at the resort, or come out here?"

"How about I come to you?"

She laughed at that. "What do you want me to make you?"

"Well.... I haven't had a Philly cheese steak in forever, and
yours are the best."

"No need for flattery, you know I'm happy to cook for
you."

"Hey, it's honesty, not flattery."

"Sure, want me to make you a key-lime too?"

"You know the answer to that, Em, but only if it's no
trouble."

"It's no trouble at all, Pete."

"In that case, yes please. I'll see you then, then."

"See you."

Emma hung up, smiling. If she could relax and enjoy it, this
could be the best summer she'd ever had. She was up here
with Gramps. She had Missy and Ben on her doorstep, Pete

coming up every weekend – and Holly next weekend, she remembered. She had her very own house, right on the beautiful lake, and to top it all off she had a wonderful, gentle, funny man around – who also happened to be the sexiest man she'd ever seen and with whom she was having lots of hot sex. If she dared to think about it, he was a man who was starting to make her feel things she'd told herself she would never feel again, making her want things that she'd taught herself didn't exist. But, no, she didn't dare to think about all of that. Stick with the hot sex. And don't mess it up, Em. Remember, live the moments, enjoy it for what it is.

Jack had the windows rolled down on the old truck, and the warm breeze felt wonderful. He'd made some good progress today. Hopefully they'd be able to break ground on Pete's place next week. It might take a while for all the paperwork to filter through, but he could get much of the groundwork done while he waited. For now he was headed back to Emma's, or at least to the RV to shower and change, and then to Emma's. He could get used to this. It would be real easy to trade the LA skyline for the mountains, the ocean for the lake, that godawful traffic on the freeway for these quiet roads and this old truck. That whole empty social life with its artificial women and fancy restaurants for dinners with beautiful Emma on her front deck.

He shook his head, smiling ruefully. Was this what Pete had meant, about achieving so much success but nothing that really mattered? He figured he'd probably feel more successful day-laboring here, if he could come home to Emma every night, than he had ever felt while building a multi-million-dollar business. Wow! He really did have it bad. At least between building Pete's house and then hopefully working out a development on Joe's land, he would be able to stay here a good long time. Enjoy this life that was suiting him so much better than the city ever had, and work on persuading Emma to trust him with her heart.

As he arrived back at the North Shore he couldn't resist stopping by to see her before going over to the RV to change. She came down the steps to greet him with a smile and a kiss.

"Hey, handsome."

What he wouldn't give to spend the rest of his life coming home to this. "Hey, beautiful. Good day?"

"Very good. You?"

"About the same."

"Would you like a beer? I'm ready for one."

"I need to go shower and change first. I just couldn't bring myself to drive by without stopping to say hi."

She smiled, looking pleased. "Well, now that you're here, at least have a cold one. I don't think we need to stand on ceremony, do you?"

He drew her towards him and kissed her. "No, baby, I don't." Once he released her, she brought two beers out. He took them and popped the tops. "A man could get used to this, you know. Coming home to a pretty lady and an ice cold beer."

She lowered her eyes then met his, smiling. "It is kind of nice, isn't it?"

"Well, let's see what we can do to make it last, shall we?"

This time she didn't meet his gaze and he knew better than to push it.

"Have you spoken to Pete today?"

"No, I need to call him later. We need to run through a few things before tomorrow. You talked to him?"

"Yes, he's coming for lunch before your meeting. He's glad to be up here for the weekend again."

Jack's face fell.

"Something wrong?"

He raised an eyebrow. "Perfect honesty?"

"Yes, please."

"It's just that I don't want to be banished back to the RV for the weekend!"

She smiled. "And why is that?"

"I think you know why."

"Perhaps you'd like to tell me why, so I'm sure."

He loved it when she teased him. It was good to know she had the confidence, and a turn on too. "Well," he began, "I'm thinking Dan and Scot will be in the RV...."

"Oh, I see. Is that all?"

"No, that is the very least of it." He came to stand behind her, wrapping his arms around her waist and lowering his mouth so he spoke right next to her ear. "You, my darling, will be up in that bed of yours with no one to protect you. I won't be able to sleep a wink for worrying about you."

"Is that so?"

"Sure is."

"Well then, how about you come to my bed with me and protect me, if that's what you're calling it. That way we'll both know I'm safe and I won't feel responsible for your loss of beauty sleep."

He hadn't expected her to let him stay while the others were around.

"So, you don't mind what the others might think about my 'protecting' you, huh?"

To his surprise, she grew serious. "I don't care what anyone thinks. We're both consenting adults and it's none of anyone else's business!" She relaxed a little. "Besides, every single one of them has sung your praises and told me to give you a chance. So they can hardly say anything. Not that they would, anyway."

"Well, alrighty then." He was pleased by her decisiveness. "I shall come to your bed and 'protect' you no matter who is around. How about that?" He gave her his best sexy smile.

She laughed. "If you keep that up, I might drag you there now." He stepped forward hopefully, but she put a hand on his chest to stop him. "Much as I would like to, I have to finish up here. So why don't you go and get your shower and call Pete while I make us some dinner?"

He took her hand from his chest and brought it to his lips. "Okay then, but I won't be long and I'm hungry." He let his gaze travel slowly down her body and smiled as he watched the flush spread over her neck and chest. He was learning what aroused her, and intended to put it to good use real soon.

Emerging from the shower, Jack dialed Pete's cell from the computer so he could finish getting ready while they talked. He toweled himself dry as it rang.

"S'up, partner?" Pete answered.

"Doing great. You?"

"Yep. Looks like the deal with Bowers is in the bag."

As they discussed the Bowers deal and a few other projects, Jack finished drying himself off and dressed in jeans and a black sweater.

"You had time to look over my proposal for tomorrow?" asked Pete.

"Went through it this afternoon. I think you've covered everything we talked about."

"Yeah."

"Yeah, but what? I know that tone." He hoped this wouldn't take long; he wanted to get back to Emma. He really was hungry and wouldn't mind at all if they skipped dinner.

"You want me to lay it on you straight?" asked Pete.

Jack frowned, "I'll be pissed if you don't!" This wasn't like Pete. Part of the reason they worked so well together as friends and as partners was that they were always honest with each other; neither pulled any punches, ever. Most of the time they seemed to read each other's thoughts anyway, but whenever they didn't, neither was afraid to tell it like it was.

"I want to be sure that you really want to go after this one?"

"Damn, Pete! You've seen all the work I've done already, the drafts of what we can do out there. I didn't do all that for fun, did I? Why would you think I'm not on board?" Then realization dawned. Pete was thinking about Emma. "Sorry, I get it."

"What do you get?"

"You're concerned that if things don't work out between me and Emma, I won't want to be tied to a development up here, right?"

"That's about it."

"Well, thanks for the concern, but I'm working my ass off here to make sure things will work out. And to be honest with you, bro, if they don't I'll be glad to still have a reason to be out here, hanging around the lake, hoping to still catch a glimpse of her! Satisfied?"

"That bad, huh?"

"You have no idea."

"Well then, you're going to hate me even more, but I have to do this."

"Do what?"

"I've asked her to have lunch with me tomorrow."

"Yeah, she said. You're coming over at noon, right?"

"Yeah, but sorry bro, you're not invited."

Jack frowned. He wasn't sure he was getting this. "Okay."

"Jack, I told you, she's like my little sister. Before we tie up several million bucks in this thing, I need to know that she's thought it through. I have to ask how *she* would deal with you still being up there if things don't work out between the two of you. Believe me, I really hope they do. But, if they don't, I don't want her feeling she has to leave because you're around. You know that's what she'd do if she were uncomfortable with it. I'm sorry, but I feel responsible for her. It's her home, and her Gramps'."

Jack was silent a long time.

"You mad, bro?"

"Nah, man, I get it. I'd do the same in your shoes. It's just...well, it's weird to think that if she runs back to her mouse hole when you ask her about it, we're going to kill the deal, right?"

"I think we'd have to, don't you?"

"I guess so."

"I feel bad about this, Jack, but I'd feel worse if it ends up with us working up there and Emma leaving because of it. We'd both hate that."

"I know, and I'm with you. But if you force her to decide right now, she might scare off just because she's not ready yet."

"I know and I'm sorry, but do you have a better idea?'

Jack racked his brain, but he had to admit that Pete was right. "The only thing I can come up with right now is to get on over to her place and continue to convince her what a great guy I am," he said with a laugh, "and to somehow add in that if she decides she doesn't want me, I'd still be a great friend to have around."

Pete snorted. "Sounds like your best plan. Good luck, bro."

Pete hung up, leaving Jack to think about their conversation. He ran his fingers through his hair as he paced the RV. Damn. He understood that, as Emma's friend, Pete wanted to be sure that he wasn't about to hurt her by committing her to either having to still be around Jack or leave if things didn't work out between them. He just hated that Pete was going to force her to think about it, and decide about it, right now. Maybe they could wait a while before pulling the trigger on the deal? Give him chance to spend more time with her first? But no, Joe wanted to sell soon and if it wasn't to them it could well be to Armstrong—had Pete thought about that?

He would just have to hope that Emma had come far enough to think of him as a real friend whom she really wouldn't mind having around, even if they weren't together. The thought made him go cold. Even after such a short time, he couldn't think about the rest of his life without her in it. Maybe he should talk to her about it tonight? Would that be fair? What could he say?

'Hey, baby, could you please decide now how you might handle our breakup if we have one, and of course I'm only asking because I don't want one'.... No, he wasn't going there! But he did want her to have more time to think about it. Not just the length of a lunch with Pete tomorrow. He dialed Pete's number again.

"S'up?"

"Okay, I feel like a schoolgirl."

"I don't think that would help your case with Em." Pete laughed.

Jack couldn't help but laugh with him. "Damn you, Pete. Take this seriously, would you. My whole life is on the line here."

"Now you sound like a schoolgirl. Quit with the melodramatics and tell me already."

"Would you call Emma now and tell her why you want to talk to her tomorrow?"

"Sure. Only reason I didn't was that I didn't want to ruin you guys' evening if it puts her in a spin."

"I'll risk it. See, this way she'll have more time to think about it. I was going to bring it up myself, but I don't want her to feel like I'm pressuring her. This way if she wants to talk to me about what you've said she can. If not, she won't even mention it."

"Okay," said Pete, "I do think it's better to give her more time. I'll call her now."

"Thanks. And Pete?"

"Yeah?"

"When you get off the phone with her, will you call me back so I can get over there?"

Pete laughed again. "Sure thing. And when I see you tomorrow can we whisper behind our hands and giggle together too?"

"I know, I know! It's ridiculous, but she's fragile. I want to do this right and I don't want to lose her."

"I know, I'm sorry. It's just so weird to see you like this. Give me ten to talk to her. I'll text you when we're done."

Jack paced the RV again. He did feel a little ridiculous. Asking his friend to call his girl had never been his style. But nothing about this was his normal style. He was dealing with a woman who ran at the slightest risk of hurt and he was in danger himself of getting very badly hurt if she ran out on him now. His impatience grew as the minutes ticked by. "Come on, Pete," he muttered. This was driving him crazy.

After fifteen of the longest minutes of his life his phone beeped.

All yours.

He locked up the RV and jumped in the truck.

Emma was in the kitchen when he arrived.

"Pizza for tonight. I hope that's all right?"

"Wonderful, thanks, and this should go pretty well with it." He presented her with a bottle of Merlot. "The winery belongs to a friend of mine up in Napa. Maybe I could take you up there to meet him one weekend?"

Her eyes shone with pleasure. "I'd like that. I love Napa."

"Let's plan on it then, shall we? Want to go in a couple of weeks, since it's Gramps' birthday next weekend?"

"Yes, let's. It'll be fun," she smiled mischievously. "We can take my car if you like?"

"Yes, Miss Douglas. The way things went yesterday, we didn't get to talk about your Mouse-mobile, but you do surprise me. We could go to Napa in it on one condition."

"What's that?"

"That I get to do some of the driving too."

She laughed. "So, you don't disapprove? Everyone else thinks I'm nuts."

"Disapprove? I'm envious! I almost bought one myself when I got to LA. Do you know how hard it is to get hold of a blue one?" He smiled. "Of course you do. You got one."

"I do and I did," she laughed. "If you tried yourself then you'll know the lengths I went to and from that you'll understand how badly I wanted it."

"Believe me, if anyone understands about getting hooked on a car, I do."

She certainly didn't seem to be put out by Pete's call. He hoped that was a good thing.

Since it was a much cooler evening they ate their pizza in the big kitchen.

"This is wonderful." Emma swirled her glass, enjoying the wine.

"I'll get you a case when we go up there. They make a great Cabernet Franc too." He loved the idea of taking her away for a weekend. Showing her his favorite haunts in Napa, showing her off to his friends up there.

"Pete called while you were gone."

Here goes. At least she's going to talk to me about it. He didn't say anything but raised an eyebrow, waiting for her to continue.

"You know he's coming for lunch tomorrow? Well, he's really coming to see if I'm okay with the whole Four Mile Creek deal."

Jack said nothing. He felt like an ass. He couldn't bring himself to ask questions he already knew the answers to.

She continued, "He thinks that if we mess this up, I might leave the lake if you're still working here."

He nodded again, he couldn't do this. "I know, Em. He told me he was going to call you about it."

"Oh."

What did that mean? He looked at her and to his surprise she laughed at him.

"You're giving me the puppy dog eyes again."

Huh? He shook his head. That time it hadn't been intentional. "I need to know what you think." His heart was pounding.

She looked puzzled, then, "Oh, you mean about Pete?"

"Yes, about whether us working out there is a bad idea?"

She reached across the table and took hold of his hand. "Jack, I told him not to be so silly, of course!"

A mixture of shock and relief rushed through him. "I'm afraid I was being the same kind of silly, baby. I was scared of what you might say."

"Oh, Jack." She squeezed his hand a little tighter. "I know I'm a bit unpredictable, but really. Like I told Pete, you're a good man, it's a good deal for you two, and for Ben. If we don't work out," she shrugged her shoulders, "this town is big enough for the both of us, and I would like to think that no matter what else happens now, we will still be friends. My little talk with Holly the other day really opened my eyes."

Jack made another mental note to thank Holly when he met her.

Emma gave him a little smile that melted his heart. "I may act like a scared little girl when it comes to relationships, but other than that I really am quite a competent, mature adult." Her words took him back to their first meeting with her juvenile banter with Pete and the cool composure afterward. He'd been so caught up in reassuring the little girl that he'd forgotten about the strong, capable woman.

"Sorry, Em. I guess I was so invested in not scaring you off that I got a little scared myself."

She rose from the table and came around to sit in his lap. Wrapping her arms around his neck, she kissed him. "It's okay, Jack. We're both learning this as we go along."

Wow, now *she* was reassuring *him*. They really were making progress.

Chapter Nineteen

Emma smiled at Pete as she watched him eat his Philly cheese steak. He was savoring every mouthful as they sat out on the deck.

"You know, for all your big company and your mega millions, you still eat like you did in the cafeteria in grade school," she teased.

He slowly finished chewing and swallowed deliberately before answering.

"Do not!" He stuck his tongue out, looking every bit the kid he'd been all those years ago.

She laughed, "So much for the suave and sophisticated Mr. Hemming."

"It's your fault, Em. You bring out the worst in me, and it's only your food that is worthy of taking my time over like this, its sooo good." He enjoyed another mouthful before asking, "So, you're sure you don't have any reservations about me and Jack working up here?"

"I'm sure, Pete. It's okay, really. I do appreciate that you would pull out of it for my sake, but there's no need."

"I would, you know. You only need to say the word and I'll pull the plug on the whole thing. Jack would too. I hope you can see by now that he would never do anything that would make you uncomfortable." He looked at her, searching her face for the truth.

"I can. That's part of why it's okay. He is a good man. Even I get that. We don't know how this will end up, but if it doesn't work out, I think we'll do okay as friends." Even as she said the words she wondered how it would feel to just be Jack's friend. Not to be able to hold him, to no longer see the lust in his eyes when he looked at her. She shook her head and, catching Pete still watching her, said, "No, no problem at all."

"I had to be sure. You know I'll do anything for you, Mouse."

"I know, Pete, and I love you too. Now, are you about ready for some of that key-lime pie?"

"Hell, yeah. And I get to eat it before anyone else gets any, right?"

He really was such a big kid. "Yes, you do. In fact this one's got your name on it. I made another for later. You are coming up here tonight?"

"I wasn't sure, didn't know what your plans would be. If you would want us all around?"

"Of course I do. Missy's bringing Scot and Dan over and I thought Ben would probably come with you two after your meeting?"

"Well, that'll be great then."

"Pete, I'm not that girl who abandons her friends when she meets a guy, and besides, that guy is your best friend, and his brother is coming up here too. If it's going to go anywhere between me and Jack it will be by him being one of the gang, not by me missing out on the gang in order to be with him. I made that mistake once, remember?"

Pete nodded. She knew he'd hated her relationship with Rob and had tried so hard to make her see sense. She wished now that she had listened to him. She smiled at that as it reminded her that she really should listen to him and these days he was encouraging her to be with Jack.

"Is it weird for you?" she asked.

"Is what weird?"

"You know, me and Jack seeing each other like this." If she was honest, she wanted some more of his encouragement.

"I don't think weird is the word.... Or maybe it is. There are so many different angles to it for me. First there's you. My little Mouse is dipping her toes into a relationship for the first time since the asshole episode, and I'm happy that you are. I want you to be happy and not die an old maid." She laughed at that. "But at the same time, I'd kill any man that hurt you. After watching what you went through before, and knowing what taking this risk is costing you, part of me wants to supervise and chaperone the whole thing. Then I remember that the guy you're with is the most decent man I've ever known, who would never hurt anyone intentionally. He is also the most protective man I've ever known. I truly would trust him with my life. But when it comes to women, I've only ever known him do superficial."

Emma's heart jumped into her mouth at that; it certainly wasn't the encouragement she'd been hoping for.

"Don't look at me like that, Mouse. I don't mean it like that. I mean, I've known him date a lot."

Oh, how she wished he'd shut up now. This was not what she wanted to hear.

"Argh! Just wait till I've finished before you jump to conclusions, Em. This isn't going where you think."

She nodded, her heart still pounding.

"I mean, he's a good-looking guy. Got a lot to offer. The personality, the lifestyle, the money and all. Lots of women want all that. But he never really seemed to want them. He dated them, but never for too long and I never saw him really into any of them."

Emma nodded, still not sure she needed to be hearing this.

"Damn. This is your fault you know, for asking."

"I know. I'm sorry. Let's leave it."

"No, I can't leave it now, Mouse, because I've given you the wrong idea and I need you to understand what I mean. Let me give this another shot, eh?"

"If you must."

"My point was, I've known him date women, but always like he was going through the motions. I've never seen him act the way he is now. He's crazy about you. He talks about you all the time, asks my opinion on stuff. See, here's an example that might make you understand. His secretary, Lexi, she's always sent his flowers for him. Birthdays, thank yous, those kind of things, she takes care of them, yeah? Well, with his dates it was the same, just some routine detail you let a good secretary handle. Then you come along, and he's bugging me the whole time; what flowers do you like, what colors do you like. He's like an excited little kid. And, I'm sorry Mouse, but I told him to let Lexi take care of it. He was horrified. It was like he was on the most important mission of his life! He had to find the perfect flowers for you to make you happy and he had to do it himself. And no, they weren't going to be delivered, not by anyone but him. I imagine you've already noticed, but he's a detail guy, at least he is when he cares about something. You'll see it in his work, when he talks about his brother, a few other things, but never before have I seen him go into detail mode for a woman."

Emma smiled, remembering his face as he'd given her the flowers, so eager to please her. "Okay, you made a much nicer point. Now can we please leave it alone?"

"Gladly," said Pete, looking relieved, "And you know, more pie would really shut me up."

She gave him more key-lime and they chatted as he ate.

"Jack's going to swing by to pick me up in a little while," said Pete looking at his watch. "Do you want me to bring anything back later?"

"If you guys would do the booze run, that'd be great. I need to catch up with Gramps this afternoon, sort out a few things for next week's cookout. Can you make it up here for Friday?"

"I'm planning to. Is Gramps looking forward to Saturday?"

"They're like two little kids, him and Joe. I don't know about a joint seventy-fifth birthday party, I think it's more like a joint seventh the way those two are carrying on."

"They both know how to enjoy themselves, that's for sure." Pete looked up. "Well, here comes my ride," he said as Jack turned into the driveway. "S'funny, you know, he drives that fancy SUV in the city, he has an Aston Martin in Texas, and yet he looks most at home in your Gramps' old truck."

Emma smiled, watching Jack get out of the truck. "He does, doesn't he?"

"And it must tell you something that your Gramps trusted him with it."

"Yes. Gramps really surprised me with that."

"He's another good judge of character, Mouse."

Emma nodded as Jack climbed the steps.

"Good lunch?" he asked.

"Good lunch," Pete affirmed. "You ready to go make a deal?"

"Sure am, just one thing first?" He came to Emma. "Kiss for good luck?"

She hooked her arms around his neck and, standing on tiptoes, pulled him down to kiss her lips.

"Oh, pur-lease!" laughed Pete, "I'd say get a room, but we have a meeting to get to. I'll be in the truck when you're done here. Later, Mouse."

"Later, Pete."

"Sorry, Em," Jack held her close, "I needed a quick kiss."

"I'm only sorry it's not a slow kiss."

His eyes softened, "Oh, baby."

"That's okay, you'll have to owe me one till later."

He ran his hand down her arm, sending a shiver all through her. "I'll pay with interest."

"I'll hold you to that."

"I'll hold you to this." He drew her against him and she looked up at him in wonder...he was so hard. "It's what you do to me," he said with a laugh.

"Perhaps later you'll let me relieve you of that problem." She brought her finger to her lips, loving the way his eyes filled with desire as she suggestively sucked her fingertip.

"Hold on, I have a meeting to cancel!"

She laughed. "No, you don't. You have to go and sit through your meeting and you have to hang out and have fun with everyone tonight. When you're done with all of that, then we can revisit this." This time she held his hand up and flicked the tip of his finger with her tongue.

He rolled his eyes back and gave a low moan. "Later, my little minx."

"Later, Mr. Benson."

Emma stood on the deck as they drove away, feeling incredibly sexy. The fact that she could arouse him so easily pleased her immensely. She may not have the hang of trust or relationships yet, but she knew she was getting rather good at the sex at least.

"So, how are Scot and Dan getting along?" Emma asked Missy as she washed some salad.

"Like a house on fire. Dan must have set out before dawn this morning to get here so early, and they've been messaging each other constantly since he left Monday. It's so nice for Scot to have someone he can work with, you know?"

"It is, and it seems to be a two way street."

"I'm not sure which one of them is more excited. And how about you? How's it going with Jack?"

Emma faced her friend and smiled. "It's good. We had a bit of a hiccup the other day, but it's all okay now, we got past it."

"Speaking of the devil, here come the three musketeers now." Jack, Pete and Ben all piled out of Gramps' truck looking very pleased with themselves.

"Now there we have three good-looking guys."

"Four, don't forget the one in the RV with Scot."

Emma raised an eyebrow, "I'll need you to elaborate on that, lady."

Missy gave her a smile and then turned to the guys. "I'm guessing from those smiles that all went well?"

"Real well," said Pete.

"Sure did," added Ben, looking happier than Emma had seen him in a long time.

"Once we get the papers drawn up we'll be partners, partner." Jack slapped Ben on the back.

The five of them ate out on the deck. Scot and Dan had disappeared into the RV once more.

"So, Mouse," said Ben, "we got everything covered for the big birthday bash next week?"

"We certainly have. I saw Gramps this afternoon and he is so excited."

"Joe's the same." Ben laughed. "Remember what we were saying about their second childhood? Looks like we were spot on. You sure you don't need anything else brought out from the resort?"

"I don't think so, but I'll check in with you midweek if that's okay? I've got to get back to the city again and there's a chance I won't make it back till Saturday morning." She caught Jack's eye as he made a sad face at her. That hurt puppy dog look he played so well melted her, even though he was only teasing.

"Is everything okay with Carla?" he asked.

"Yes, she's doing what she does and trying to throw another project my way. And I do have to meet up with Brad. I promised I'd go over his spec script with him before the end of the month, that's what may take the time, but I can't let him down." Brad was another screenwriter she had worked with on several occasions. They'd known each other since her early days in the city, so though the timing wasn't perfect, she was determined to help him out this week, as he had done for her so often in the past. "It's just such a pain to have to make that drive again. It's getting old already."

"Tell me about it," said Pete, "I'm loving being here on the weekends, but I'm not loving the eight hours on the road each time."

"It'd only take about forty-five minutes in the air," said Jack.

"Mind reader. I was going to ask you why we still have the plane based in Houston. Now you're not there and Nate is closing out the Allen project, perhaps it's time we hangar it in Santa Monica? That would make my weekends a lot easier – and any time you two need to get back to the city."

"I won't be able to do anything this week," Jack looked at Emma apologetically.

"Don't worry about me, I'm fine driving."

He looked at Pete, "I've got Nate out in Miami till the first, but after that we can get it out here. That work for you?"

"Sounds great."

"Okay, I'll put Lexi on it on Monday morning."

Pete gave Emma a knowing look and she smiled to herself. That was merely a detail to hand over to his secretary.

"Thanks for another great dinner, Em," said Ben. The others all muttered their agreement. "I was wondering if I could take care of tomorrow night? We've got a couple of big parties coming in and I need to be around, but I still want to hang with you guys. Is everyone up for dinner at the Boathouse on me?"

They all agreed it would be fun to have a night at the resort and, despite Emma's protests that she really didn't mind, good to give her a night off from cooking.

Chapter Twenty

Emma, Missy and Ben sat out on the Boathouse deck. The restaurant was packed.

"We've got a big reunion upstairs," said Ben, "And this lot," he nodded through the doors that had been slid back to create a huge indoor-outdoor space, "this is the usual Saturday night crowd plus a girls night out."

Two long banquet tables of already rowdy women were making quite a racket.

Missy laughed. "They'll be hunting in packs later, Ben. You'll have to watch yourself."

"I've already had to dodge a few," he grinned. "Looks like the guys won't get away unscathed either."

Emma followed his eyes to where Jack and Pete were crossing the parking lot on their way to join them. Her heart fluttered as she watched them walk, Jack so tall, dark and muscular in his dark jeans with a black shirt and black boots. Pete, just as tall and muscular, handsome in a fairer way, wore a white shirt. They made quite a pair. A group of girls wolf whistled as they passed, making Missy and Ben laugh. Emma's stomach churned, though. As they came through the bar she watched as a tall, dark-haired beauty in a tiny mini skirt approached Jack and put a hand on his arm. She leaned towards him and said something. Emma's heart was pounding now. This was the effect he had on women. She watched him shake his head and shrug; the woman looked disappointed. As they kept walking Pete said something to Jack and the two of them laughed. Emma excused herself and headed to the ladies room before they reached the table.

She closed herself in a cubicle and stood shaking. Breathing deeply she tried to tell herself that she was just being silly. Jack had done nothing. It wasn't his fault he was gorgeous and women wanted to be with him. It didn't help that the ways she tried to rationalize it to herself were all things that Rob had said to her when he tried to explain the women always around him. On Rob's lips it'd all been lies. She shuddered. It may not be Jack's fault that it happened to him, but she'd bet it happened a lot. Spending their time alone together had been wonderful, but if they were going to have a real relationship, they'd be out amongst people like this all the time. Could she handle it? She hated how much it reminded her of Rob, of how stupid she had been. Blind. She'd been so proud that she was the one he'd chosen, not realizing until it was too late that he hadn't chosen at all. He'd kept pursuing every opportunity that presented itself. Of all those adoring women in their circle he'd slept with half a dozen of them in the short time they were married.

She took another deep breath, reminding herself: that was Rob, and this is Jack. Jack is a good man. He's not like that.

She unlocked the cubicle and ran cold water over her wrists, waiting for her heartbeat to return to normal. She looked at herself in the mirror—Not too shabby, she thought, trying to calm herself down, boost herself back up. And it was true. She'd left her hair down and wavy tonight. Her black sleeveless top was classy, showing off her light tan. The shiny crystal heart tied on a black leather thong sat at her throat, drawing attention to just a hint of cleavage displayed beneath it. She was wearing her favorite jeans—at least they'd become her favorites since the other day when Jack had commented how nicely they showed off her backside. She'd finished the outfit off with her black cowboy boots. Yes, not too shabby at all. As she took in the overall effect in the mirror, she realized that she and Jack were dressed pretty much identically and smiled.

"Okay, pull yourself together and get back out there."

She gave herself an encouraging smile in the mirror, pleased that she had been able to talk herself down and not go with her first instinct and run away home.

When she returned to the table the others were all chatting, except Jack who was sitting in her seat looking glum. As she reached the table he stood and folded her in his arms, kissing her full on for all the world to see. Keeping his arms wrapped around her he sat back down, pulling her with him to sit in his lap. He held her there, refusing to let her move.

"Hey, Mouse," laughed Pete, "How's it going?"

"I'd be better if I could sit in a chair."

Jack wrapped his arms tighter, surrounding her with his size, scent and warmth. "I am a chair!"

She had to laugh and she felt him relax a little. "You are not a chair."

He rested his chin on her shoulder. "Maybe not, but this is where you are sitting until I'm sure you're not going to bolt for the mouse hole."

"Why would I do that?"

"You tell me."

"I had to visit the ladies."

"Uh-huh?

"Uh-huh!"

"So, you're okay then?"

"I came back all by myself, didn't I?"

"You sure did," said Pete, "I would have put money on you being halfway back to North Cove by now."

Emma looked at Pete. "You stay out of this, Hemming."

"I would if I were you," said Ben.

"See, Ben's on my side," Emma smiled. "He's the only guy around here who'll stick up for me!"

"I wouldn't say that," said Jack, and as he held her tighter in his lap, she could feel his hardness pressing up against her. She was speechless a moment. They were all smiling at her and Jack was, well, wanting her like that, right in front of them all and they didn't know it. Oh my!

"You're not going to run, then?" he asked.

"I am not, but I would like a beer."

"Sorry, darlin', but I'm not going near that bar again tonight." They all laughed at that.

Ben raised his arm and caught the bartender's attention. "I think we'll go with table service tonight."

"I knew I liked this guy," said Jack, loosening his hold on her long enough to offer Ben a fist bump.

A server brought their drinks and took their food order.

"Are you going to let me sit down?" asked Emma.

"You are sitting down."

"I mean on a chair of my own."

"I told you, I am a chair and I'm all yours."

She relaxed against him, liking the sound of that in spite of herself. "Then I guess I'm staying put."

He put his head on her shoulder again. "That's what I needed to hear."

"When do you have to go to the city, Em?" asked Missy.

"Thursday, and I might have to stay Friday night too, depending on how long it takes with Brad."

"Are you coming?" Pete asked Jack. "Show your face in the office?"

"I can't, I'm meeting with Meyers on Thursday afternoon."

Emma was disappointed. It would be nice to make the drive with Jack, and nice not to have to spend the night, maybe two, away from him.

"Is your friend, Holly coming back up with you for the party?" asked Missy.

"We haven't worked it out yet. I'd rather get back Friday if I can, but she can't come till Saturday and she doesn't really like to drive by herself."

"I can understand that," said Missy.

"She can ride with me if it will help, Mouse," offered Pete.

Emma's eyes sparkled. "Well, if I do bring her I was going to ask you to take her back with you on Sunday. I just didn't think you'd want to drive her up here since you don't know her yet."

"Oh, you'll love her," said Missy, "she's great."

"Of course I don't mind," said Pete, "if it'll help you out, and get you back to lover boy here sooner."

Jack wrapped himself around her again. "Yes, you come home. Let Pete bring Holly." He looked at Pete. "Holly is a very cool lady, I'm sure you'll like her."

Emma looked at him over her shoulder, "But you've never met her."

"I know, but she's already helped me out, hasn't she?"

Emma remembered that she'd told him how Holly had given her a few home truths. "Yes, I guess she has."

"That's settled then," said Pete. "Let me know how you want to work it."

The server returned with their food. "Are you going to let me sit down?" she asked Jack.

"Maybe. If you sit between me and Pete and don't run off."

She laughed. "I'm not going to run away, I promise."

He'd done such a good job of reassuring her that he only had eyes for her, that all uneasiness had faded away while she sat on his lap.

"Okay, then," he let her slide down into the empty chair beside him, "but I'm watching you."

After they'd eaten, the band started up.

"Let me know what you think of them," said Ben. "I like their sound and they're a good bunch of guys. I may keep them around for the summer." He went off to check on his staff.

"Dance with me, Pete?" Missy dragged Pete to the dance floor.

Emma watched as many of the women in the large party eyed Pete appreciatively. Though from the way they behaved, she was sure anyone who didn't know them would think he and Missy were a couple, and a very beautiful couple at that.

As he so often seemed to, Jack read her thoughts. "Those two look good together, has there ever been anything between them?"

"God, no," she laughed. "That would be almost incestuous! We've all been such good friends for so long."

"So none of you were ever involved?"

"Well, Ben and I dated for a little while in high school." She couldn't read the look on his face. "Not for long though, we were meant to be friends, not anything else."

At that moment Ben returned. "So what do you think of the band?"

"They're great. I think you should keep them around."

"I'm thinking I will."

Missy and Pete returned. "They are good," Missy agreed, "very danceable."

"Yeah," said Pete, "too danceable, she's worn me out. I need beer."

"I think we need to test drive them too," Ben said to Emma, then he looked at Jack, "Mind if I borrow your lady?"

"The lady does as she pleases," he smiled.

Ben led her out onto to the dance floor. "Just wanted to make sure you're okay, Mouse."

"Thanks, Ben. I'm okay now. I did nearly leave though. I know it's silly, but it reminded me so much of Rob and all the awful times."

"I thought as much." He stroked her hair in a gesture that had calmed her since they were kids, as concerned and gentle as he'd been when she was the new kid in class and scared out of her wits. She'd been so grateful for his friendship then and still was now. "You looked like someone had stuck a dagger through your heart. Just like you did after Rob."

"That bad?"

"Maybe worse. If it's any consolation, Jack looked just as devastated when you got up and left. I think he would have chased you into the ladies room if Pete hadn't made him wait."

Emma smiled. "Thanks Ben. You're such a good friend."

"Always have been, always will be. Uh-oh, I may need to go and sort that out," he nodded to where the bartender was beckoning to him.

Emma returned to the table and Jack stood. "May I?"

"Why of course."

They returned to the dance floor where he held her close, though a little stiffly.

She looked up at him, surprised by the tension. "Are you all right?"

"I'm good, baby. You?"

She nodded and rested her cheek against his chest, but he still felt tense and she could hear his heart beating loudly. "What is it, Jack?"

He met her eyes and held them with his own. "I guess I'm having a taste of what you go through and I'm not liking it."

"What do you mean?"

"Two minutes after you tell me you used to date Ben, he whisks you away to dance. You looked so happy and so comfortable together, I guess I'm feeling a little jealous. You've shared a lifetime together and I'm the new kid in town, trying to edge my way in."

She was shocked by his revelation, but touched by his honesty. She looped her arms up around his neck as the band began to play a slow ballad. He circled her waist and held her close.

"I'm sorry, baby."

"You have nothing to be sorry for. It actually feels kind of nice to know that you get it. Especially since you know you have nothing to worry about. Ben is my friend. You are the only man I have dared to take a chance on." She decided against adding that if this didn't work out, she wouldn't be taking any more. He lowered his head and kissed her deep and slow as they turned around the dance floor.

~ ~ ~

"Em, Em!" called Missy as they returned to the table. "You have to come see Nessa, she's getting married."

"Oh, dear God. Why on Earth would she want to do that?"

"Come on, she's with Leah and Cindy over there and don't you dare try to talk her out of it. Pretend to be happy for her, admire the ring, you know, do the things normal people do when they hear someone got engaged." Emma rolled her eyes at Pete as Missy dragged her away to visit with their old school friends.

Pete looked at Jack and grimaced when he saw his friend's face. "Guess you didn't need to hear that?"

"She's anti-marriage!?"

"It wasn't exactly good to her."

"But that was the man, not the institution!"

"You know that and I know that, but Emma is convinced that marriage is a special form of torture designed to ruin lives."

"Oh, man!" Jack hadn't considered that.

Pete came and sat next to him, looking concerned, "You're not going to tell me you're thinking along those lines?"

Jack closed his eyes and sighed. He rubbed his hand over his face and then met Pete's eyes. "You're my partner and my best friend Pete. I'm not going to lie to you. Wouldn't get away with it if I tried. So, honestly? I can hardly think of anything else!"

Pete's face broke into a huge grin. "I knew you had it bad, but marriage?"

"You know, before I met Emma, my response to hearing that someone was getting married was pretty much the same as hers was just now—what do they want to do that for? But now, man, now all I can think about is making her my wife, coming home to her at night, building a life together, maybe having a couple of kids. Can you imagine a baby girl with her blond hair and green eyes? A little boy...." He stopped short and looked at Pete. "So, now you know."

"So what are you going to do?"

Jack shook his head. "I'm open to suggestions. I thought I had my work cut out for me already, given what she went through before, but now it seems that I also have to convince her that marriage is something she should consider." He looked up as Emma and Missy came back, "Wish me luck, Bro. I think I'm going to need it."

Pete slapped his back, "I'll do all I can."

"What are you two up to?" asked Emma.

Jack grabbed her hand and pulled her back into his lap. "Talking business," he said. "I have a pretty big problem I need to work on and Pete is helping me figure it out."

She smiled at him and planted a kiss on his lips. "I'm sure you'll work it out, you're a very talented man, and really, if you and Pete are both on the case I can't imagine there is any problem that could ever be too much for the two of you to solve."

Jack caught Pete's eye as he smiled at her. "I hope you're right, baby. I really hope you're right."

Chapter Twenty-One

The late afternoon sun danced on the lake as Emma and Jack sat out on the beach.

"It was a good weekend."

"It was," Jack agreed.

They'd had brunch at the grill with everyone this morning, then Jack and Dan had gone off together, which Emma had been pleased to see. Now everyone was returning to their lives, ready for another work week. She was glad that for her that would mean sitting out on the deck, tapping out the story in her head that was now impatient to be told. Jack put an arm around her shoulders, sending a thrill through her as it always did. She leaned her head on his shoulder and sighed, content.

"Can I ask you something, Mouse?"

She nodded.

"Last night, when you heard your friend was getting married, you didn't seem too pleased for her."

Emma snorted. "Why would I be? The poor girl doesn't know what she's letting herself in for!"

"And what's that?"

"Misery! Jack, the whole thing is horrible!"

"Is it really, Em?" He turned her to face him. "Wouldn't you say you're biased?"

She frowned. "Of course I am. I've been married remember?"

"How could I forget?" he asked, through gritted teeth.

"What does that mean?" She was getting a little agitated now, sitting up.

He drew her back down to his shoulder, trying to soothe her. "Baby, it makes me sad that you dismiss marriage as a whole because of what that man did to you."

"That's the one thing I'm grateful to that man for! He opened my eyes to it all. We women tend to have an unrealistic view of the whole marriage deal and that view doesn't match what men want from it at all. Take Nessa last night. There she is, showing off her ring. To her it's a symbol of love, but to the great bumbling idiot sitting next to her it's a symbol to tell other men to keep their hands off—this one is taken, guys. It's also a status symbol; women think the bigger the diamond, the more he loves her. Men think the bigger the diamond, the more people will think of him as successful, that he can afford it. And do you know what else pisses me off?" she continued, gathering steam now. "He's not wearing an engagement ring to let the world know, to mark him as hers. I bet he won't even wear a wedding ring. Most men don't you know. You see, marriage means the woman is off the market, but not the man. Still, we women do check for a ring, because we respect it when it's there. I'm sure that's why men don't wear them. Even when I first met you, I surprised myself because, before we had even gotten up off the floor, I had checked your left hand for a wedding band! And that woman? Last night? In the bar with you? She checked your left hand before she came to talk to you—I saw her!" She finally ran out of steam and sat staring at him.

"Finished?"

"Yes, sorry."

"No need to be. I wanted to know what you thought. You sure told me."

"Well, marriage is not a good thing."

"Baby, can you maybe see that marriage is only as good or bad as two people make it? You were with a bad man, so that marriage could never have been anything but bad." He waited, but she said nothing. "But when you have two good people together, who both want it and are both prepared to work at it, marriage could be the best thing to happen to a person." He turned her to face him again and looked into her eyes. "Emma, I'm a good man."

Her eyes darted around his face, a tiny line creasing between her brows. "What...what are you saying, Jack?"

"I'm saying I love you, Emma."

Tears welled in her eyes and he held her close, hoping he hadn't done the wrong thing.

She lifted her head. "Jack...I...."

"It's okay. You don't need to say anything. I just need you to know."

He kissed her slowly, owning her with his mouth, relieved to feel her respond. He stood silently and offered her his hand. When she took it he led her up to the house, up to the bedroom. Still without a word he lifted her onto the bed and undressed her, slowly, gently. Once they were both naked he positioned himself above her, kissing her until she writhed underneath him, panting and thrusting her hips up, needing him to be inside her. He lifted his head and, holding her eyes with his own, entered her with one deep thrust. She gasped as he filled her and he held himself back as she came, loving the way he could take her there so easily. When she opened her eyes he held her gaze and thrust deep again, setting up an insistent rhythm, all the while looking deep into her eyes, trying to convey to her with his mind and his body all that those three little words were too small to say. As she began to tighten around him he told her again, "I love you, Emma," then he let her carry him away as they came together, soaring to a place he'd never been, a place where only she could take him on a tide of pure ecstasy. When they came back to their senses he gathered her in his arms and held on, hoping that he was holding on to the rest of his life.

Emma couldn't keep her mind on her writing. Jack had gone to meet with the crew who would soon be starting work on the construction of Pete's house. They'd made love all night long, drifting off to sleep then finding each other again, coming together in a union like nothing she'd ever experienced. He'd shown her the truth of his words, of his heart, with his body. She'd clung to him as he'd taken her over and over again, uttering his love, giving her his love and asking for nothing. She'd tried to speak, still not knowing what to say, but needing to say something to this wonderful man as he gave her his heart. She sighed as she remembered his eyes full of love as he'd placed a finger to her lips and then kissed away the words that wouldn't come.

He loved her? He loved her! One part of her wanted to dance and sing and tell the world. Another part sat back, watching cynically. Rob said he loved you too. You believed him, look how that worked out. But this was Jack, and Jack was a good man. Funny, protective, so charismatic and so darned sexy! She sighed again at all the things that made so many women want him. But he only wanted her, he'd told her that. Did she love him? Her heart pounded at the question. What was the point in even asking it? What would it mean if she did? In her experience love only led to pain and loss. She didn't think she could stand to go through that again. Staring out at the lake she admitted to herself that, despite all of that, despite all the reasons that she couldn't, yes she did love him. She didn't have to let that mean she would put herself in a position to get hurt, but no matter how hard she tried to avoid it, she had fallen in love with the man.

They'd eaten a quiet dinner on the deck. Jack seemed to be trying to keep everything light and upbeat tonight.

"Want to go pebble hunting?" he asked.

Emma smiled. "Why not."

She loved to walk the shoreline looking for pretty stones, and she found it so endearing that Jack shared this simple pleasure. They walked in the fading light, each with quite a collection of stones.

"Do you think we've got enough?" she asked.

He grinned at her. "Let's find one more special one each, then we can sit on the deck and go through our treasure."

She laughed. "You really are a big kid sometimes, you know."

"I know, but little treasures can be the most important things in life."

She laughed again, touched by his sentimentality but a little afraid to show how much. "Whatever you say, Mr. Benson."

They continued their walk, scanning the shoreline. A few minutes later she spotted a beautiful rose quartz glistening at the water's edge. Jack had spotted it in the same moment and their hands met as they both reached for it, laughing. He let her take it and she held it up in the last glow of the sunset.

"Isn't it beautiful, Jack?"

"It's perfect. Told you we'd find one last special one and that's the one we were looking for."

"Come on then, let's go back up. You light the torches and I'll get the wine."

Once they were settled on the deck they went through their haul. Emma laid out her finds on one side of the table and Jack placed his on the other. She placed the last one in the middle. They had some larger stones that Emma placed on the rail around the deck.

"Here," she said, "we can decorate with them."

"What about these?" Jack held out a handful of smaller pebbles.

"Ooh, I know." She went inside and returned with a couple of round, goldfish bowl vases. "We can collect and decorate." She scooped most of the pebbles into the vases.

Jack spread out a few of the smaller stones on the table. "Which do you like best?""

She touched the one in the middle of the table, the one they had found together. "This one, it's beautiful."

He smiled at her. "It is and it's ours; not in my pile, not in your pile."

"Yes, it's ours, it's special." She was still surprised that he would be so sentimental over a pebble.

"Would you mind very much if I hang on to it?" he asked.

"Of course not." She watched amused as he pulled his wallet from his back pocket and carefully stored the little stone inside a zippered section, his big hands surprisingly delicate.

He met her eyes and laughed with a shrug. "You already told me I'm a big kid, and that's precious treasure."

"Whatever you say."

He grinned. "Then I say come here and kiss me, woman." He stood and held his arms out to her and Emma happily did as he said.

~ ~ ~

"I can take everything to Gramps' house Saturday morning," said Ben.

Emma had come into town to pick up a few groceries and was having a quick coffee with Ben before she headed home.

"That would be great, if you don't mind. I'm really hoping to get back on Friday night, but if I do have to stay over it will be a rush on Saturday to drive back and get everything sorted in time."

"Don't sweat it, Mouse. I can cover it."

"Thanks. You know, I'm really looking forward to it."

"Me too. Be nice to see the old guys having fun, and I've laid on extra cover at the resort for the day, so I shouldn't have to run back here."

They were planning an afternoon and evening cookout at Gramps' place. The two men had lived around the lake all of their long lives. Both were well known and liked within the community.

"I reckon we'll have a really good turnout," said Ben, "And the band are really looking forward to it, it's something a bit different for them."

"I'll bet it is. Are you keeping them for the season after all?"

"Yeah, they're a good fit at the resort and they're good guys, too. I think you'll like them."

"Well, maybe we should have them up to North Cove one night for dinner with everyone, introduce them around."

"That'd be great, let me know when."

"Let's get Saturday taken care of then we'll see. For now though, I'd better get going. I've got an early start tomorrow."

"Okay, Mouse. Call me and let me know when you're coming back so we can sort the details."

"Will do." She hugged Ben and headed back to her car.

~ ~ ~

At home she found a note from Jack taped to the screen door.

Dinner at my place tonight?

xXx

She smiled. He was determined to cook for her in that motor coach. She called his cell.

"Hey baby."

"Hey you."

"So, will you have dinner over here with me?"

"If you really want me to. You know I have to leave early in the morning."

"I know. I thought maybe you could stay here tonight. Pack your bag before you come?"

"I could," she said, a little surprised. She'd grown used to Jack staying at the house with her.

"Go on. Live a little. Come and camp out with me."

She laughed, thinking of the luxury coach. "Okay then, I suppose I can rough it with you for one night."

"Excellent! See you in a little while then."

"Bye."

When she arrived at the RV, Jack was sitting on the step talking on his cell phone. He smiled up at her.

"Yes, like I told you. No, the second one." He listened a moment then looked up at her again. She tried not to think that his eyes looked wary, but they certainly seemed to.

"I can't.

No, I can't right now," this time a little more forcefully.

"No.

Yes." Now he seemed agitated, quite unlike him.

"Look, we'll discuss this tomorrow.

I told you, I can't right now."

Emma started to feel a little uncomfortable. She started to walk down toward the beach, not wanting to intrude on what appeared to be a private conversation.

"Look, I've got to go. I'll call you in the morning, bye."

He came after her. "Sorry about that." He bent to kiss her.

She gave him a quick peck then stepped away, feeling a little tense. "Sorry, I didn't mean to interrupt you."

"Oh, that? That was nothing." He ran his fingers through his hair, a gesture she'd come to recognize when he was uncomfortable.

"Is everything okay?"

"Everything's fine." He didn't meet her eye. "Come on in and see what I'm making us." He reached for her hand and she decided it best to leave it at that. She was no doubt being silly again, right?

Inside, the RV smelled wonderful. "Chili?"

"Yes, ma'am," he drawled, "a big ole Texas chili for my lil lady."

She laughed, starting to relax. "I may have to rope you in to making some for Saturday. Gramps loves a good chili."

"Consider it done. I'd love to make him some. It'd be nice to contribute to his party."

"You're on then. As much as you can make, there will be a lot of people to feed."

"Your wish is my command, purdy lady." He made her laugh with his deep Texan drawl.

"I forget most of the time that's where you're from."

He smiled. "So do I, these days. Want some wine?"

"I'd love some of that Merlot you brought the other day."

"Coming right up."

"Could I run through to the bathroom?" she started toward the back of the coach, but he blocked her way.

"Give me two minutes, would you? It's a bit messy back there, I need to tidy up. You arrived a little earlier than I expected, sorry." He went into the master bedroom and closed the door behind him.

What on Earth was he playing at? She'd never known him make any kind of mess, or be untidy in any way. He was meticulously neat. Even here in the kitchen where he'd been cooking, you couldn't tell because he cleaned as he went. But apparently he had something to hide in his bedroom.

Emma frowned, she didn't like this. She remembered there was another bathroom anyway. She stepped inside and closed the door. Don't get worked up, she told herself. It's not like he's Rob, trying to explain stray earrings in the bed. She shuddered at the memory. This is Jack. He loves you, remember? Hearing his deep voice echo in her mind, "I love you, Emma," she smiled. If he was hiding anything back there it was probably another surprise for her.

She emerged from the bathroom to find him back in the kitchen, stirring the chili.

"Sorry about that," he didn't look up.

"That's okay. I used the other one. Are you sure everything's all right?"

He finally met her eye and gave her the smile she now knew so well. "Yeah, baby. I'd be better with a hug, though."

She wrapped her arms around him and held him close, surprised to feel his heart pounding. He bent his head to kiss her and soon any questions left her mind along with everything else except the feel of his lips on hers.

~ ~ ~

"Gramps will absolutely love this," she said after they'd eaten the chili. "It's wonderful."

"Then I'll be more than happy to make him some. I know Dan will love it, too. I used to make it all the time when we were kids."

She raised an eyebrow. "You cooked as a kid?"

"Yeah," he shrugged, not offering anything further. "Anyway, do you want to watch a movie tonight?"

She looked at him. This was something different.

"Honestly? It's an excuse to get you to come lie on that big bed with me."

That was more likely.

"See, I'll have to spend the next two nights alone in there."
He gave her the puppy dog eyes and she melted.

"I'll try to get back for Friday night."

"Even so. I wanted you to stay here with me tonight so
that while you're gone, I can smell you on the pillows and
remember you in that bed with me."

"You are a big softie!"

He shrugged, "Only when it comes to you, baby. So what
do you say? I'm beat and I think it'd be kinda nice to spend an
evening lying around with you." He let his eyes trail over her,
"Maybe make out?"

Emma could think of nothing she would like more.

In the bedroom he'd made a mountain of pillows on the
huge bed.

"How about you get comfy and pick us out a movie while I
fix us some dessert?"

He returned with a bowl of fresh strawberries and a bowl
of melted chocolate.

"Oh my!"

"You like?"

"I like."

He dipped a strawberry and fed it to her.

"Oh, Jack that's wonderful."

"See, I may not bake, but I can still do desserts."

"You certainly can." She dipped another and popped it into
his mouth. He caught her hand and licked a drop of chocolate
from her wrist, sending shivers all though her.

"Ooh, this could get messy," she laughed.

"I'm hoping so."

He dipped a finger into the chocolate and dabbed it onto
her lips. Holding her eyes, he licked it away then nibbled on

her lower lip before he slowly explored her mouth with his own. Emma felt the now familiar ache for him between her legs, her breasts tingling, hopeful for his touch. She was so glad she hadn't freaked out over that phone call earlier and his mad dash back here had probably been simply to pile up the pillows. She wouldn't have wanted to miss out on this, on having Jack, strawberries and melted chocolate all in the same bed with the whole night ahead of them. She tangled her fingers in his hair as he kissed her and when they finally came up for air she couldn't deny that it was love in those gorgeous eyes that were looking at her. Nor could she deny that she loved him right back. It scared her; she had no idea what to do with it, but she loved him with all her heart and soul.

"What is it, Em?"

"Nothing." How could she speak those words to him when she didn't know what they could mean?

"Okay then."

He fed her another strawberry, a little frown on his face. But she knew how to distract him by now. She slid her hands inside his shirt and stroked his abs, loving the way the hard muscles trembled at her touch. A look of lust replaced his frown. She removed his shirt, smiling at him mischievously. She dipped a finger in the warm chocolate and coated his nipples, then delicately lapped them clean with her tongue.

"Oh my God, Emma," he groaned, reaching for her, eager to return the favor.

She pulled away and smiled at him. "You're beat, remember? And you made dinner. I think perhaps you should lay back and let me work tonight."

She wanted to make this about his pleasure as he always did for her. He'd been so gentle and understanding in loving her.

She may not be able to say the words he wanted to hear, but she knew she could show him with her body. She stood and undressed before him, loving the way he devoured her with his eyes. He reached for her again, but she pushed him back down on the pillows.

"Lie back and relax."

She covered his nipples with the chocolate again and as her tongue licked him clean her hands unfastened his belt and jeans. Even as he kicked them off she took hold of him and began to stroke gently as she kissed her way down his stomach. She dabbed some chocolate on the very tip of him. He gave a low growl as she flicked her tongue over him.

"Mm, tastes good." She kept up her stroking as she took him into her mouth. He tensed and lay completely still.

"Em, stop. I don't want...."

Keeping her mouth close to him so the breath of her words fanned him, she smiled up at him. "I do want, Jack. I want chocolate." She smeared it all over him, amazed as he grew even bigger and harder in her hand. She gently sucked at the end of him, "And I want this. Anyway, this is between me and him," his cock surged in her hand, "and he doesn't want me to stop, do you?"

She addressed the question to his erection and returned to her task of cleaning away the chocolate with her tongue. Jack moaned and lay back. She felt him relax, pleased he was giving in to her. She held him in both hands and trailed her tongue up him over and over again.

His hands tangled in her hair, "Oh God, Emma!" His voice cracked on her name as she took him deep in her throat and swirled her tongue over him. She raised her gaze to see him and their eyes locked as he thrust his hips up. Again she felt totally empowered as she commanded his release and he gave in, letting her carry him away as he cried out her name and his love. When she came back up beside him, his chest was still heaving. He wrapped her in his arms. "Oh my God, Emma!"

"You like?" she smiled, pleased with herself.

"I more than like!" He nuzzled his lips to her neck and his fingers found her heat. "Will you ride me, baby?" he pulled her on top of him. "Let me do the work this time?"

"You sure you want me up here then?"

"I want you right there." He sat up against the pillows, carrying her with him. Bringing his knees up behind her he brought her face to face with him. "Hi," he smiled.

"Hello." As she sat astride him he kissed her long and hard, filling his hands with her breasts, making her moan though the kisses, amazing her by how quickly she could feel him grow hard again. Without leaving her lips he stroked his hands down to her hips and lifted her, ready to receive him.

"Lean back on me, baby."

She leaned back against his legs and gasped as he thrust up inside her. In this position he was deeper than he'd ever been. She marveled again at the size of him. He held her hip with one hand, steadying her to receive his thrusts, while with his other hand he sought her heat, stroking the sensitive flesh even as she stretched around him. At the pressure of his thumb against the bud of her arousal, she felt the heat tear through her as she came. He'd hardly gotten started as she rode the sensations that carried her away. As soon as she opened her eyes she found him smiling at her and his fingers returned to their work. She couldn't believe she was so close again already as he circled his thumb.

"Jack," she moaned as he carried her stroke by stroke through her second orgasm.

When she returned to earth he was still smiling at her.

"Come with me, baby?"

"I don't know if I can."

"You can." His eyes were filled with a mixture of lust, love and determination as he placed both hands on her hips and pulled her down to receive his thrusts. She felt him pulsating inside her, growing hotter and harder at every stroke. The intensity of his emotion and the sheer size of him made her feel as though he filled every fiber of her being. He moaned and she felt him explode inside her, and every fiber exploded with him as he swept her away through a third mind-blowing, soul-stealing orgasm. As she collapsed onto his chest his arms came around her once more.

"I love you, Emma."

"I love you, Jack."

The words came straight from her heart before her mind had chance to censor them. She tensed, immediately regretting that she'd spoken them out loud. Jack flipped her over and lay on top of her, brown eyes shining happily.

"Run that by me one more time?"

She sighed; there was no point denying it. "I love you, Jack."

He kissed her long and deep. "You've made me the happiest man alive."

"Jack, don't get carried away. I didn't mean to say it."

He looked down at her, smile gone. "You're not saying you don't love me?"

She shook her head.

"No, you're not or no, you don't?"

"No, I'm not."

His smile returned. "Then nothing else matters."

"But, Jack, I don't know what I can do with it."

"What do you want to do with it?"

"Right now I want to run and hide, it scares me so much!"

"But you haven't run yet, Em. You're still here. You came to me," he grinned, "came for me, came with me. Told me you love me and you haven't run away!"

She couldn't help but smile at the triumphant look on his face. "I can't exactly run. I don't know if you've noticed, but I have two hundred pounds of man lying on top of me."

He looked down and laughed, pretending surprise. "Why, yes you do. Isn't that handy?" He made no effort to move. "Baby, you don't have to know what to do with it. That's how love works, we can figure it out together. Just relax. Keep giving me the chance to show you that I'm for real. Show you all that we could share?"

She nodded.

"You have to know how happy it makes me?"

She nodded again.

"Tell me one more time?" he asked, eyes crinkling in that sexy grin.

She wrapped her arms around him and looked into his eyes. "I love you, Jack."

"And I love you, baby."

Chapter Twenty-Two

"Do you really have to go?"

They'd had breakfast and Emma was getting her things together, ready to head to the city.

"You know I do. Can't you come too?"

He thought about it for a moment. He could probably see Meyers next week, but he needed to finish last night's phone call with Laura. He needed to get over to the mall where he had some important shopping to do, too. Could he do that in the city if he went with Emma?

"It's okay," she said, "I know you've got work to do, probably best not. I'll try my hardest to get back tomorrow, but really I think I will have to stay till Saturday morning."

"And condemn me to two nights alone, in this thing?" he joked.

"You'll survive."

"I suppose." He pulled her close for a lingering kiss. "You drive safely, my little Mouse, and hurry back to me."

"I will."

He walked her out to her car. He wanted her to tell him again that she loved him, but he didn't want to say it first just so that she would respond in kind. He still couldn't quite believe that she'd come so far so soon. Although he knew he still had an uphill climb ahead, he felt that it was all possible now. It would just take time and patience on his part.

She put her bag in the car and kissed him one last time. Her green eyes met his. "I do love you, Jack."

"And I love you, baby. With all my heart."

As he watched her drive away he smiled to himself. This was going better than he'd dared to hope. While she was gone he had some important business to take care of. He pulled his cell phone from his back pocket.

"Laura? Hey sweetie. Sorry about last night. Yeah, Emma showed up earlier than I expected."

After talking to Laura he decided to go and see Gramps before he did anything else. If this was going to work it was really important that the old guy be on his side. After that he should still have time to get to the mall and back before his meeting with Meyers.

He found Gramps sitting out on his front porch, drinking coffee and eating doughnuts.

"Want to join me, son?"

"I'd love to."

Gramps brought him out a coffee, "Help yourself," he said nodding toward the doughnuts.

Jack smiled, "Thanks, but I think I'll pass. After last week those things have lost their appeal."

Gramps grinned at him. "Yeah, but it all worked out, eh son?"

"It did. And in big part thanks to you. I've been wanting to thank you."

Gramps tapped the side of his nose with his finger. "Say no more."

Jack smiled gratefully, glad he didn't have to spell it out, though he had been fully prepared to.

"So, what brings you out here? Has she gone into hiding again?"

"No, sir. She's gone down to the city, but she's not hiding. She's doing her very best to face her fears and give me a chance."

"That's good to hear. So what's the question? I can see plain as day you've got one and it's a big 'un, ain't it?"

Jack nodded; only the biggest question of his whole life. He looked the old man in the eye. "Sir, I've come to ask your permission to ask her to marry me."

Gramps smirk faded and he looked away. Jack's heart sank. Surely he wasn't going to say no?

"Jack, you're a fine man. I like you, I think you know that."

Jack nodded, not sure he wanted to hear the 'but' that he knew was coming.

"Nothing would please me better than to see you marry the girl." He smiled at the thought. "That sure would make an old man happy, but I'm guessing you haven't heard her thoughts on marriage?"

"I have."

"And yer still asking my permission?"

"She's blaming marriage for what Rob did. A marriage is defined by the two people that make it. For Emma and me it would be great."

"I don't disagree with you, son. I know the truth of what you're saying. Hell, I lived it for forty-five years, a wonderful marriage with a wonderful woman. I just don't know that you can convince Emma of the truth of it."

Jack sighed, "I don't know that I can either, but I'll die trying. I guess that's what I want your permission and your blessing, to do."

"That's the easy part. You can have them by the bucket load." He patted Jack on the back. "I'm guessing a man like you would have a plan. What have you got in mind?"

Jack told him what he was planning and when he'd finished, Gramps sat smiling. "You're a smart one, son. How could any woman say no?" His eyes darkened. "If any woman could though, it's Em."

"I know, but I have to try."

"Well, I'm with you all the way. I'll help any way I can."

"Thank you."

"No, son. Thank you. I'm not going to be around forever. It's been weighing on me heavy that when I'm gone she'll have no one left. I mean, she's got the gang and they'll always be there for her, but no one of her own. No one who will love her and look out for her like I do, like you do."

"I just hope she'll let me."

Emma had spent the afternoon with Carla in a totally non-productive meeting about a movie she knew would never get off the ground. Why, oh why, had she even agreed to come? Old habits were hard to break, she supposed. When Carla set up a meeting, she came running, even though all she really wanted these days was to be left to write her novel, up at the lake – with Jack. She hoped tomorrow's session helping Brad go through his spec script would prove to be more worthwhile.

As she let herself into her apartment she felt as though she'd been away from it for months, not just a couple of weeks. She was so grateful to Holly for keeping an eye on the place for her. Her friend had left a note propped on the kitchen counter.

Call me when you get in – if you're not too tired. Holly x

She picked up the phone.

"Hey, how are you?"

"I'm great. I got done early with Carla so I'm home already. Do you want to come over for dinner?"

"Of course I do. I'll take your cooking over mine any day of the week."

"Come on over as soon as you're ready. I'll get to work."

She ran to the grocery store on the corner, another of the reasons she loved her apartment. She picked up some chicken breasts and everything else she would need and was home again within fifteen minutes. As she chopped mushrooms her cell phone rang. Jack.

"Hey you!"

"Hey baby. How did your day go?"

She told him about the meeting with Carla. "It was a big waste of time really."

"Well, I'm glad she didn't offer you some tempting project to drag you back to the city for any longer than this. One night is enough."

"Two, remember?" She was still hoping to leave tomorrow evening, but she didn't want to say so in case her work with Brad ran on.

"Two then, but I know you'll be back for sure on Saturday."

"I will. How about you, how did your day go?"

"Oh, I've been real busy. I got lots of important business taken care of," he sounded very pleased with himself.

The doorbell rang. "Hold on. Holly's at the door." She let her friend in.

"I'll let you go then, babe. Say hi to Holly for me. Can I call you tomorrow?"

"Yes, please."

"Okay, I love you, babe."

"I love you too, Jack." As Emma hung up Holly's face was a picture. "Did I really just hear you say that?"

Emma nodded.

"Well, what the...? Less than a week ago you were convinced he'd only wanted you for the sex and had then done a runner."

"I know, I know. But then a dear friend of mine gave me a severe talking to and told me to grow up. I've been working on doing that and this is the result. Thank you."

Holly gave her a big hug. "You are most welcome. I can't believe that our little chat led to this. Want to tell me all about it?"

"There's not really much to tell, Holly. Other than I am scared to death. Almost every instinct I have is telling me to run like crazy, as far and as fast as I can away from him. But part of me wants to run to him. At the moment that part is winning, but I don't know for how long."

"Well, good for you, girl. I can't wait to meet him."

"Hm, about getting you up there. I would like to get back tomorrow if I can get done early enough."

"I can drive myself then, early Saturday morning. I really do need to work on that."

"Yes, you do, but not this weekend. I fixed you up with a ride, just in case."

"A ride?"

"Yes, Pete is happy to bring you with him if I have to leave early."

"Emma!"

"What? It makes all kinds of sense. I can get back to Jack and you two can get to know each other on the way up."

"I've never met the guy."

"You'll love him. He's great company."

"Perhaps so, but you don't want the first time you meet a person to be on a four-hour road trip!"

"It'll be fine. He really doesn't mind. He's glad to help me out."

"And what if I mind? Does he know you're trying to set us up?"

Emma grinned. "He has no clue!"

"Oh, Em!"

"Say you will? Of course, if you really don't want to then I can leave Jack all alone for another night and stay until Saturday, just so that I can take you."

Holly laughed. "Great, you don't give me much choice, do you?"

"Is that a yes?"

"That's a yes, but I'm not happy about it."

"Oh, you will be. Seriously, Pete is great fun, a really nice guy. There are so few of us real people in this town, we have to stick together."

"Well, I guess that's true."

"I already gave him your number so he can call and arrange to pick you up, though there's still a chance that you'll be coming with me if I can't get out of here tomorrow."

"Okay, whatever works."

By three o'clock on Friday Emma was still waiting for Brad to finish his script meeting and get back to her. It looked like she'd be here for the night. She'd have to pass the Phoenix building on her way to Brad's so she decided to stop by and see Pete. At least she'd be closer by the time Brad was free. As she pulled into the visitor spaces at the front of the building, her cell phone rang.

"Hey you."

"Hey baby."

She looked at the parking space a few yards away. J. Benson C.O.O. "You have great timing, I just pulled up next to your parking space."

"You did?"

"Yes, I'm still running around and I'm stopping in to see Pete."

"Why don't you park in my space then? What's mine is yours."

"Hold on, I might just do that." She smiled, surprised at how much she liked the idea. She backed up and then pulled the car into his slot. "There, now I'm invading your space."

"See, I can take care of you even when I'm not there. Hey, if you're going in anyway, would you mind stopping by to see Lexi? She was going to give some files to Pete for me, but you could get them, if you wouldn't mind?"

"Of course." She was curious to meet his secretary, hoping that she wasn't one of the leggy brunette beauties he seemed to attract. How many men had something going on with their secretary? She stopped herself before she could get carried away. "I don't mind at all."

"Will you be back tonight?"

"I don't think so, I haven't even gotten to see Brad yet."

"Too bad." He sounded disappointed.

"I know. I'm sorry. How about I come straight to you in the morning, say hello before my crazy day begins?"

"Yeah, do that," he heaved an exaggerated sigh, "it'll give me something to look forward to as I spend another night all by myself in that big old coach, lonely and alone."

She laughed. "Isn't Dan arriving tonight? You could go into town and see him. I'm sure Missy would be glad to see you, and Ben for that matter."

"I might do that."

"Well, I'll be back early anyway."

"Okay, baby. I'll see you in the morning. Hurry home to me."

"Bye, Jack."

Judy looked up as she walked in. "Oh, hi Emma. Does he know you're coming?"

"No, I thought I'd just stop in. Is he busy?"

"He's got someone with him, but they should be done in ten minutes, and then he's free till four fifteen."

"I'll wait then if that's all right. Actually, could you tell me where Lexi's office is? Jack asked me to pick up some files from her."

"I can do better than tell you," smiled Judy, "I'll walk you over. How is Jack? We haven't seen him in a couple of weeks."

Emma wondered if Judy knew about her and Jack. She'd known Pete's secretary for years, liked her, yet now she felt a little uncomfortable, not knowing quite what to say. "He seems to be getting a lot done with Pete's place."

"Oh good."

Well, what else was she supposed to say? That he looked much more relaxed up there? That the fresh air and beautiful scenery seemed to suit him? That, considering all the great sex she was providing him with, he was doing very well, thank you? She blushed as they walked down the corridor where the plush carpet and wood paneling made her think of an exclusive club. She'd always thought that about Pete's office, but now she realized it was Jack's office too. The place he spent his days, working with Pete.

They arrived at a door, "Here we are then," said Judy as she knocked and went in. A woman, in her early fifties, Emma guessed, was talking on the phone. "I'd better get back," said Judy. "I'll see you in a little while." She showed Emma to a large chair and left.

The woman finished the call and came around her desk, beaming. "So you're the beautiful Emma! So nice to meet you, honey!"

The force of her friendly Texan drawl surprised Emma. She smiled back, a little uncertain.

"Oh, he just called, said you'd be coming." Lexi had curly red hair and bright blue eyes. Emma liked her immediately. "Would you mind if I give you a big old hug, honey?" She'd wrapped her arms around her before Emma had chance to reply. The hug felt like coming home, and Emma found herself hugging right back, feeling tears prick behind her eyes as she wondered what it would have been like to have grown up knowing a mother's hugs. She didn't have time to pursue sad thoughts though. Lexi was so warm and bubbly.

"The man is crazy about you, hon."

Emma blushed again, wishing she could control the blood that infused her face so often since she'd met Jack.

"Look at you! Blushing like a schoolgirl, aren't you just the sweetest thing!"

"I, um...." She was completely thrown. She'd had visions of some tall, smoky beauty, eyeing her coolly, and instead here she was with this welcoming motherly figure doting on her.

"Oh, don't you mind me. I'm a bit much for some folk."

"Oh, no," said Emma, "It's not that, it's just...."

"I'm not what you were expecting, right? You thought his secretary might be one of those stick insects." She laughed, a sound so infectious that Emma joined her, shaking her head.

"Don't tell him, but yes, I was a little nervous to meet you."

"Don't you worry that pretty little head of yours. Like I said, the man is crazy about you. In all my years I've never known him to be like this. And honey, we go back a long ways, me and Jack. His momma's my best friend—we went to school together—and I've done Jack's books for him since before he was old enough to file. When he was setting up Phoenix with Pete, he brought me with him. I was worried about him for a while there, we were buzzing around in that plane of his so much—Houston, Miami, New York—I didn't know my tail from my elbow, and he was burning out fast. Pete thought getting him to LA might fix him, but you know, even though it's not been so crazy since we set down here, this city isn't a good fit for him." She smiled, nodding at Emma. "But these last few weeks, he's doing much better, and that's all down to you."

"I think being out at the lake is really suiting him." Emma pictured him walking on the beach, relaxed and smiling, the tension gone from his face.

"I think being with you is what's suiting him. He's laughing again, back to being a big old goofball. I was starting to think he'd gone and grown up on me, but now he's happy."

Emma smiled, touched, though a little overwhelmed, by Lexi's forthright approach. "Well, we have been having fun."

Lexi frowned. "He's got a whole lot more than just fun on his mind honey, what are you scared of?"

Emma was shocked to be asked outright like that. She looked down at her nails then up at Lexi, who watched her with a reassuring smile. "Sorry, I told you I can be a bit much. It's none of my business, I guess I'm getting a little carried away. Don't let me scare you off. Here," she picked up a bunch of files from her desk, "these are what he's after." She gave Emma another hug. "I'll be seeing you again, Miss Emma, and you can call me any time you want."

"Thank you, it's so lovely to meet you."

"You too, hon, you too."

Emma started towards the door.

"Hang on." Lexi took a business card from her desk and wrote her number on the back. "I'm guessing you know the office number well enough, but that's my cell on the back, and you can bet your tail I've never given that to none of those stick insects!" She laughed. "And don't be so scared. If you ask me it's him as is most likely to get his heart broken, and I'm hoping that won't happen. You take care now and don't forget, call me any time."

Emma walked back to Pete's office, trying to process her meeting with Lexi. She was certainly a larger than life personality. She liked her immensely, and it seemed Jack had told her at least some of what was going on between them.

"What is going on between us?" she wondered. "Whatever it is, it's good. Just leave it at that for now."

She turned over the business card. And now she had a new ally, that could only be a good thing, right?

"Mouse!" Pete grinned as she arrived back at his office. "Didn't expect to see you today."

"Well, I was in the neighborhood and it's been too long, I haven't seen you since Sunday," she laughed.

He nodded at the files she was carrying. "And he's got you running errands for him now, I see."

"He asked me to pick them up since I was here."

"Good, saves me having to remember."

"I met Lexi."

"Don't worry about her, her bark is worse than her bite."

"I can't imagine her barking or biting. Are we talking about the same person? That bubbly Texan lady who kept hugging me?"

Pete laughed. "She likes you then."

"It would seem so. You mean she's not always like that?"

Pete looked a little uncomfortable.

"What?"

"Well, she's kind of like, you know, the gatekeeper. Or in her case, Jack's guard dog!"

"Oh," realization dawned, "you mean she's usually fending his girlfriends off, not being nice to them?"

"Oh, Mouse, I didn't mean it like that, don't get...."

"It's all right, Pete, really. I'm trying very hard to be more mature about these things. Of course he's had other girlfriends," she smiled, "Lexi called them stick insects."

Pete laughed at that.

"I have to deal with the positives. Lexi is lovely and she likes me. And, for the time being at least, Jack doesn't have other girlfriends, because he's with me."

"Wow! You are getting grown up, Mouse. I'm impressed."

"Me too. It's not easy, but I'm working on it."

"Well, good for you, and you picked the right guy. You have to know he'd never mess around on you?"

"I hope you're right, Pete. I don't think I could handle that."

"You've got nothing to worry about there, Em."

At that moment, Emma's phone rang. She put the files down and checked the display, "Would you excuse me a minute, Pete?"

"Sure, use the meeting room if you like."

Emma stepped through the double doors. "Hey, Brad, are you all done?"

"I'm so sorry, Em. They're picking me to pieces. I don't think I'll see daylight for another century at this rate."

"Oh, okay."

"Is it a problem?"

"No, of course not. No problem. Call me Monday then?"

"You mean if the script police let me out of here by then?"

"Well, I'm sure they'll come around. Try to have a good weekend, okay?"

"Thanks, Em. You too, I'll be in touch."

She hung up, slightly stunned to realize she didn't have any more plans for the day. Looking around, she realized she was standing in the spot where she'd knocked Jack over. She smiled, remembering the feel of his arm around her and her first look into his deep brown eyes. And now she got to go home to him! She stepped back into Pete's office.

"My meeting just canceled."

"You don't look disappointed."

"Because, if you really don't mind bringing Holly, this means I can go home now."

"You know I don't mind. I'll call her when I get done here."

"Thanks Pete, you're the best."

He smiled, "Anything for you, Em." He checked his watch, "If you get going now you might still catch dinner with lover boy."

She grinned back at him. "You don't need to tell me twice," she hugged him. "I'm off. I'll see you in the morning."

He laughed as she hurried to the door. "Yeah, see you then. You drive safe though, no speeding tickets, okay?"

"Yes, Boss!"

Chapter Twenty-Three

After she'd left the worst of the traffic behind, Emma called Holly.

"Hey sweetie."

"Hey, I'm sorry, but I'm leaving tonight."

"No problem. I kind of knew you would. I'll bet Jack's pleased."

"I haven't told him. When I talked to him this afternoon I still thought I'd have to stay and he was teasing me about abandoning him. I'm going to surprise him, tell him he made me feel too guilty to leave him all alone."

Holly laughed, "I'm sure he'll love that."

"I hope so."

"I'll see you tomorrow then."

"Thanks Holly. Pete said he'd call you later about picking you up. Be warned, he usually leaves early."

"Hey, I'm just the hitchhiker. I'll do whatever he says."

"Don't tell him that," laughed Emma, "you'll give him all kinds of ideas!"

"Honestly, Em! Leave it alone. I'll see you tomorrow."

"Bye."

It was almost eight thirty when Emma turned onto North Shore; the traffic out of the city was always worse on Fridays. Her heart did that happy little skitter as she pulled into her driveway. She'd decided to leave the car here and walk down the beach to see Jack at the RV. She'd spent much of the drive up thinking about what she would say, how she could tease him about having to come back to him, just so he wouldn't have to spend the night alone. She really was pleased with herself. She was going along with all of this, not over-thinking everything and instead listening to the part of her that didn't want to run scared. She left her bag in the car, not wanting to waste time taking it inside. She set out down the path to the beach. Looking out at the last of the evening sun she felt so happy.

Then she froze.

At the far end of the beach she saw Jack. He was with a woman. Emma began to shake as she watched them walk side by side at the water's edge, their dark heads close together as they talked. Jack said something and the woman laughed and punched his arm. She was tall and slender with long dark hair—a stick insect! Jack held something out and the woman looked at it and nodded. He laughed. He looked so happy. She saw him shrug and grin that sexy grin. The woman reached up and hugged him and he hugged her right back. He really did look so very happy. Emma's heart was pounding in her ears. No. No. No! She turned and ran for her car. She couldn't stand to see any more.

She drove out onto the unpaved road that led back to the freeway. She had no idea where she was going as she swiped at the tears rolling down her face. How could he? On her beach, *their* beach! Where they'd walked so many times, held hands, collected pebbles. She began to sob as she drove. "Oh, Jack!" She pulled over, no longer able to see the road. She sat there a long time until the sobs subsided. How could he do that to her? Why tell her he loved her? How could she have been so wrong?

She heard Pete's voice, just hours ago saying, "You have to know he'd never mess around on you."

Lexi's voice, "The man is crazy about you."

Jack himself, "Hurry home to me, baby."

Ha! Why, Jack? Because if I'm not quick enough you'll have to find someone else to warm your bed?

Only this afternoon she'd been so taken in by him she'd told Pete he didn't have any other girlfriends. How wrong she'd been. How wrong they'd all been!

It was getting dark. She didn't know what to do. She couldn't sit here all night and she certainly didn't want to go home. She didn't want to risk seeing them again, or risk Jack seeing her. What would he do? Would he try to hide the woman, pretend there was nothing going on? Or would he be like Rob and tell her she was being ridiculous? After all, she'd left him alone for two nights, what did she expect? How she wished she'd called to tell him she was coming back. But, no, then she wouldn't have known. He'd still be keeping this woman secret somewhere. Who was she? Where had she come from? Was she a tourist he'd picked up at the lake, or a girlfriend who had come out to visit him? Whoever she was, she was welcome to him.

It was fully dark now. If she couldn't go home, where could she go? Not to Gramps, he'd know there was something wrong and she didn't want to upset him, especially not tonight, before his party. Missy? No. Dan would be there. Okay, then.

Ben. He had a spare room in his apartment...she could stay there. Then they could get everything ready together in the morning too. She took a deep breath. This would not spoil the party. She wouldn't let it.

She started the car and dialed Ben, her hands still shaking. His voice over the speakers sounded reassuring, so familiar.

"Hey Mouse."

"Hey Ben."

"What time will you be over tomorrow?"

"Would it be okay if I come tonight?"

"Sure, what do you need?"

"A place to stay."

"What's up, Em?"

"I'll tell you when I get there."

"Do you want to come to the restaurant?"

"Can I meet you at the apartment, in about fifteen minutes?"

"Of course. Em, are you all right?"

"Not really, no. I'll see you in a few." She stifled another sob as she hung up and headed down the west shore. He'd sounded so concerned...why couldn't she have fallen in love with Ben? He was good-looking and successful too, but more importantly he was honest and trustworthy and, like Missy and Pete, he loved her and he'd always been there for her. Protected her from pain instead of inflicting it.

She arrived at the resort and hurried past the restaurant where the band was playing out on the deck and the Friday night crowd danced. She ran up the stairs to Ben's apartment and knocked. He let her in, his face full of concern.

"What's going on, Em?"

She burst into tears and he wrapped her in a hug.

"Shh, it's okay, little Mouse. It's okay. It'll all be okay." He stroked her hair and held her gently as she cried and cried. Eventually she pulled herself together.

"Thanks, Ben. I'm so sorry."

"I'm here for you, Em. We all are. Is this a whiskey night?"

She nodded and gave him a small smile. The four of them had a tradition of whiskey nights whenever one of them hit a bump in the road of life. He brought a bottle of whiskey and two glasses.

"Want to sit outside?"

She nodded. They sat on his balcony directly above the lake and he poured two glasses. Emma downed hers in one gulp.

"Whoa, slow down, Mouse. Are you going to talk to me?"

She nodded pushing her glass forward for a refill.

"Have you eaten, before we go pouring whiskey down you?"

"No," she realized she hadn't eaten since breakfast. "I don't think I could."

"No more of the strong stuff until you at least try. Let me call down and order you something. Then you have to tell me what's going on." He called down and ordered her a sandwich and fries. "I can go straight down and get that for you now. Will you be okay a minute?"

"Yes, I've got to make a quick call anyway." She wanted to let Holly know to come straight to Ben's in the morning, she didn't want her going to the house.

"Hey sweetie, I didn't expect to hear from you tonight. Did Jack like his surprise?"

At that the tears came again. "Jack had a surprise of his own and I didn't like it at all."

"What happened?"

She told Holly what she'd seen. "So it seems he really wasn't able to get through two nights alone."

"Oh, sweetie, I'm so sorry. Perhaps there's some explanation." She didn't sound convinced.

"Even if there was I wouldn't want to hear it. I'm staying at Ben's tonight, so could you get Pete to drop you here in the morning?"

"Okay."

"But don't tell him why. I don't know what he'll make of this and to be honest, I don't even want to know."

"Em, don't you think you should talk to him? Don't you think he'd want to know, help straighten this out?"

"I don't want to deal with him. I don't want to deal with any of it. Promise me you won't say anything."

Ben came back out and put her food down in front of her.

"Promise me?"

"Okay then."

"Thank you. I've got to go. I'll see you tomorrow."

"You get some rest tonight. You'll be all right, Em."

"Thanks Holly, bye."

"Here you go," said Ben. "You have to eat something."

"Thanks." She stared at the plate.

"Well, go on then. Two fries before I refill you."

She ate two fries, then pushed her glass forward. He topped it up and she took a long swig.

"Take it easy though. Remember we've got a party to run tomorrow. Now are you going to tell me what's happened?"

She took a deep breath and told him about coming back to surprise Jack and everything she'd seen on the beach. "So it was me that got the surprise," she finished.

Ben sipped his whiskey frowning. "It doesn't sound right, Em."

"It damn well didn't look right either, Ben!"

"No, I mean he's genuinely crazy about you."

"Yeah. I've heard that a lot lately. Perhaps he's just crazy about her too, whoever she is."

Ben ignored that. "I can't believe he'd do that. I really can't."

"Well, I don't want to, but I saw them."

"But did you see them, like, kiss or anything. What did they actually do?"

Emma groaned, not wanting to have to relive the memory. "I saw them walking on the beach together, laughing and joking. She punched his arm, she hugged him and he hugged her back, very enthusiastically. And he looked really, really happy." Her voice cracked as she remembered just how happy he had looked with that woman in his arms. She took another slug of her whiskey.

"Slow down with that stuff and eat some of your sandwich. Did you see them do anything that, say, you and I wouldn't do?"

Emma thought about that. "I suppose not."

"Well then!" Ben shrugged as if that were some kind of explanation.

"Well then what?"

"I don't know, but I think there has to be some innocent explanation, I really do."

"Oh, Ben. You're as bad as I used to be. You want to believe the best of people. But I've already learned the hard way that you can't do that, because if you do you end up getting your heart broken."

"I'm sorry."

"It's not your fault. I should have known better. I just wanted to believe. I'd even started to think that maybe...but no. This is life kicking my ass, reminding me that I wasn't meant to have that kind of happiness." She downed some more whiskey.

"Em, that's not true. You so deserve happiness and you will find it. And think about it. If anyone saw the way we are together, or you and Pete or me and Missy, they might get the wrong idea if they didn't know the whole story."

"But what could his story be, Ben? That he has a dear lifelong friend, who he never mentioned and who just happened to drop by the minute I was out of town?"

"I know it doesn't look good, but I simply cannot buy that he would do that, Em. I can't. Why don't you call him?"

"Are you crazy? I don't want to talk to him!"

"But maybe...."

"Please, leave it. I don't want to talk to him, and I don't want to talk about him. I'm here and I've got you and Missy and Pete and Gramps. I don't need anyone else."

"Have you told Pete?"

She looked at him, "What do you think? He'll be here in the morning, that's soon enough. And don't you dare call him."

"I didn't say anything about calling him."

"You didn't need to. I've known you since we were eight years old and I can read you like a book!"

He gave her a sheepish grin. "Really not allowed to call him?"

"Nope."

"Missy?"

"Nope."

She gave him a grim smile. "And no texting either. You're stuck with this one and all you have to do is change the subject and keep the whiskey coming." She held out her now empty glass.

"No deal." He pointed at her mostly untouched plate, "You get through at least half the sandwich and some more fries." He moved the bottle to the floor by his feet. "Until then don't talk to me about whiskey."

She smiled, grateful to have him to turn to. She munched on the sandwich. At first she'd thought she wouldn't be able to eat a thing, but once she started she realized how hungry she was. She also needed something to soak up the whiskey that was already going straight to her head. Ben's cell rang.

"What's up?

Can't Kallen do it?

Tell him.... No forget it. I'll be down in a minute."

He came back to the table. "Sorry Mouse, but I'm going to have to go and help out. The new credit card software has a glitch and I keep having to reset it."

"No problem," she reached for the bottle again, "I'm fine."

"Tell you what, why don't you come down with me? It'll take a little while and I really don't want to leave you up here by yourself."

"What's up? Don't trust me with your whiskey?"

"No, I don't." He grinned. "Come on. I'd rather get you a small one at the bar than leave you up here with a whole bottle. Come listen to the band."

"Give me a minute?" She went into the bathroom and rinsed her tear-stained face. "Make that two minutes," she shouted as she applied fresh lipstick and mascara.

"Uh-oh, war paint," said Ben when she came out.

"Just cover-up so I don't frighten your customers away."

"Em, you're beautiful, even when you've been crying."

"See, that's why you're my best friend. You always know the right thing to say."

"Come on. I need to get down there and sort this out."

Ben got her settled at the end of the bar near the servers' station. She had a great view of the band and was out of the way from the crowd of locals and tourists all enjoying a Friday night out. She sipped her whiskey and tried to enjoy the music. They were really good. Five guys who all sang and between them played lead, bass, keyboards, drums and saxophone, exchanging instruments according to the song. Gramps would like some of the older songs they played. She tried to focus on Gramps and the party, not wanting to let images of Jack and that woman crowd into her head. That was how she'd eventually learned to cope with her grief as a child. After months of abject misery she'd discovered that if she focused completely on something else she could shut out the pain for a little while. She knew now that it wasn't really 'coping' but at least it was a way of surviving. As a child she'd started to write, had been able to lose herself in the worlds and characters she created. Right now she focused on listening to the band, deciding on what songs she could ask them to play for Gramps. She hadn't had chance to talk to them yet; Ben had taken care of all that.

She clapped as they finished a number. Catching the lead singer's eye she smiled at him. He looked back at her a long time as they started in to the next song. Uh-oh! Don't need to be going there. She jumped as Ben put a hand on her shoulder.

"You doing okay?"

"I am doing just fine." She was aware that her speech may, possibly, be a tiny bit slurred. "I'll be better when you bring me another."

Ben shook his head, "I think you may have had enough already."

She put her arms around his neck and smiled at him sweetly. "I promise I'll be good and anyway, it will help me sleep. You don't want to have to listen to me crying all night do you?"

He pursed his lips then smiled. "One last small one and no more."

"Thank you, Ben. You're such a good friend."

He returned as the band was finishing their set and taking a break. As he placed the whiskey in front of her, the lead singer came over to join them.

"Hi, Ben. I haven't been introduced to your girlfriend." He held out his hand to Emma. "I'm Chase, nice to meet you."

"This is Emma, and she's not my girlfriend."

"I don't have a boyfriend!" declared Emma.

Ben looked at her and shook his head. "Don't mind her, she's had a bad day."

Chase looked from Ben to Emma, obviously trying to figure out what was going on between the two of them. "Should I disappear?"

"No, sorry," said Ben, "stay and have a drink with us. Emma is one of my oldest friends." She nodded solemnly at Chase who smiled back at her. "And," continued Ben, "she may want to take note of the fact that the way you behave with your close friends can sometimes look to other people like you are a couple."

"Yeah, sorry about that. I thought you were together."

"Nope," smiled Emma. "Ben is far too good for me!"

Ben dug her in the ribs. "No more whiskey for you," he laughed.

"Hm, I may have had enough. Anyway," she turned to Chase, "we need to talk about what we're going to do tomorrow."

He smiled and raised his eyebrows looking from her to Ben and back. "You want to do something with me tomorrow?"

She nodded again and Ben laughed. "Emma here is responsible for the other half of tomorrow's party, though at the moment I don't think she's responsible for anything at all!"

She smiled sweetly. "The only whiskey I drank was the whiskey you gave me, Ben. Nothing else, nothing at all!" She swayed slightly on her stool making the two guys laugh.

"Don't mind her. This is not normally our Em. You won't believe the Emma you see tomorrow. This is a very rare occasion. Like I say, she had a bad day."

"The worst day," said Emma, "but my old pal Ben is getting me through it." She slapped him on the back.

Chase laughed. "Well, I'd say your old pal Ben is a true friend and a true gentleman."

"Oh, he is. I'm so lucky to have to him."

"I'd better get back to it. I'll see you tomorrow."

"See you tomorrow, Chase."

As he got back on stage ready to start the next set, Chase watched Ben persuade the curvy little blonde that it was time to leave. Ben truly was a gentleman and she was lucky to have him around. She was beautiful, and with that figure she turned quite a few heads as they left. He'd bet Ben was one of a very small handful of guys who'd make sure she got home safe and wouldn't take advantage. Would he be one himself if he got the chance? Watching her cross the parking lot with Ben's arm around her as she swayed, he had to admit he'd be tempted— she was hot. As they launched into the first song he realized he was looking forward to tomorrow a whole lot more now. And hoping she'd still be as much fun when she was sober.

~ ~ ~

Ben put an arm around Emma's shoulders as he led her out of the bar. She leaned against him as they crossed the parking lot back to his apartment. Two of the guys from the marina were standing out there smoking. As they passed them Emma smiled up at Ben blearily.

"Thank you, Ben. Thank you for letting me stay with you tonight."

One of the guys smiled at Ben. "You have yourself a good night there, boss!" They both laughed.

"Oh, we are," said Emma. "My Ben is so good to me."

"Come on," said Ben, not wanting this to look any worse than it already did. He led her up the stairs to his apartment. Inside he deposited her on the bed in the guest room. "You need anything, Mouse?"

"I'm fine."

"You sleep it off, or your head won't be fine in the morning."

"She was a stick insect, Ben. That's what he likes!"

Ben shook his head. "We'll talk about it tomorrow, Mouse. Get some sleep."

He didn't need to tell her twice, she had already drifted off.

Chapter Twenty-Four

Jack woke early as usual. He stretched across the bed, wishing Emma was there to hold. He pulled her pillow towards him, breathing in the faint scent of summer breeze that lingered from the night she'd spent here with him. His longing for her grew under the sheet as he remembered that night, and the chocolate and....

Time for a shower, a cold one at that! She'd be back soon, or at least he hoped so. She hadn't answered last night when he'd called. He figured her meeting had run on as she'd feared. He'd call her after his shower. She'd definitely be on the road by then, if she wasn't already. He couldn't wait to see her; today was a big day. A jolt of apprehension ran through him. What if it was too soon? Would it be better to wait a while longer? No, he didn't want to wait. Couldn't wait. The sooner he did this the better. It was, after all, only the first step on a long road still to travel.

He showered and made coffee then went outside to call her. Still no reply. Surely she should be on the road by now. He went back into the RV where Laura was up and fixing herself a coffee.

"Morning, sweetie. Did you sleep okay?"

"Like a log, thanks. You?"

"Not too well. I guess I'm kind of nervous."

"I can't wait to meet her," Laura smiled. "Finally, the woman who can make you nervous...she must really be something special."

"Oh, she is. You'll adore her."

"It's obvious you do. What time is she getting back?"

"I don't know. She's not picking up yet. Listen, when you're ready would you mind if I drop you off with Dan and Missy? I'd kind of like to have her to myself for a little while and I know today is going to get crazy with the party."

"I was going to suggest it."

While Laura got ready, Jack tried Emma's cell again. This time it didn't even ring, just went straight to voice mail. He decided to call Pete and see what time he was arriving. He didn't need to ask outright, but he was pretty sure Emma would come up in the conversation. He smiled as he dialed. If he had to he'd ask, but he'd rather avoid the ribbing if he could.

The drive was going much better than Holly had expected. She stole a sideways glance at Pete. Emma hadn't been kidding, he was gorgeous. Tall and tan with dark blond hair, just a tiny touch of gray at the temples. He had intense blue eyes and chiseled features, a strong jaw and a tiny dimple on his chin that softened the overall impression of a strong and powerful personality. His easy smile that she'd already seen so often transformed what could be a formidable persona into something much more friendly and reassuring.

He'd picked her up this morning and been the perfect gentleman, carrying her bag, making sure she was all set before they started out. He was one of those rare men who put you right at ease, striking up easy conversation, making it comfortable to be around him. She'd soon felt like they were old friends. If she weren't so worried about Emma, she'd be really enjoying this. She'd been tempted a few times now to tell him about Emma's distraught call last night. She knew how much he cared about their shared friend. But she'd promised Em she wouldn't say anything, so she kept quiet, but she wasn't liking it one bit.

Pete's phone buzzed.

"Do you mind?"

"No, of course, go ahead."

Pete touched the screen and Holly's heart sank as the name, Jack, appeared.

"Hey, bro. You're on speaker with me and Holly."

"Hey Pete. Hi Holly."

"Hi Jack."

"You on the way?"

"Sure am, shouldn't be too long now. Oh and don't let me forget, I've got those files you wanted."

"I thought Em got them?"

Pete laughed. "She did, but she was in such a hurry to get back to you she left them in my office."

"What do you mean?" Jack's voice sounded odd.

Holly swallowed. This wasn't good. It looked like she may not be able to keep that promise to say nothing.

"When she got the call that her meeting was canceled she was out the door like a shot. Hoping to get back to you in time for dinner."

"She left to come back here? Pete, she's not here. She's not been answering her cell!"

"Oh God," said Pete, "You don't think she's...."

Holly couldn't stand anymore.

"She's okay," she broke in.

"Where the hell is she?" both men asked at once.

"I think you need to talk to her about that, not me."

"I would if I could get hold of her!" Jack's voice boomed through the speakers.

Pete had pulled over to the side of the road and turned to face her. He put a hand on her arm and said, "I think you'd better tell us." He rolled his eyes toward the phone. "We need to know."

Holly felt like she was being asked to toss a hand grenade into the situation, but she knew she had no choice. She swallowed again and said, "She spent the night with Ben."

"*What?*" Jack's voice resonated throughout the truck.

"I mean at Ben's place," Holly was aware too late of what her words had implied.

"Why?" again Jack and Pete spoke in perfect unison. Under other circumstances it would be quite comical, but there was nothing funny about this. She still wanted to keep her promise to Emma.

"Because she was upset."

"What upset her?" asked Jack.

Holly looked at Pete, not wanting to cause or witness what might happen between the two men.

Jack's voice came again, sounding desperate this time. "Please Holly, could you tell me whatever you know?"

He certainly didn't sound like a no-good cheat. He sounded like a man in love. She looked at Pete and mouthed "I'm sorry." He shrugged and smiled, nodding encouraging her to speak.

"She wanted to surprise you last night."

Jack groaned.

"Do I need to say any more?"

"Probably not, but I think you should."

As Pete looked at her puzzled, Holly continued. "When she got back to the house she saw you on the beach with a woman, laughing and hugging. I don't think I need to tell you what that did to her."

Silence buzzed in the speakers.

"What woman?" asked Pete.

"Laura came up with Dan." Jack's voice sounded hollow.

"Oh, okay. How come?"

"I had her make something for me."

"You did??"

"Yes. But, Holly, why did she go to Ben and not Missy or Gramps?" Now he sounded agitated.

"I don't know, Jack. But I really only meant to say she spent the night at his place not, you know, with him."

"But do you know that?" It was more of a plea than a question.

"Take it easy, bro. I know that."

"I've gotta go. I've got to straighten this out."

"Don't go getting your wires crossed, I'm telling you there is no way she was *with* Ben."

There was another long silence before Jack's voice came again. "Whatever you say. I need to go find her."

"Good luck, bro. I'll see you soon."

Holly looked at Pete. He didn't seem too put out.

"So who is Laura?"

"So why didn't you tell me?"

They both spoke at once.

"Sorry," said Pete. "You go first."

"It's okay." She couldn't look away from the intense blue gaze that seemed to lock onto her own eyes and pin her down. "I didn't say anything because she made me promise not to. I told her there might be an innocent explanation, but you know what she's like. She didn't want to talk about it, think about it or deal with it."

Pete let out a short sigh of exasperation. "Oh, I do know what she's like. But this time I can see it from her point of view, how it must have looked. Just when she's trying to be so brave about trusting him."

"So who is this Laura?"

"She's his cousin. More like a little sister really, they're that close. She lives in San Francisco, designs jewelry. He set her up with her own studio a couple of years ago and she's made quite a name for herself."

Holly frowned. "He said she'd come because he'd had her make something for him. You don't think...?"

"I'm hoping not. I mean he has heard Em's view on marriage, but I do know that's what he wants and he's one determined son...." He stopped himself short. Holly appreciated that it even occurred to him that perhaps he shouldn't finish that sentence.

"No need to hold back on my account, sweetie. I've heard them all and use some of them on the bad days. And you were at least calling him a son and not a mother." She enjoyed the surprise on his face at that. "Let's just hope he had her make a nice necklace or bracelet, shall we?"

Pete laughed. "We can hope, but I have a feeling this is going to be a very long and eventful weekend."

Holly nodded, wondering just what might be in store.

"I'll tell you what, though. I'm in no hurry to get there. I'd rather wait until our star-crossed lovers work this out for themselves. Shall we stop for some breakfast?"

Holly hesitated, feeling she should get to Emma, but then again, Jack was on that same mission. She wouldn't be needed for a while yet. She smiled at Pete. "Why the hell not. I'm hungry."

Chapter Twenty-Five

Jack stuck his head back in the RV. "Are you ready, Laura? I've got to go."

She came to the door, bag in hand. "What's the matter?" He hurried her out and ran to the truck. Laura jumped in the passenger seat as he started the ignition and slammed it in gear. "Jack? What on Earth is the matter?"

Jack couldn't believe this was happening. He should have told Emma that Laura was coming. He didn't need to tell her why! But no, he'd been so caught up in his plan, he'd wanted to keep it all secret. Dammit! Why hadn't he thought of this, remembered that with Em everything had to be up front and in the open, even if it was meant to be a surprise! He looked at Laura.

"Emma came back last night. Apparently she saw us on the beach together and got the wrong idea."

Laura looked puzzled. "But surely that's an easy fix? Once she knows who I am—and especially once she knows why I came?"

Jack ran his fingers through his hair, adrenaline coursing through him. "It's not that easy with Emma, She's kind of...." What exactly was she? "She's scared of getting hurt. She was married," he grimaced, "to a real bastard. He destroyed her belief in men and marriage. So, even when she knows the truth, seeing us like that, and what she's no doubt been thinking all night, she might just...."

He rubbed a hand over his face, not wanting to think what she might just do. Run back into her mouse hole, never to come out again? Then there was what she might have already done. His heart pounded and he grasped the steering wheel with white knuckles as Holly's words echoed, "She spent the night with Ben."

She wouldn't. Ben was her friend, like Pete. Pete had reassured him she wouldn't have, but he couldn't shift the thought. The little pang of jealousy he'd felt watching her dance with Ben that night gnawed at him, threatening to eat him alive if he didn't get a grip. He banged his fist on the steering wheel.

"Take it easy, big guy. She might just be relieved that it was all a misunderstanding."

He shook his head. "I'd love to believe that, but I won't hold my breath on it." Damn. Now he even sounded like Emma, wanting to believe in a positive outcome but instead filled with dread that he'd have to face the worst and deal with the pain. He needed to find her, explain to her and hope that she could get past it. He clenched his jaw, and hoped against hope that she hadn't already tried to get past it—with Ben!

Arriving in town, he screeched to a halt outside Missy's. Laura jumped out.

"Go find her, Jack. It'll be all right. You'll see."

He drove off without a word, headed for the resort. He parked the truck and strode into the restaurant.

"Is Ben around?"

The bartender shook his head. "He's not working today, he's got Joe's party."

"Do you know if he's left yet?"

"Not sure. He was headed down to check on the marina first. You may catch him down there."

Jack tried to calm himself as he walked down the pier to the little office at the end. He mustn't take it out on Ben, just find out what the deal is.

"Is Ben here?" he asked a guy who was tying up one of the rental boats.

"Not seen him, and I don't really expect to this morning."

"I thought he was supposed to be here?"

The man grinned. "Maybe so, but I think he had a heavy night. Last time I saw him he had his hands full with a hot little blonde number, taking her upstairs."

"To his apartment?"

The man nodded and gave him a raunchy grin. "Lucky bugger!"

Jack turned away before he was tempted to wipe that grin off his face. He ran back up the pier, across the parking lot and up the stairs to Ben's apartment. He hammered on the door. "Ben! Ben!"

One of the band shouted up from behind a van they were loading in the parking lot. "You won't find him, no matter how loud you bang. He's gone over to set up a party. You can follow us if you like, that's where we're headed."

"Thanks. I know where it is." He ran back to the truck and shot off, tires screeching again.

~ ~ ~

Emma pegged a bright plastic tablecloth to one of the long tables they had set up. Her head was pounding, but she was determined to keep busy, determined nothing was going to spoil Gramps' and Joe's party. In that respect, everything was coming together nicely. Gramps had seemed concerned about her first thing, but she'd reassured him with a half-truth. She was a little worse for wear after a whiskey night with Ben. He'd smiled at that, knowing the tradition and no doubt assuming it was Ben's sorrows they'd been drowning. She'd muttered something about Jack having business to take care of this morning, suffering a wave of nausea as she thought of the business he'd been taking care of last night. She really couldn't afford to think about it, about him. If he did show his face she'd simply tell him they were done and she didn't want to talk to him. Today was about Gramps and Joe.

She saw Ben pull up. He waved and came down to where she was decorating tables.

"How you feeling, Mouse?"

"Like I drank too much whiskey."

"There's a reason for that."

"Don't remind me!"

"Have you talked to anyone yet?"

"I turned my phone off."

"Emma! You're going to have to deal with this, you know."

"Maybe, but not today. Today we have a party to organize and nothing is going to get in the way of that."

Ben shook his head. "And what about when Pete gets here?"

"I'm not going to mention it."

"Don't you think he'll kind of notice something's up when you're not with Jack?"

"I told you Ben, I just can't deal with it."

"You're not going to have any choice though, once everyone arrives. Jack doesn't know you saw him, so he's going to be looking for you and remember, you don't really know what you saw. You might want to check that out."

"I don't want to check it out. It doesn't matter. Whatever it was, I'm done. I can't do this!"

"Whatever you say, Mouse." Ben was clearly exasperated.

"Please don't be mad at me, I couldn't stand that on top of everything."

"Come here." He gave her a hug and she felt tears well in her eyes again as she hugged him back. "I'm not mad at you, Mouse. I'm frustrated. I want to see you work this out and be okay."

"Will you settle for me being okay? I'll be okay if we get everything sorted out here and put on a really good day for Gramps and Joe."

"All right then. What do we still need?"

"I think we're pretty much covered. Tables are almost done. Food is sorted." She refused to think about the chili Jack was supposed to make. "Chase and Robin have been setting up the stage and the rest of the band are on their way over."

As if hearing his name, Chase stood up from his work on the stage and came over to them.

"Morning, Ben."

"Hey. Is everything set?"

"We're getting there. I may need to run some more cable, but I'll handle it. How's everything else"

"Pretty good, right Em?"

She nodded, "I may need to go to the hardware store for some more helium for the balloons, but other than that we're good."

"I could take you?" offered Chase. "I could pick up more cable."

Emma thought about it. She'd been aware of Chase watching her all morning as he'd worked on building the stage. But he was friendly enough and with her head thumping she really didn't feel much like driving. "Okay, thanks. Do you want to go now?"

"Yep," he grinned. "I'll just tell Robin, the others should be here any minute."

Emma climbed into Chase's truck and they set off for town. Halfway down West Shore Road she saw Gramps' truck flying along in the opposite direction. As it whizzed past them she caught a glimpse of Jack, face set as he grasped the steering wheel.

"Maniac!" laughed Chase. "I guess you get the crazies out here too."

"We certainly do." She tried to calm the butterflies in her stomach, wondering if he was headed to Gramps', and hoping he wasn't. At least she was out of the way, for now.

Jack stopped the truck in a cloud of dust when he saw Ben. He jumped out.

"Ben!"

What was that look on his face? Jack couldn't read it. Certainly not happy to see me, he thought as he strode towards Ben, determined not to lose his cool while he figured out what was going on. Ben looked decidedly uncomfortable as he approached.

"Where's Emma?"

"She's not here right now, Jack."

"Where the hell has she been?" He resisted asking what he really wanted to know.

"She stayed at my apartment last night, she was in a bit of a state." Jack glowered at him. "Jack, what the hell is going on?'

"I was about to ask you the same thing!"

"Me? I'm picking up the pieces after your girlfriend saw you getting friendly with some woman on the beach last night!"

"Friendly, yes. Nothing else. Dammit, Ben! She's my cousin!"

"Ah," Ben smiled. "I told her it couldn't be what she thought."

"You did?"

"Of course I did. I've seen you with her, man. I know the score."

"So you weren't... You didn't..." Jack really didn't want to say what he'd suspected.

Ben understood though. "God no!" He shook his head as if the thought freaked him out. "I'll admit I love Em, but love her like a sister." He smiled at Jack. "Not love her like you love her. You do, don't you?"

Jack nodded. Ben's words had knocked all the fire out of him. "I do. Listen, I'm sorry, man. I got a little crazy there."

Ben put a hand on his back. "Say no more. I understand. Besides, it's not me you need to be talking to, is it?"

"No, but do you think she'll even listen to me, let me explain? "

Ben's face didn't offer him much hope. "I'd like to offer you words of encouragement, but she's shut down. Says no matter what really happened, she doesn't want to know. She's done."

Much as he'd been expecting that, Jack really didn't want to hear it. "Where is she?"

"She's gone into town, but before she left she was saying she's not going to deal with it today. Today's about the old guys. She's turned her phone off and won't talk to anyone."

"Oh, man. What about Gramps, does he know?"

"No, he was worried about her, but she passed it off as a whiskey hangover, which isn't a lie."

Jack raised an eyebrow, "Whiskey?"

"It's what we've always done when one of us is down." He smiled, "She's a very endearing drunk, you know."

"I only hope I get the chance to see it someday. Listen, I'm going to talk to Gramps before she gets back." Seeing a look of concern cross Ben's face, he said, "Don't worry I won't upset him. He and I had some plans of our own for today so I have to let him know what's going on."

Ben still didn't like it. "All she's been saying is that today is about him having a good time and she doesn't want him upset. That's why she didn't come here last night."

That made more sense, but if only she had, Gramps could have set her straight!

"Honestly, I know what I'm doing, Ben. Don't sweat it."

Jack found Gramps down on the dock, hiding out.

"Morning, son," he grinned. "You ready for our big day?"

"Not quite. We've got a bit of a problem." He hated to see the old man's smile fade.

"Uh-oh. I thought she wasn't right. What's happening?"

Jack told him everything that had happened and how Ben had told him about Emma deciding she just wasn't going to face it.

"Aw, son. Do you think you can get past this one? It might be too much for her."

Jack hated to see the old man look so sad. He'd been as excited as Jack himself about today. "I have to Gramps. I have to, but I might need your help."

"Anything at all, you name it. What have you got in mind?"

Jack explained the plan he was cobbling together, hoping he knew Emma well enough for it to work.

"If anything will work, that will. You really got her figured, don't you son?"

"I hope so, Gramps."

Gramps went back up to the house and Jack stayed down on the dock, wanting to stay out of the way. He didn't feel nearly as confident as he'd led Gramps to believe. Where was Pete anyway? He should be here by now. He was going to need his help, and Holly's for that matter. He dug his phone from his pocket and called Pete.

"How'd it go?"

"It hasn't yet. I haven't seen her. I thought you'd be here by now."

"We stopped for breakfast. We'll be there soon."

"Well hurry up, will you? I need you and Holly in my corner.... Oh, shit!"

"What?"

Jack watched as Emma climbed out of a truck, the driver coming around to help her with some bags. He put a hand on her back and she smiled at him. Jack gripped his phone tighter.

"She's arrived and she's with some guy. It's the singer from the band. He's all over her!" Jack couldn't believe his eyes. The guy was flirting with her and she was going right along with it.

"I gotta go!"

"Take it easy, Jack! Don't do anything stupid. I'll be there as soon as I can."

"Emma!" He covered the ground between them in no time.

"Hello, Jack. How are you?"

Whatever reaction he'd been expecting, this certainly wasn't it. No scared little mouse, no tears, no anger, no nothing. Just greeting him as she would any of her friends on an ordinary day.

"Em, I need to talk to you." He eyed the singer, hoping he'd get the idea and leave them alone.

"I'm busy right now. Chase and I have been shopping." She held up the bags as if that explained everything.

"Em, we need to talk. Now."

"She said she's busy." Chase stepped forward.

Jack glowered at him. "This is none of your business. Give us a minute."

Chase looked at Emma, infuriating Jack. So help him, if the guy didn't get away from her in the next minute! He gritted his teeth. Calm down.

"It's okay Chase, thanks."

The guy walked away, throwing a look back at Jack, as if to make sure Emma was really going to be okay. How the hell did he think he was the one looking out for her? That was Jack's job!

"What are you doing with him?" That wasn't the first thing he'd meant to say, but he couldn't help it.

The look she gave him slayed him. In a matter of seconds he saw pain, anger and sadness in those green eyes before they shuttered him out.

"I don't think that's any of your business, not after last night. If I still cared, I could ask you the same question, what were you doing with her?"

"Em," he reached out to take her hand, but she pulled away from him. "I wish you had asked me that question, instead of assuming the worst. If you had I could have told you, she's my cousin. She came up with Dan."

He watched the shock register on her face, but she didn't soften.

"I'm glad you have your family out to visit. Now if you don't mind, I've still got a lot to do."

"Baby, I know it must have been awful for you and I'm so sorry. I should have told you she was coming, but I have a surprise for you and she was helping me with it. Please, Em, now you know the truth, let's get past this." He held her eyes, hoping he could break down the walls she'd put back up. His heart leaped as her eyes softened.

"I'm glad it wasn't what it looked like. But," why was there always a 'but'? "Jack, it's made me realize, I'm not brave enough. I can't risk that kind of hurt and you don't need this kind of drama. I'm sorry, but we're done."

It was only what he'd expected, but the pain of those last two words struck through to his soul.

"But, Emma. I love you." He reached for her hand again and this time she let him.

Her eyes filled with tears. "I'm sorry, Jack. I can't do this."

"Then tell me you don't love me."

She met his eyes as the tears spilled down her cheeks. His heart stopped and he held his breath, praying that she wouldn't be able to say it. She shook her head and turned and ran. Damn! The only hope he had left was that she hadn't been able to make herself say she didn't love him.

Chapter Twenty-Six

Emma wiped at her face before entering the house then ran up the stairs and into her childhood bedroom. Her heart was racing. She was his cousin! Not some stick insect he'd picked up. Like Ben said, they hadn't done anything she and Pete wouldn't do. He hadn't betrayed her at all! She shook her head sadly. But the whole thing had shown her how much pain she was risking if she allowed herself to love him. Ha! Allowed herself? She had no choice in the matter.

She saw his face, his big brown eyes full of love and pain of his own. "Tell me you don't love me." And she hadn't been able to say it. She couldn't lie to him because she did love him. But that didn't mean she had to live it. She could bury it, get on with her life alone, like she had been doing until the day she'd knocked him down in Pete's office. She didn't have to expose herself to more pain. She took a deep breath, trying to steady herself. She needed to get back downstairs; there was still a lot to do. This was Gramps' day. The bedroom door opened and Gramps stuck his head round.

"Can I come in, Sunshine?"

"Of course." She tried to pull herself together.

"Are you going to be a brave little mouse?"

She looked at him questioningly.

"I know all about it, Em."

"He told you?" Emma couldn't believe it. How could Jack upset Gramps today of all days? "I'm sorry, Gramps. He shouldn't have said anything to you." She was surprised by the stern look on his face.

"Don't you go blaming him. It's you that's upset me."

She was horrified by that. "How?"

"Because you didn't come to your old Grampy and let me talk some sense into you!" His eyes twinkled. "If you'd come to me instead of Ben we could've had all this straightened out last night."

"You knew?"

"Sure did!"

"Oh."

"I was in on it from the start."

"In on what?"

"You'll have to talk to Jack if you want to know that. Let's just say I was in on what he had planned till you went and spoiled it all."

Tears pricked her eyes for what felt like the millionth time that day. "I spoiled everything?" She was stunned.

"Yes, you did, Em. By being too scared to actually live."

"No, Gramps. Jack spoiled it all by...."

"By what, Sunshine?" His voice was gentler now. "By having his cousin over? Yeah that was unforgivable. By wanting to set up a surprise for you? How terrible of him. Think about it, Sunshine. You're the one created a problem by being too scared to talk to him. And you're the one who is making it worse by choosing to hold on to your fear instead of holding on to your man."

She stared at him. Gramps hadn't told her off for years, yet here he was telling her this was all her fault.

"I'm sorry, Gramps."

"Sure you are. But sorry doesn't change anything does it, Em? You know that better than anyone. It's what you do with sorry that makes the difference. You think on that one, Sunshine. Now, I've got a party to get on with. You'd better pull yourself together and come see your friends."

Once he'd gone downstairs, Emma sat on her old bed, thinking about what he'd said. He was right. She had created the problem. What if she'd been brave enough to just walk down to the beach last night? But she hadn't. Would she ever get that far past her fears? Be that brave? She looked at herself in the mirror, then closed her eyes. Give up the fear, or give up Jack; it was that simple.

When she went back outside she saw that Holly and Pete had arrived. They were sitting at one of the tables with Ben and Jack. Holly was laughing at something Jack had said. She couldn't not greet them. She tried to catch Holly's eye, but couldn't. Gathering her strength she went to join them.

"Hey, you made it."

Holly hugged her, then Pete stood up and wrapped her in his bear hug.

"Hey, Mousey. Everything okay?"

"Fine thanks Pete. I've still got a lot to do though. Holly, would you mind giving me a hand?"

"Anything I can do?" asked Jack.

Oh, how she wished he would make this easy and go away. "I don't think so, thank you."

Pete laughed. "Oh, come on Em. Give it up, will you? He's done nothing wrong."

"Yeah, didn't I tell you?" Ben smiled at her.

She stared at the three of them, lost for words, then turned on her heel and walked away, toward the dock.

Holly came after her. "Are you okay, sweetie?"

"Not really, no."

"What do you need me to do?"

"Come and help me fill some balloons. I wanted to get you away from him, really."

"Emma, he's gorgeous. You've got yourself one delicious man there. And he's such a sweetheart."

"Holly! You know what happened."

Holly stared at her. "Yeah. You saw him with his cousin and got the wrong idea. No biggie, right?"

"No biggie!? I thought he was...." She couldn't even bring herself to say it.

"Yes, but he wasn't, was he? It was a thought and it was wrong. Now you know, you can let it go, right?"

Emma grappled with this. Could it really be as easy as that?

"You're not making this a big deal, are you?"

"Well, it is a big deal to me," she stammered.

"Are you determined not to be happy or something? Look at him!"

She looked to find Jack watching her. He gave her a little smile and her heart did its customary skitter in response.

"Are you saying you would rather run scared than have that man in your life? Because if you are, you're not just dealing with past emotional baggage, you are most definitely certifiable!"

"But...."

"But what, sweetie?"

"Oh, Holly. I don't know, I just don't know."

"What's to think about, really?"

"Whether I can survive the pain."

"What pain? Do you mean the pain you imagine if he somehow hurts you?"

Emma nodded.

"Then tell me this. What about the very real pain you will put you both through if you give up on him now? Could you love him any more than you already do?"

Emma shook her head.

"Then why on Earth not live it, Em? Love him, let him love you—do what we all have to do. Love like you've never been hurt."

"You're supposed to be on my side," was all Emma could think to say.

"For goodness sake, Em, I am. I'm trying to stop you from making the biggest mistake of your life!"

"The biggest mistake of my life was getting married!" Emma blurted out.

Holly took her arm and led her further away, down to the water's edge. "Your biggest mistake, so far, wasn't getting married, but marrying the wrong man, and believe me, it would be an even bigger mistake to not even give the right man a chance."

Emma stared out at the lake. She needed time to think about Holly's words.

"Hey, Em!" At the sound of her name she looked back, and realized she wasn't going to get that time. Missy had arrived with Scot and Dan, and with them was the woman from the beach. Emma's head pounded again. How she wished she could just run. Run away from it all, not have to deal with any of it, with any of them. Jack had joined them as they all trooped down to the dock where she and Holly were sitting.

"I've got a car load of goodies," said Missy as she hugged her. "Is everything okay?"

"I think so," Emma replied as she hugged Scot.

Next came Dan. "Are you alright?"

She nodded, not trusting her voice. His shy concern touched her heart. As he let her go she came face to face with the cousin.

"This is Laura," said Jack. Emma was struck by her resemblance to both Benson brothers as Laura clasped her hand in both of her own.

"It's so nice to finally meet you. I've heard so much about you."

Jack shrugged behind her. "Apparently I talk about you. A lot."

"An awful lot," added Dan.

Emma attempted a smile that she hoped didn't look as frozen as it felt. "Welcome. I hope you enjoy the party. I have to.... Missy. Let me show you where to put everything." She grabbed Missy's arm and marched her back to her car.

"Should be a great day for it, Mouse."

"Oh my God! Not you too?"

"Me too what?"

"Acting like everything is all fine and dandy and normal. Tell me this is some sort of conspiracy?"

Missy looked at her. "I heard you downed some whiskey last night. Are you still sloshed?"

"No. I just don't understand why you're all making out that everything is fine and normal."

"Well, isn't it?"

Emma was starting to wonder herself. She looked back at the others. They were all talking and smiling. Once again she found Jack's eyes on her. He gave her that little smile and a beseeching look, the puppy dog one. She looked away.

"Is it really no big deal that I came home and found him on the beach with a woman?"

"With his cousin, you mean?" laughed Missy. "I can see how it would have freaked you out, but you know who she is now. And if you'd come to me last night, Dan or I could have told you."

Emma closed her eyes. "So I went to the only person who didn't know what was going on?"

"Looks that way. Anyway, it was a mix up and it's all cleared up now, right?"

"Oh, Miss. I'm so confused."

"What about?"

Were they all blind, or was she really creating a problem that only existed in her mind? Even if she was, did that make it any less real?

"Miss, I'm waiting and hoping that he'll go away, accept that it's over. Yet all of you are making out that everything is peachy, or at least it should be."

"Over?" Missy looked genuinely stunned. "Em, why?"

"Because last night made me realize how much he could hurt me."

"But he didn't hurt you. You hurt yourself by believing the worst, don't you see that?"

"Yes, I do. But...but...."

She couldn't even remember her own 'but' at this point. And there he was again, watching her. He let his eyes travel over her and she was helpless. Even her body was on his side as she felt the familiar flush creep over her under his gaze. She turned away without meeting his eye.

Missy pulled the last of the boxes from her car. "Sounds like you're all out of buts, so why don't you stop looking for them and enjoy yourself? I don't get it Mouse, why don't you just enjoy him and all that he's offering you?"

Chapter Twenty-Seven

More people had been arriving and now there was quite a crowd, sitting at the long tables, down at the dock, or standing by the stage where the band was doing a sound check. Gramps and Joe were holding court on the front porch, telling stories to their gang of buddies and an ever-changing group of well-wishers. Emma smiled, relaxing a little, glad they were having a good time. She saw Holly and Pete walking down by the water's edge, Holly animated as she talked to him. Pete seemed intrigued, nodding and laughing, perhaps her plan for them might work out. Missy was sitting with Dan and Scot at one of the tables, the two of them seemingly explaining something to her. They looked like a family sitting there like that. Emma smiled at the thought; wouldn't that be something? She found Ben at the grill, working a dozen burgers.

"I'd say it's a success so far, Mouse."

"The old guys are certainly enjoying themselves."

"So is everyone else, and the band should be starting up soon."

She looked at the stage where Chase was going through his final checks. He'd been so nice to her this morning. As she watched, Jack approached him.

"Uh-oh." Ben followed her gaze. "He wasn't happy to see you with Chase this morning."

"It's none of his business."

Ben gave her a look, "Forgive me for putting it bluntly, Em, but who have you been sleeping with these last few weeks?"

She felt her face color.

"And Chase was a bit hands-on with you when you got back from the store. Any guy in Jack's position would see it as his business."

"Chase was being nice and besides, Jack was...."

"Jack was what? Hanging out with his cousin?"

"Yes, but I thought he was...."

"Yeah, you thought, but you were wrong—as I did try to tell you that you might be. And now you know better, so what's the problem?"

Emma watched Jack and Chase talk, the tension between them obvious even from this distance. Chase was a handsome man, but next to Jack he was just another guy. They exchanged a few heated words and she tensed, watching them square off. Oh no! Then Jack said something that seemed to diffuse it. Chase laughed and nodded. Jack held out his hand and Chase shook it. They talked for a few moments and then walked over to the electrical control box and Jack started working on it.

"Why not talk to him?"

"You said that last night."

"I did, and imagine all the trouble we could have saved if you'd listened then!"

She certainly wasn't going to talk to him while he was with Chase. No, she needed some alone time to think about all this. Perhaps now she could sneak upstairs for a few minutes.

"There's my Mouse," shouted Gramps as she tried to slip into the house. "Give me a few minutes fellas." He followed her inside.

"You figured it out yet, Em?"

"Gramps, I haven't had chance to even think, everyone's too busy making out like it's nothing."

"It doesn't have to be anything, like I told you. It's only a problem if you make it one."

"Gramps I'm going upstairs. I need to think."

"Okay, Mousey. But don't miss too much of my party will you? It's a good 'un. And when you're done with your thinking, will you ask Jack about my Texas chili? I been looking forward to getting my gums around that."

She exhaled and looked at him. "Really?"

"Really! It'll ruin my day if I don't get none."

She headed up the stairs and closed herself in the bedroom. Gramps knew which buttons to push. They were all on Jack's side! Was she really being so completely blind? And how the devil was she supposed to figure anything out when she knew she'd have to go and talk to him? She may as well get that over with first. She went back downstairs and out into the throng. There were people milling everywhere now. The band had started up, not too loud, thank goodness.

Pete appeared out of the crowd. "You've done a great job, Em. It's going great."

"Thanks."

"What are you up to?"

She scanned the faces. "Looking for Jack."

He grinned. "You finally come to your senses then?"

She scowled at him. "Don't you start, too. I need to talk to him about chili. I bet he didn't even make it, though."

"He did. Enough to feed the whole of Texas from what Laura said."

"Why didn't he bring it then?"

"Err, perhaps because he was in a panic this morning trying to hunt his lady down and explain to her that she hadn't seen what she thought she had?"

Emma tutted. "I don't want to hear it Pete. I've had enough. You're all on his side so why don't you find him and ask him to get the chili for Gramps."

She felt the tears coming yet again.

"C'mere, Em." He put an arm around her shoulders. "We're all on your side, we all love you and we want to see you happy. It's just that you're so scared you can't see straight and we can be objective because it's not our hearts that are on the line here. I'm not going to keep on at you. You already know what I think. But I'm not going to find him for you either. You need to talk to him yourself." He planted a kiss on the top of her head. "Be a brave little Mouse, in fact be Super-Mouse and kick your fear in the ass! Grab your chance at happiness, Em. We don't get many chances in this life and if you pass them up, you may never get them again. Look, he's over there." He pointed up the driveway to where Jack was standing, watching her yet again. He raised a hand and smiled. "Go on, Em."

Her heart pounded as she walked to him. Just the chili, that's all she needed to talk to him about.

"Hey, baby." Jack tried to sound much more confident than he felt. She looked terrified. He just wanted to hold her, reassure her, protect her from everything she feared so much.

"I've only come to ask about the chili. Gramps was looking forward to it." She wouldn't meet his eye.

"Sorry, I left in a bit of a rush this morning."

She said nothing.

"It's all ready, in the RV. Em, will you come with me to get it?"

"I don't think so."

He hadn't expected a yes. "Baby, I know you. I understand how much what you thought you saw last night must have hurt you. I even understand why you feel you need to run and hide from me, but please, can we talk about it?"

"There's nothing to talk about. I've said all I'm going to say."

"Perhaps, but what about what I still have to say?"

She finally met his eye. "What's left to say, Jack? It's over."

He watched the tears fill her eyes and wanted so badly to take her in his arms and make her smile again. "I still have a lot left to say and I think you owe it to me to hear me out. Please ride back out there with me."

"I can't."

"Why not?"

"Because...because I need to be here."

This was good. She was making excuses, not saying she didn't want to.

"What do you need to do?" He swept his arm out over the party, "Everyone's happy, everything's covered, there's really nothing for you to do."

"I can't. I need to be by myself."

"You'd really rather be alone than be with me?"

She looked away.

"I only want you to be happy, Em. I love you. If you're
sure you're happier by yourself, I'll leave you alone. I'll fetch
Gramps' chili and then I'll go and stay out of your way. You
don't ever have to be around me again if you don't want to."
His heart was racing, this was a huge gamble. "In case you do
though, I'm going to wait at the RV a while. If you have any
doubts at all about being better off without me, if you want to
hear what I still have to say, then you come up there, okay? If
you're not there by four I'll know you're not coming." He
hooked his thumb under her chin and tipped her face to meet
his eyes. "Please come, baby." He leaned in as if to kiss her,
but stopped an inch from her lips. "I'll be waiting for you."
Then he was gone.

Emma watched as the old truck turned out of the driveway.
The tears were escaping now, flowing freely down her cheeks.
She was trembling. She'd thought he was going to kiss her and
if he had, she wouldn't have stopped him. Feeling him so near,
his big reassuring presence surrounding her, she'd felt safe
again. Not scared. Safe. She longed to feel his arms around
her. His lips on hers. And now he'd gone. What had he said?
"You don't ever have to be around me again." Could she really
stand to be without him? What did he still have to say? She
needed to think. Maybe now she could get back to her old
bedroom and attempt to make sense of it all.

She managed to slip into the house unnoticed. In the quiet
of her old room she heaved a big sigh. Was she really being as
silly as they were all making out? Of all of them, Jack was the
only one who seemed to understand how much the whole
thing had thrown her. Did she really want to run from the one

person in the world who understood her so well? And if she felt so safe with him near, was he really the cause of her fear or perhaps the only one who could help her conquer it?

There was a tap on the door then Gramps appeared. "You going to see about my chili?"

"Jack's gone to get it."

Gramps smile vanished. "He's gone? And you didn't go with him?"

She shook her head.

"Oh, Sunshine." Gramps looked on the verge of tears himself.

"What, Gramps?"

"It's okay, Em. I thought, well, I hoped...."

"What?"

"I thought you'd at least go and talk to him."

She hung her head.

"Em, go talk to him."

"I can't! It's your party, I can't leave."

"Course you can. Especially since I'm asking you to. Please, Em?"

How could she tell him no? She checked her watch: three forty, she could still get there in time. "If you're sure?"

The twinkle returned to his eyes. "I'm damned sure, little Mouse. Now git!"

She hugged him and ran for her car.

Jack paced the beach. Four o'clock was approaching way too fast. Was she really not coming? He couldn't imagine what he'd do if she didn't. No, there was still time. She'd come. He had to believe it. He touched the two little boxes in his pocket. This was the beginning, not the end. He strained his ears, hoping that was a car he heard out on the road. He checked, five till four, please God, let it be her! A huge smile spread across his face as her car appeared. As she pulled up next to the truck he ran up the beach and was there by the time she got out.

"You came!"

"I came."

She was keeping her distance, but she was here!

"Jack, I don't think I can do this, but you're right. I do owe it to you to hear you out."

He stopped himself from taking her in his arms and kissing her as he so wanted to. He had to get this right. His whole future depended on him doing so.

"Thanks, Em. I need to explain. I'm so, so sorry that my having Laura out here caused you so much pain. I know what it must've done to you."

He was surprised to see a small smile play on her lips.

"What, baby?"

She gave a sad little shrug. "You're the only one who really does understand."

"That's because I know you, and I love you." He took her hand. "Come walk with me?" His heart filled with hope as she let him lead her down to the beach.

"Baby, I know how hard it is for you to trust and I know the pain you've lived through. Whenever you've let yourself love someone, you've suffered so badly. I think I can understand. You see, I loved my dad so much. All I ever wanted was for him to love me back, but instead he beat me. He beat Dan and my mom, too, till I got big enough to get in the way. It's not the same as losing your folks, I know. And it's not the same as your horrible marriage. But I do know something about what it's like to love someone, to want and need their love in return, only to find that you don't get it. That all you do get is pain. What you went through taught you that it's better not to love or trust at all. What I went through taught me that love and trust should be earned, not given blindly. Some people will never be worthy of them, but when you find the ones who are, you let yourself love them with all that you are, you cherish them and protect them."

She was looking up at him, tears in her eyes.

He stepped closer. "I love you and trust you. I love you with all that I am and I want to cherish you and protect you. I've tried so hard to earn your love and trust. Can you really tell me you don't love me?"

The tears rolled down her cheeks as she looked into his eyes. She shook her head and threw herself into his arms. He closed his eyes and held her tight as she clung to him, sobbing. Eventually he lifted her chin and found her green eyes finally meeting his gaze.

"I can't tell you that, because I do love you, Jack."

That was all he needed to hear. His lips found hers in a long, tender kiss. Her arms came up around his neck as she kissed him back. Feeling her soft and warm in his arms he swore he'd never let her go.

Chapter Twenty-Eight

Emma clung to Jack as she kissed him. She wanted to melt into him and the safety she felt in his arms. He'd never said too much about his dad before, but now she understood. He'd known pain too. He'd just found a different way to deal with it. A better way. It was a long time before that kiss ended.

She finally looked up at him. "I've been so afraid of you hurting me, I didn't feel safe. But now you are the only place I do feel safe." His smile and the love in his eyes told her everything.

"I'll keep you safe, Em. As long as you'll let me. There's something I need to ask you."

She nodded, feeling at this moment, she'd do anything, tell him anything he asked. He went down on one knee and smiled up at her.

Oh no! Her heart was in her mouth. Anything but this! I thought he understood me!

"Jack, I...." she began, feeling herself starting to shake all over.

"Please, Em," he took her hand. "Trust me? Hear me out?"

She swallowed hard and nodded, still trembling. She loved him with all her heart, but this? She couldn't.

He squeezed her hand. "Baby, I'm not asking you to marry me." Her panic subsided a little. "Yet." He held up a little box, "But I am asking you to wear my ring. He gave her the box. Inside it was the most unusual and beautiful ring she'd ever seen. A beautiful rose quartz shone as the centerpiece of a flower, surrounded by petals of marquise cut diamonds. The gold band was inlaid with tiny pave diamonds.

"Jack," she gasped. "It's beautiful! It's a daisy!"

"I know," he smiled. "It's our pebble at the center, too."

She looked at him in wonder, "Really?"

"Yes, baby, really. It's why Laura's here. She made it."

She was amazed, admiring the perfect craftsmanship. Then she remembered. "But, Jack. What...?"

"Don't panic. I do know you and I do understand. It's not an engagement ring. It's a good old-fashioned promise ring. All I'm asking of you is that you will promise to think about marrying me."

Tears filled her eyes once more.

"Don't say no yet, Em."

"I wasn't about to. I'm just so amazed by you."

"So you will think about it?"

She nodded.

With a huge grin he took the ring out of the box. "It comes with a couple of conditions, though. Once I put this ring on your finger, you have to promise me that any time you get scared you will talk to me before you run. Remember that I might be the best place for you to run to. You think you can do that?"

"I'll try."

"No, not try, Em. It's crucial. I have and I will work my ass off to earn your trust, but you've got to give me a chance, yes?"

"Yes."

"And the other condition is that you really will think about marrying me. I know that's a stretch for you right now. But I think that deep down you still believe in forever as much as I do, and that means marriage."

She nodded again. He really did know her. A tiny voice in the back of her mind was shouting for joy, doing cartwheels. Maybe, just maybe, she really would get married and find it to be the wonderful union she used to believe in. How could it be anything else with Jack?

"So, knowing what this proposal means, do you accept?"

"Yes, Jack. Yes I do!"

He slid the ring onto her wedding finger and stood up. She jumped on him, wrapping her arms and legs around him. He kissed her then put her back down. She held out her hand to admire the ring, it was so beautiful.

"You like?"

"I more than like. I love it. And I love you! That's really our pebble?"

He looked so pleased with himself. "Didn't I tell you it was precious treasure?"

She laughed. "You certainly did!"

"And you were so adamant about engagement rings and flashy diamonds, I knew I had to come up with something unique. Every time you look at it, Em, I want you to remember what you told me about daisies."

She looked at him. Did he remember every little detail? He grinned as if he'd read her mind once more.

"Em, you're the best thing that's ever happened to me. I intend to spend the rest of my life with you and I'm a detail guy, so you may as well get used to it."

He was unbelievable. She really did feel like the luckiest woman on Earth. "What did I tell you about daisies, Jack, that inspired this beautiful ring?"

He came to stand behind her and she relaxed against him, loving the feel of him.

"You said," he dropped a kiss on her shoulder, "that daisies always make you happy. I wanted the ring to make you happy, but more importantly to remind you that I can make you happy, if you give me the chance."

She looked down at the ring sparkling on her finger. "I believe it will do that, Jack."

"Good," he held her closer. "You also said that daisies always look like they're nodding and smiling. When you look at your daisy ring I want you to think of me and everyone else who loves you—Gramps, Pete, Missy, Ben, Holly, all of us smiling and nodding at you in encouragement. You can do this, Emma. Don't be scared. It'll be okay, just trust, love."

This time her tears were happy ones as she twisted around and held him tight. "What did I ever do to deserve you?"

"You suffered too much too soon, so life sent you a big old Texan with a big old heart whose mission is to ensure that you know only happiness for the rest of your days."

"I love you, Mr. Big Old Texan."

"And I love you, my purdy little lady, with all of my heart and soul. But I'm not done yet. There's one more thing that you told me about daisies. You said all that other stuff may sound goofy, but you have to take your happiness where you find it. The ring is a reminder that you've found it if you want it."

"I really have found happiness with you."

"And now it's my job to make sure that you don't get scared and run away from it."

"I would never have believed that a ring could say so much."

He gave her a mysterious smile. "Rings can say all sort of things, you taught me that with your lecture about them. There is another ring involved in this proposal, Em."

He took a second box from his pocket. She couldn't gauge the look on his face, was he nervous? He held out the box to her.

"This may be presumptuous of me, but go ahead and open it and I'll explain."

She popped the box open and saw a broad, plain gold, man's wedding band. Her eyebrows knit together.

"I don't understand."

"Remember you said men don't wear engagement rings, or even wedding bands in most cases? But that women check for them and respect them if they're there?"

She nodded, starting to understand.

"Well, if you want me, if you'll have me, I want to wear one. I want to tell the world that my heart is spoken for, and that I'm off the market! I want to wear your ring."

She laughed, "But it's not my ring."

"But it is, Em. I could hardly ask you to pick me one up while you were in the city, could I?"

She laughed again.

"But maybe it's a dumb idea."

"Oh, Jack no, it's a lovely idea. I love it, I really do. It's just, well, are you sure?"

"Never been more sure of anything in my life, babe."

She took the ring from the box then hesitated.

"Please, Em. I want to."

She slid the ring onto his finger and he held it up for them both to admire.

"That feels good, it feels right. Of course, if it doesn't feel like 'your' ring you could always get me one yourself. But please can it be a big one like this, so it's noticeable?"

"You're kidding me, right?"

"I am not! I'm deadly serious. I have big hands. I don't want some skinny little piece of wire you can't notice. I want a big heavy duty band that shouts out loud, 'I am very married!'"

"Spoken for. Not married."

"Not yet, but when you do marry me, I'll be the most married man ever."

"Okay, but can we drop the 'M' word for now and enjoy this part?"

"Nope." He held her close. "Married. That's what we're going to be, as soon as you get your head around it. And I'm going to campaign shamelessly."

She smiled, thrilled by his exuberance, even if she really did need more time to get past her views on marriage. He held his hand up again, showing off his ring.

"You'd better get used to the idea, Em, because you are going to marry me."

"Enough 'M' word for now, okay?" she laughed. "Anyway, weren't you saying something about having big hands?" She knew the perfect way to distract him. "I may have a use for those."

She faced him and taking both his hands she placed them on her backside. He cupped her and pulled her against him. She reached up around his neck and molded herself to him as he kissed her hungrily. Holding her in those big hands he lifted her so he could better push his desire against her. She lifted her legs and wrapped them around his waist as he started walking with her back to the RV.

Jack didn't put her down until they reached the bedroom. He was deeply aroused; every step of the way he'd been pressing into her as she clung to him with her legs wrapped around his waist. He felt himself grow even harder at the desire in her eyes as he laid her on the bed. He soon had them both out of their clothes. Once he did he stood and held out his hand, pulling her to her feet to join him.

"These big hands haven't quite finished yet."

She gasped as he cupped her butt cheeks again and lifted her. Her legs came back around him, opening herself up to him, this time with nothing between them. She nibbled at his neck as he pressed her back against the wall and spread her wider with his hands. Her eyes flew open as he nudged into her.

"Jack!"

"Is this okay, baby?"

She nodded, her skin flushed, nipples erect.

Unable to wait any longer he slid deep inside. She let out a long low moan and he felt her tighten around him.

"I love you, Em," he rasped as he moved inside her. With just a couple of strokes he felt her tense.

He heard her, "I love you too, Jack," and let himself go with her, seeing stars as he exploded.

Once he was able to move his legs again, he carried her back to the bed. She rolled over and drew him on top of her.

"More," she breathed.

"You are insatiable, you know that?"

"It's all your fault. I was never like this till I met you. But now I can't get enough of you."

Jack was amazed how quickly he recovered around her. Her words had him almost ready again.

"I promise I'll make it a lifelong endeavor to make sure you do get enough of me."

"Starting now?" She held her arms up and rubbed against him, spreading her legs to receive him.

"Starting right now," he breathed as he slid back inside her. He circled her nipple with his thumb, capturing her mouth with his as he moved slowly and deliberately. As he heard her breathing change and muscles tense in anticipation, he withdrew from her. He smiled as she opened her eyes and thrust her hips up to him.

"Come back! I thought you were going to make sure I have enough?"

"Patience, baby." He held her eyes as he gave her what she wanted, deep and hard, then slowly, despite her writhing desperately beneath him. Sweat rolled down his back from the effort this restraint was costing him, but the look of exquisite desperation on her face encouraged him to torment her. As he felt her get closer he pulled out again.

"Jack, please, I want you."

He kissed her and she thrust her hips back up to him. He lifted his head.

"Jack what are you doing to me?" She ran her hands down his back and cupped his ass, trying to draw him back.

"I love you, baby."

"Jack, I *need* you. Now!"

They were the words he'd wanted to hear. He drove deep and she came as he did, her immediate release encouraging him on. He didn't break his rhythm, just kept working her as she floated away gasping, again and again. As she came back to Earth he was still thrusting deep.

"What did you say, baby?"

"I...I...." Her eyes glazed as another orgasm took her. She was totally at his mercy as he swept her along. "I need you, Jack!" He felt her whole body quiver as he kept up the wild thrust of his hips. When she opened her eyes again, he smiled.

"Jack, I need you.... Go with me...Jack!"

He was amazed as he felt her tighten again and this time he let himself go with her in a whole body orgasm that shook him from his head to his toes. Eventually he lay still, heart pounding, breathing hard.

"I take it you like feeling needed?" she asked, her head on his shoulder.

An aftershock rippled through him at the sensation of her breath on his ear.

"Ooh," she gasped as it took her, too. "I'll take that as a yes!"

He rolled over and pulled her into his arms. "I suppose I should warn you that I do apparently have some caveman in me, yes."

She laughed. "You mean like picking up your woman and carrying her off to your bed?"

"Yes," he nuzzled her neck. "I do, and I should put you on notice that I am liable to do that on occasion."

"No complaints here. In fact I rather like it."

"Good. And yes, I do like to be needed. I don't suppose it's very PC of me, but I like it and I like to protect and provide for the people I love. To date that has been my mom and Dan, and Laura and her mom. But you, my little Mouse, you are the one I want to spend my whole life taking care of, and thinking that you need me makes me feel happy."

"And horny?"

He laughed. "Yes. And horny. Very horny."

"I'm glad." She held her hand up and looked at the ring. "It's so beautiful, Jack, and so very thoughtful."

He smiled, "I'm glad you like it. An awful lot of thought did go into it, Em. You have no idea how much. I wanted it to be right."

"It's perfect, just perfect." She took his hand and looked at the heavy gold band. "And you really want to wear that? You don't have to, you know. I'm not that bad, am I?"

"You are not 'bad' at all. If you'd asked me to wear it, I probably would have freaked out. But when you talked about your friend's engagement ring, it really made me think. I've never been a jewelry guy, but this is something I want to do. As long as you don't think it's too weird?"

"I don't. If I'm honest it makes me very happy. I suppose it's a bit like your caveman confession. I don't want or mean to be insecure, or jealous, or possessive or any of those other unattractive things, but knowing you choose to wear that—to reassure me and to tell the world—Jack, it makes me love you even more." She snuggled closer to him.

"You know, speaking of telling the world, hadn't we better get back to the party?"

"Oh, my goodness! I'd completely zoned out of the rest of the world."

"And Gramps is waiting for more than his chili."

She looked at him. "He was in on this with you?"

Jack grinned and nodded. "I could hardly ask you to marry me without getting his permission, could I? To think about marrying me, I mean," he corrected himself quickly as he saw her frown.

"You asked his permission?"

"Sure did. And as you may have noticed, he really is on my side! He even helped me with damage control today." He grinned, loving the shocked look on her face. "You know, I really don't think he'd care if we went back without the chili, as long as we show him these." He held up their joined hands with the rings.

"You! You mean the pair of you set me up?"

Jack shrugged. "I prefer to say 'collaborated in your best interests.'"

She laughed even as she tried to look cross with him.

"You're not going to be mad at them, are you?"

"Them? I thought we were talking about Gramps."

He feigned innocence. "Well, of course we were."

"Jack!"

"What?"

"Who else knew?"

"Knew what?"

"Were they all in on it?"

"Not at first," he pulled her towards him. "They only want you to be happy, Em. Please don't be mad."

"I'm not. I suppose I feel a bit, well, foolish!"

"You were being foolish, but it's okay. I forgive you!"

She had to laugh. "You're certainly used to getting what you want, aren't you?"

"Yup. And I want you, Em. And I want you to marry me, so say you will?"

She pulled away from him. "I told you once before, Jack. I can't change just like that, in an instant."

"I'm sorry, baby, I know. I didn't mean to push." He was mad at himself. He knew better than that.

She must have noticed. "No, *I'm* sorry." She kissed him and gave him a little smile. "I'm not saying no, and that's major progress."

"I know, baby and that makes me happy."

She kissed him again. "It doesn't even horrify me, like it would have only a week ago. But, please, give me time to think about it?"

"That's all I'm asking Em." He smiled, hoping to make her laugh again. "How often am I allowed to ask?"

"Not too often."

"Only every five minutes?"

She rolled her eyes. "Give me a couple of months?"

"Hours?"

"Months!"

"Days?"

"Months!"

"Once a week?"

She laughed, "You don't give up do you?"

"Never."

"How about once a month?"

It was much better than he'd expected. "Done!"

"Hm, did I just walk myself into that?"

"Well, to be fair I may have led you a little."

"Jack Benson, you are impossible!"

"No, my love, you are impossible, but I'm working on getting you past it." He nuzzled into her neck. "And while you think about it, think about this—Emma Benson—how do you like the sound of that?" He watched her face, then grinned. "You like it don't you?!"

She nodded her head shyly.

"Well, as soon as you're ready, baby. And you know, whenever you are ready you can always just tell me, you don't have to wait for me to ask again."

"Okay, Jack. I get the idea. Will you let it go for now so we can get back to the party?"

"I'll let it go, but I'm not ready to let you go, yet." He turned her on her back.

"We really should...."

He held her hands above her head and devoured her with the look he knew would leave her with no choice. Positioning himself above her he kissed her and let his hands roam over her. A few minutes later, when she was breathing hard he lifted his head. "Did you say we have to go?"

"No, we can't go yet."

"Why not, baby?" He shifted his weight and coaxed her with his thumb.

"Mmm," she moved her hips in time with his caresses.

"Should I stop?"

"No, don't stop!"

"Why not?"

"Because I need you. I need you now."

He reached underneath, cupping her and lifting her hips up to meet him as he slid inside her. "You need this?"

"Yes!"

He rode her hard as she willingly gave herself up to him. She ran her nails down his back, urging him on, then she dug them hard into his ass, sending him over the edge, taking her with him as they soared together.

"Note to self," she murmured once she had her breath back. "Tell him you need him and he's all yours."

He laughed. "He's all yours anyway, but tell him you need him and you'd better not have anywhere else you need to be for a while, because you can bet he's going to satisfy that need."

"I am well and truly satisfied, but now I think we do have somewhere else we need to be."

~ ~ ~

Before they got back in the truck, Jack fished his cell phone from his pocket.

"I want to let Gramps know it's okay. I don't want him worrying any longer."

Emma watched him dial a number from memory.

"Hey, Gramps, it's me.

Yeah, it's all good.

Yeah, we'll be back soon.

Yes it is. See you soon."

Emma stared at him. "He gave you his cell phone number? And he actually answered it?"

Jack grinned, "I told you, he's my buddy!"

He was adorable when he was so pleased with himself. She looked down at the ring on her finger; it was so beautiful. Everything it represented was even more beautiful.

"Not having second thoughts, are you?" Jack looked worried.

"No, my goodness, no! I was thinking how wonderful you are!" The smile on his face warmed her heart. She could do this. For him, with him, she could do anything. "It's so beautiful, Jack. How did Laura ever come up with it? I don't think I've ever seen a daisy ring before."

He shrugged. "She's so good at that stuff. You know, Em, I really would like you to meet her properly. It wasn't exactly easy earlier—on any of us."

"I'm sorry."

"No need. Let's talk to her before the party is over, I think you'll like her."

Emma shuddered as she thought about last night, and what she thought she'd been watching. "Can I ask you something?"

"Anything."

"Last night on the beach. When I saw you. You held something out to show Laura and she hugged you."

"I'm sorry, Em. I guess that really didn't look good. We were looking at your ring."

"The thing that threw me so badly was that when you hugged her back you looked so very happy."

Jack pulled the truck over to the side of the road and turned to face her. Taking both her hands, he held her eyes. "Baby, that's because I *was* so very happy. We were looking at your ring and she said it was a very special piece. I told her it had to be, since my whole future was riding on it. She hugged me and told me there was no way you would turn me down. I believed that, Em. That's what made me so happy." He lifted her hand to his lips, "And what's making me so happy right now is that you didn't turn me down."

Emma returned his smile as relief flooded through her. He'd been happy about her! She looked at the heavy band on his finger. He'd done so much to reassure her, to help her through her fears. He didn't dismiss them as silly like everyone else had—even though, she acknowledged, they kind of were. To her the fear of more emotional pain was very real, but Jack understood and he was doing so much to work with her. For a moment she imagined the wedding she used to dream of, out on Gramps' dock. She could see Jack standing there waiting for her, so handsome, so happy. Pete standing beside him. She shook her head as cold fingers of dread crept down her spine. Not yet, but maybe, with time, maybe she might get that dream back.

"I'm so glad you didn't give up on me, Jack."

"I never will, baby. No matter how scared you get or how far you run." He kissed her hand. "But you know it really would be nice if you could work with me a little. And don't forget, wearing that ring means you have to talk to me before you run, right?"

"Right." She hoped he realized how big a commitment that was for her.

Chapter Twenty-Nine

Jack had to park the truck out by the gate, there were so many people at Gramps' place now. He carried a huge catering-sized bowl of chili and Emma brought the smaller one he'd made just for Gramps.

"Here's my Sunshine," beamed Gramps as they came up onto the porch. "Got anything to tell us, Mouse?"

Emma looked around at all the smiling faces looking at her expectantly. Pete and Holly, Ben, Missy, Dan and even Scot were all up on the porch with the old timers.

She laughed. "You set me up, all of you!"

"We helped you along, Mouse," said Pete, "since you were messing it up by yourself."

They all laughed.

"Wait while we take these in, Hemming," she said.

Jack followed her into the kitchen where they handed the chili over. He pulled her to him.

"Are you all right with this?"

"Oh, don't worry. I can take it—and I can give it out too!"

She wasn't about to be heckled by her friends, no matter how well meaning. Jack grinned as he followed her back out to the porch. She didn't get chance to give any of them a piece of her mind.

"Come here!" shouted Gramps. She went to him and he wrapped her in a big hug. For the second time today she saw tears in his eyes.

"Best birthday present I could have gotten," he said. They all cheered.

"You too," he held his arm out to Jack and gave him a hug as well. "You've made this old man real happy, son."

"I've made this not-so-old man very happy too," Jack smiled. "And I intend to make that young lady there very happy for the rest of her life. I couldn't have done it without you though, Gramps."

"Yes, apparently he couldn't." Emma tried to look angry, but she couldn't manage it, she was too happy.

"Someone get these two a drink," said Gramps.

Pete passed them a couple of cold beers.

"To Emma and Jack!" Gramps raised his glass.

"Emma and Jack," they all repeated.

"So," asked Pete, his eyes gleaming with mischief, "do I hear wedding bells?"

Emma's heart sank as all eyes turned to her. She didn't know what to say that wouldn't spoil the moment. She needn't have worried, though, as Jack put an arm round her.

"Distant ones," he smiled. "But they're getting closer. I'd like to propose a toast of my own." He raised his bottle and smiled round at them, "Here's to persistence!"

Everyone laughed. "Persistence!"

Emma let out the breath she'd been holding and raised her bottle to his. He was smiling down at her as they chinked their beers together. "Persistence, baby. You'd better get used to it."

"I think I'm starting to."

After they'd sat with Gramps for a while, they left him and Joe to enjoy their chili and went to join the others who had claimed the picnic bench down on the dock. The band was going strong and a growing crowd swayed in front of the stage. Ben shifted up to make room for them. Jack sat on the end and pulled Emma down onto his lap, wrapping an arm around her waist.

"Come on then," said Holly as they sat down, "let's see this ring."

"Were you in on this too?" Emma asked, remembering Holly's words earlier about what might really be the biggest mistake of her life.

"Hey, I'm only the city-girl come visiting, remember, don't look at me."

"Nicely dodged," laughed Emma as she held out her hand.

"Oh, Em! It's gorgeous!" cried Missy.

"No need to act like you haven't already seen it," Emma arched an eyebrow. "I know you were all in on it."

"Honestly, I hadn't," laughed Missy. "He wouldn't show any of us. You had to see it first."

She looked at Jack and he shrugged. "Laura was the only one to see it and she kind of had to." He nodded to where Laura sat at the far end of the table next to Dan. Emma met her eyes, hoping to make up for being so rude earlier.

"It's beautiful Laura, you are very talented. Thank you. I asked Jack how you came up with such a unique design."

Laura smiled back at her warmly. "Oh, the design was all Jack. He knew exactly what he wanted, right down to the cut of the stone."

Emma looked up at him in surprise. "You?"

His eyes crinkled as he gave her the smile she had come to love so much.

"I'm a man of many talents." As he said it he held her closer and she felt him hard against her, reminding her of another of his talents. She met his eyes and laughed.

"So you keep proving!"

"You came up with that all by yourself?" asked Holly, amazed. "How?"

"I guess I know what I like and I know how to get it."

Emma felt his arm tighten around her. "I can vouch for that," she said, making them all laugh again.

Missy was still examining the ring. "It's spectacular." She looked at Laura, "I don't know how you do it. The craftsmanship, the petals. You've set each one so perfectly."

Laura laughed. "Yes, all eleven of them according to my cousin's strict requirements. No working with even numbers or anything to make my life easier."

Pete looked at Jack. "This should be good. I know the way you design. Every detail is crucial, so there has to be a reason for eleven petals"

"It didn't have to be eleven," said Jack, pretending to be absorbed in examining his fingernails.

Laura laughed again. "No, that's true, it could have been nine or fifteen, just as long as it wasn't unlucky thirteen or, worse still, an even number of them."

"Come on," said Pete, "spill it, Benson. Why did it have to be an odd number of petals?"

Emma looked at him, intrigued, and he surprised her by giving her a quick kiss. Then he looked at the others, gave an exaggerated sigh and rolled his eyes.

"Okay, then. I'll tell." He looked around the table. "Ladies, you'll love this and sorry guys, but you'll probably think I'm a sad sack."

"Now I really have to know," Pete said with a laugh.

Jack looked at Holly and Missy. "Okay, what did you used to do with daisies when you were a little girl?"

"Make daisy chains?" asked Holly.

He shook his head.

"Oh, I know. The old 'he loves me, he loves me not,'" said Missy.

"That's it!" said Jack, grinning at them. Holly and Missy stared at him blankly while Pete groaned and Emma snuggled a little closer, not understanding either.

"Think about it," said Jack. "You pull off the first petal and what do you say?"

"He loves me," said Emma.

He turned and kissed her and his "Yes, he does baby," had them all laughing.

"Come on, people! Think this through. If there were an even number of petals, then it would end on 'he loves me not!'" He wrapped both arms around her. "And *that* will *never* be true."

"Oh my Lord!" exclaimed Laura. "And I thought you were just being picky."

"I was. But with very good reason."

Emma felt tears prick her eyes again. He kept on surprising her with the depth of his thoughtfulness. She would never have come up with that herself, but she could well imagine that at some point she would have played the childish game with her ring. If she'd done it at a time when she was ready to run, what conclusion would she have drawn if the ring had told her 'he loves me not?'

The realization of just how well he understood her and the lengths he would go to shifted something deep inside. She looked around at the others and knew what she had to do.

"Ladies," she said, "would you mind coming up to the house with me?"

"Sure, what do you need?" asked Missy as she and Holly rose from the table.

"You too, please." Emma smiled at Laura, who hadn't moved.

As Emma went to stand herself, Jack pulled her back down to his lap. "What are you up to?"

"Something I need to check on." She smiled and kissed the little frown between his brows. "We'll be back in little while with Gramps. In fact, would you guys do me a favor and stand up when you see us bringing him down here?"

"Of course," said Pete. "Are we singing Happy Birthday?"

"No, we're saving that for later. I have a gift for him that I'd like you all to see."

Jack watched as Emma walked up to the house. He was pleased to see her link arms with Laura, the two of them smiling and talking as they went. Had it really only been a few hours since he'd thought he had lost her completely? Now she was wearing his ring, making friends with Laura, and promising to think about marrying him! He knew it would take time, but patience and persistence were his specialties! He finally believed they would get there. One day she really would be his wife.

"Congratulations, bro!" Pete broke into his thoughts. "You weren't kidding about the Benson persistence, were you?"

"I had my doubts for a while there, Pete. I thought I'd screwed it all up! Thanks for helping nudge her along." He looked at Ben. "And thank you. For last night, as well as today."

"No worries," smiled Ben. "I'm glad to see it working out for the two of you."

"Me too," added Dan.

"Are you going to be my Uncle Jack now?" asked Scot.

Jack smiled at him; he really liked the kid. "I hope so, Scot. Someday soon."

He was surprised to see Dan put an arm around the boy's shoulders and say, "We'll have to find a way to make that happen, huh, Scot?"

Damn! Was he imagining it or was Dan talking about taking an entirely different route to making him Scot's Uncle? He'd been so caught up in everything with Emma, he hadn't been paying so much attention to his little brother—and Missy! He'd have to talk to him about that.

Right now wasn't the time. He could see Emma and Gramps up on the porch. The old guy took her arm as they came down the front steps.

"Come on guys," said Jack as he stood up. "She's bringing Gramps."

Pete came to stand beside him as Emma and Gramps started down toward the dock, picking their way through the crowd followed by Missy, Holly and Laura.

~ ~ ~

Emma was surprised how confident she felt holding on to Gramps' arm as they walked down to the little dock. Jack stood there waiting, Pete at his side, both of them smiling, just as she'd imagined. Ben, Dan and Scot stood off to one side, the sun shining brightly on the lake behind them. It looked like the wedding she had dreamed of, the man who loved her waiting as Gramps walked her to him. The closer she got, the happier she felt. When she had imagined this scene, the cold fingers of dread and doubt had crept in, but that was in her mind. Her fears were only real in her mind. She'd learned that much today. Once she got out of her head and into her life there was only happiness, she understood that now. In her life, if she allowed it, there really could be happiness—happiness and love with this wonderful man who was offering her another chance at them. She only had to be brave enough to take it.

With every step toward the dock, Emma became more sure of what she was about to do. As she stopped in front of Jack she smiled at him. Gramps let go of her arm and turned to Holly, grinning.

"See, she brings me down here 'cos she says she's got a gift for me and she's so lovestruck she's forgotten I'm even here!"

"Oh, I've not forgotten," smiled Emma.

"Well, where is it then?" Gramps looked around.

"It's right here," she said as she wrapped her arms around Jack's waist and looked up into his eyes.

Gramps cocked his head to one side, looking puzzled. Jack closed his arms around her, looking mystified himself. He made her feel so safe. If she'd needed any final encouragement for what she was about to do, she found it in the love that shone from his eyes as he looked down at her.

"What do you mean, Em?" he asked.

"I mean, yes, Jack!"

"Yes?"

"Yes, I will marry you!"

He crushed her to him and found her lips with his own. Even as she was lost in that kiss she could hear Gramps give a little whoop as Missy, Holly and Laura all squealed with excitement.

When Jack finally let her go, the others crowded around them with hugs and slaps on the back. Gramps was practically dancing with delight as Jack shook his hand one more time.

"We did it, son! We did it!"

Jack still looked stunned, even as he grinned from ear to ear. The two men she loved most in the world were happier than she had ever seen them. She herself felt only happiness, the doubt and fear that had haunted her all her life were gone. She could do this. With Jack she could do it. She really could love like she'd never been hurt;

;

A Note from SJ

I hope you enjoyed visiting Summer Lake and getting to know the locals. Please let your friends know about the books if you feel they would enjoy them as well. It would be wonderful if you would leave me a review, I'd very much appreciate it.

To come back to the lake to catch up with the gang and get to know more couples as they each find their happiness, you can check out the rest of the series on my website

www.SJMcCoy.com

Pete and Holly are up next in Work Like You Don't Need the Money.

Alternatively take a look at the "Also By" page to see if any of my other series appeal to you – I have a couple of freebie series starters so you can take them for a test drive in ebook format from all the major online retailers. You can find all the information you need on that on my website.

There are a few options to keep up with me and my imaginary friends:

The best way is to join up on the website for my Newsletter. Don't worry I won't bombard you! I'll let you know about upcoming releases, share a sneak peek or two and keep you in the loop for a couple of fun giveaways I have coming up :0)

You can join my readers group to chat about the books on Facebook or just browse and like my Facebook Page

I occasionally attempt to say something in 140 characters or less(!) on Twitter

And I'm always in the process of updating my website at www.SJMcCoy.com with new book updates and even some videos. Plus, you'll find the latest news on new releases and giveaways in my blog.

I love to hear from readers, so feel free to email me at AuthorSJMcCoy@gmail.com.. I'm better at that! :0)

I hope our paths will cross again soon. Until then, take care, and thanks for your support—you are the reason I write!

Love

SJ

PS Project Semicolon

You may have noticed that the final sentence of the story closed with a semi-colon. It isn't a typo. Project Semi Colon is a non-profit movement dedicated to presenting hope and love to those who are struggling with depression, suicide, addiction and self-injury. Project Semicolon exists to encourage, love and inspire. It's a movement I support with all my heart.

"A semicolon represents a sentence the author could have ended, but chose not to. The sentence is your life and the author is you."

                                         - Project Semicolon

This author started writing after her son was killed in a car crash. At the time I wanted my own story to be over, instead I chose to honour a promise to my son to write my 'silly stories' someday. I chose to escape into my fictional world. I know for many who struggle with depression, suicide can appear to be the only escape. The semicolon has become a symbol of support, and hopefully a reminder – Your story isn't over yet

Also by SJ McCoy

Summer Lake Series
Love Like You've Never Been Hurt (FREE in ebook form)
Work Like You Don't Need the Money
Dance Like Nobody's Watching
Fly Like You've Never Been Grounded
Laugh Like You've Never Cried
Sing Like Nobody's Listening
Smile Like You Mean It
The Wedding Dance
Chasing Tomorrow
Dream Like Nothing's Impossible
Ride Like You've Never Fallen
Live Like There's No Tomorrow
The Wedding Flight

The Davenports
Oscar
TJ
Reid

The Hamiltons
Cameron and Piper in Red wine and Roses
Chelsea and Grant in Champagne and Daisies
Mary Ellen and Antonio in Marsala and Magnolias
Marcos and Molly in Prosecco and Peonies
Coming Next
Grady

Remington Ranch Series
Mason (FREE in ebook form) and also available as Audio
Shane
Carter
Beau
Four Weddings and a Vendetta

A Chance and a Hope
Chance is a guy with a whole lot of story to tell. He's part of the fabric of both Summer Lake and Remington Ranch. He needed three whole books to tell his own story.
Chance Encounter
Finding Hope
Give Hope a Chance

Summer Lake Seasons
A return to the wonderful small town so many readers have grown to love. We'll see our old friends around town and they'll feature to a greater or lesser extent in the new stories. I want you to be able to catch up on their lives if you know them - and to not feel like you're missing anything if you didn't read the original series.

Angel and Luke in Take These Broken Wings

About the Author

I'm SJ, a coffee addict, lover of chocolate and drinker of good red wines. I'm a lost soul and a hopeless romantic. Reading and writing are necessary parts of who I am. Though perhaps not as necessary as coffee! I can drink coffee without writing, but I can't write without coffee.

I grew up loving romance novels, my first boyfriends were book boyfriends, but life intervened, as it tends to do, and I wandered down the paths of non-fiction for many years. My life changed completely a few years ago and I returned to Romance to find my escape.

I write 'Sweet n Steamy' stories because to me there is enough angst and darkness in real life. My favorite romances are happy escapes with a focus on fun, friendships and happily-ever-afters, just like the ones I write.

These days I live in beautiful Montana, the last best place. If I'm not reading or writing, you'll find me just down the road in the park - Yellowstone. I have deer, eagles and the occasional bear for company, and I like it that way :0)

Massapequa Public Library
523 Central Avenue
Massapequa, NY 11758
(516) 798-4607

Made in the USA
Middletown, DE
23 June 2019